The item should be returned or renewed by the last date stamped below.

Dylid dychwelyd neu adnewyddu'r eitem erbyn y dyddiad olaf sydd wedi'i stampio isod.

MALPAS

To renew visit / Adnewyddwch ar
www.newport.gov.uk/libraries

ALSO BY NICK RENNISON

Freud and Psychoanalysis
Peter Mark Roget – The Man Who Became a Book
Robin Hood – Myth, History & Culture
A Short History of Polar Exploration
Bohemian London

The Rivals of Sherlock Holmes
The Rivals of Dracula
Supernatural Sherlocks
More Rivals of Sherlock Holmes
Sherlock's Sisters

AMERICAN SHERLOCKS

★ ★ ★ ★   STORIES FROM   ★ ★ ★ ★

THE GOLDEN AGE OF THE AMERICAN DETECTIVE

edited and introduced by

NICK RENNISON

NO EXIT PRESS

First published in 2021 by No Exit Press,
an imprint of Oldcastle Books Ltd,
Harpenden, UK

noexit.co.uk
@noexitpress

ISBN
978-0-85730-439-1 (print)
978-0-85730-440-7 (epub)

2 4 6 8 10 9 7 5 3 1

Typeset in 11.1 on 12.5pt Bembo
by Avocet Typeset, Bideford, Devon, EX39 2BP
Printed and bound in Great Britain by Clays Ltd, Elcograf S.p.A.

Contents

Introduction 7

Uncle Abner
Created by Melville Davisson Post
The Doomdorf Mystery 13

Bromley Barnes
Created by George Barton
Adventure of the Cleopatra Necklace 27

Mr Barnes and Mr Mitchel
Created by Rodrigues Ottolengui
The Montezuma Emerald 39

Nick Carter
Created by John R Coryell
**An Uncanny Revenge, or Nick Carter and the Mind
Murderer** 52

Thornley Colton
Created by Clinton H Stagg
The Flying Death 103

LeDroit Conners
Created by Samuel Gardenhire
The Park Slope Mystery 134

CONTENTS

Elinor Frost
Created by Carolyn Wells
Christabel's Crystal 161

Philo Gubb
Created by Ellis Parker Butler
Philo Gubb's Greatest Case 175

Clare Kendall
Created by Arthur B Reeve
The Mystery of the Stolen Da Vinci 192

Craig Kennedy
Created by Arthur B Reeve
The Azure Ring 207

Madelyn Mack
Created by Hugh Cosgro Weir
Cinderella's Slipper 228

Jigger Masters
Created by Anthony M Rud
The Affair at Steffen Shoals 262

Quincy Adams Sawyer
Created by Charles Felton Pidgin
The Affair of Lamson's Cook 276

Violet Strange
Created by Anna Katharine Green
The Second Bullet 296

Professor Augustus SFX Van Dusen ('The Thinking Machine')
Created by Jacques Futrelle
The Problem of the Opera Box 316

INTRODUCTION

We all have a picture in our minds of the archetypal detective of American fiction. The hardboiled, wisecracking private eye, walking a city's mean streets. Dashiell Hammett's Sam Spade, Raymond Chandler's Philip Marlowe or one of the hundreds, probably thousands, of other gumshoes who have trodden in their footsteps. But that style of detective only came into being in the late 1920s and early 1930s, most influentially in Hammett's novels and in the pages of the legendary magazine *Black Mask*. American crime fiction has a much longer history.

It really begins with Edgar Allan Poe. (The history of most genre fiction in the USA really begins with Edgar Allan Poe.) Claims for precedence have been made on behalf of earlier works such as Charles Brockden Brown's 1799 novel *Edgar Huntly* and some of Nathaniel Hawthorne's shorter fiction. However, it was Poe who established many of the tropes of crime fiction which are still being used by writers today. In three short stories published in the 1840s – 'The Murders in the Rue Morgue', 'The Mystery of Marie Rogêt' and 'The Purloined Letter' – he created the templates for much of what was to come. The locked-room mystery; the story based on a true crime; the clues, sometimes hidden in plain sight, which point towards a satisfying explanation of what initially seems inexplicable; the bumbling police outshone by the brilliant amateur. All of these derive ultimately from what Poe himself called his 'tales of ratiocination'. His character C Auguste Dupin is the archetype of the detective hero with superior powers of deduction and his influence on later creations, most notably Sherlock Holmes, is clear.

Yet Poe's impact was not markedly felt in his own country in the decades immediately following his death in 1849. There are stories and novels from the 1850s and 1860s which can be classed retrospectively as crime fiction. *The Dead Letter* of 1866 by Seeley Regester (the pseudonym of the woman writer Metta Victoria Fuller Victor), for instance, is the story of the narrator's quest to track down a murderer. Another female author, Harriet Spofford, created what was arguably one of the first 'series' detectives in history in Mr Furbush who appeared in several stories published in *Harper's New Monthly Magazine*. However, the genre Poe had pioneered did not gain much more than a toehold in the traditional publishing houses and magazines of the American literary world.

It was in the more downmarket arena of the so-called 'dime novel' that the figure of the detective finally emerged from the wings and, often enough, took centre stage. The equivalent of the British 'penny dreadful', the dime novel began to flourish in the 1860s. The first example of the genre is usually said to be *Malaeska, the Indian Wife of the Great Hunter*, written by a prolific author and editor, Ann S Stephens, and published by the firm of Beadle & Adams in 1860. Thousands of titles followed in the last decades of the nineteenth century and the opening ones of the twentieth. Several factors fuelled this explosion in cheap genre fiction. Literacy levels began to increase around the time of the American Civil War and continued to do so in the years between 1870 and 1900. At the same time, new printing technologies meant that publishers could issue more books at cheaper prices.

As the title of Ann Stephens's original dime novel indicates, tales of Native Americans and what was increasingly becoming known as the 'Wild West' were popular. The army scout and bison hunter William Cody was transformed into the national hero 'Buffalo Bill' by the adventures attributed to him in stories by writers such as Ned Buntline and Prentiss Ingraham. Other genres thrived as well. One of these was the detective novel. Characters like 'Old Sleuth', 'Lady Kate, the Dashing Female Detective', 'Sam Strong the Cowboy Detective' and 'Old King Brady' battled bad guys in stories that made up in lively action for what they lacked in literary sophistication. However, the major detective to emerge from the dime novel was Nick Carter.

After his first appearance in the *New York Weekly* in 1886, Carter soon graduated to his own series, the *Nick Carter Weekly*. A square-jawed, two-fisted, all-American hero, Carter proved to be a character of astonishing longevity. Transformed into a kind of sub-James Bond figure, he appeared in dozens of cheap paperbacks in the 1960s and new stories about him were still appearing in the early 1990s. In his earliest incarnations, he was kept busy righting wrongs across America and around the world in a series of breath-taking and occasionally fantastical adventures. He gathered about him a small platoon of willing assistants and faced a rogues' gallery of memorable opponents, including the supervillain Doctor Quartz, Dazaar the Arch Fiend, and Zanoni the Woman Wizard. Authors such as Frederick van Rensselaer Day, George C Jenks and Thomas C Harbaugh churned out scores of stories which were published anonymously or attributed to the fictional 'Chick Carter', Nick's adopted son. After the success of Sherlock Holmes in America, Carter evolved into a more traditional gentleman detective, mainly operating in New York, and I have included a typical tale from this period in this anthology.

During the heyday of the dime novel, crime fiction gradually gained popularity in more upmarket fiction. Many of these new crime novels, appearing under the imprint of publishers who would have turned their noses up at the likes of Nick Carter and 'Old Sleuth', were by women writers. *The Leavenworth Case*, for example, was the work of Anna Katharine Green, a Brooklyn-born author who turned to fiction after failing to make much of a mark as a poet. First published in 1878, this introduced a detective from the New York Metropolitan Police Force named Ebenezer Gryce who went on to feature in a number of Green's later novels. Although *The Leavenworth Case* is very much a novel of its time, it continued to have an influence well into the twentieth century. Agatha Christie later cited the book as an inspiration for her when she was just setting out on her career. (Green herself was still writing in the 1920s and created other recurring characters, including nosy spinster Amelia Butterworth, a prototype Miss Marple, and Violet Strange, a wealthy young New Yorker moonlighting as a detective, who features in one of the stories in this anthology.)

The Leavenworth Case was a bestseller and other crime novels of the 1870s and 1880s made their mark. By the early 1890s the figure of the fictional detective was firmly established with readers of both 'downmarket' and 'upmarket' literature. However, one character was about to change the ways in which they all imagined that figure. His name, of course, was Sherlock Holmes. His impact was to be felt almost as profoundly in the USA as it was in Britain. Although the first Holmes tale, the novel *A Study in Scarlet*, had to wait more than two years for an American edition, the stories after that appeared almost simultaneously in the UK and across the Atlantic. Indeed, in some instances, Americans could enjoy Holmes's latest adventure before his home readership. Some of the stories later collected in *The Return of Sherlock Holmes*, for example, were published in the US *Collier's* magazine a week or two prior to their appearances in the UK *Strand Magazine*.

The Sherlock Holmes effect was soon evident. Just as in Britain, scores upon scores of rivals made their bow in books and magazines in the years between 1880 and 1920. Of the characters who feature in the stories in this anthology, it is difficult to believe that Bromley Barnes, LeDroit Conners, Craig Kennedy and others would have been created in quite the same way without the influence of Doyle's great detective. They all carry echoes of the man from Baker Street's genius and personality. And Ellis Parker Butler's Philo Gubb, the inept 'hero' of a series of comic crime stories, may be the polar opposite of Doyle's hero in terms of intellectual prowess but even he was an avowed admirer of Holmes.

A host of other American fictional detectives, not included in this anthology, largely for reasons of space, also operate in the shadow of Sherlock. 'Average' Jones, the creation of the muckraking journalist Samuel Hopkins Adams, may seem something of an original in that he comes across all his cases through the classified ads of the daily newspapers but even that idiosyncrasy is an echo of Holmes's abiding interest in the agony column of *The Times*. Luther Trant, the so-called 'psychological detective' who was the invention of William MacHarg and Edwin Balmer, was hailed in the magazine that published their first story in 1909 as propounding a 'new detective theory... as important as Poe's deductive theory of ratiocination'. Yet readers of Conan Doyle could have pointed to the pages of *The Strand Magazine* and justifiably disputed its novelty.

All these detectives, whether included in this anthology or not, had distinctly American attributes but equally they all owed something to the man from Baker Street. Only a handful of characters escaped the influence of Conan Doyle almost entirely. Perhaps the most original of all the American detectives of this period was Uncle Abner, the creation of the lawyer and author Melville Davisson Post. Post turned to the past as the setting for the 22 stories which feature his God-fearing hero, dispensing wisdom and justice as he rides through the backwoods of West Virginia in the years before the American Civil War, under the admiring gaze of the narrator, his young nephew Martin. Although largely forgotten today, the Uncle Abner stories have had many admirers over the years since their first publication. In 1941, Howard Haycraft, one of the first literary critics to take crime fiction seriously, called Post's character 'the greatest American contribution' to the cast list of detective fiction since Poe's C Auguste Dupin. The opening story in *American Sherlocks*, I hope, will introduce Uncle Abner to new readers.

Even readers with a wide-ranging knowledge of the genre have a tendency to assume that little American crime fiction of any interest appeared in the eighty or so years between Poe's stories and 1920s novels by such writers as SS Van Dine, creator of Philo Vance, and Dashiell Hammett, whose first book, *Red Harvest*, was published as that decade came to an end. One aim of my anthology is to show how wrong that assumption is. There are many crime stories from the period between 1880 and 1920 which are well worth discovering. Stories of women detectives like Hugh Cosgro Weir's Madelyn Mack and Anna Katharine Green's Violet Strange. Stories of hyper-cerebral geniuses like Jacques Futrelle's 'Thinking Machine', Professor Augustus SFX Van Dusen. Stories of pioneering scientific criminologists like Arthur Reeve's Craig Kennedy. From the blind detective Thornley Colton to the retired Secret Service agent Bromley

Barnes, the pages of American magazines were filled with intriguing characters whose exploits remain very enjoyable. Here are fifteen of them.

UNCLE ABNER

Created by Melville Davisson Post (1869–1930)

Melville Davisson Post was born in West Virginia, the son of a wealthy landowner. He practised law for some years and during this time he published his first stories – about the unscrupulous lawyer Randolph Mason. After giving up the law because of ill-health, Post became one of the most popular American mystery writers of the first decades of the twentieth century. For some years after his death, following a fall from his horse, he was regularly cited in studies and histories of the genre. Yet today he is hardly known. Post created a number of detectives (Sir Henry Marquis of Scotland Yard, a French policeman named Jonquelle) but his most admired and original character was Uncle Abner, a shrewd, God-fearing West Virginian backwoodsman solving mysteries in pre-Civil War America, who appeared in 22 stories published between 1911 and 1928. Eighteen of them were collected in Uncle Abner, Master of Mysteries, *published in 1918. These tales, most of them narrated by Abner's admiring young nephew Martin, are very much of their time (some of the language used about black Americans can be off-putting for modern readers) but they are also very skilfully constructed and remain compelling reading. 'The Doomdorf Mystery', a clever variant on the locked-room tale, is one of the best of them.*

THE DOOMDORF MYSTERY

The pioneer was not the only man in the great mountains behind Virginia. Strange aliens drifted in after the Colonial wars. All foreign armies are sprinkled with a cockle of adventurers that take root and remain. They were with Braddock and La Salle, and they rode north out of Mexico after her many empires went to pieces.

I think Doomdorf crossed the seas with Iturbide when that ill-starred adventurer returned to be shot against a wall; but there was no Southern blood in him. He came from some European race remote and barbaric. The evidences were all about him. He was a huge figure of a man, with a black spade beard, broad, thick hands, and square, flat fingers.

He had found a wedge of land between the Crown's grant to Daniel Davisson and a Washington survey. It was an uncovered triangle not worth the running of the lines; and so, no doubt, was left out, a sheer rock standing up out of the river for a base, and a peak of the mountain rising northward behind it for an apex.

Doomdorf squatted on the rock. He must have brought a belt of gold pieces when he took to his horse, for he hired old Robert Steuart's slaves and built a stone house on the rock, and he brought the furnishings overland from a frigate in the Chesapeake; and then in the handfuls of earth, wherever a root would hold, he planted the mountain behind his house with peach trees. The gold gave out; but the devil is fertile in resources. Doomdorf built a log still and turned the first fruits of the garden into a hell-brew. The idle and the vicious came with their stone jugs, and violence and riot flowed out.

The government of Virginia was remote and its arm short and feeble; but the men who held the lands west of the mountains against the savages under grants from George, and after that held them against George himself, were efficient and expeditious. They had long patience, but when that failed they went up from their fields and drove the thing before them out of the land, like a scourge of God.

There came a day, then, when my Uncle Abner and Squire Randolph rode through the gap of the mountains to have the thing out with Doomdorf. The work of this brew, which had the odors of Eden and the impulses of the devil in it, could be borne no longer. The drunken negros had shot old Duncan's cattle and burned his haystacks, and the land was on its feet.

They rode alone, but they were worth an army of little men. Randolph was vain and pompous and given over to extravagance of words, but he was a gentleman beneath it, and fear was an alien and a stranger to him. And Abner was the right hand of the land.

It was a day in early summer and the sun lay hot. They crossed through the broken spine of the mountains and trailed along the river in the shade of the great chestnut trees. The road was only a path and the horses went one before the other. It left the river when the rock began to rise and, making a detour through the grove of peach trees, reached the house on the mountain side. Randolph and Abner got down, unsaddled their horses and turned them out to graze, for their business with Doomdorf would not be over in an hour. Then they took a steep path that brought them out on the mountain side of the house.

A man sat on a big red-roan horse in the paved court before the door. He was a gaunt old man. He sat bare-headed, the palms of his hands resting on the pommel of his saddle, his chin sunk in his black stock, his face in retrospection, the wind moving gently his great shock of voluminous white hair. Under him the huge red horse stood with his legs spread out like a horse of stone.

There was no sound. The door to the house was closed; insects moved in the sun; a shadow crept out from the motionless figure, and swarms of yellow butterflies manoeuvred like an army.

Abner and Randolph stopped. They knew the tragic figure – a circuit rider of the hills who preached the invective of Isaiah as though he were the mouthpiece of a militant and avenging overlord; as though the government of Virginia were the awful theocracy of the Book of Kings. The horse was dripping with sweat and the man bore the dust and the evidences of a journey on him.

'Bronson,' said Abner, 'where is Doomdorf?'

The old man lifted his head and looked down at Abner over the pommel of the saddle.

'"Surely,"' he said, '"he covereth his feet in his summer chamber."'

Abner went over and knocked on the closed door, and presently the white, frightened face of a woman looked out at him. She was a little, faded woman, with fair hair, a broad foreign face, but with the delicate evidences of gentle blood.

Abner repeated his question.

'Where is Doomdorf?'

'Oh, sir,' she answered with a queer lisping accent, 'he went to lie down in his south room after his midday meal, as his custom is; and I went to the orchard to gather any fruit that might be ripened.' She hesitated and her voice lisped into a whisper: 'He is not come out and I cannot wake him.'

The two men followed her through the hall and up the stairway to the door.

'It is always bolted,' she said, 'when he goes to lie down.' And she knocked feebly with the tips of her fingers.

There was no answer and Randolph rattled the doorknob.

'Come out, Doomdorf!' he called in his big, bellowing voice.

There was only silence and the echoes of the words among the rafters. Then Randolph set his shoulder to the door and burst it open.

They went in. The room was flooded with sun from the tall south windows. Doomdorf lay on a couch in a little offset of the room, a great scarlet patch on his bosom and a pool of scarlet on the floor.

The woman stood for a moment staring; then she cried out:

'At last I have killed him!' And she ran like a frightened hare.

The two men closed the door and went over to the couch. Doomdorf had been shot to death. There was a great ragged hole in his waistcoat. They began to look about for the weapon with which the deed had been accomplished, and in a moment found it – a fowling piece lying in two dogwood forks against the wall. The gun had just been fired; there was a freshly exploded paper cap under the hammer.

There was little else in the room – a loom-woven rag carpet on the floor; wooden shutters flung back from the windows; a great oak table, and on it a big, round, glass water bottle, filled to its glass stopper with raw liquor from the still. The stuff was limpid and clear as spring water; and, but for its pungent odor, one would have taken it for God's brew instead of Doomdorf's. The sun lay on it and against the wall where hung the weapon that had ejected the dead man out of life.

'Abner,' said Randolph, 'this is murder! The woman took that gun down from the wall and shot Doomdorf while he slept.'

Abner was standing by the table, his fingers round his chin.

'Randolph,' he replied, 'what brought Bronson here?'

'The same outrages that brought us,' said Randolph. 'The mad old circuit rider has been preaching a crusade against Doomdorf far and wide in the hills.'

Abner answered, without taking his fingers from about his chin:

'You think this woman killed Doomdorf? Well, let us go and ask Bronson who killed him.'

They closed the door, leaving the dead man on his couch, and went down into the court.

The old circuit rider had put away his horse and got an ax. He had taken off his coat and pushed his shirtsleeves up over his long elbows. He was on his way to the still to destroy the barrels of liquor. He stopped when the two men came out, and Abner called to him.

'Bronson,' he said, 'who killed Doomdorf?'

'I killed him,' replied the old man, and went on toward the still.

Randolph swore under his breath. 'By the Almighty,' he said, 'everybody couldn't kill him!'

'Who can tell how many had a hand in it?' replied Abner.

'Two have confessed!' cried Randolph. 'Was there perhaps a third? Did you kill him, Abner? And I too? Man, the thing is impossible!'

'The impossible,' replied Abner, 'looks here like the truth. Come with me, Randolph, and I will show you a thing more impossible than this.'

They returned through the house and up the stairs to the room. Abner closed the door behind them.

'Look at this bolt,' he said; 'it is on the inside and not connected with the lock. How did the one who killed Doomdorf get into this room, since the door was bolted?'

'Through the windows,' replied Randolph.

There were but two windows, facing the south, through which the sun entered. Abner led Randolph to them.

'Look!' he said. 'The wall of the house is plumb with the sheer face of the rock. It is a hundred feet to the river and the rock is as smooth as a sheet of glass. But that is not all. Look at these window frames; they are cemented into their casement with dust and they are bound along their edges with cobwebs. These windows have not been opened. How did the assassin enter?'

'The answer is evident,' said Randolph: 'The one who killed Doomdorf hid in the room until he was asleep; then he shot him and went out.'

'The explanation is excellent but for one thing,' replied Abner: 'How did the assassin bolt the door behind him on the inside of this room after he had gone out?'

Randolph flung out his arms with a hopeless gesture.

'Who knows?' he cried. 'Maybe Doomdorf killed himself.'

Abner laughed.

'And after firing a handful of shot into his heart he got up and put the gun back carefully into the forks against the wall!'

'Well,' cried Randolph, 'there is one open road out of this mystery. Bronson and this woman say they killed Doomdorf, and if they killed him they surely know how they did it. Let us go down and ask them.'

'In the law court,' replied Abner, 'that procedure would be considered sound sense; but we are in God's court and things are managed there in a somewhat stranger way. Before we go let us find out, if we can, at what hour it was that Doomdorf died.'

He went over and took a big silver watch out of the dead man's pocket. It was broken by a shot and the hands lay at one hour after noon. He stood for a moment fingering his chin.

'At one o'clock,' he said. 'Bronson, I think, was on the road to this place, and the woman was on the mountain among the peach trees.'

Randolph threw back his shoulders.

'Why waste time in a speculation about it, Abner?' he said. 'We know who did this thing. Let us go and get the story of it out of their own mouths. Doomdorf died by the hands of either Bronson or this woman.'

'I could better believe it,' replied Abner, 'but for the running of a certain awful law.'

'What law?' said Randolph. 'Is it a statute of Virginia?'

'It is a statute,' replied Abner, 'of an authority somewhat higher. Mark the language of it: "He that killeth with the sword must be killed with the sword."'

He came over and took Randolph by the arm.

'Must! Randolph, did you mark particularly the word "must"? It is a mandatory law. There is no room in it for the vicissitudes of chance or fortune. There is no way round that word. Thus, we reap what we sow and nothing else; thus, we receive what we give and nothing else. It is the weapon in our own hands that finally destroys us. You are looking at it now.' And he turned him about so that the table and the weapon and the dead man were before him. '"He that killeth with the sword must be killed with the sword." And now,' he said, 'let us go and try the method of the law courts. Your faith is in the wisdom of their ways.'

They found the old circuit rider at work in the still, staving in Doomdorf's liquor casks, splitting the oak heads with his ax.

'Bronson,' said Randolph, 'how did you kill Doomdorf?'

The old man stopped and stood leaning on his ax.

'I killed him,' replied the old man, 'as Elijah killed the captains of Ahaziah and their fifties. But not by the hand of any man did I pray the Lord God to destroy Doomdorf, but with fire from heaven to destroy him.'

He stood up and extended his arms.

'His hands were full of blood,' he said. 'With his abomination from these groves of Baal he stirred up the people to contention, to strife and murder. The widow and the orphan cried to heaven against him. "I will surely hear their cry," is the promise written in the Book. The land was weary of him; and I prayed the Lord God to destroy him with fire from heaven, as he destroyed the Princes of Gomorrah in their palaces!'

Randolph made a gesture as of one who dismisses the impossible, but Abner's face took on a deep, strange look.

'With fire from heaven!' he repeated slowly to himself. Then he asked a question. 'A little while ago,' he said, 'when we came, I asked you where Doomdorf was, and you answered me in the language of the third chapter of the Book of Judges. Why did you answer me like that, Bronson? – "Surely he covereth his feet in his summer chamber."'

'The woman told me that he had not come down from the room where he had gone up to sleep,' replied the old man, 'and that the door was locked. And then I knew that he was dead in his summer chamber like Eglon, King of Moab.'

He extended his arm toward the south.

'I came here from the Great Valley,' he said, 'to cut down these groves of Baal and to empty out this abomination; but I did not know that the Lord had heard my prayer and visited His wrath on Doomdorf until I was come up into these mountains to his door. When the woman spoke I knew it.' And he went away to his horse, leaving the ax among the ruined barrels.

Randolph interrupted.

'Come, Abner,' he said; 'this is wasted time. Bronson did not kill Doomdorf.'

Abner answered slowly in his deep, level voice:

'Do you realize, Randolph, how Doomdorf died?'

'Not by fire from heaven, at any rate,' said Randolph.

'Randolph,' replied Abner, 'are you sure?'

'Abner,' cried Randolph, 'you are pleased to jest, but I am in deadly earnest. A crime has been done here against the state. I am an officer of justice and I propose to discover the assassin if I can.'

He walked away toward the house and Abner followed, his hands behind him and his great shoulders thrown loosely forward, with a grim smile about his mouth.

'It is no use to talk with the mad old preacher,' Randolph went on. 'Let him empty out the liquor and ride away. I won't issue a warrant against him. Prayer may be a handy implement to do a murder with, Abner, but it is not a deadly weapon under the statutes of Virginia. Doomdorf was dead when old Bronson got here with his Scriptural jargon. This woman killed Doomdorf. I shall put her to an inquisition.'

'As you like,' replied Abner. 'Your faith remains in the methods of the law courts.'

'Do you know of any better methods?' said Randolph.

'Perhaps,' replied Abner, 'when you have finished.'

Night had entered the valley. The two men went into the house and set about preparing the corpse for burial. They got candles, and made a coffin, and put Doomdorf in it, and straightened out his limbs, and folded his arms across his shot-out heart. Then they set the coffin on benches in the hall.

They kindled a fire in the dining room and sat down before it, with the door open and the red firelight shining through on the dead man's narrow, everlasting house. The woman had put some cold meat, a golden cheese and a loaf on the table. They did not see her, but they heard her moving about the house; and finally, on the gravel court outside, her step and the whinny of a horse. Then she came in, dressed as for a journey. Randolph sprang up.

'Where are you going?' he said.

'To the sea and a ship,' replied the woman. Then she indicated the hall with a gesture. 'He is dead and I am free.'

There was a sudden illumination in her face. Randolph took a step toward her. His voice was big and harsh.

'Who killed Doomdorf?' he cried.

'I killed him,' replied the woman. 'It was fair!'

'Fair!' echoed the justice. 'What do you mean by that?'

The woman shrugged her shoulders and put out her hands with a foreign gesture.

'I remember an old, old man sitting against a sunny wall, and a little girl, and one who came and talked a long time with the old man, while the little girl plucked yellow flowers out of the grass and put them into her hair. Then finally the stranger gave the old man a gold chain and took the little girl away.' She flung out her hands. 'Oh, it was fair to kill him!' She looked up with a queer, pathetic smile.

'The old man will be gone by now,' she said; 'but I shall perhaps find the wall there, with the sun on it, and the yellow flowers in the grass. And now, may I go?'

It is a law of the story-teller's art that he does not tell a story. It is the listener who tells it. The story-teller does but provide him with the stimuli.

Randolph got up and walked about the floor. He was a justice of the peace in a day when that office was filled only by the landed gentry, after the English fashion; and the obligations of the law were strong on him. If he should take liberties with the letter of it, how could the weak and the evil be made to hold it in respect? Here was this woman before him a confessed assassin. Could he let her go?

Abner sat unmoving by the hearth, his elbow on the arm of his chair, his palm propping up his jaw, his face clouded in deep lines. Randolph was consumed with vanity and the weakness of ostentation, but he shouldered his duties for himself. Presently he stopped and looked at the woman, wan, faded like some prisoner of legend escaped out of fabled dungeons into the sun.

The firelight flickered past her to the box on the benches in the hall, and the vast, inscrutable justice of heaven entered and overcame him.

'Yes,' he said. 'Go! There is no jury in Virginia that would hold a woman for shooting a beast like that.' And he thrust out his arm, with the fingers extended toward the dead man.

The woman made a little awkward curtsy.

'I thank you, sir.' Then she hesitated and lisped, 'But I have not shoot him.'

'Not shoot him!' cried Randolph. 'Why, the man's heart is riddled!'

'Yes, sir,' she said simply, like a child. 'I kill him, but have not shoot him.'

Randolph took two long strides toward the woman.

'Not shoot him!' he repeated. 'How then, in the name of heaven, did you kill Doomdorf?' And his big voice filled the empty places of the room.

'I will show you, sir,' she said.

She turned and went away into the house. Presently she returned with something folded up in a linen towel. She put it on the table between the loaf of bread and the yellow cheese.

Randolph stood over the table, and the woman's deft fingers undid the towel from round its deadly contents; and presently the thing lay there uncovered.

It was a little crude model of a human figure done in wax with a needle thrust through the bosom.

Randolph stood up with a great intake of the breath.

'Magic! By the eternal!'

'Yes, sir,' the woman explained, in her voice and manner of a child. 'I have try to kill him many times – oh, very many times! – with witch words which I have remember; but always they fail. Then, at last, I make him in wax, and I put a needle through his heart; and I kill him very quickly.'

It was as clear as daylight, even to Randolph, that the woman was innocent. Her little harmless magic was the pathetic effort of a child to kill a dragon. He hesitated a moment before he spoke, and then he decided like the gentleman he was. If it helped the child to believe that her enchanted straw had slain the monster – well, he would let her believe it.

'And now, sir, may I go?'

Randolph looked at the woman in a sort of wonder.

'Are you not afraid,' he said, 'of the night and the mountains, and the long road?'

'Oh no, sir,' she replied simply. 'The good God will be everywhere now.'

It was an awful commentary on the dead man – that this strange half-child believed that all the evil in the world had gone out with him; that now that he was dead, the sunlight of heaven would fill every nook and corner.

It was not a faith that either of the two men wished to shatter, and they let her go. It would be daylight presently and the road through the mountains to the Chesapeake was open.

Randolph came back to the fireside after he had helped her into the saddle, and sat down. He tapped on the hearth for some time idly with the iron poker; and then finally he spoke.

'This is the strangest thing that ever happened,' he said. 'Here's a mad old preacher who thinks that he killed Doomdorf with fire from Heaven, like Elijah the Tishbite; and here is a simple child of a woman who thinks she killed him with a piece of magic of the Middle Ages – each as innocent of his death as I am. And yet, by the eternal, the beast is dead!'

He drummed on the hearth with the poker, lifting it up and letting it drop through the hollow of his fingers.

'Somebody shot Doomdorf. But who? And how did he get into and out of that shut-up room? The assassin that killed Doomdorf must have gotten into the room to kill him. Now, how did he get in?' He spoke as to himself; but my uncle sitting across the hearth replied:

'Through the window.'

'Through the window!' echoed Randolph. 'Why, man, you yourself showed me that the window had not been opened, and the precipice below it a fly could hardly climb. Do you tell me now that the window was opened?'

'No,' said Abner, 'it was never opened.'

Randolph got on his feet.

'Abner,' he cried, 'are you saying that the one who killed Doomdorf climbed the sheer wall and got in through a closed window, without disturbing the dust or the cobwebs on the window frame?'

My uncle looked Randolph in the face.

'The murderer of Doomdorf did even more,' he said. 'That assassin not only climbed the face of that precipice and got in through the closed window, but he shot Doomdorf to death and got out again through the closed window without leaving a single track or trace behind, and without disturbing a grain of dust or a thread of a cobweb.'

Randolph swore a great oath.

'The thing is impossible!' he cried. 'Men are not killed today in Virginia by black art or a curse of God.'

'By black art, no,' replied Abner; 'but by the curse of God, yes. I think they are.'

Randolph drove his clenched right hand into the palm of his left.

'By the eternal!' he cried. 'I would like to see the assassin who could do a murder like this, whether he be an imp from the pit or an angel out of Heaven.'

'Very well,' replied Abner, undisturbed. 'When he comes back tomorrow I will show you the assassin who killed Doomdorf.'

When day broke they dug a grave and buried the dead man

against the mountain among his peach trees. It was noon when that work was ended. Abner threw down his spade and looked up at the sun.

'Randolph,' he said, 'let us go and lay an ambush for this assassin. He is on the way here.'

And it was a strange ambush that he laid. When they were come again into the chamber where Doomdorf died he bolted the door; then he loaded the fowling piece and put it carefully back on its rack against the wall. After that he did another curious thing: He took the blood-stained coat, which they had stripped off the dead man when they had prepared his body for the earth, put a pillow in it and laid it on the couch precisely where Doomdorf had slept. And while he did these things Randolph stood in wonder and Abner talked:

'Look you, Randolph... We will trick the murderer... We will catch him in the act.'

Then he went over and took the puzzled justice by the arm.

'Watch!' he said. 'The assassin is coming along the wall!'

But Randolph heard nothing, saw nothing. Only the sun entered. Abner's hand tightened on his arm.

'It is here! Look!' And he pointed to the wall.

Randolph, following the extended finger, saw a tiny brilliant disk of light moving slowly up the wall toward the lock of the fowling piece. Abner's hand became a vise and his voice rang as over metal.

'"He that killeth with the sword must be killed with the sword." It is the water bottle, full of Doomdorf's liquor, focusing the sun... And look, Randolph, how Bronson's prayer was answered!'

The tiny disk of light traveled on the plate of the lock.

'It is fire from heaven!'

The words rang above the roar of the fowling piece, and Randolph saw the dead man's coat leap up on the couch, riddled by the shot. The gun, in its natural position on the rack, pointed to the couch standing at the end of the chamber, beyond the offset of the wall, and the focused sun had exploded the percussion cap.

Randolph made a great gesture, with his arm extended.

'It is a world,' he said, 'filled with the mysterious joinder of accident!'

'It is a world,' replied Abner, 'filled with the mysterious justice of God!'

BROMLEY BARNES

Created by George Barton (1866–1940)

A former Secret Service agent with thirty years' experience, Bromley Barnes is supposedly retired from US government work but government seems incapable of functioning well without him. In the stories by George Barton, the sophisticated Mr Barnes, a collector of first editions and connoisseur of fine living, is regularly called back to deal with sensitive investigations in both Washington and New York. He looks into the mysterious death of an inventor, identifies the source of a series of White House leaks and thwarts a bomb attack on the National Arsenal. Many of the tales in the 1918 volume The Strange Adventures of Bromley Barnes *are closer to spy fiction than crime fiction but 'Adventure of the Cleopatra Necklace', in which Bromley Barnes tracks down the man who stole a priceless Ancient Egyptian artefact from the renowned 'Cosmopolitan Museum', is a fairly traditional detective story. Barnes, who also appeared in a 1920 novel entitled* The Pembroke Mason Affair, *was the creation of George Barton, a regular contributor to story magazines throughout the first three decades of the twentieth century. In addition, Barton compiled a number of non-fiction works with titles such as* Adventures of the World's Greatest Detectives, Celebrated Crimes and Their Solutions, *and* The World's Greatest Military Spies and Secret Service Agents.

ADVENTURE OF THE CLEOPATRA NECKLACE

It doesn't pay to advertise – always. At least that was the conclusion of the trustees of the great Cosmopolitan Museum after the antiquarians of the country were thrown into a state of hysteria over the strange disappearance of the Cleopatra necklace. The sensational business started with a newspaper paragraph in the *Clarion*, reading something like this:

'The trustees of the Cosmopolitan Museum have added to the collection of curios in Egyptian Hall a rare old necklace which they say belonged, beyond the shadow of a doubt, to the famous sorceress of the Nile. As a relic of the civilization which existed three thousand years before Christ, the collar is naturally priceless. Its intrinsic value is placed at $30,000.'

The announcement brought a crush of visitors to Egyptian Hall. The curator, Dr Randall-Brown, had provided a strong plate glass case for the precious relic, and had given it the place of honor in the very center of the marble-tiled hall. The collar of the late – very late – Queen of Egypt reposed on a velvet-covered stand which displayed its rare qualities to excellent advantage. The setting was of some curious metal that was neither gold nor silver, but the necklace itself was a collection of amethysts, pearls and diamonds.

Egyptian Hall was one of a number of large rooms in the Cosmopolitan Museum, which was part of the educational system of the famous University where some eighteen hundred young men, from all parts of the world, were preparing themselves for their attack on the world. The Cosmopolitan Museum, it might be added, was regarded as burglar-proof, as well as fire-proof. One watchman was employed during the day and another by night. George Young, the day watchman, also acted as a sort of guide, and when the trouble came he admitted that he had not remained in Egyptian Hall continuously; that, at one time, he had been out of the room for fifteen minutes.

It was Dr Randall-Brown, the curator, who first made the astonishing discovery. He had brought a connoisseur from Harvard to look at the treasure.

'You will notice,' said the curator, gloating over the prize as only an antiquarian can, 'that there are three pearls, three amethysts and three diamonds in succession, and after that they come in twos and then in ones.'

But even as he spoke, he realized that this orderly arrangement no longer existed. One of the amethysts had been misplaced.

Filled with the gloomiest forebodings, he examined the outside of the case. Casually, all seemed well, but the use of a magnifying glass proved that the twelve screws which fastened the case to the flat table, on which it reposed, had been disturbed.

'Close the doors,' cried the curator, nervously, 'and we'll look into this business.'

The case was opened and the astounding discovery was made that someone had taken the stones from the priceless Cleopatra necklace and had substituted paste diamonds and imitation gems in their place.

The news, which leaked out in spite of the caution of the trustees, made a tremendous sensation. The telegraph and the cable were called into requisition to beseech the police everywhere, and the learned men of the world, to join in the search for the missing treasure. Dealers in precious stones and pawnbrokers were given the description of the gems taken from the necklace, with instructions to arrest the first person who offered such stones for sale. Their curious size and shape, it was added, would make their identification comparatively easy.

The local police made a determined effort to locate the stolen property and to unravel the mystery of the robbery. Everyone connected with the museum, in any capacity whatever, was subjected to a rigid inquiry but without result. The curator and the trustees wrung their hands in despair. They were estimable gentlemen, but their brows were so high and their intellects so keen that they were absolutely helpless in solving everyday problems of life. The University was becoming the laughing stock of the world. It was inconceivable, said outsiders, that such a crime could be committed without the police speedily detecting the criminal.

It was at this stage of the game that Barnes, going into the *Clarion* office, met his friend Curley, of that paper, and was given this command: 'Solve the museum mystery.' He had been given many difficult orders in the past, but this seemed the most impossible of all. Perhaps they were trying to have some fun with him at the office. 'If so,' he said to himself, 'I'll put the laugh on the other side.'

That afternoon he called up Dr Randall-Brown and told him

that he had been commissioned to solve the mystery. The learned curator smiled through his perplexity and said fervently:

'Do so, and you'll win my everlasting gratitude.'

'But,' insisted Barnes, 'I must have your authority to cross-examine the employees and to conduct the investigation in any way I see fit.'

'You have all that,' replied the doctor. 'I'll see that no obstacles are placed in your way.'

The first thing that Barnes considered was the substitution of the fake necklace for the real one in the day time. He interrogated George Young, the day watchman, at some length, and that officer persisted in his statement that his longest length of absence from Egyptian Hall was for fifteen minutes.

'Didn't you go out for luncheon?'

'No, sir; I carried it with me as usual and ate it at that little desk over in the corner of the room, where I had a full view of the case containing the relic.'

'Have you had many visitors?'

'Yes, sir; especially since the necklace came.'

'How many at one time?'

'The number varied. Sometimes the room was crowded, and again there would be only two or three.'

The detective reflected that it might have been possible for a trained gang of thieves to do the job in fifteen minutes. One man might have stood guard at the door while a half-dozen confederates unscrewed the case and made the substitution. But, of course, they would be subjected to interruption. Altogether, Barnes felt rather skeptical about his theory.

His next move was to put Adam Markley, the night watchman, through the third degree. The results were far from satisfactory, Adam Markley had been with the museum for fifteen years, and his reputation for integrity was very high. Indeed, he almost took a childish interest in the rare objects that were in his charge. He was an illiterate man, but what he lacked in education he supplied with enthusiasm and devotion to duty.

Dr Randall-Brown shook his head smilingly when Barnes spoke of the night watchman.

'It's all right to put him on the griddle,' he said, 'but you might as well suspect me as old Adam Markley.'

'I do suspect you,' began the detective.

The venerable Egyptologist gave a start of surprise. He spoke sharply:

'Well of all the cheeky —'

Barnes lifted an interrupting hand.

'I suspect you and everyone connected with this place,' he finished. 'You know,' he added, 'I am working on the French principle that you're all guilty until you prove your innocence.'

'Ah,' was the relieved reply, 'that's different, but I'm sure you're wasting your time on the night watchman.'

Adam Markley told his story in a straightforward way, and although he was called upon to repeat it, he never once deviated from any of the essential details. He was cherubic in appearance, and in spite of his years, his cheeks were round and rosy, and his blue eyes looked out at his inquisitor with child-like innocence and freshness. He constantly ran his hand through his brown hair, and his manner seemed to say, 'Why don't you look for the thief instead of bothering with me?'

Barnes, not content with examining the employees, made an exhaustive investigation into their antecedents. He paid particular attention to the two watchmen. Young, he found, was a married man with a large family living in a modest house in the suburbs. Markley resided in bachelor apartments in the city, living comfortably but inexpensively. Those who knew him were loud in his praise. Some of his older friends recalled him as a child. He had a brother, and the two of them, with long brown curls and rosy cheeks, went about hand in hand like two babes in the wood. The brother, who, unfortunately, had left the straight and narrow path, was now living in the West.

Adam Markley, in the course of his examination, let fall one remark which Barnes thought might develop into a clue. He said that Professor von Hermann had paid five or six visits to the museum and had stood before the case containing the necklace like a man fascinated. Professor von Hermann was one of the world's greatest archaeologists, and there is no doubt that he keenly felt the disappointment which comes to such a man when a rival – even though that rival be an institution – secures the prize he covets. Barnes, in the course of his investigation, learned that the professor, on one occasion, had told a friend that the only thing he needed to complete his own collection was just such a necklace as the trustees of the Cosmopolitan Museum had fondly believed to be safe in Egyptian Hall. Barnes called at the professor's home with the idea of gaining some impressions of the venerable connoisseur, but that gentleman bluntly informed him through a servant that he 'had no time to give to gossiping detectives.'

Barnes relished this greatly, and made a mental resolution to remember the eccentricity – or worse – of the savant at the proper time and place. In the meantime he called upon the curator of the museum for the purpose of asking some further questions.

'Well, my man,' cried Dr Randall-Brown, with wet-blanket cordiality, 'I suppose you've come to tell me you're stumped.'

'Nothing of the kind,' protested the detective.

'You haven't found the thief?'

'No,' admitted Barnes, 'not yet, but I've got a bully good theory.'

'What is it?'

'I'm not ready to give it out. What I want to know from you is whether you haven't forgotten to tell me something.'

'Sir!' exclaimed the doctor, with a rising and highly indignant inflection, 'I've told you all I know.'

'You were in your office in this building the day before the theft was discovered? '

'I was.'

'Did anything unusual occur?'

'No, sir.'

'You stepped out of your office for a few minutes?'

'Yes, I was in and out several times.'

'And once, when you returned, you found a young man fumbling in the drawer of your desk?'

The curator's face lengthened.

'You're right, Barnes, I forgot all about that. It seemed such a trifling matter.'

'It's the trifles that count, doctor. Who was the young man?'

'I never learned. He ran out as I came in. I imagine it was one of the students from the University.'

'Wasn't he dark-complexioned?'

'Now that you mention it, I believe that he was.'

'Haven't they some Egyptian students in the University?'

'By Jove, they have five or six. My boy, I believe you're on the right track!'

Barnes sighed. 'I doubt it, but I've got to clean all of these things up, you know.'

'Shall I send for the Egyptian students?'

'No – at least not at present. By the way, do you know Professor von Hermann?'

'Yes.'

'Has he ever said anything about the necklace?'

'Yes, he told me that his collection was incomplete without it and that our collection was incomplete without his Egyptian antiquities. He wondered if the trustees would consider a suggestion to sell him the necklace. I told him the proposition was preposterous.'

'He thought the collection should be merged?'

'Exactly, only his plan would be to have the tail wag the dog.'

Six days had now gone and Barnes apparently was no nearer the truth than he had been in the beginning. Every day regularly he reported at the *Clarion* office and found against his name on the assignment book in the *Clarion* office the command, 'Solve the museum mystery.' The city editor, in his dry mirthless way, did his best to tease the emergency man.

'If you want to give up the assignment, Barnes,' he said, 'I'll let you report the meetings of the Universal Peace Union.'

'No,' said the baited one, clicking his teeth with determination, 'I'll finish this job first if you don't mind.'

That night he enlisted the aid of his friend and fellow worker, Clancy.

'You needn't tell me what you want,' said the loyal Con, 'I'll go with you anywhere without asking questions.'

At midnight the two of them were prowling about the dark stone walls of the Cosmopolitan Museum. The place was on the outskirts of the city, and at that hour was lonely and deserted. A dim light shone from one of the small windows near the entrance. It was too high for either of them to look inside.

'I'd give a dollar for a soap box or something to stand on,' grunted Barnes.

Clancy never hesitated for an instant.

'Let's play horsey,' he said.

'What do you mean?'

'Why, I'll get down on my hands and knees,' quoth the faithful one, 'and you can stand on my back and peep inside.'

It was no sooner said than done. The improvised stand proved to be just the right height.

By clutching the window sill with his fingertips Barnes was able to draw himself up and peer into the little room that led to the museum.

There sat old Markley tilted back in a chair with his feet on the window ledge reading a book. A half smile wreathed his cherubic face, and he had the appearance of a man who, as one of our Presidents once remarked, was 'at peace with the world and the rest of mankind.'

There was certainly nothing to excite suspicion in appearance or the action of the venerable person, and yet the mere sight of him seemed to throw Barnes into a state of intense excitement

'I've got it! I've got it!' he whispered hoarsely to his friend, as he jumped from Clancy's willing back.

'Got what?'

'Never mind,' was the impatient retort as he grabbed his associate by the coat sleeve, 'come with me.'

'What are you going to do now?' ventured Clancy.

'Commit burglary, I hope,' ejaculated Barnes fervently.

Clancy looked at Barnes with real concern. He wondered whether he could, by any possibility, be taking leave of his senses. In spite of this momentary doubt he followed his friend with the blind devotion which was his most becoming trait. Soon after leaving the museum they were able to get a cab and in a little while the vehicle, pursuant to Barnes's directions, drew up in front of Adam Markley's lodgings.

'This is the part of the job that I dislike, but desperate cases require desperate methods.'

'How in the world can you get in?'

'This is one feature of the case where credit belongs to the police department. They secured skeleton keys in order to search old Markley's rooms.'

'Then what's the use of your doing it over again?'

'Oh, they might have forgotten something,' was the laughing rejoinder.

The two men entered the house noiselessly, crept silently up the stairs and soon found themselves in the modest habitation of the old watchman. It consisted of a bedroom and a sitting room. Barnes paid no attention to the sleeping chamber, but proceeded at once to the living apartment. This was plainly but comfortably furnished. A roll-top desk stood in one comer and a big Morris chair in the other. The left wall contained some family photographs, and Barnes gazed long and earnestly at one of these representing two young men. The other wall held a large engraving of General Grant on horseback. Presently Barnes went to the desk. It was locked. Without any evidence of compunction he pulled out a sharp instrument and began to twist the lock.

'You're going pretty far,' said Clancy gravely.

'Yes,' retorted the irrepressible one, 'and the farther I go the more I learn.'

The lock yielded and the top rolled up. Barnes grabbed a handful of papers and went through them like a conjurer doing a trick. Finally he reached a little yellow slip. He read what was written on the sheet and gave a gurgle of delight. He hastily slipped all the papers back in place and pulled the desk down in a way that automatically locked it, and cried out cheerfully:

'We're through, Clancy, old boy; nothing to do until tomorrow.'

After breakfast next day Barnes called Dayton, Ohio, on the long-distance telephone. It took him some time to get the person he wanted, but by noon his face was wreathed in smiles.

'It's all right,' he exclaimed gaily to Clancy, 'I want you to meet me at Markley's room the day after tomorrow at eight o'clock in the morning.'

'Why?'

'Oh, we're going to have a little surprise party.'

At the hour appointed Barnes and Clancy were at the modest quarters of the old watchman. So was Dr Randall-Brown. The curator was annoyed.

'I don't like this,' he exclaimed testily. 'I don't relish the idea of breaking into a man's rooms without absolute proof.'

Barnes smiled.

'If we had absolute proof, we wouldn't have to do it.'

'Well, what do you expect to prove by coming here?'

'That depends entirely on the result of my experiment. We'll know all about it in a few minutes.'

As he spoke, heavy footsteps were heard on the stairway, and in a few minutes Markley entered the room. He seemed dazed at the unexpected sight of strangers in his apartments.

'What's – what's the meaning of this?' he stammered.

'You know,' said Barnes, sharply.

'I don't,' he retorted with a trace of defiance.

Barnes advanced until he stood directly in front of the old man. He pointed an accusing finger at him. He spoke sternly.

'I charge you with the theft of the Cleopatra necklace from the Cosmopolitan Museum!'

The color slowly receded from the cheeks of the man's cherubic face. He sank weakly into the easy chair. It was some moments before he spoke, and then it was in a hushed and trembling voice.

'Where's – where's your proof?'

'In the necklace itself – we've found its hiding place.'

The man's glance went waveringly about the room, and then it halted and rested on the engraving of General Grant. Barnes had been watching him like a hawk, and upon that significant halt he rushed over to the picture.

'Yes,' he said, as if answering a question, 'it does hang a bit crooked,' and, as he straightened the frame, there was a crashing sound from behind the engraving and a small woollen bag fell to the floor.

Barnes picked it up quickly, and opening the top emptied the contents on the table. There before the astonished gaze of the onlookers, were the pearls, amethysts and diamonds that had composed the Cleopatra necklace.

Markley lay back in his chair, too stupefied to speak. Dr Randall-Brown broke forth in a cry of anguish.

'This is horrible! No one living could have convinced me that Adam Markley was a thief!'

'He isn't,' said Barnes, coolly.

The curator pointed a despairing finger at the gems and then at the cowering man in the chair.

'There,' he cried angrily, 'how do you explain this evidence away?'

Barnes paused for a moment as though listening, and then said:

'If I'm not mistaken, the explanation will be here in a moment.'

He had scarcely ceased speaking when the door opened, and in walked a rosy-cheeked, brown-haired, cherubic-faced person. The detective gave a wave of his hand in the direction of the newcomer.

'Gentlemen,' he said, with something like dramatic effect, 'let me present to you Mr Adam Markley.'

Every one shouted with surprise.

'But who,' exclaimed Dr Randall-Brown, pointing to the creature in the arm chair, 'is this man?'

'That,' said Barnes, 'is Jim Markley, thief and general all-round confidence man. He had been living in Dayton, O., but when he read of your $30,000 necklace he couldn't resist the temptation to come here and get it. How he got it is a long story that will have to be told in the court, but in the meantime it is sufficient for you to know that he first had his twin brother lured away from here and then, clothing himself in his gray uniform, personated him at the museum and easily got away with the gems during the night.'

While he talked the two brothers were staring at each other. Adam's eyes were humid with unshed tears, but the face of the black sheep now betrayed only cynical indifference. The resemblance between the two was remarkable. They were as much alike as two peas in a pod. After the necessary formalities had ended, they separated, one to take his place in a felon's dock, the other to resume his position as a faithful and trusted employee.

That night Clancy ventured to question Bromley Barnes.

'I thought at first,' he said, 'that the culprit was either the student who was found going through Dr Randall-Brown's desk, or Professor von Hermann, the Egyptologist.'

Barnes shook his head.

'The boy was hunting for a set of questions to be used in the coming examination, while the sight of the necklace simply caused Professor von Hermann to give his rare collection to the Cosmopolitan Museum.'

'You got your clue the night you peeped in at Markley, didn't you?' persisted Clancy.

'I did,' was the reply, 'and the clue was in the book he was reading. I knew that Adam Markley could scarcely write his own name and that he could read only with great difficulty. Therefore, when I discovered that watchman reading the second volume of Gibbon's *Decline and Fall of the Roman Empire* with ease, I knew he wasn't Adam Markley. The rest was easy. The finding of the telegram that lured Adam to Dayton, and then getting into communication with him over the long-distance telephone was simply a matter of course.'

'What's the moral as far as Jim Markley is concerned?'

'I don't know,' grinned Barnes, 'unless it's the old one "where ignorance is bliss 'tis folly to be wise."'

MR BARNES and MR MITCHEL

Created by Rodrigues Ottolengui (1861–1937)

Born in Charleston, South Carolina but long resident in New York, Rodrigues Ottolengui devoted most of his energies to his career as a dentist. When he died in 1937, obituaries concentrated more on his decades-long editorship of a dental journal and his pioneering use of X-rays in orthodontics than they did on the four novels and a collection of short stories that he published in the 1890s. However, the stories, featuring the professional detective Mr Barnes and the wealthy amateur Mr Mitchel, were not completely forgotten. Ellery Queen mentioned them in an influential list of great crime fiction published in the 1940s and they have continued to find readers who enjoy detective stories from that period. 'The Montezuma Emerald', in which Mr Barnes comes to believe that his friend and crime-solving partner has been brutally murdered by a Mexican gangster in search of a priceless jewel, is one of the best of Ottolengui's tales.

THE MONTEZUMA EMERALD

'Is the Inspector in?'

Mr Barnes immediately recognised the voice, and turned to greet the speaker. The man was Mr Leroy Mitchel's English valet. Contrary to all precedent and tradition, he did not speak in cockney dialect, not even stumbling over the proper distribution of the letter W throughout his vocabulary. That he was English, however, was apparent to the ear, because of a certain rather attractive accent, peculiar to his native island, and to the eye because of a deferential politeness of manner, too seldom observed in American servants. He also always called Mr Barnes 'Inspector', oblivious of the fact that he was not a member of the regular police, and mindful only of the English application of the word to detectives.

'Step right in, Williams,' said Mr Barnes. 'What is the trouble?'

'I don't rightly know, Inspector,' said Williams. 'Won't you let me speak to you alone? It's about the master.'

'Certainly. Come into my private room.' He led the way and Williams followed, remaining standing, although Mr Barnes waved his hand towards a chair, as he seated himself in his usual place at his desk. 'Now then,' continued the detective, 'what's wrong? Nothing serious, I hope?'

'I hope not, sir, indeed! But the master's disappeared!'

'Disappeared, has he!' Mr Barnes smiled slightly. 'Now, Williams, what do you mean by that? You did not see him vanish, eh?'

'No, sir, of course not. If you'll excuse my presumption, Inspector, I don't think this is a joke, sir, and you're laughing.'

'All right, Williams,' answered Mr Barnes, assuming a more serious tone. 'I will give your tale my sober consideration. Proceed!'

'Well, I hardly know where to begin, Inspector. But I'll just give you the facts, without any unnecessary opinions of my own.'

Williams rather prided himself upon his ability to tell what he called 'a straight story'. He placed his hat on a chair, and, standing behind it, with one foot resting on a rung, checked off the points of his narrative, as he made them, by tapping the palm of one hand with the index finger of the other.

'To begin then,' said he. 'Mrs Mitchel and Miss Rose sailed for England, Wednesday morning of last week. That same night, quite unexpected, the master says to me, says he, "Williams, I think you have a young woman you're sweet on down at Newport?" "Well, sir," says I, "I do know a person as answers that description," though I must say to you, Inspector, that how he ever came to know it beats me. But that's aside, and digression is not my habit. "Well, Williams," the master went on, "I shan't need you for the rest of this week, and if you'd like to take a trip to the seashore, I shan't mind standing the expense, and letting you go." Of course, I thanked him very much, and I went, promising to be back on

Monday morning as directed. And I kept my word, Inspector; though it was a hard wrench to leave the young person last Sunday in time to catch the boat; the moon being bright and everything most propitious for a stroll, it being her Sunday off and all that. But as I said, I kept my word, and was up to the house Monday morning only a little after seven, the boat having got in at six. I was a little surprised to find the master was not at home, but then it struck me as how he must have gone out of town over Sunday, and I looked for him to be in for dinner. But he did not come to dinner, nor at all that night. Still, I did not worry about it. It was the master's privilege to stay away as long as he liked. Only I could not help thinking I might just as well have had that stroll in the moonlight, Sunday night. But when all Tuesday and Tuesday night went by, and no word from the master, I must confess that I got uneasy; and now here's Wednesday noon, and no news; so I just took the liberty to come down and ask your opinion in the matter, seeing as how you are a particular friend of the family, and an Inspector to boot.'

'Really, Williams,' said Mr Barnes, 'all I see in your story is that Mr Mitchel, contemplating a little trip off somewhere with friends, let you go away. He expected to be back by Monday, but, enjoying himself, has remained longer.'

'I hope that's all, sir, and I've tried to think so. But this morning I made a few investigations of my own, and I'm bound to say what I found don't fit that theory.'

'Ah! You have some more facts! What are they?'

'One of them is this cablegram that I found only this morning under a book on the table in the library.' He handed a blue paper to Mr Barnes, who took it and read the following, on a cable blank:

'Emerald. Danger. Await letter.'

For the first time during the interview, Mr Barnes's face assumed a really serious expression. He studied the dispatch silently for a full minute, and then, without raising his eyes, said:

'What else?'

'Well, Inspector, I don't know that this has anything to do with the affair, but the master had a curious sort of jacket, made of steel links, so tight and so closely put together, that I've often wondered what it was for. Once I made so bold as to ask him, and he said, said he: "Williams, if I had an enemy, it would be a good idea to wear that, because it would stop a bullet or a knife." Then he laughed, and went on, "Of course, I shan't need it for myself. I bought it when I was abroad once, merely as a curiosity." Now, Inspector, that jacket's disappeared also.'

'Are you quite sure?'

'I've looked from dining room to garret for it. The master's derringer is missing, too. It's a mighty small affair. Could be held in the hand without being noticed, but it carries a nasty-looking ball.'

'Very well, Williams, there may be something in your story. I'll look into the matter at once. Meanwhile, go home, and stay there so that I may find you if I want you.'

'Yes, sir; I thank you for taking it up. It takes a load off my mind to know you're in charge, Inspector. If there's harm come to the master, I'm sure you'll track the party down. Good morning, sir!'

'Good morning, Williams.'

After the departure of Williams, the detective sat still for several minutes, lost in thought. He was weighing two ideas. He seemed still to hear the words which Mr Mitchel had uttered after his success in unravelling the mystery of Mr Goldie's lost identity. 'Next time I will assign myself the chief role,' or words to that effect, Mr Mitchel had said. Was this disappearance a new riddle for Mr Barnes to solve? If so, of course, he would undertake it as a sort of challenge which his professional pride could not reject. On the other hand, the cable dispatch and the missing coat-of-mail might portend ominously. The detective felt that Mr Mitchel was somewhat in the position of the fabled boy who cried 'Wolf' so often, that when at last the wolf really appeared, no assistance was sent to him. Only Mr Barnes decided that he must chase the 'wolf', whether it be real or imaginary. He wished, though, that he knew which.

Ten minutes later he decided upon a course of action, and proceeded to a telegraph office, where he found that, as he had supposed, the dispatch had come from the Paris firm of jewellers from which Mr Mitchel had frequently bought gems. He sent a lengthy message to them, asking for an immediate reply.

While waiting for the answer, the detective was not inactive. He went direct to Mr Mitchel's house, and once more questioned the valet, from whom he obtained an accurate description of the clothes which his master must have worn, only one suit being absent. This fact alone seemed significantly against the theory of a visit to friends out of town. Next, Mr Barnes interviewed the neighbours, none of whom remembered to have seen Mr Mitchel during the week. At the sixth house below, however, he learned something definite. Here he found Mr Mordaunt, a personal acquaintance, and member of one of Mr Mitchel's clubs. This gentleman stated that he had dined at the club with Mr Mitchel on the previous Thursday, and had accompanied him home, in the neighbourhood of eleven o'clock, parting with him at the door of his own residence. Since then he had neither seen nor heard from him. This proved that Mr Mitchel was at home one day after Williams went to Newport.

Leaving the house, Mr Barnes called at the nearest telegraph office and asked whether a messenger summons had reached them during the week, from Mr Mitchel's house. The record slips showed that the last call had been received at twelve-thirty a.m. on Friday. A cab had been demanded, and was sent, reaching the house at one o'clock. At the stables, Mr Barnes questioned the cab-driver, and learned that Mr Mitchel alighted at Madison Square.

'But he got right into another cab,' added the driver. 'It was just a chance I seen him, 'cause he made as if he was goin' into the Fifth Avenoo; but luck was again him, for I'd scarcely gone two blocks back, when I had to get down to fix my harness, and while I was doin' that, who should I see but my fare go by in another cab.'

'You did not happen to know the driver of that vehicle?' suggested Mr Barnes.

'That's just what I did happen to know. He's always by the Square, along the curb by the Park. His name's Jerry. You'll find him easy enough, and he'll tell you where he took that fly bird.'

Mr Barnes went down town again, and did find Jerry, who

remembered driving a man at the stated time, as far as the Imperial Hotel; but beyond that the detective learned nothing, for at the hotel no one knew Mr Mitchel, and none recollected his arrival early Friday morning.

From the fact that Mr Mitchel had changed cabs, and doubled on his track, Mr Barnes concluded that he was after all merely hiding away for the pleasure of baffling him, and he felt much relieved to divest the case of its alarming aspect. However, he was not long permitted to hold this opinion. At the telegraph office he found a cable dispatch awaiting him, which read as follows:

'Montezuma Emerald forwarded Mitchel tenth. Previous owner murdered London eleventh. Mexican suspected. Warned Mitchel.'

This assuredly looked very serious. Casting aside all thought of a practical joke, Mr Barnes now threw himself heart and soul into the task of finding Mitchel, dead or alive. From the telegraph office he hastened to the Custom House, where he learned that an emerald, the invoiced value of which was no less than twenty thousand dollars, had been delivered to Mr Mitchel in person, upon payment of the custom duties, at noon of the previous Thursday. Mr Barnes, with this knowledge, thought he knew why Mr Mitchel had been careful to have a friend accompany him to his home on that night. But why had he gone out again? Perhaps he felt safer at a hotel than at home, and, having reached the Imperial, taking two cabs to mystify the villain who might be tracking him, he might have registered under an alias. What a fool he had been not to examine the registry, as he could certainly recognise Mr Mitchel's handwriting, though the name signed would of course be a false one.

Back, therefore, he hastened to the Imperial, where, however, his search for familiar chirography was fruitless. Then an idea occurred to him. Mr Mitchel was so shrewd that it would not be unlikely that, meditating a disappearance to baffle the men on his track, he had registered at the hotel several days prior to his permanently stopping there. Turning the page over, Mr Barnes still failed to find what he sought, but a curious name caught his eye.

'Miguel Palma – City of Mexico.'

Could this be the London murderer? Was this the suspected
Mexican? If so, here was a bold and therefore dangerous criminal
who openly put up at one of the most prominent hostelries.

Mr Barnes was turning this over in his mind, when a diminutive
newsboy rushed into the corridor, shouting:

'Extra Sun! Extra Sun! All about the horrible murder. Extra!'

Mr Barnes purchased a paper and was stupefied at the headlines.

ROBERT LEROY MITCHEL DROWNED! His Body
Found Floating in the East River. A DAGGER IN HIS
BACK INDICATES MURDER.

Mr Barnes rushed out of the hotel, and, quickly finding a cab,
instructed the man to drive rapidly to the morgue. On the way, he
read the details of the crime as recounted in the newspaper. From
this he gathered that the body had been discovered early that
morning by two boatmen, who towed it to shore and handed it
over to the police. An examination at the morgue had established
the identity by letters found on the corpse and the initials marked
on the clothing. Mr Barnes was sad at heart, and inwardly fretted
because his friend had not asked his aid when in danger.

Jumping from the cab almost before it had fully stopped in
front of the morgue, he stumbled and nearly fell over a decrepit-
looking beggar, upon whose breast was a printed card soliciting
alms for the blind. Mr Barnes dropped a coin, a silver quarter,
into his outstretched palm, and hurried into the building. As he
did so he was jostled by a tall man who was coming out, and who
seemed to have lost his temper, as he muttered an imprecation
under his breath in Spanish. As the detective's keen ear noted the
foreign tongue an idea occurred to him which made him turn and
follow the stranger. When he reached the street again he received
a double surprise. The stranger had already signalled the cab
which Mr Barnes had but just left, and was entering it, so that he
had only a moment in which to observe him. Then the door was
slammed, and the driver whipped up his horses and drove rapidly
away. At the same moment the blind beggar jumped up, and ran in
the direction taken by the cab. Mr Barnes watched them till both

cab and beggar disappeared around the next corner, and then he went into the building again, deeply thinking over the episode.

He found the morgue-keeper, and was taken to the corpse. He recognised the clothing at once, both from the description given by Williams, and because he now remembered to have seen Mr Mitchel so dressed. It was evident that the body had been in the water for several days, and the marks of violence plainly pointed to murder. Still sticking in the back was a curious dagger of foreign make, the handle projecting between the shoulders. The blow must have been a powerful stroke, for the blade was so tightly wedged in the bones of the spine that it resisted ordinary efforts to withdraw it. Moreover, the condition of the head showed that a crime had been committed, for the skull and face had been beaten into a pulpy mass with some heavy instrument. Mr Barnes turned away from the sickening sight to examine the letters found upon the corpse. One of these bore the Paris postmark, and he was allowed to read it. It was from the jewellers, and was the letter alluded to in the warning cable. Its contents were:

'Dear Sir – As we have previously advised you, the Montezuma emerald was shipped to you on the tenth instant. On the following day the man from whom we had bought it was found dead in Dover Street, London, killed by a dagger-thrust between the shoulders. The meagre accounts telegraphed to the papers here state that there is no clue to the assassin. We were struck by the name, and remembered that the deceased had urged us to buy the emerald, because, as he declared, he feared that a man had followed him from Mexico, intending to murder him to get possession of it. Within an hour of reading the newspaper story, a gentlemanly-looking man, giving the name of Miguel Palma, entered our store, and asked if we had purchased the Montezuma emerald. We replied negatively, and he smiled and left. We notified the police, but they have not yet been able to find this man. We deemed it our duty to warn you, and did so by cable.'

The signature was that of the firm from which Mr Barnes had received the cable in the morning. The plot seemed plain enough now. After the fruitless murder of the man in London, the Mexican had traced the emerald to Mr Mitchel, and had followed it across the water. Had he succeeded in obtaining it? Among the things found on the corpse was an empty jewel-case, bearing the name of the Paris firm. It seemed from this that the gem had been stolen. But if so, this man, Miguel Palma, must be made to explain his knowledge of the affair.

Once more visiting the Imperial, Mr Barnes made inquiry, and was told that Mr Palma had left the hotel on the night of the previous Thursday, which was just a few hours before Mr Mitchel had undoubtedly reached there alive. Could it be that the man at the morgue had been he? If so, why was he visiting that place to view the body of his victim? This was a problem over which Mr Barnes puzzled, as he was driven up to the residence of Mr Mitchel. Here he found Williams, and imparted to that faithful servant the news of his master's death, and then inquired the address of the family abroad, that he might notify them by cable, before they might read the bald statement in a newspaper.

'As they only sailed a week ago today,' said Williams, 'they're hardly more than due in London. I'll go up to the master's desk and get the address of his London bankers.'

As Williams turned to leave the room, he started back amazed at the sound of a bell.

'That's the master's bell, Inspector! Someone is in his room! Come with me!'

The two men bounded upstairs, two steps at a time, and Williams threw open the door of Mr Mitchel's boudoir, and then fell back against Mr Barnes, crying: 'The master himself!'

Mr Barnes looked over the man's shoulders, and could scarcely believe his eyes when he observed Mr Mitchel, alive and well, brushing his hair before a mirror.

'I've rung for you twice, Williams,' said Mr Mitchel, and then, seeing Mr Barnes, he added:

'Ah, Mr Barnes! You are very welcome. Come in. Why, what is the matter, man? You are as white as though you had seen a ghost.'

'Thank God you are safe,' fervently ejaculated the detective, going forward and grasping Mr Mitchel's hand. 'Here, read this, and you will understand.' He drew out the afternoon paper and handed it to him.

'Oh, that!' said Mr Mitchel carelessly. 'I've read that. Merely a sensational lie, worked off upon a guileless public. Not a word of truth in it, I assure you.'

'Of course not, since you are alive; but there is a mystery about this which is yet to be explained.'

'What? A mystery, and the great Mr Barnes has not solved it! I am surprised. I am, indeed. But then, you know, I told you after Goldie made a fizzle of our little joke that if I should choose to play the principal part you would not catch me. You see, I have beaten you this time. Confess. You thought that was my corpse which you gazed upon at the morgue?'

'Well,' said Mr Barnes reluctantly, 'the identification certainly seemed complete, in spite of the condition of the face, which made recognition impossible.'

'Yes; I flatter myself the whole affair was artistic.'

'Do you mean that this whole thing is nothing but a joke? That you went so far as to invent cables and letters from Paris just for the trifling amusement of making a fool of me?'

Mr Barnes was evidently slightly angry, and Mr Mitchel, noting this fact, hastened to mollify him.

'No! No! It is not quite so bad as that,' he said. 'I must tell you the whole story, for there is yet important work to do, and you must help me. No, Williams, you need not go out. Your anxiety over my absence entitles you to a knowledge of the truth. A short time ago I heard that a very rare gem was in the market, no less a stone than the original emerald which Cortez stole from the crown of Montezuma. The emerald was offered in Paris, and I was notified at once by the dealer, and authorized the purchase by cable. A few days later I received a dispatch warning me that there was danger. I understood at once, for similar danger has lurked about other large stones which are now in my collection. The warning meant that I should not attempt to get the emerald from the Custom House until further advices reached me, which would indicate the exact nature of the danger. Later, I received the letter which was found on the body now at the morgue, and which I suppose you have read?'

Mr Barnes nodded assent.

'I readily located the man Palma at the Imperial, and from his openly using his name I knew that I had a dangerous adversary. Criminals who disdain aliases have brains, and use them. I kept away from the Custom House until I satisfied myself that I was being dogged by a veritable cut-throat, who, of course, was the tool hired by Palma to rob, perhaps to kill me. Thus acquainted with my adversaries, I was ready for the enterprise.'

'Why did you not solicit my assistance?' asked Mr Barnes.

'Partly because I wanted all the glory, and partly because I saw a chance to make you admit that I am still the champion detective baffler. I sent my wife and daughter to Europe that I might have time for my scheme. On the day after their departure I boldly went to the Custom House and obtained the emerald. Of course I was dogged by the hireling, but I had arranged a plan which gave him no advantage over me. I had constructed a pair of goggles which looked like simple smoked glasses, but in one of these I had a little mirror so arranged that I could easily watch the man behind me, should he approach too near. However, I was sure that he would not attack me in a crowded thoroughfare, and I kept in crowds until time for dinner, when, by appointment, I met my neighbour Mordaunt, and remained in his company until I reached my own doorway late at night. Here he left me, and I stood on the stoop until he disappeared into his own house. Then I turned, and apparently had much trouble to place my latch-key in the lock. This offered the assassin the chance he had hoped for, and, gliding stealthily forward, he made a vicious stab at me. But, in the first place, I had put on a chain-armour vest, and, in the second, expecting the attack to occur just as it did, I turned swiftly and with one blow with a club I knocked the weapon from the fellow's hand, and with another I struck him over the head so that he fell senseless at my feet.'

'Bravo!' cried Mr Barnes. 'You have a cool nerve.'

'I don't know. I think I was very much excited at the crucial moment, but with my chain armour, a stout loaded club in one hand and a derringer in the other, I never was in any real danger. I took the man down to the wine cellar and locked him in one of the vaults. Then I called a cab, and went down to the Imperial, in search of Palma; but I was too late. He had vanished.'

'So I discovered,' interjected Mr Barnes.

'I could get nothing out of the fellow in the cellar. Either he cannot or he will not speak English. So I have merely kept him a prisoner, visiting him at midnight only, to avoid Williams, and giving him rations for another day. Meanwhile, I disguised myself and looked for Palma. I could not find him. I had another card, however, and the time came at last to play it. I deduced from Palma's leaving the hotel on the very day when I took the emerald from the Custom House that it was prearranged that his hireling should stick to me until he obtained the gem, and then meet him at some rendezvous, previously appointed. Hearing nothing during the past few days, he has perhaps thought that I left the city, and that his man was still upon my track. Meanwhile I was perfecting my grand coup. With the aid of a physician, who is a confidential friend, I obtained a corpse from one of the hospitals, a man about my size whose face was battered beyond recognition. We dressed him in my clothing, and fixed the dagger which I had taken from my would-be assassin so tightly in the backbone that it would not drop out. Then one night we took our dummy to the river and securely anchored it in the water. Last night I simply cut it loose and let it drift down the river.'

'You knew of course that it would be taken to the morgue,' said Mr Barnes.

'Precisely. Then I dressed myself as a blind beggar, posted myself in front of the morgue, and waited.'

'You were the beggar?' ejaculated the detective.

'Yes! I have your quarter, and shall prize it as a souvenir. Indeed, I made nearly four dollars during the day. Begging seems to be lucrative. After the newspapers got on the street with the account of my death, I looked for developments. Palma came in due time, and went in. I presume that he saw the dagger, which was placed there for his special benefit, as well as the empty jewel-case, and at once concluded that his man had stolen the gem, and meant to keep it for himself. Under these circumstances he would naturally be angry, and therefore less cautious, and more easily shadowed. Before he came out, you turned up and stupidly brought a cab, which allowed my man to get a start of me. However, I am a good runner, and as he only rode as far as Third Avenue, and then took the elevated railroad, I easily followed him to his lair. Now I will explain what I wish you to do, if I may count on you?'

'Assuredly!'

'You must go into the street, and when I release the man in the cellar, you must track him. I will go to the other place, and we will see what happens when the men meet. We will both be there to see the fun.'

An hour later, Mr Barnes was skilfully dogging a sneaking Mexican, who walked rapidly through one of the lowest streets on the East side, until finally he dodged into a blind alley, and before the detective could make sure which of the many doors had allowed him ingress, he had disappeared. A moment later a low whistle attracted his attention, and across in a doorway he saw a figure which beckoned to him. He went over and found Mr Mitchel.

'Palma is here. I have seen him. You see I was right. This is the place of appointment, and the cut-throat has come here straight. Hush! what was that?'

There was a shriek, followed by another, and then silence. 'Let us go up,' said Mr Barnes.

'Do you know which door?'

'Yes; follow me.'

Mr Mitchel started across, but just as they reached the door footsteps were heard rapidly descending the stairs. Both men stood aside and waited. A minute later a cloaked figure bounded out, only to be gripped instantly by those in hiding. It was Palma, and he fought like a demon, but the long, powerful arms of Mr Barnes encircled him, and, with a hug that would have made a bear envious, the scoundrel was soon subdued. Mr Barnes then manacled him, while Mr Mitchel ascended the stairs to see about the other man. He lay sprawling on the floor, face downward, stabbed in the heart.

NICK CARTER

Created by John R Coryell (1851-1924)

Nick Carter has been a presence in American popular culture for more than 130 years. He began life as the central figure in a newspaper serial entitled 'The Old Detective's Pupil, or The Mysterious Crime of Madison Square' which appeared in the New York Weekly *in 1886. Its author was John R Coryell, a prolific writer of dime novels. The character proved popular and was soon the headline act in his own* Nick Carter Weekly. *Over the decades, Carter evolved and changed, turning from dime novel hero to Sherlockian consulting detective to hardboiled private eye. In the 1960s, he was even relaunched as a James Bond-style secret agent, also known as the Killmaster, who appeared in more than 200 cheap paperbacks. He has been the star of comic strips, comics, radio series, movies and TV shows. There have been literally thousands of Nick Carter stories, nearly all of them the work of the mostly unidentified writers who followed Coryell. The one below was published in 1914 and it is described as 'edited' by Chick Carter, the detective's adopted son. Its real author is unknown. It has many of the regularly recurring characteristics of a Nick Carter story: a mad mastermind as its villain; a New York setting; and the detective's own peculiar combination of deductive ability and a liking for a good bout of fisticuffs. Carter uses his intelligence and wit to track down 'the mind murderer' of the subtitle but the story ends with a terrific no-holds-barred punch-up between the good guys and the bad guys which goes on for several pages.*

AN UNCANNY REVENGE, or NICK CARTER AND THE MIND MURDERER

I

The members of Nick Carter's household all happened to meet at the breakfast table that morning – a rather unusual circumstance.

The famous New York detective sat at the head of the table. Ranged about it were Chick Carter, his leading assistant; Patsy Garvan, and the latter's young wife, Adelina, and Ida Jones, Nick's beautiful woman assistant.

It was the latter who held the attention of her companions at that moment. She was a little late, and had just seated herself. Her flushed cheeks and sparkling eyes gave no hint that she had reached the house – they all shared the detective's hospitable roof – a little after three o'clock that morning.

'You good people certainly missed a sensation last night,' she declared. 'It was the strangest thing – and one of the most pitiable I ever beheld!'

Nick, who had been glancing at his favorite newspaper, looked up.

'What do you mean?' he asked.

It was Ida's turn to show surprise.

'Is it possible you don't know, any of you?' she demanded, looking around the table. 'Haven't you read of Helga Lund's breakdown, or whatever it was?'

Helga Lund, the great Swedish actress, who was electrifying New York that season in a powerful play, *The Daughters of Men*, had consented, in response to many requests, to give a special midnight performance, in order that the many actors and actresses in the city might have an opportunity to see her in her most successful role at an hour which would not conflict with their own performances.

The date had been set for the night before, and, since it was not to be exclusively a performance for professionals, the manager of the theater, who was a friend of Nick Carter's, had presented the detective with a box.

Much to Nick's regret, however, and that of his male assistants, an emergency had prevented them from attending. To cap the climax, Adelina Garvan had not been feeling well, so decided not to go. Consequently, Ida Jones had occupied the box with several of her friends.

Nick shook his head in response to his pretty assistant's question.

'I haven't, anyway,' he said, glancing from her face back to his paper. 'Ah, here's something about it – a long article!' he added. 'I hadn't seen it before. It looks very serious. Tell us all about it.'

Ida needed no urging, for she was full of her subject.

'Oh, it was terrible!' she exclaimed, shuddering. 'Helga Lund had been perfectly wonderful all through the first and second acts. I don't know when I have been so thrilled. But soon after the third act began she stopped right in the middle of an impassioned speech and stared fixedly into the audience, apparently at someone in one of the front rows of the orchestra.

'I'm afraid I can't describe her look. It seemed to express merely recollection and loathing at first, as if she had recognized a face which had very disagreeable associations. Then her expression – as I read it, at any rate – swiftly changed to one of frightened appeal, and then it jumped to one of pure harrowing terror.

'My heart stopped, and the whole theater was as still as a death chamber – at least, the audience was. Afterward I realized that the actor who was on the stage with her at the time had been improvising something in an effort to cover up her lapse; but I don't believe anybody paid any attention to him, any more than she did. Her chin dropped, her eyes were wild and seemed ready to burst from their sockets. She put both hands to her breast, and then raised one and passed it over her forehead in a dazed sort of way. She staggered, and I believe she would have fallen if her lover in the play hadn't supported her.

'The curtain had started to descend, when she seemed to pull herself together. She pushed the poor actor aside with a strength that sent him spinning, and began to speak. Her voice had lost all of its wonderful music, however, and was rough and rasping. Her grace was gone, too – Heaven only knows how! She was positively awkward. And her words – they couldn't have had anything to do with her part. They were incoherent ravings. The curtain had started to go up again. Evidently, the stage manager had thought the crisis was past when she began to speak. But when she only made matters worse, it came down with a rush. After a maddening delay, her manager came out, looking wild enough himself, and announced, with many apologies, that Miss Lund had suffered a temporary nervous breakdown.'

Nick Carter had listened intently, now and then scanning the article which described the affair.

'Too bad!' he commented soberly, when Ida had finished. 'But haven't you any explanation, either? The paper doesn't seem to have any – at least, it doesn't give any.'

A curious expression crossed Ida's face.

'I had forgotten for the moment,' she replied. 'I haven't told you one of the strangest things about it. In common with everybody else, I was so engrossed in watching Helga Lund's face that I didn't have much time for anything else. That is why there wasn't a more general attempt to see whom she was looking at. We wouldn't ordinarily have been very curious, but she held our gaze so compellingly. I did manage to tear my eyes away once, though; but I wasn't in a position to see – I was too far to one side. She appeared to be looking at someone almost on a line with our box, but over toward the other side of the theater. I turned my glasses in that direction for a few moments and thought I located the person, a man, but, of course, I couldn't be sure. I could only see his profile, but his expression seemed to be very set, and he was leaning forward a little, in a tense sort of way.'

Nick nodded, as if Ida's words had confirmed some theory which he had already formed.

'But what was so strange about him?' he prompted.

'Oh, it doesn't mean anything, of course,' was the reply; 'but he bore the most startling resemblance to Doctor Hiram Grantley. If I hadn't known that Grantley was safe in Sing Sing for a long term of years, I'm afraid I would have sworn that it was he.'

The detective gave Ida a keen, slightly startled look.

'Well, stranger things than that have happened in our

experience,' he commented thoughtfully. 'I haven't any reason to believe, though, that Grantley is at large again. He would be quite capable of what you have described, but surely Kennedy would have notified me before this if –'

The telephone had just rung, and, before Nick could finish his sentence, Joseph, his butler, entered. His announcement caused a sensation. It was:

'Long distance, Mr Carter. Warden Kennedy, of Sing Sing, wishes to speak with you.'

The detective got up quickly, without comment, and stepped out into the hall, where the nearest instrument of the several in the house was located.

Patsy Garvan gave a low, expressive whisper.

'Suffering catfish!' he ejaculated. 'It looks as if you were right, Ida!'

After that he relapsed into silence and listened, with the others. Nick had evidently interrupted the warden.

'Just a moment, Kennedy,' they heard him saying. 'I think I can guess what you have to tell me. It's Doctor Grantley who has escaped, isn't it?'

Naturally, the warden's reply was inaudible, but the detective's next words were sufficient confirmation.

'I thought so,' Nick said, in a significant tone. 'One of my assistants was just telling me of having seen, last night, a man who looked surprisingly like him. When did you find out that he was missing? ... As early as that? ... I see... Yes, I'll come up, if necessary, as soon as I can; but first I must set the ball rolling here. I think we already have a clue. I'll call you up later... Yes, certainly... Yes, goodbye!'

A moment later he returned to the dining room.

'Maybe your eyes didn't deceive you, after all, Ida,' he announced gravely. 'Grantley escaped last night – in time to have reached the theater for the third act of that special performance, if not earlier. And it looks as if he subjected one of the keepers of the prison to an ordeal somewhat similar to that which Helga Lund seems to have endured.'

II

'What do you mean by that, chief?' demanded Chick.

'Kennedy says that one of the keepers was found, in a peculiar sort of stupor, as he calls it, in Grantley's cell, after the surgeon had gone. He had evidently been overpowered in some way, and his keys had been taken from him. Kennedy assumes, rightly enough, I suppose, that Grantley lured him into the cell on some pretext, and then tried his tricks. The man is still unconscious, and the prison physician can do nothing to help him. Kennedy wants me to come up.'

'But I don't see what that has to do with Helga Lund,' objected Chick. 'Even if it was Grantley that Ida saw – which remains to be proved – I don't see any similarity. He didn't render her unconscious, and, anyway, he wasn't near enough to –'

'Think it over, Chick,' the detective interrupted. 'The significance will reach you, by slow freight, sooner or later, I'm sure. I, for one, haven't any doubt that Ida saw the fugitive last night. If so, Grantley did a very daring thing to go there without any attempt at disguise – not as daring as might be supposed, however. He doubtless counted on just what happened. If anyone who knew him by sight had noticed him in the theater, the supposition would naturally be that it was a misleading resemblance, for the chances were that anyone who would be likely to know him would be aware of his conviction, and be firmly convinced that he was up the river.

'There doesn't seem to be any doubt that he disguised himself carefully enough for his flight from Sing Sing, and covered his tracks with unusual care, for Kennedy has been unable to obtain any reliable information about his movements. If he was at the play, we may be sure that he restored his normal appearance deliberately, in defiance of the risks involved, in order that one person, at least, should recognize him without fail – that person being Helga Lund. And that implies that he was again actuated primarily by motives of private revenge, as in the case of Baldwin.

'The scoundrel seems to have a supply of enemies in reserve, and is willing to go to any lengths in order to revenge himself upon them for real or fancied grievances. If he's the man who broke up Lund's performance last night, it is obvious that he knew of the special occasion and the unusual hour before he made his escape. In fact, it seems probable that he escaped when he did for the purpose of committing this latest outrage. Even if his chief object has been attained, however, I don't imagine he will return to Sing Sing and give himself up. We shall have to get busy, and, perhaps, keep so for some time. Plainly, the first thing for me to do is to seek an interview with Helga Lund, if she is in a condition to receive me. She can tell, if she will, who or what it was that caused her breakdown. If there turns out to be no way of connecting it with Grantley, we shall have to begin our work at Sing Sing. If it was Grantley, we shall begin here. Did you see anything more of the man you noticed, Ida?'

'Nothing more worth mentioning. He slipped out quickly as soon as the curtain went down; but lots of others were doing the same, although many remained and exchanged excited conjectures. I left the box when I saw him going, but by the time I reached the lobby he was nowhere in sight, and I couldn't find any one who had noticed him.'

'Too bad! Then there's nothing to do but try to see Helga. The rest of you had better hang around the house until you hear from me. Whatever the outcome, I shall probably want you all on the jump, before long.'

Nick hastily finished his breakfast, while his assistants read him snatches from the accounts in the various morning newspapers. In that way he got the gist of all that had been printed in explanation of the actress's 'attack' and in regard to her later condition.

All of the accounts agreed in saying that Helga Lund was in seclusion at her hotel, in a greatly overwrought state, and that two specialists and a nurse were in attendance.

The prospect of a personal interview with her seemed exceedingly remote; but Nick Carter meant to do his best, unless her condition absolutely forbade.

★★★★

Doctor Hiram A Grantley was very well, if not favorably, known to the detectives, in addition to thousands of others.

For a quarter of a century he had been famous as an exceptionally daring and skilful surgeon. In recent years, however, his great reputation had suffered from a blight, due to his general eccentricities, and, in particular, to his many heartless experiments upon live animals.

At length, he had gone so far as to perform uncalled-for operations on human beings in his ruthless search for knowledge.

Nick Carter had heard rumors of this; and had set a trap for Grantley. He had caught the surgeon and several younger satellites red-handed.

Their victim at that time was a young Jewish girl, whose heart had been cruelly lifted out of the chest cavity, without severing any of the arteries or veins, despite the fact that the girl had sought treatment only for consumption.

Grantley and his accomplices had been placed on trial, charged with manslaughter. The case was a complicated one, and the jury disagreed. The authorities subsequently released the prisoners in the belief that the chances for a conviction were not bright enough to warrant the great expense of a new trial.

Nevertheless, as a result of the agitation, a law was passed, which attached a severe penalty to all such unjustifiable experiments or operations on human beings.

After a few weeks of freedom, Grantley had committed a still more atrocious crime. His victim in this instance had been one of the most prominent financiers in New York, J Hackley Baldwin, who had been totally blind for years.

For years Grantley had been nursing two grievances against the afflicted millionaire. Under pretense of operating on Baldwin's eyes – after securing the financier's complete confidence – he had removed parts of his patient's brain.

Owing to Grantley's great skill, the operation had not proved fatal; but Baldwin became a hopeless imbecile.

Nick Carter and his assistants again captured the fugitive, who had fled with his assistant, Doctor Siebold. This pair was locked up, together with a nurse and Grantley's German manservant, who were also involved.

To these four defendants, Nick presently added a fifth, in the person of Felix Simmons, another famous financier, who had been a bitter rival of Baldwin's for years, and who was found to have aided and abetted the rascally surgeon.

It was a startling disclosure, and all of the prisoners were convicted under the new law and sentenced to long terms of confinement.

That had been several months before; and now Doctor Grantley was at large again, and under suspicion of having been guilty of some strange and mysterious offense against the celebrated Swedish actress, who had never before visited this country.

****

Nick had learned from the papers that Helga Lund was staying at the Wentworth-Belding Hotel. Accordingly, he drove there in one of his motor cars and sent a card up to her suite. On it he scribbled a request for a word with one of the physicians or the nurse.

Doctor Lightfoot, a well-known New York physician, with a large practice among theatrical people, received him in one of the rooms of the actress's suite.

He seemed surprised at the detective's presence, but Nick quickly explained matters to his satisfaction. Miss Lund, it seemed, was in a serious condition. She had gone to pieces mentally, passed a sleepless night, most of the time walking the floor, and appeared to be haunted by the conviction that her career was at an end.

She declared that she would not mind so much if it had happened before any ordinary audience, but as it was, she had made a spectacle of herself before hundreds of the members of her own profession. That thought almost crazed her, and she insisted wildly that she would never regain enough confidence to appear in public again.

If that was the case, it was nothing short of a tragedy, in view of her great gifts.

Doctor Lightfoot hoped, however, that she would ultimately recover from the shock of her experience, although he stated that it would be months, at least, before she was herself again. Meanwhile, all of her engagements would have to be cancelled, of course.

In response to Nick's questions, the physician assured him that Helga Lund had given no adequate explanation of her startling behavior of the night before. She had simply said that she had recognized someone in the audience, that the recognition had brought up painful memories, and that she had completely forgotten her lines and talked at random. She did not know what she had said or done.

Her physicians realized that she was keeping something back, and had pleaded with her to confide fully in them as a means of relieving her mind from the weight that was so evidently pressing upon it. But she had refused to do so, having declared that it would serve no good purpose, and that the most they could do was to restore her shattered nerves.

The detective was not surprised at this attitude, which, as a matter of fact, paved the way to an interview with the actress.

'In that case I think you will have reason to be glad I came,' he told Doctor Lightfoot. 'I believe I know, in general, what happened last night, and if you will give me your permission to see Miss Lund alone for half an hour, I have hope of being able to induce her to confide in me. My errand does not reflect upon her in any way, nor does it imply the slightest danger or embarrassment to her, so far as I am aware. My real interest lies elsewhere, but you will readily understand how it might help her and reinforce your efforts if I could induce her to unbosom herself.'

'There isn't any doubt about that, Carter,' was the doctor's reply; 'but it's a risky business. She is in a highly excitable state, and uninvited calls from men of your profession are not apt to be soothing, no matter what their object may be. How do you know that some ghost of remorse is not haunting her? If so, you would do much more harm than good.'

'If she saw the person I think she saw in the audience last night,' Nick replied, 'it's ten to one that the remorse is on the other side – or ought to be. If I am mistaken, a very few sentences will prove it, and I give you my word that I shall do my best to quiet any fears my presence may have aroused, and withdraw at once. On the other hand, if I am right, I can convince her that I am her friend, and that I know enough to make it worth her while to shift as much of her burden as possible to me. If she consents, the tension will be removed at once, and she will be on the road to recovery. And, incidentally, I shall have gained some very important information.'

The detective was prepared, if necessary, to be more explicit with Doctor Lightfoot; but the latter, after looking Nick over thoughtfully for a few moments, gave his consent.

'I've always understood that you always know what you are about, Carter,' he said. 'There is nothing of the blunderer or the brute about you, as there is about almost all detectives. On the contrary, I am sure you are capable of using a great deal of tact, aside from your warm sympathies. My colleague isn't here now, and I am taking a great responsibility on my shoulders in giving you permission to see Miss Lund alone at such a time. She is a great actress, remember, and, if it is possible, we must give her back to the world with all of her splendid powers unimpaired. She is like a musical instrument of incredible delicacy, so, for Heaven's sake, don't handle her as if she were a hurdy-gurdy!'

'Trust me,' the famous detective said quietly.

'Then wait,' was the reply, and the physician hurried from the room.

Two or three minutes later he returned.

'Come,' he said. 'I have prepared her – told her you are a specialist in psychology, which is true, of course, in one sense. You can tell her the truth later, if all goes well.'

III

Nick was led through a couple of sumptuously furnished rooms into the great Swedish actress's presence.

Helga Lund was a magnificently proportioned woman, well above medium height, and about thirty years of age.

She wore a loose, filmy negligee of silk and lace, and its pale blue was singularly becoming to her fair skin and golden hair. Two thick, heavy ropes of the latter hung down far below her waist.

She was not merely pretty, but something infinitely better – she had the rugged statuesque beauty of a goddess in face and form.

She was pacing the floor like a caged lioness when Nick entered. Her head was thrown back and her hands were clasped across her forehead, allowing the full sleeves to fall away from her perfectly formed, milk-white arms.

'Miss Lund, this is Mr Carter, of whom I spoke,' Doctor Lightfoot said gently. 'He believes he can help you. I shall leave you with him, but I will be within call.'

He withdrew softly and closed the door. They were alone.

The actress turned for the first time, and a pang shot through the tender-hearted detective as he saw the tortured expression of her face.

She nodded absent-mindedly, but did not speak.

'Miss Lund,' the detective began, 'I trust you will believe that I would not have intruded at this time if I hadn't believed that I might possibly possess the key to last night's unfortunate occurrence, and that –'

'You – the key? Impossible, sir!' the actress interrupted, in the precise but rather labored English which she had acquired in a surprisingly short time in anticipation of her American tour.

'We shall soon be able to tell,' Nick replied. 'If I am wrong, I assure you that I shall not trouble you any further. If I am right, however, I hope to be able to help you. In any case, you may take it for granted that I am not trying to pry into your affairs. I have seen you on the stage more than once, both here and abroad. It is needless to say that I have the greatest admiration for your genius. Beyond that I know nothing about you, except what I have read.'

'Then, will you explain – briefly? You see that I am in no condition to talk.'

'I see that talking, of the right kind, would be the best thing for you, if the floodgates could be opened, Miss Lund,' Nick answered sympathetically. 'I shall do better than explain; with your permission, I shall ask you a question.'

'What is it?'

'Simply this: Are you acquainted with a New York surgeon who goes by the name of Doctor Grantley – Hiram A Grantley?'

The actress, who had remained standing, started slightly at the detective's words. Her bosom rose and fell tumultuously, and her clenched hands were raised to it, as Ida Jones had described them.

A look of mingled amazement and fright overspread her face.

Nick did not wait for her to reply, nor did he tell her that it was unnecessary. Nevertheless, he had already received his answer and it gave him the greatest satisfaction.

He was on the right track.

'Before you reply, let me say this,' he went on quickly, in order to convince her that she had nothing to fear from him: 'Grantley is one of the worst criminals living, and it is solely because our laws are still inadequate in certain ways that he is alive today. As it is, he is a fugitive, an escaped prisoner, with a long term still to serve. He escaped last night, but he will undoubtedly be caught soon, despite his undeniable cleverness, and returned to the cell which awaits him. Now you may answer, if you please.'

He was, of course, unaware of the extent of Helga Lund's knowledge of Grantley. It might not be news to her, but he wished – in view of the actress' evident fear of Grantley – to prove to her that he himself could not possibly be there in the surgeon's interest.

His purpose seemed to have been gained. Unless he was greatly mistaken, a distinct relief mingled with the surprise which was stamped on Helga's face.

'He is a – criminal, you say?' she breathed eagerly, leaning forward, forgetful that she had not admitted any knowledge of Grantley at all.

'You do not know what has happened to Doctor Grantley here in the last year?'

'No,' was the reply. 'I have never been in America before, and I have never even acted in England. I do not read the papers in English.'

'You met Grantley abroad, then, some years ago, perhaps?'

The actress realized that she had committed herself. She delayed for some time before she replied, and when she did, it was with a graceful gesture of surrender.

'I will tell you all there is to tell, Mr Carter,' she said, 'if you will give me your word as a gentleman that the facts will not be communicated to the newspapers until I give you permission. Will you? I think I have guessed your profession, but I am sure I have correctly gauged your honor.'

'I promise you that no word will find its way, prematurely, into print through me,' Nick declared readily. 'I am a detective, as you seem to have surmised, Miss Lund. I called on you, primarily, to get a clue to the whereabouts of Doctor Grantley, but, as I told you, I am confident that it will have a beneficial effect on you to relieve your mind and to be assured, in return, that Grantley is a marked and hunted man, and that every effort will be made to prevent him from molesting you any further.'

'Thank you, Mr Carter,' the actress responded, throwing herself down on a couch and tucking her feet under her.

The act suggested that her mental tension was already lessened to a considerable degree.

'There is very little to tell,' she went on, after a slight pause, 'and I should certainly have confided in my physicians if I had seen any use in doing so. It is nothing I need be ashamed of, I assure you. I did meet Doctor Grantley – to my sorrow – five years ago, in Paris. He was touring Europe at the time, and I was playing in the French capital. He was introduced to me as a distinguished American surgeon, and at first I found him decidedly interesting, despite – or, perhaps, because of – his eccentricities. Almost at once, however, he began to pay violent court to me. He was much older than I, and I could not think of him as a husband without a shudder. With all his brilliancy, there was something sinister and cruel about him, even then. I tried to dismiss him as gently as I knew how, but he would not admit defeat. He persisted in his odious attentions, and one day he seized me in his arms and was covering my face and neck with his detestable kisses, when a good friend, a young Englishman, was announced. My friend was big and powerful, a trained athlete. I was burning with shame and rage. I turned Doctor Grantley over to his tender mercies and left the room. Doctor Grantley was very strong, but he was no match for the Englishman. I am afraid he was maltreated rather severely. At any rate, he was thrown out of the hotel, and I did not see him again until last night. He wrote me a threatening letter, however, to the effect that he would have his revenge some day and ruin my career.

'I was greatly frightened at first, but, as time passed and nothing happened, I forgot him. Last night, those terrible, compelling eyes of his drew mine irresistibly. I simply had to look toward him, and when I did so, my heart seemed to turn to a lump of ice. I forgot my lines – everything. I knew what he meant to do, but I could not resist him. He was my master, and he was killing my art, my mastery. I was a child, a witless fool, in his hands. My brain was in chaos. I tried to rally my forces, to go on with my part, but it was impossible. I did manage to speak, but I do not know what I said, and no one will tell me. Doubtless, I babbled or raved, and the words were not mine. They were words of delirium, or, worse still, words which his powerful brain of evil put into my mouth.'

Helga Lund halted abruptly and threw out her hands again in an expressive gesture.

'That is all, Mr Carter,' she added. 'It was not my guilty conscience which made me afraid of him, you see. As for his whereabouts, I can tell you nothing. I did not know that he had been in trouble, although I am not surprised. I had neither heard nor seen anything of him since he wrote me, five years ago. Consequently, I fear I can be of no assistance to you in locating him – unless he should make another attempt of some sort on me, and Heaven forbid that!'

'I have learned that he was here last night,' said Nick, 'and that is all I hoped for. That will give us a point of departure. I assure you that I greatly appreciate your confidence, and that I shall not violate it. With your permission I shall tell your physicians just enough, in general terms, to give them a better understanding of your trouble. It will be best, for the present, to let the public believe that you are the victim of a temporary nervous breakdown, but I should strongly advise you to allow the facts to become known as soon as Grantley is captured. It will be good advertising, as we say over here, and, at the same time, it will stop gossip and dispel the mystery. It will also serve to reassure your many admirers, because it will give, for the first time, an adequate explanation, and prove that the cause of your mental disturbance has been removed.'

The actress agreed to this, and Nick Carter took leave of her, after promising to apprehend Grantley as soon as possible and to keep her informed of the progress of his search.

Before he left the hotel he had a short talk with Doctor Lightfoot, which gave promise of a more intelligent handling of the case, aside from the benefit which Helga Lund had already derived from her frank talk with the sympathetic detective.

The man hunt could now begin in New York City, instead of at Ossining, and, since the preliminaries could be safely intrusted to his assistants, Nick decided to comply with Warden Kennedy's urgent request and run up to the prison to see what he could make of the keeper's condition.

IV

The great detective set his men to work and called up the prison before leaving New York. As a result of the telephone conversation, the warden gave up the search for the fugitive in the neighborhood of Ossining.

Ossining is up the Hudson, about an hour's ride, by train, from the metropolis. It did not take Nick long to reach his destination.

He found Warden Kennedy in the latter's office, and listened to a characteristic account of Doctor Grantley's escape, which – in view of the fugitive's subsequent appearance at the theater – need not be repeated here.

Bradley, the keeper, was still unconscious, and nobody seemed to know what was the matter with him. Nick had a theory, which almost amounted to a certainty; but it remained to confirm it by a personal examination.

The warden presently led the way to the prison hospital, where the unfortunate keeper lay. No second glance was necessary to convince the detective that he had been right.

The man was in a sort of semi-rigid state, curiously like that of a trance. All ordinary restoratives had been tried and had failed, yet there did not appear to be anything alarming about his condition.

The prison physician started to describe the efforts which had been made, but Nick interrupted him quietly.

'Never mind about that, doctor,' he said. 'I know what is the matter with him, and I believe I can revive him – unless Grantley has blocked the way.'

'Is it possible!' exclaimed Kennedy and the doctor, in concert. 'What is it?' added the former, while the latter demanded: 'What do you mean by "blocking the way"?'

'Your ex-guest hypnotized him, Kennedy,' was the simple reply, 'and, as I have had more or less experience along that line myself, I ought to be able to bring Bradley out of the hypnotic sleep, provided the man who plunged him into it did not impress upon his victim's mind too strong a suggestion to the contrary. Grantley has gone deep into hypnotism, and it is possible that he has discovered some way of preventing a third person from reviving his subjects. There would have been nothing for him to gain by it in this case, but he may – out of mere malice – have thrown Bradley under a spell which no one but he can break. Let us hope not, however.'

'Hypnotism, eh?' ejaculated Kennedy. 'By the powers, why didn't we think of that, doctor?'

The prison physician hastily sought an excuse for his ignorance, but, as a matter of fact, he could not be greatly blamed. He was not one of the shining lights of his profession, as his not very tempting position proved, and comparatively few medical practitioners have had any practical experience with hypnotism or its occasional victims.

Nick Carter, on the other hand, had made an exhaustive study of the subject, both from a theoretical and a practical standpoint, and had often had occasion to utilize his extensive knowledge.

While Warden Kennedy, the physician, and a couple of nurses leaned forward curiously, the detective bent over the figure on the narrow white bed and rubbed the forehead and eyes a few times, in a peculiar way.

Then he spoke to the man.

'Come, wake up, Bradley!' he said commandingly. 'I want you! You're conscious! You're answering me. You cannot resist! Get up!'

And to the amazement of the onlookers, the keeper opened his eyes in a dazed, uncomprehending sort of way, threw his feet over the edge of the bed, and sat up.

'What is it? Where have I been?' he asked, looking about him. And then he added, in astonishment: 'What — what am I doing here?'

'You've been taking a long nap, but you're all right now, Bradley,' the detective assured him. 'You remember what happened, don't you?'

For a few moments the man's face was blank, but soon a look of shamed understanding, mingled with resentment, overspread it.

'It was that cursed Number Sixty Thousand One Hundred and Thirteen!' he exclaimed, giving Grantley's prison number. 'He called to me, while I was making my rounds — was it last night?'

Nick nodded, and the keeper went on:

'What do you know about that! Is he gone?'

This time it was the warden who replied.

'Yes, he's skipped, Bradley; but we know he was down in New York later in the night, and Carter here can be counted on to bring him back, sooner or later.'

Kennedy had begun mildly enough, owing to the experience which his subordinate had so recently undergone, but, at this point, the autocrat in him got the better of his sympathy.

'What the devil did you mean, though, by going into his cell, keys and all, like a confounded imbecile?' he demanded harshly. 'Isn't that the first thing you had drilled into that reinforced-concrete dome of yours — not to give any of these fellows a chance to jump you when you have your keys with you? If you hadn't fallen for his little game —'

'But I didn't fall for nothing, warden!' the keeper interrupted warmly. 'I didn't go into his cell at all. I know better than that, believe me!'

'You didn't – what? What are you trying to put over, Bradley?' Kennedy burst out. 'You were found in his cell, with the door unlocked and the keys gone, not to mention Number Sixty Thousand One Hundred and Thirteen, curse him! Maybe that ain't proof.'

'It ain't proof,' insisted the keeper, 'no matter how it looks. He called to me, and I started toward the grating to see what he wanted. He fixed his eyes on me, like he was looking me through and through, and made some funny motions with his hands. I'll swear that's all I remember. If I was found in his cell, I don't know how I got there, or anything about it, so help me!'

The warden started to give Bradley another tongue-lashing, but Nick interposed.

'He's telling the truth, Kennedy,' he said.

'But how in thunder –'

'Very easily. It hadn't occurred to me before, but it is evident that Grantley hypnotized him through the bars and then commanded him to unlock the door and come inside. There is nothing in hypnotism to interfere; on the contrary, that would be the easiest and surest thing to do, under the circumstances. Grantley is too clever to try any of the old, outworn devices – such as feigning sickness, for instance – in order to get a keeper in his power. All that was necessary was for him to catch Bradley's eye. The rest was as easy as rolling off a log. When he got our friend inside, he put him to sleep, took his keys and his outer clothing, and then – goodbye, Sing Sing! It's rather strange that he succeeded in getting away without discovery of the deception, but he evidently did; or else he bribed somebody. You might look into that possibility, if you think best. The supposition isn't essential, however, for accident, or good luck, might easily have aided him. As for the means he used to cover his trail after leaving the vicinity of the prison, we need not waste any time over that question. Fortunately, we have hit upon his trail down the river, and all that remains to do is to keep on it, in the right direction, until we come up with him. It may be a matter of hours or days or months, but Grantley is going to be brought back here before we're through. You can bank on that, gentlemen. And when I return him to you it will be up to you to take some extraordinary precautions to see that he doesn't hypnotize any more keepers.'

'I guess that's right, Carter,' agreed Warden Kennedy tugging at his big moustache. 'Bolts and bars are no good to keep in a man like that, who can make anybody let him out just by looking at him and telling him to hand over the keys. I suppose I'd have done it, too, if I'd been in Bradley's place.'

'Exactly!' the detective responded, with a laugh. 'You couldn't have helped yourself. Don't worry, though. I think we can keep him from trying any more tricks of that sort, when we turn him over to you again.'

'Hanged if I see how, unless we give him a dose of solitary confinement, in a dark cell, and have the men blindfold themselves when they poke his food in through the grating.'

'That won't be necessary,' Nick assured the warden as he prepared to leave. 'We can get around it easier than that.'

Half an hour later Nick was on his way back to New York City.

He was not as light-hearted or confident as he had allowed Warden Kennedy to suppose, however.

The fact that Grantley had turned to that mysterious and terrifying agency, hypnotism, with all of its many evil possibilities, caused him profound disquiet.

Already the fugitive had used his mastery of the uncanny force in two widely different ways. He had escaped from prison with startling ease by means of it, and then, not content with that, he had hypnotized a famous actress in the midst of one of her greatest triumphs – for Nick had known all along that Helga Lund had yielded to hypnotic influence.

If the escaped convict kept on in the way he had begun, there was no means of foretelling the character or extent of his future crimes, in case he was not speedily brought to bay.

V

Grantley's trail vanished into thin air – or seemed to – very quickly.

Nick Carter and his assistants had comparatively little trouble in finding the hotel which the fugitive had patronized the night before, but their success amounted to little.

Grantley had arrived there at almost one o'clock in the morning and signed an assumed name on the register. He brought a couple of heavy suitcases with him.

He had not been in prison long enough to acquire the characteristic prison pallor to an unmistakable degree, and a wig had evidently concealed his closely cropped hair.

He was assigned to an expensive room, but left his newly acquired key at the desk a few minutes later, and sallied forth on foot.

The night clerk thought nothing of his departure at the time, owing to the fact that the Times Square hotel section is quite accustomed to the keeping of untimely hours.

That was the last any of the hotel staff had seen of him, however. His baggage was still in his room, but, upon investigation, it was found to contain an array of useless and valueless odds and ends, obviously thrown in merely to give weight and bulk. In other words, the suit cases had been packed in anticipation of their abandonment.

It seemed likely that the doctor had had at least one accomplice in his flight, for the purpose of aiding him in his arrangements. But not necessarily so.

If he had received such assistance, it was quite possible that one of the six young physicians, who had formerly been associated with him in his unlawful experiments, had lent the helping hand.

Nick had kept track of them for some time, and now he determined to look them up again.

It was significant, however, that Grantley had, apparently, made no provision for the escape of Doctor Siebold, his assistant, who had been in Sing Sing with him.

In the flight which had followed their ghastly crime against the blind financier, Siebold had shown the white feather, and it was easy to believe that the stern, implacable Grantley had no further use for his erstwhile associate.

There was no reason to doubt that the escaped convict had gone directly to the theater after leaving the hotel. But why had he gone to the latter at all, and what had become of him after he had broken up Helga Lund's play?

There was no reasonable doubt that Grantley had disguised himself pretty effectually for his flight from Ossining to New York, and yet the night clerk's description was that of Grantley himself.

It followed, therefore, that the fugitive had already shed his disguise somewhere in the big city. But why not have gone directly from that stopping place, wherever it was, to the theater?

Nick gave it up as unimportant. The hotel episode did not seem to have served any desirable purpose, from Grantley's standpoint, unless on the theory that it was simply meant to confuse the detectives.

However that might be, it would be much more worthwhile to know what the surgeon's movements had been after his dastardly attack on the actress.

Had he gone to another hotel, in disguise or otherwise? Had he returned to his former house in the Bronx, which had been closed up since his removal to Sing Sing? Had he left town, or – well, done any one of a number of things?

There was room only for shrewd guesswork, for the most part.

An exhaustive search of the hotels failed to reveal his presence at any of them that night or later. The closed house in the Bronx was inspected, with a similar result.

That was about as far as the detective got along that line. Nick had a feeling that the fellow was still in New York. He had once tried to slip away in an unusually clever fashion, and had come to grief. It was fair to assume, therefore, that he would not make a second attempt, especially in view of the fact that the metropolis offers countless hiding places and countless multitudes to shield a fugitive.

If he was still in the city, though, he was almost unquestionably in disguise; and he could be counted on to see that that disguise was an exceptionally good one.

Certainly, the prospect was not an encouraging one. The proverbial needle in a haystack would have been easy to find in comparison.

And, meanwhile, Helga Lund would not know what real peace of mind was until she was informed that her vindictive persecutor had been captured.

Three days was spent in this fruitless tracking, and then, in the absence of tangible clues, the great detective turned to something which had often met with surprising success in the past.

He banished everything else from his mind and tried to put himself, in imagination, in Doctor Grantley's place.

What would this brilliant, erratic, but misguided genius, with all of his unbridled enmities and his criminal propensities, have done that night, after having escaped from prison and brought Helga Lund's performance to such an untimely and harrowing close?

It was clear that much depended on the depth of his hatred for the actress who had repulsed him five years before. Undoubtedly his enmity for the beautiful Swede was great, else he would not have timed his escape as he had done, or put the first hours of his liberty to such a use.

But would he have been content with what he had done that first night? If he had considered his end accomplished, he might have shaken the dust of New York from his feet at once. On the other hand, if his thirst for revenge had not yet been slaked, it was probable that he was still lurking near, ready to follow up his first blow with others.

The more Nick thought about it the more certain he became that the latter supposition was nearer the truth than the former. Grantley had caused Helga Lund to break down completely before one of the most important and critical audiences that had ever been assembled in New York, to be sure, but, with a man of his type, was that likely to be anything more than the first step? He had threatened to ruin her career, and he was nothing if not thorough in whatever he attempted. Therefore – so Nick reasoned – further trouble might be looked for in that quarter.

The thought was an unwelcome one. The detective had taken every practicable precaution to shield Helga from further molestation, but he knew only too well that Grantley's attacks were of a sort which usually defied ordinary safeguards.

The possibility of new danger to the actress spurred Nick on to added concentration.

Assuming that Grantley was still in New York, in disguise, and bent upon inflicting additional injury on the woman he had once loved, where would he be likely to hide himself, and what would be the probable nature of his next move?

The detective answered his last question first after much weighing of possibilities.

Grantley was one of the most dangerous of criminals, simply because his methods were about as far removed as possible from the ordinary methods of criminals. He had confined himself, thus far, to crimes in which he had made use of his immense scientific knowledge, surgical and hypnotic.

Accordingly, the chances were that he would work along one of those two lines in the future, or else along some other, in which his special knowledge would be the determining factor.

Moreover, since his escape, he had repeatedly called his mastery of hypnotism to his aid. That being so, Nick was inclined to believe that he would continue to use it, especially since Helga had shown herself so susceptible to hypnotic influence.

Could the detective guard against that?

He vowed to do his best, notwithstanding the many difficulties involved.

But it was not until he had carefully balanced the probabilities in regard to Grantley's whereabouts that Nick became seriously alarmed.

As a consequence of his study of the problem, an overwhelming conviction came to him that it would be just like the rascally surgeon to have gone to Helga's own hotel, under another name.

The luxurious Wentworth-Belding would be as safe for the fugitive as any other place, providing his disguise was adequate –

safer, in fact, for it was the very last place which would ordinarily fall under suspicion.

In addition to that great advantage, it offered the best opportunity to keep in touch with developments in connection with the actress's condition, and residence there promised comparatively easy access to Helga when the time should come for the next act in the drama of revenge.

This astounding suspicion had sprung up, full-fledged, in Nick's brain in the space of a second. The detective knew that his preliminary reasoning had been sound, however, and based upon a thorough knowledge of Grantley's characteristic methods.

It was staggering, but his keen intuition told him that it was true. He was now certain that Grantley would be found housed under the same huge roof as his latest victim, and that meant that Helga's danger was greater than ever.

The next blow might fall at any minute.

It was very surprising, in fact, that Grantley had remained inactive so long.

The detective hastily but effectively disguised himself, left word for his assistants, and hurried to the hotel – only to find that his flash of inspiration had come a little too late.

Helga Lund had mysteriously disappeared.

VI

Doctor Lightfoot, the actress's physician, was greatly excited and had just telephoned to Nick's house, after the detective had left for the hotel.

The doctor had arrived there about half an hour before, for his regular morning visit. To his consternation he had found the night nurse stretched out on Helga Lund's bed, unconscious, and clad only in her undergarments.

The actress was nowhere to be found.

The anxious Lightfoot was of very different caliber from the prison physician at Sing Sing. He had recognized the nurse's symptoms at once, and knew that she had been hypnotized.

He set to work at once to revive her and succeeded in doing

so, after some little delay. As soon as she was in a condition to question, he pressed her for all the details she could give.

They were meager enough, but sufficiently disquieting. According to her story, a man whom she had supposed to be Lightfoot himself had gained entrance to the suite between nine and ten o'clock at night.

He had sent up Doctor Lightfoot's name, and his appearance, when she saw him, had coincided with that of the attending physician. He had acted rather strangely, to be sure, and the nurse had been surprised at his presence at that hour, owing to the fact that Lightfoot had already made his two regular calls that day.

Before her surprise had had time to become full-fledged suspicion, however, the intruder had fixed her commandingly with his eyes and she had found herself powerless to resist the weakness of will which had frightened her.

She dimly remembered that he had approached her slowly, nearer and nearer, and that his gleaming eyes had seemed to be two coals of fire in his head.

That was all she recalled, except that she had felt her senses reeling and leaving her. She had known no more until Doctor Lightfoot broke the dread spell, almost twelve hours afterward.

She had met the bogus Lightfoot in one of the outer rooms of the suite, not in the presence of the actress. Miss Lund had been in her bedroom at the time, but had not yet retired.

The nurse was horror-stricken to learn that her patient was missing, and equally at a loss to explain how she herself came to be without her uniform.

But Doctor Lightfoot possessed a sufficiently analytical mind to enable him to solve the puzzle, after a fashion, even before Nick arrived.

The detective had told him that the sight of an enemy of the actress had caused her seizure, and it was easy to put two and two together. This enemy had doubtless made himself up to represent the attending physician, had hypnotized the nurse, and then passed on, unhindered, to the actress's room.

He had obviously subdued her in the same fashion, after which he had removed the unconscious nurse's uniform and compelled Helga to don it.

The doctor remembered now that the two women were nearly alike in height and build. The nurse had dark-brown hair, in sharp contrast to Helga's golden glory; but a wig could have remedied that. Neither was there any similarity in features, but veils can be counted on to hide such differences.

Doctor Lightfoot, despite his alarm, was rather proud of his ability to reason the thing out alone. He had no doubt that Helga Lund, under hypnotic influence, had accompanied the strange man from the hotel, against her will.

It would have been very easy, with no obstacle worth mentioning to interpose. No one who saw them would have thought it particularly strange to see the nurse and the doctor leaving together. At most, it would have suggested that they were on unusually good terms, and that he was taking her out for an airing in his car.

The keen-witted physician had progressed thus far by the time Nick arrived, but he had not yet sought to verify his deductions by questioning any of the hotel staff.

Nick listened to his theory, put a few additional questions to the nurse, and then complimented Doctor Lightfoot on his analysis.

'That seems to be the way of it,' the detective admitted. 'A light, three-quarter-length coat, which the nurse often wore over her uniform, is also missing, together with her hat. The distinctive nurse's skirt would have shown beneath the coat and thereby helped the deception.'

Confidential inquiries were made at once, and the fact was established that the two masqueraders – one voluntary and one involuntary – had left the building about ten o'clock the night before.

The supposed Lightfoot had arrived in a smart, closed town car, which had been near enough to the physician's in appearance to deceive the carriage starter. The chauffeur wore a quiet livery, a copy of that worn by Lightfoot's driver. The car had waited, and the two had ridden away in it.

That was all the hotel people could say. The night clerk had thought it odd that Miss Lund's nurse had not returned, but it was none of his business, of course, if the actress's physician had taken her away.

It was of little importance now, but Nick was curious enough to make inquiries, while he was about it, which brought out the fact that a man had registered at the hotel the morning after the affair at the theater, and had paid his bill and left the evening before.

It might have been only a coincidence, but certain features of the man's description, as given, left room for the belief that Doctor Grantley had really been at the Wentworth-Belding during that interval.

But where was he now, and what had he done with the unfortunate actress?

Such as it was, the slender clue furnished by the closed car must be followed up for all it was worth.

That was not likely to prove an easy matter, and, unless Grantley had lost his cunning, the trail of the machine would probably lead to nothing, even if it could be followed. Nevertheless, there seemed to be nothing else to work on.

The chauffeur of the car might have been an accomplice, but it was not necessary to suppose so. It looked as if the wily Grantley had hunted up a machine of the same make as Doctor Lightfoot's, and had engaged it for a week or a month, paying for it in advance.

There are many cars to be had in New York on such terms, and they are extensively used by people who wish to give the impression, for a limited time, that they own a fine car.

It is a favorite way of overawing visitors, and chauffeurs in various sorts of livery go with the cars, both being always at the command of the renter.

It would not, therefore, have aroused suspicion if Grantley had furnished a livery of his own choice for his temporary chauffeur.

The first step was to ascertain the make of Doctor Lightfoot's car. Another make might have been used, of course, but it was not likely, since the easiest way to duplicate the machine would have been to choose another having the same lines and color.

'Mine is a Palgrave,' the physician informed Nick, in response to the latter's question.

'Humph! That made it easy for Grantley,' remarked the detective; 'but it won't be so easy for us. The Palgrave is the favorite car for renting by the week or month, and there are numerous places where that particular machine might have been obtained. We'll have to go the rounds.'

Nick and his assistants set to work at once, with the help of the telephone directory, which listed the various agencies for automobiles. There were nearly twenty of them, but that meant comparatively little delay, with several investigators at work.

A little over an hour after the search began, Chick 'struck oil.'

Grantley, disguised as Doctor Lightfoot, had engaged a Palgrave town car of the latest model at an agency on 'Automobile Row,' as that section of Broadway near Fifty-ninth Street is sometimes called.

The machine had been engaged for a week – not under Lightfoot's name, however – and Grantley had furnished the suit of livery. The car had been used by its transient possessor for the first time the night before, had returned to the garage about eleven o'clock, and had not since been sent for.

The chauffeur was there, and, at Nick's request, the manager sent for him.

The detective was about to learn something of Grantley's movements; but was it to be much, or little?

He feared that the latter would prove to be the case.

VII

The detective had revealed his identity, and the chauffeur was quite willing to tell all he knew.

He had driven his temporary employer and the woman in nurse's garb to the Yellow Anchor Line pier, near the Battery. Grantley – or Thomas Worthington, as he had called himself in this connection – had volunteered the information that his companion was his niece, who had been sent for suddenly to take care of someone who was to sail on the *Laurentian* at five o'clock in the morning.

Both of the occupants of the car had alighted at the pier, and the man had told the chauffeur not to wait, the explanation being that he might be detained on board for some time.

The pier was a long one, and the chauffeur could not, of course, say whether the pair had actually gone on board the vessel or not. He had obeyed orders and driven away at once.

Neither the man nor the woman had carried any baggage. The chauffeur had gathered that the person who was ill was a relative of both of them, and that the nurse's rather bewildered manner was due to her anxiety and the suddenness of the call.

That was all Nick could learn from him, and an immediate visit to the Yellow Anchor Line's pier was imperative.

There it was learned that a man and woman answering the description given had been noticed in the crowd of people who had come to bid goodbye to relatives and friends. One man was sure he had seen them enter a taxi which had just dropped its passengers. When interrogated further, he gave it as his impression that the taxi was a red-and-black machine. He naturally did not notice its number, and no one else could be found who had seen even that much.

A wireless inquiry brought a prompt reply from the *Laurentian*, to the effect that no couple of that description was on board, or had been seen on the vessel the night before.

It was clear that Grantley had made a false trail, for the purpose of throwing off his pursuers. It had been a characteristic move, and no more than Nick had expected.

The detective turned his attention to the taxi clue. Red and black were the distinctive colors of the Flanders-Jackson Taxicab Company's machines. Consequently, the main garage of that concern was next visited.

Luckily, the man at the pier had been right. One of the company's taxis had been at the Yellow Anchor Line pier the previous night, and had picked up a couple of new passengers there, after having been dismissed by those who had originally engaged it.,

Nick obtained the name and address of the chauffeur, who was off duty until night. He was not at home when the detective called, but, after a vexatious delay, he was eventually located.

A tip loosened his tongue.

'I remember them well, sir,' he declared. 'The man looked like a doctor, I thought, and, if I'm not mistaken, the woman had on a nurse's uniform under her long coat. I couldn't see her face, though, on account of the heavy veil she wore. She acted queer – sick or something. The fellow told me, when they got in, to drive them to the Wentworth-Belding, but when I got up to Fourteenth Street, he said to take them to the Metropolitan Building. I did, and they got out. That's all I know about it. I drove them to the Madison Square side, and they had gone into the building before I started away, but that's the last I saw of them.'

'Well, we've traced them one step farther, Chick,' Nick remarked to his first assistant as they left, 'but we haven't tracked them down, by a long shot. Grantley doubtless went through the Metropolitan Building to Fourth Avenue. There he either took the subway, hailed another taxi, or – hold on, though! Maybe there's something in that! I wonder –'

'Now, what?' Chick asked eagerly.

'You remember Doctor Chester, one of the six young physicians who was mixed up with Grantley in that vivisection case?'

'Of course I do,' his assistant answered. 'He has taken another name and given up his profession – on the surface, at least. He's living on East Twenty-sixth Street –'

'Exactly – a very few blocks from the Metropolitan Building!' interrupted his chief.

'You mean –'

'I have a "hunch", as Patsy would call it, that Grantley has taken Helga Lund to Chester's house. Chester has rented one of those old-fashioned, run-down bricks across from the armory. It's liable to be demolished almost any day, to make way for a new skyscraper, and he doubtless gets it for a song. He can do what he pleases there, and I wouldn't be surprised to find that Grantley had been paying the rent in anticipation of something of this sort. They undoubtedly think that we lost sight of Chester long ago.'

'By George! I'll wager you're right, chief!' exclaimed Chick. 'The fact that we've traced Grantley to the Metropolitan Building certainly looks significant, in view of Chester's house being so near to it. It's only about five minutes' walk, and a man with

Grantley's resourcefulness could easily have made enough changes in his appearance and that of Miss Lund, while in the Metropolitan Building, to have made it impossible for the two who entered Chester's house to be identified with those who had left the Wentworth-Belding an hour or so before.'

'That's the way it strikes me,' agreed the detective. 'And, if the scoundrel took her there last night, they are doubtless there now. I think we're sufficiently justified in forcing our way into the house and searching it, and that without delay. We don't know enough to take the police into our confidence as yet; therefore, the raid will have to be purely on our own responsibility. We must put our theory to the test at once, however, without giving Grantley any more time to harm the actress. Heaven knows he's had enough opportunity to do so already!'

'Right! We can't wait for darkness or reinforcements. It will have to be a daylight job, put through just as we are. If we find ourselves on the wrong scent, Chester will be in a position to make it hot for us – or would be, if he had any standing – but we'll have to risk that.'

'Well, if Chester – or Schofield, as he is calling himself now – is tending to his new business as a commercial chemist, he ought to be away at this hour. That remains to be seen, however. I imagine, at any rate, that we can handle any situation that is likely to arise. If time were not so precious, it would be better to have some of the other boys along with us, but we don't know what may be happening at this very moment. Come on. We can plan our campaign on the way.'

A couple of tall loft buildings had already replaced part of the old row of houses on the north side of Twenty-sixth Street, beginning at Fourth Avenue. Nick and his assistant entered the second of these and took the elevator to one of the upper floors, from the eastern corridor of which they could obtain a view of the house occupied by young Doctor Chester, together with its approaches, back and front.

The house consisted of a high basement – occupied by a little hand laundry – and three upper stories, the main floor being reached by a flight of iron steps at the front.

Obviously, there was no exit from the body of the house at the rear. There was only a basement door opening into the tiny back yard, and that was connected with the laundry.

The detective decided, as a result of their general knowledge of such houses, not to bother with the back at all. Their plan was to march boldly up the front stairs, outside, fit a skeleton key to the lock, and enter the hall.

They argued that, owing to the fact that the basement was sublet, any crooked work that might be going on would be likely to be confined to the second or third floor to prevent suspicion on the part of those connected with the laundry.

Therefore, they hoped to find the first floor deserted. If that were the case, it was improbable that their entrance would be discovered prematurely.

There was, doubtless, a flight of steps at the rear of the house, leading down to the laundry from the first floor; but they were practically certain that these rear stairs did not ascend above the main floor. If they did not, there was no way of retreat for the occupants of the upper part of the house, except by the front stairs, and, as the detective meant to climb them, it seemed reasonable to suppose that Grantley, Chester & Company could easily be trapped.

Nick and Chick returned to the street and made their way, without the slightest attempt at concealment, toward the suspected house.

They met no one whose recognition was likely to be embarrassing, and saw no face at the upper windows as they climbed the outer steps.

They had already seen to it that their automatics were handy, and now Nick produced a bunch of skeleton keys and began fitting them, one after another.

The fifth one worked. They stepped into the hall as if they belonged there – taking care to make no noise, however – and gently closed the doors behind them.

The adventure was well under way, and, technically speaking, they were already housebreakers.

VIII

The house in which Nick and Chick found themselves had been a good one, but it was now badly in need of repair.

The main hall was comparatively wide for so narrow a building, and a heavy balustrade fenced off the stairs on one side.

The detectives paused just inside the door and listened intently. The doors on the first floor were all closed and the rooms behind them appeared to be untenanted. At any rate, all was still on that floor. Subdued noises of various sorts floated down to them from above, however, seemingly from the third floor.

They looked at each other significantly. Evidently, their theory had been correct – to some extent, at least.

They approached each of the doors in turn, but could hear nothing. Under the stairway they found the expected door leading down to the basement, but, as it was locked, and there was no key, they paid no further attention to it.

Instead, they started to mount the front stairs to the second floor. The stairway was old and rather creaky, but the detectives knew how to step in order to make the least noise. Consequently, they gained the next landing without being discovered.

Here they repeated the tactics they had used below, with a like result. The sounds of voices and footfalls were louder now, but they all came from the third floor. The second seemed to be as quiet as the first.

The doors on the second floor, like those on the first, were all closed, but Nick ascertained that at least one of them was unlocked.

That fact might be of great advantage in preventing discovery, in case anyone should start down unexpectedly from the third floor, for the halls and stairs offered no place of concealment.

The detectives noiselessly removed their shoes before attempting the last flight, and placed them inside the unlocked room, which they noiselessly closed again.

They were now ready for the final reconnaissance.

By placing the balls of their stockinged feet on the edges of the steps, they succeeded in mounting to the third floor without making any more noise than that produced by the contact of their clothing.

A slight pause at the top served to satisfy them that the noises all proceeded from one room at the front of the house. They were already close to the door of this room, and they listened breathlessly.

Words were plainly audible now, punctuated at frequent intervals by loud bursts of laughter.

It sounded like a merrymaking of some kind. What was going on behind that closed door? Had they made a mistake in entering the house and wasted precious time in following a will-o'-the-wisp, when Helga Lund might be even then in the greatest danger?

Nick and his assistants feared so, and their hearts sank heavily.

But no. The next words they heard reassured, but, at the same time, startled them. The voice was unmistakably Grantley's.

'That's enough of pantomime,' it said, with a peculiar note of cruel, triumphant command. 'Now give us your confession from *The Daughters of Men* – give it, but remember that you are not a great actress, that you are so bad that you would be hooted from the cheapest stage. Remember that you are ugly and dressed in rags, that you are awkward and ungainly in your movements, that your voice is like a file. Remember it not only now, but always. You will never be able to act. Your acting is a nightmare, and you are a fright – when you aren't a joke. But show us what you can do in that confession scene.'

Nick and Chick grew tense as they listened to those unbelievable words, and to the heartless chuckles and whisperings with which they were received. Apparently there were several men in the 'audience' – probably Chester and some of Grantley's other former accomplices. .

The meaning was plain – all too plain.

The proud, beautiful Helga Lund was once more under hypnotic influence, and Grantley, with devilish ingenuity, was impressing suggestions upon her poor, tortured brain, suggestions which were designed to rob her of her great ability, not only for the moment, but, unless their baneful effect could be removed, for all the rest of her life.

She, who had earned the plaudits of royalty in most of the countries of Europe, was being made a show of for the amusement of a handful of ruthless scoffers.

It made the detectives' blood boil in their veins and their hands clench until their knuckles were white, but they managed somehow to keep from betraying themselves.

The employment of hypnotism in such a way was plainly within the scope of the new law against unwarranted operations or experiments on human beings, without their consent; but it was necessary to secure as much evidence as possible before interfering.

To that end Nick Carter took out of a pocket case a curious little instrument, which he was in the habit of calling his 'keyhole periscope.'

It consisted of a small black tube, about the length and diameter of a lead pencil. There was an eyepiece at one end. At the other a semi-circular lens bulged out.

It was designed to serve the same purpose as the periscope of a submarine torpedo boat – that is, to give a view on all sides of a given area at once. The exposed convex lens, when thrust through a keyhole or other small aperture, received images of objects from every angle in the room beyond, and magnified them, in just the same way as the similarly constructed periscope of a submarine projects above the level of the water and gives those in the submerged vessel below a view of all objects on the surface, within a wide radius.

Nick had noted that there was no key in the lock of the door. Taking advantage of that fact, he crept silently forward, inserted the wonderful little instrument in the round upper portion of the hole, and, stooping, applied his eye to the eyepiece.

He could not resist an involuntary start as he caught his first glimpse of the extraordinary scene within.

The whole interior of the room was revealed to him. Around the walls were seated three young men of professional appearance. Nick recognized them all. They were Doctor Chester, Doctor Willard, and Doctor Graves, three of Grantley's former satellites.

They were leaning forward or throwing themselves back in

different attitudes of cruel enjoyment and derision, while Grantley stood at one side, his hawk-like face thrust out, his keen, pitiless eyes fixed malignantly on the figure in the center of the room.

Nick's heart went out in pity toward that pathetic figure, although he could hardly believe his eyes.

It was that of Helga Lund, but so changed as to be almost unrecognizable.

Her splendid golden hair hung in a matted, disordered snarl about her face, which was pale and smudged with grime. She was clothed in the cheapest of calico wrappers, hideously colored, soiled and torn, beneath which showed her bare, dust-stained feet.

She had thrown herself upon her knees, as the part required; her outstretched hands were intertwined beseechingly, and her wonderful eyes were raised to Grantley's face. In them was the hurt, fearful look of a faithful but abused dog in the presence of a cruel master.

Her tattered sleeves revealed numerous bruises on her perfectly formed arms.

The part of the play which Grantley had ordered her to render was that in which the heroine pleaded with her angry lover for his forgiveness of some past act of hers, which she had bitterly repented.

She was reciting the powerful lines now. They had always held her great audiences breathless, but how different was this pitiable travesty!

It would have been hard enough at best for her to make them ring true when delivered before such unsympathetic listeners and in such an incongruous garb, but she was not at her best. On the contrary, her performance was infinitely worse than anyone would have supposed possible.

She had unconsciously adopted every one of the hypnotist's brutal suggestions.

There was not a vestige of her famous grace in any of her movements. The most ungainly slattern could not have been more awkward.

Her words were spoken parrot-like, as if learned by rote, without the slightest understanding of their meaning. For the most part, they succeeded one another without any attempt at emphasis, and when emphasis was used, it was invariably in the wrong place.

It was her voice itself, however, which gave Nick and Chick their greatest shock.

The Lund, as she was generally called in Europe, had always been celebrated for her remarkably musical voice; but this sorry-looking creature's voice was alternately shrill and harsh. It pierced and rasped and set the teeth on edge, just as the sound of a file does.

Nothing could have given a more sickening sense of Grantley's power over the actress than this astounding transformation, this slavish adherence to the conditions of abject failure which he had imposed upon her.

It seemed incredible, and yet, there it was, plainly revealed to sight and hearing alike.

A subtler or more uncanny revenge has probably never been conceived by the mind of man. The public breakdown which Grantley had so mercilessly caused had only been the beginning of his scheme of vengeance.

He doubtless meant to hypnotize his victim again and again, and each time to impose his will upon her gradually weakening mind, until she had become a mere wreck of her former self, and incapable of ever again taking her former place in the ranks of genius.

There was nothing impossible about it. On the contrary, the result was a foregone conclusion if Grantley were left free to continue as he had begun.

The very emotional susceptibility which had made Helga Lund a great actress had also made her an easy victim of hypnotic suggestion, and if the process went on long enough, she would permanently lose everything that had made her successful.

Outright murder would have been innocent by comparison with such infernal ingenuity of torture. It seemed to Nick as if he were watching the destruction of a splendid priceless work of art.

He had seen enough.

He withdrew the little periscope from the keyhole and

straightened up. One hand went to his pocket and came out with an automatic. Chick followed his example.

They were outnumbered two to one, but that did not deter them.

Helga must be rescued at once, and her tormentors caught red-handed.

IX

What was to be done, though?

To burst into the room and seek to overpower the four doctors then and there, in Helga's presence, would place the actress in additional danger.

Nick was convinced, however, that that risk would have to be run. He had seen evidences that more than one of the men were tiring of the cruel sport, and it might now come to an end at any moment.

He swiftly considered two or three possible plans for drawing the four away from their victim, but rejected them all. They would only increase the danger of a slip of some sort, and he was bent upon capturing the four, as well as releasing the actress.

Furthermore, he did not believe that even Grantley would dare to harm Helga further in his presence, even if the fortunes of war should give the surgeon a momentary opportunity.

He, accordingly, motioned to his assistant to follow close behind him, and laid his left hand on the knob.

He turned it noiselessly, and was greatly relieved to find that the door yielded. Their advent would be a complete surprise, therefore, and would find the four totally unprepared.

Nick paused a moment, then flung the door back violently and strode into the room.

Grantley was the ringleader, the most dangerous of the lot at any time, and the fact that he was an escaped convict would render his resistance more than ordinarily desperate. The periscope had told Nick where the fugitive stood, and thus the detective was enabled to cover him at once with the unwavering muzzle of the automatic.

'Hands up, Grantley! Hands up, everybody!' cried Nick, stepping a little to one side to allow Chick to enter.

His assistant took immediate advantage of the opening and stepped to his chief's side, with leveled weapon. Chick's automatic was pointed at Doctor Chester, however. After Grantley, the man whose house had been invaded was naturally the one who was likely to put up the hardest fight.

The guilty four were spellbound with astonishment and fear for a moment, then the three younger ones jumped to their feet like so many jacks-in-the-box. Grantley had already been standing when the detectives broke in.

'Did you hear me, gentlemen?' Nick demanded, crooking his finger a little more closely about the trigger. 'I said "Hands up!" and it won't be healthy for any of you to ignore the invitation. One – two – three!'

Before the last word passed his lips, however, four pairs of hands were in the air. Doctor Willard's had gone up first, and Grantley's last.

'Thank you so much!' the detective remarked, with mock politeness. 'Now, if you will oblige me a little further, by lining up against that right wall, I shall be still more grateful to you. Kindly place yourselves about two feet apart, not less. I want you, Number Sixty Thousand One Thirteen' – Grantley winced at his prison number – 'at this end of the line, next to me, with Chester, alias Schofield, next; Graves next to him, and Willard last. You see, I haven't forgotten any of my old friends.'

This disposition of the trapped quartet was designed to serve two purposes. In the first place, it would remove them from proximity to Helga Lund, who, crouched in the middle of the floor, was watching the detectives with bewildered, uncomprehending eyes. In the second place, it would enable Chick to handcuff them one by one, while Nick stood ready to fire, at an instant's notice, on any one who made a false move.

It looked, for the time being, as if the capture would be altogether too easy to have any spice in it, but the detectives did not make the mistake of underrating their adversaries – Grantley, especially.

91

To be sure, they were probably unarmed, and had been taken at such a disadvantage that they would hardly have had an opportunity to draw weapons, even if they had worn them. Still, any one of a number of things might happen.

The four doctors had been caught 'with the goods,' as the police saying is, and they might be expected to take desperate chances as soon as they had had time to collect their scattered wits and to realize the seriousness of their plight.

Nick Carter had shown his usual generalship in the orders he had given so crisply.

Grantley himself, the most to be feared of the lot, was to be placed nearest to the detective, where Nick could watch him most narrowly. That was not all, however. The detective meant that Chick should handcuff Grantley first, and thus put the leader out of mischief at the earliest opportunity.

After him, Chester was to be disposed of, and the two that would then remain were comparatively harmless in themselves.

Grantley doubtless saw through Nick's tactics from the beginning, and if the detective could have caught the gleam behind the wily surgeon's half-closed lids, he would have known that Grantley thought he saw an opportunity to circumvent those tactics.

With reasonable promptness, hands still in the air, Grantley started to obey the detective's order. He moved slowly, grudgingly, his face distorted with rage and hate.

Chester started to follow the older man toward the wall but Chick halted him.

'Hold up, there, Schofield-Chester!' the young detective ordered. 'One at a time, if you don't mind!'

He wished to prevent the confusion that would result from the simultaneous movement of the four scoundrels.

Chester paused with a snarl, and Grantley went on alone. He was making for the corner nearest to Nick, who still stood close to the door. In doing so, he was obliged to pass in front of the detective.

It had been no part of Nick's plan to have the fugitive take to that corner, and he suddenly realized that the criminal was crossing a little too close to him for safety.

'Here, keep to the left a little –' he began sharply, when Grantley was about four feet away.

But before he could complete his sentence, the escaped convict ducked and threw his body sidewise, the long arms were already above his head and he left them where they were. Their abnormal length helped to bridge the distance between him and Nick as he flung himself at the detective.

Nick guessed the nature of the move, as if by instinct, and when he fired, which he did immediately, it was with depressed muzzle. He had allowed, in other words, for the swift descent of Grantley's body.

In spite of that, however, the bullet merely plowed a furrow across the criminal's shoulder and back, as he dropped. It did not disable him in the least, and, before Nick could fire again, Grantley's peculiar dive ended with a vicious impact against his legs, and claw-like hands gripped him about the knees in an effort to pull him down.

The convict's daring act broke the spell which had held his companions. Without waiting to see whether Grantley's move was to prove successful or not, the three of them threw themselves bodily upon Chick, while the latter's attention was diverted for a moment by his chief's peril.

Doctor Chester, who had been looking for something of the sort from Grantley, was the first to pounce upon Nick's assistant. He gripped Chick's right wrist and began to twist it in an attempt to loosen the hold on the weapon.

'Help Grantley, Willard,' he directed, at the same time, between his clenched teeth. 'Graves and I can handle this fellow, I guess.'

Willard started for Nick, while Graves shifted his attack, and, edging around behind Chick, seized him by the shoulders. At the same moment he placed one knee in the small of the young detective's back.

There could be only one result.

Chick was bent painfully back until his spine felt as if it was about to crack in two; then, in his efforts to relieve the strain, he lost his footing and went down, with Chester on top of him, and still clinging doggedly to his wrists.

A few feet away Nick was being hard pressed by two other rascals.

The pendulum of chance had swung the other way, and things looked very dubious for the detectives – and for what was left of Helga Lund!

X

Chick had thrown himself to one side to ease the pressure on his back. Accordingly, he struck the floor on his left side.

Chester and Graves dropped heavily upon him before he had more than touched the boards, the former at his feet, the latter on his shoulders.

Their bony knees crushed him down, and Graves used his weight to try to pull Chick over on his back.

Nick's assistant had twisted his left wrist out of Chester's grasp as he fell, but the renegade physician had clung for dear life to the hand which held the automatic.

Chick allowed himself to be pulled over on his back – for a very good reason. His free arm had been under him as he lay on his side, and he wanted an opportunity to use it.

Graves grabbed at it at once, but Chick stretched it – all but the upper arm – out of his antagonist's reach.

Graves would have to lean far over Chick in order to reach the latter's left wrist, and, in so doing, he would expose himself not a little. Or else he would be obliged to edge around on his knees, behind Chick's head.

He chose to try the latter manoeuvre, but Chick feinted with his left arm. Graves dodged, and Chick's hand darted in behind the other's guard, grasping Graves firmly by the hair.

Almost at the same instant the young detective jerked his right foot loose and gave the startled Chester a tremendous kick in the stomach.

The master of the house gave a grunt and doubled up like a jack-knife. His grip on Chick's right wrist relaxed simultaneously, and its owner tore it away.

Chester had involuntarily lurched forward, and the act had

brought his head well within the reach of Chick's right hand, which was now once more at liberty.

While Nick's assistant held the struggling Graves at arm's length by the hair, with one hand, he brought down the butt of the automatic, with all the strength he could bring to bear, on Chester's lowered poll.

He had juggled the weapon in a twinkling, so that it was clubbed when it descended. The blow was surprisingly effective, considering the circumstances.

Chester groaned and toppled forward, over Chick's legs.

The detective's assistant was ready to follow up his advantage at once. He wriggled about until he was facing Graves, and then he began pulling that individual toward him by the hair.

Tears of pain were in Graves's eyes, and he struck out blindly in a desperate effort to break Chick's relentless hold. The attempt was a failure, however. Despite all of Graves's struggles, he was irresistibly drawn nearer and nearer. The fact that he wore his hair rather long helped Chick to maintain his grip.

Presently the young physician's head was near enough to allow Chick to strike it with his clubbed weapon. He drew the latter back for the blow, but his enemy, seeing what was coming, suddenly changed his tactics.

Instead of trying to pull away any more, he ducked and threw himself into Chick's arms.

The revolver butt naturally missed its mark and, for a time, they fought at too close quarters to permit such a blow to be tried again.

Graves had seized Chick around the body as he closed in, and he drew himself close, burying his head on Chick's chest. Chick still maintained his hold of his opponent's hair, however, and now retaliated by rolling over on Graves, working his feet from under the unconscious Chester as he did so.

Graves snuggled as close as he could to avoid the dreaded blow, but Chick, now being on top, was able to hold Graves's head on the floor by main force, while he arched his own powerful back and began to tear his body from his antagonist's straining arms.

Graves was game; there was no doubt about that. The pulling of his hair must have been torture to him, but he did not relinquish his hold about Chick's waist.

His eyes were closed, his face drawn and twisted with pain, but he clung obstinately, and without a whimper.

Slowly but surely, nevertheless, Chick raised himself, and the space between their laboring breasts widened. Graves's hold was being loosened bit by bit, but it had not broken.

As a matter of fact, Chick did not wait for it to break. It was not necessary, for one thing; and for another, he realized that it would be a kindness to Graves to end the painful struggle as soon as possible.

Accordingly, as soon as he had raised himself enough to deliver a reasonably effective blow with the clubbed automatic, he struck downward, with carefully controlled aim and strength.

The butt of the little weapon landed in the middle of the physician's forehead. A gasp followed, and the tugging arms fell away.

Chick had floored his two opponents.

He got quickly to his feet and looked to see if Nick needed him. Chester and Graves ought to be handcuffed before they had time to revive, but that could wait a little if necessary.

It was well that Chick finished his business just when he did, for Nick was in trouble.

Doctor Grantley was not an athlete, and his long, lanky build gave little promise of success against Nick Carter's trained muscles and varied experience in physical encounters of all sorts.

On the other hand, the convict was possessed of amazing wiriness and endurance, and, although he was not cut out for a fighting man, his keen, quick mind made up for most of his bodily deficiencies.

His original attack, for instance, was an example of unconventional but startlingly successful strategy. On the surface, it would have seemed that such a man, without weapons, had precious little chance of gaining any advantage over Nick Carter, armed as the latter was, and a good four feet away.

But Grantley followed up his impetuous dive in a most surprising way. His long arms closed about Nick's legs, but, instead of endeavoring to pull the detective down in the ordinary way, Grantley unexpectedly plucked his legs apart with all his strength.

The detective's balance instantly became a very uncertain quantity, for the surgeon's abnormally long, gorilla-like arms tore his legs apart and pushed them to right and left with astonishing ease.

Nick felt like an involuntary Colossus of Rhodes as he was forced to straddle farther and farther. He threw one hand behind him to brace himself against the wall, reversed his automatic and leaned forward, bent upon knocking the enterprising Grantley in the head.

The fugitive had other plans, however. Just as Nick bent forward, Grantley suddenly thrust his head and shoulders between the detective's outstretched limbs, and heaved upward and backward.

The detective was lifted from his feet and pitched forward, head downward. His discomfiture was a decided shock to him, but he neither lost his presence of mind nor his grip on his weapon.

Had he struck on his head and shoulders, as Grantley evidently intended he should, the result might have been exceedingly disastrous. The detective would almost certainly have been plunged into unconsciousness, and his neck might easily have been broken.

Nick saw his danger in a flash, though, drew his head and shoulders sharply inward and downward, and at the same time grasped one of Grantley's thighs with his left hand.

The result would have been ludicrous under almost any other circumstances. The detective's lowered head went, in turn, between Grantley's legs, and their intertwined bodies formed a wheel, such as trained athletes sometimes contrive.

This countermove of Nick's was as much of a surprise to the surgeon as the latter's curious mode of attack had been to the detective.

They rolled over and over a couple of times, until Nick, finding himself momentarily on top, brought them to a stop. So awkward were their positions that neither was able to strike an effective blow at the other.

Nick had the upper hand temporarily, however, and proceeded

to wrench himself loose. He had been busily engaged in this when Willard had rushed to Grantley's assistance.

That put still another face on the situation at once.

XI

The newcomer saw his opportunity and snatched up a chair as he rushed toward the tangled combatants.

Nick heard him coming, but did not have time to extricate himself from Grantley's dogged grasp.

He raised his weapon, though, and was about to fire at Willard, when he saw that the latter was directly between him and Helga Lund. Under the circumstances, the detective did not dare to fire for fear of hitting the actress.

He kept Grantley down as best he could with his left hand, and waited for Willard with his right hand still extended, holding the automatic.

He might have an opportunity to fire but, if not, he could at least partially ward off the expected blow from the chair.

Just as Willard paused and swung the chair aloft, Grantley managed partially to dislodge the detective, with the result that Nick was obliged to lower his right arm quickly. Otherwise he would undoubtedly have lost his balance completely, and the surgeon-convict would have had the upper hand in another second or two.

This involuntary lowering of Nick's guard served the purpose that Grantley had intended. Willard's cumbersome weapon descended with uninterrupted force on the detective's shoulders and the back of his head.

Nick lowered the latter instinctively, and thus saved himself the worst of the blow. Nevertheless, the impact of the chair was stunning in its force.

The detective felt his senses reeling, but he somehow managed to retain them and to grasp the chair, which he blindly wrenched from Willard's grasp.

As he did so, however, Grantley succeeded in throwing him off and scrambling to his feet. Nick followed his example almost simultaneously, dropped his revolver into his pocket – for fear it would fall into the hands of one of his enemies – and, grasping the heavy chair with both hands, whirled it about his head.

His two antagonists dodged it hurriedly, thus clearing a space about him. Their blood was up, however – especially Grantley's – and they felt sure that the detective had by no means recovered from the blow.

'Catch the chair, Willard!' cried Grantley.

The younger physician obeyed instantly, grasping the round of the chair with both hands, and thus preventing Nick from using it to any advantage.

The detective shoved it forward into the pit of Willard's stomach, but the newcomer managed to retain his hold.

He guessed that Grantley merely meant him to keep Nick busy in front, in order to allow of a rear attack; and such was the case.

While the detective was occupied with Willard, Grantley stole behind him and plunged his hand into Nick's pocket, in search of the automatic.

The detective was obliged to let go of the chair and clamp his hand on Grantley's wrist. He was still feeling very groggy as a result of the punishment he had recently received, and a thrill of apprehension went through him.

Grantley's hand was already deep in his pocket, grasping the butt of the weapon; and there was nothing about the wrist hold to prevent the criminal from turning the muzzle of the automatic toward his side and pulling the trigger.

Incidentally, Nick foresaw that he could not hope to hold the chair with one hand. Willard would twist it away and turn it upon him.

He was right. That was precisely what Willard did. Nick let go just in time to escape a sprained, if not broken wrist, and dodged back.

In order to keep his hand in Nick's pocket, Grantley was then obliged to circle about, between the detective and Willard. That saved Nick from the latter for the moment, and, simultaneously, the detective shifted his hold from Grantley's wrist to his hand, pressing his thumb in under the latter in such a way that it prevented the hammer of the automatic from descending.

He was just in time, for Grantley pulled the trigger almost at the same moment. Thanks to Nick's foresight, however, the weapon did not go off.

Grantley cursed under his breath, but he had not emptied his bag of tricks. He suddenly drove his head and shoulders in between Nick's right arm and side, and threw his own left arm around, with a back-hand movement, in front of the detective's body.

The move threw the detective backward, over Grantley's knee, which was ready for him. At the same time, the criminal, whose right hand had remained on the weapon in Nick's pocket, began to draw the automatic out and to the rear.

In other words, he was forcing the detective in one direction with the left arm and working the revolver in the other with his right. It was manifestly impossible for Nick to stand the two opposing pressures for long.

Either he must break the hold of Grantley's left arm, which pressed across his chest like an iron band, or else he must let go of the weapon.

The former seemed out of the question in that position; and to relinquish his hold on the revolver meant a shot in the side, which, with Grantley's knowledge of anatomy, would almost certainly prove fatal.

Backward went Nick's straining right arm, inward turned the hard muzzle of the weapon. Grantley was twisting the automatic now, hoping to loosen the detective's grasp all the quicker.

Something was due in a few moments, and it promised to be a tragedy for the detective.

Then, to cap the climax, Willard circled about the two combatants, like a hawk ready to swoop down on its prey, and, seeing Nick's head protruding from under Grantley's left arm, hauled off and let drive with the chair.

The surgeon received part of the blow, but Nick's head stopped enough of it to end the strange tussle.

The detective crumpled up, but Grantley held him from the floor and wrested the weapon from the nerveless fingers. He withdrew it from Nick's pocket and put it to the detective's left breast, determined to end it all, without fail.

It was at that supreme moment that Chick charged up and took a hand.

Nick's assistant reached Willard first. The latter's back was toward him, and he was just in the act of drawing back the chair. Chick's clubbed weapon descended on his head without warning, and Willard pitched forward on his face.

It was not until then that Chick saw the automatic at his chief's breast. There was no time to reach Grantley – not a second to waste.

The young detective did what Nick and his men seldom allowed themselves to do – he turned his automatic around again and shot to kill.

Nick's own life depended upon it, and there was nothing else to do.

The bullet struck Grantley full between the eyes, and the escaped convict dropped without a sound.

The battle was over and won.

★★★★

Doctor Hiram A Grantley – so called – master surgeon and monster of crime, would never return to Sing Sing to serve out his unexpired term; but neither would he trouble the world, or Helga Lund, again.

If the truth were known, it would doubtless be found that Warden Kennedy heaved a sigh of profound relief when he heard of Grantley's death. It left no room for anxiety over the possibility of another hypnotic escape.

Doctors Chester, Willard, and Graves were speedily brought to trial, and they were convicted of aiding and abetting the deceased Grantley in an illegal experiment in hypnotism on the person of the great Swedish actress.

As for Helga Lund, she was a nervous wreck for nearly a year, but gradually, under the care of the best European physicians, she recovered her health and her confidence in herself.

She has now returned to the stage, and Nick Carter, who has

seen her recently in Paris, declares that she is more wonderful than ever.

He wishes he could have spared her that last humiliating ordeal, but she is wise enough to know that, but for him and Chick, the man she had despised would have made his dreadful vengeance complete.

THORNLEY COLTON

Created by Clinton H Stagg (1888–1916)

If Clinton Stagg had not died in a car accident at the age of only 27, his name might well be much more familiar to readers of crime fiction today than it is. Even in the short career he had, he produced a large number of stories and magazine articles and, at the time of his death, he had just moved to Hollywood to work as a screenwriter. It was while he was driving along a road in Santa Monica that his car overturned and he and a fellow writer who was his passenger were killed. Some of Stagg's best fiction featured the blind detective Thornley Colton, a wealthy New Yorker who takes on cases purely for the intellectual interest they offer. Known as 'The Problemist', Colton is one of a number of blind detectives in early crime fiction (Ernest Bramah's tales of Max Carrados appeared about the same time in the UK) and, like all of them, he is able to solve the mysteries he tackles through high intelligence and the fact that his other senses have been heightened by his disability. The Thornley Colton stories were first published in 1913 in People's Ideal Fiction Magazine *and were collected in book form after Stagg's death. Plausibility wasn't always Stagg's strongpoint in his plotting but, as 'The Flying Death' shows, his stories were lively and full of colour and invention.*

THE FLYING DEATH

I

The last sobbing notes of the violin died away. Slowly, reverently, the girl lowered the bow and lifted her chin; the throat-filling hush wrought by the conjuring of her music became wild, unrestrained applause as the spell broke. The beating surges of sound from the gallery, the balcony, the floor seemed to frighten her a little; the frail body in its simple white frock shrank before it; but the girlish lips smiled bravely as she bowed her way to the wings.

Clamorous, insistent, the applause continued. She reappeared; silence came as she lifted the violin to her chin. The lilting fantasy of a folk-song rollicked from under the dancing bow. Once more came the enthusiastic outburst when she finished. She gestured her thanks, smiled an instant at the upper right-hand box, laughed and kissed her hand to the lone occupant of lower left and ran from the stage.

'Sheer genius, Sydney!' murmured Thornley Colton, in expression of the reverence good music always aroused in him; for music, to the blind man, held all the pleasures that painting, sculpture, and beautiful architecture hold for those whom God has given sight. Now his whole face, from the high forehead to the lean, cleft chin, was alight; even the sightless eyes seemed to shine behind the great blue circles of the smoked-glass, tortoise-shell-rimmed library spectacles that accentuated the striking whiteness of his face and hair.

'Wonderful!' breathlessly agreed the red-cheeked, black-haired Sydney Thames, secretary and constant companion of the blind man.

'It makes my woids muss up when I try to talk,' gulped The Fee, freckle-faced, red-haired, blue-eyed boy, who had become a member of the Colton household at the conclusion of a particularly baffling murder case. Thornley Colton laughed softly and pushed back his chair. Then real alarm came to the boy's voice. 'Gee, yuh ain't goin' now?' he pleaded. 'They's a coupla comedy acr'bats an' a wop knife t'rower yet!'

'We'll wait,' promised Colton, as he made room for a pale-faced young man who had just risen to hurry past him and out of the box.

The problemist moved his chair farther back, and whispered to Sydney. 'Our friend who just left seems to be troubled with a mighty bad case of nerves,' he observed. 'My cane could feel his chair trembling under him the whole time the girl was playing. He seemed to jump a foot when she left the stage that last time, and he's been muttering under his breath ever since. What happened?'

'I'd say he was wildly in love with her, and madly jealous of someone else,' accounted Sydney. 'She smiled up at him an instant after that last encore, but she immediately turned and kissed her hand to the man in the lower left-hand box. If ever black rage shone in a man's face it was on that of our neighbour. He isn't more than twenty-two or three, and he doesn't look as if he had ever learned to curb a nasty temper.'

'He left as if he were going in search of someone's heart blood,' smiled the blind man, leaning back in his chair.

One of the comedy acrobats had just succeeded in pushing the other from a high table, and was joyously dancing on his rubber stomach, to the great delight of The Fee, and some fourteen or fifteen hundred others.

'You don't happen to know the occupant of lower left?' asked Colton. Somehow the thought of sordid jealousy of two men, and a girl whose witchery could produce such music, seemed to jar.

Sydney gazed covertly down at the occupant of lower left. He was a big-bodied man, and fat.

There were fleshy pouches of good living and bad drinking under his eyes; but no dissipation could hide the iron will, the dominant arrogance the heavy chin showed. He sat back in the deep box, the black of his evening clothes verging into the black of the heavy velvet hangings that covered the wall behind him. The white expanse of shirt front contrasted strikingly with the sombre background; one white fist rested on the back of a gold chair.

'It's James P Cartwright, the theatrical manager!' returned Sydney suddenly. 'Her manager!' he supplemented in sudden anger as he compared the innocent girlishness of the violinist and the coarse grossness of the recognized man in the box. Sydney Thames deified all women from afar, for he had forbidden himself the joys of propinquity, because he could never forget that he had no name but that of the English river on the banks of which Thornley Colton had found him, a bundle of dirty baby-clothes, years before.

'Cartwright has an unenviable reputation among his women of

the stage,' muttered Colton. The smile was gone from the thin, expressive lips now.

The rocking notes of the fantastic folk-song still haunted him; the sobbing cadence of the piece she had played before was in his mind: an omen of tragedy. A soul that could conjure music like that – and a Cartwright, who, gossip said, demanded his price for others' success!

The two comedy acrobats had disinterred themselves from an avalanche of chairs and a table; the first to his feet had been promptly knocked down by the other, and dragged off the stage by his heels, while The Fee and a few hundred others shouted and clapped their approval. A card announced Signor Delvetoi and his marvellous whirling knives.

Sydney, watching the occupant of the lower left, saw him take out a big watch impatiently, lean ponderously back in a chair, and summon an usher. The uniformed man came, listened a moment, nodded, and opened the door at the stage end of the box, to reappear a moment later and whisper his message, or news. Cartwright nodded, and turned his attention idly toward the stage, where the signor sent a whirling knife toward the high boards before which his yellow-haired partner had set a red apple swinging on a long string. The knife point thudded into the wood; the cut string parted, and the apple rolled to the stage floor.

'Gee, that's some stunt!' ecstatically exclaimed The Fee, as he enthusiastically described the feat of the black-bearded signor to Colton.

A handful of playing cards flurried before the wooden stop. Three whirling knives shot across the whole length of the stage; three cards were pinned fast, and the assistant held them up triumphantly to show the pierced ace spots.

Cartwright inclined his head in a nod of grudging approval, then turned quickly as he heard the door that led back to the stage open. Sydney saw the girl who had played appear in her street clothes, a simple white shirt waist and dark skirt, her coat thrown over her arm. He gritted his teeth at the greeting she gave the theatrical manager, and as he saw the flush of happiness on the winsome face, while the thick lips of the man grinned as he took her coat. Cartwright jerked his thumb toward the stage where the dexterous signor had just succeeded in planting five knives in a black spot not bigger than a half dollar.

He pulled his chair close to that of the girl, and they sat talking; the girl with many pretty, unconscious gestures, the man listening, with a jerky nod now and then. They were in the rear of the box, not three feet from the heavy velvet hangings that covered the wall back of them. They could not be seen from the body of the theatre, but from the upper box opposite, where Sydney sat, everything in their box was visible.

Sydney interrupted The Fee's excited description of the signor's act long enough to tell the news to Colton; and he made no excuse for his spying. The blind man nodded grimly, and continued his patient listening to The Fee, who was having the time of his young life. The signor, in his suit of black silk and his black, pointed beard, had performed miracles with the whirling knives. Now the boy waited breathlessly for this last feat, because the soft music of the orchestra told him it would be the best of all. A huge frame was being lowered from the flies. The blond assistant stepped to the small shelf, thrust her hands through the leather loops, and stood against the golden back, arms spread wide, feet apart. The signor brought his table of glittering knives to the footlights; the frame and the assistant swung aloft. The lights went out. Darkness for a few brief seconds, then the calcium from the balcony outlined the suspended woman and the gold background.

'Ah!' The Fee's gasp swelled a thousand others, as the knife shot into the calcium beam from the darkness below, whirled with a thousand silver fires, and buried its point in the wood, blade grazing the cheek of the woman. A few seconds of breathless suspense, and another followed, to graze the ear. Even Sydney forgot the man and girl in the box as he watched the whirling blades. The weirdness of the thing held him fascinated; the knives, hurled from the hands of the man who was invisible in the darkness below the single light beam, pin-wheeled through the light to find their place unerringly.

Then something caused Sydney Thames to turn his eyes again to the lower box. At the instant a flash of lurid light leaped from the darkness, silhouetting with startling vividness the seated man and girl. The roar of a pistol came to his ears; and while the light cut the darkness he saw behind the seated man and girl the face of the youth who had been in the box with them; the man whose jealousy had been shown so plainly.

Pandemonium followed instantly. A chair crashed over in the darkness across the theatre; clear above the cries of the panic-stricken men and women came the scream of a man:

'My God! I didn't do it! I didn't! I didn't!'

The scream stopped. 'Lights!' frenziedly called someone from the darkness.

They came. In the box opposite, Sydney Thames saw Cartwright struggling with the man whose face he had seen so distinctly in the pistol's flash. On the floor of the box, face downward, was the girl of the violin. Between her shoulders, on the white shirt waist, was a widening splotch of crimson.

II

The girl was dead. The white-coated ambulance surgeon who examined her had shaken his head, and refused to take her in the ambulance. The morgue waggon had taken the body but a short time after the police reserves had beaten their way through a mob of thousands to arrest the white-faced, hysterical prisoner, who cried his innocence through lips battered by the fist of Cartwright.

In the precinct station the prisoner had collapsed, and Cartwright told his story. He had heard a slight noise, and swung around in his chair. At that instant came the flash of the pistol behind him. He heard the man drop it, and he leaped to grapple with him. Yes, he knew the prisoner; name was Nelson, a half-baked kid, who had bothered Miss Reynolds for months. Yes, this was Miss Reynolds's first engagement; her first appearance on any stage. He was her manager. No, nothing else. Emphatically!

The prisoner, brought around roughly, swore that he was innocent. He had known Miss Reynolds for months, they had been friends in Europe. She had asked him to be present at her first appearance, and at the end of her act he had gone to meet her at the stage entrance. It was there that he was told that she had an engagement with Cartwright. That this made him wild with jealousy he admitted; he knew Cartwright by reputation, and Miss Reynolds was but a girl, innocent, unsophisticated.

He had walked around outside the theatre for about fifteen minutes, then he had decided to go to the box and demand an explanation. The theatre was in darkness for the knife-throwing act, but he knew his way. His hand had been on the black velvet hangings when he stopped. And the revolver flash had come from the air not a foot ahead of him. No, he could not explain how the shot had been fired. No one could have moved from the spot where the pistol had been, because the weapon dropped on his toe!

He was taken away to a cell on a charge of murder.

Cartwright, leaving the station when the last of the curious crowd had drifted away, seemed to have aged ten years since the tragedy. He was haggard, the grim, hard smile that had been characteristic was gone, his big hands trembled. He tried in vain to get permission to remove the girl's body from the morgue immediately. But the law demanded that the coroner see it first; and the official was out of town.

Cartwright remembered his political friends. He tried to locate a dozen over the telephone and failed. Then, by chance, he met the one man in the city who could help him; the one man among the four millions whom he could trust: Theodore Rogers, the theatrical lawyer, a friend for thirty years.

He tried to tell Rogers what he wanted, but his nervousness made his words a jumble.

'What is it, Jim? What's the trouble?' Rogers shook him, and he looked into his eyes anxiously.

Cartwright told him of the shooting. 'And, by God, Ted!' he finished passionately. 'I won't rest a minute till I see that devil in the electric chair! God! To kill a girl like that!'

The lawyer looked at him curiously. This was not the cool, suave Cartwright he had known so long.

Cartwright read the look on the lawyer's face, and the thoughts behind it. 'Not that! I swear it's not that, Ted!' he choked.

'Come, have a drink,' pleaded Rogers, pulling him toward the lighted entrance of a rathskeller.

'With that girl on a slab in the morgue?'

'One drink,' insisted Rogers. 'You are worse than useless this way. Come!'

He dragged Cartwright down the steps. The clock over the bar said half-past two, and the leather-seated booths were in darkness. But drinks could be had. The barman dozed, and the lone waiter yawned as he carried a tray toward the booths in the rear. Rogers led the theatrical man to a seat at the side of the room in front of the bar, ordered whisky, and waited patiently until Cartwright had gulped down the liquor.

'Now tell me about it, Jim,' demanded Rogers.

Cartwright, as near the end of the leather seat as he could get, glanced at the dark booths in the back, then turned and surveyed the front of the place. The rathskeller was empty, except for the dozing barman and the waiter, who had gone into one of the front booths to figure his day's checks.

'Don't think – what you've been thinking about me and that girl, Ted.' There was almost pathetic pleading in the manager's voice; it was pitched so low that even the lawyer at the other side of the narrow table could scarcely hear. 'She was – a daughter to me – the daughter of the only woman I ever loved.'

Rogers stared. This from the man Broadway thought it knew!

'Remember twenty years ago?' continued Cartwright, in that same low, pleading voice.

'The girl I took away from Kelly, that drunken burlesque magician?'

The lawyer nodded, a look of understanding in his eyes.

'You know we loved each other, and we ran away; she, and I, and the six months old kid,' he went on. 'You know how she died: killed in the C & O wreck two hours out of Chicago, two hours after we started – and the kid under her body, alive! I guess that's what woke me up. All I thought about after that was making money for the kid. I put her with good people, and I didn't tell them who she was, or who I was. When she got old enough to understand, I adopted her legally. But she never knew who her father and mother were. I couldn't tell her about the drunken sot that died in the Chicago alcoholic ward. A thing like that would have spoiled her.

'She was born with music in her. I kept her away from me and the people that knew me. I sent her abroad. And tonight was her try-out! I wanted to see if she could face the lights, because I wouldn't have her laughed at by the highbrows if she couldn't make good. And she did! God, how they went wild! I wouldn't tell a soul that she was my adopted daughter – until tomorrow. Now –' He fingered his whisky glass with twitching hands.

Theodore Rogers, whose heart was reputed to be of stone, felt a lump in his throat. He pushed his gloves from the table, so in bending he would get the needed instant to hide his feelings. Something made him jerk up his head! He saw –

The roar of the pistol in his ears deafened him. He cried out as the long-barrelled gun recoiled across the table and struck him, butt foremost, on the chest. His glass was crashed to a hundred pieces as the pistol fell on the table before him. The white shirt front of Cartwright was black, a small circle of fire glowed in the linen; on his face was an awful look of horror as his head pitched forward on his arms.

And then Rogers understood what his eyes had first seen; the picture that had lasted but the hundredth part of a second, perhaps, but which would be graven on his mind for a lifetime.

He had seen the pistol against Cartwright's heart, with nothing to hold it there; the recoil of the explosion had driven it across the table before it fell, because no human hand had grasped it; no finger had pulled the trigger!

III

In the darkness of his library Thornley Colton paced back and forth. The cigarette-end glowed and died as he puffed thoughtfully. Each detail of the girl's murder at the theatre, described to him by the excited Sydney, while panic had raged above them and below them in the playhouse the night before, was being visualized by the wonderful brain that so unerringly found logic in seeming absurdity; explanation in apparent impossibility – because that brain had never been tricked by seeing eyes.

The murder of the girl had moved him mightily; the stilling forever of that wonderful music seemed more a crime against the world than against an individual. And as he paced the curtained room the mosaics of detail became a complete picture, and he knew – knew – that the man who had left their box so hurriedly the night before; the man whom Sydney had seen fire the shot, was guiltless of the murder!

He turned to face the door as hurried footsteps proclaimed to his trained, supersensitive ears that Sydney Thames was approaching.

'Cartwright has been murdered!' cried the red-cheeked secretary breathlessly. 'It happened too late for the morning papers, but The Fee got some early extras of the evening editions with full details.'

'Where? How?' asked Colton.

'In an up-town rathskeller. He was shot by Theodore Rogers, the lawyer.'

'He was not,' corrected the blind man quietly,

'How did you hear of it?' demanded Sydney, in surprise.

'This is the first intimation I had of such a thing, but your statement was just a little too positive; your voice told me that you believe Rogers guilty because of the utter impossibility of the story he must have given the police.'

Sydney flushed. 'But his story is crazy, insane!' he insisted.

'Perhaps if I heard it –' suggested Colton.

Excitedly, with utter disbelief in his voice, Sydney Thames told of the unheld pistol Rogers swore he saw; of its firing with no finger near the trigger; of its recoil, and fall.

'Of course the police arrested him,' continued Sydney. 'Cartwright held a lot of Rogers's paper. That's the motive. They've got a clear case, as clear as the one against the love-crazed kid who shot the violinist.'

'Just as clear,' echoed Colton slowly. Then: 'But haven't you withheld the fact that the pistols used in both murders are exactly alike?'

'How – did you know – that?' gasped Sydney. Many times he

had heard the blind man make such amazing statements, but they always startled him.

'Because both crimes were committed by the same man in the same way!'

'But Nelson, the kid who shot the girl, was locked up in a cell,' protested Thames.

'Exactly,' admitted the blind man. 'But he killed Cartwright as surely as he murdered the girl.'

It was several seconds before the meaning of that sentence struck Sydney. 'He shot that girl in the back!' rebelled Thames. 'I saw his face over the flash of the pistol. Even he admits that no one else could have fired it, because it fell on his toe!'

'Rogers swears that no one did fire the bullet which killed Cartwright,' reminded Colton. 'And the pistol fell on the table in front of him.'

'That's impossible,' asserted Thames emphatically. 'Someone must have held the gun. Someone must have pulled the trigger. There can be no explanation of what he says he saw. The days of ghosts and black magic have passed.'

'But not the days of black murder,' retorted Colton. 'There is no black art, ghosts, or hypnotism in the murders of last night. The method is unique, that's all.'

He picked up the slim, hollow stick he always carried. 'I'm going to find that murderer,' he said. 'A man who could kill a girl like that is either a fiend or a hideous blunderer. I think it's the latter. Will you call the machine?'

The big automobile was always ready for instant service, day or night, and ten minutes later they were on their way down town. Beside the driver, eager-eyed, joyful, was The Fee. Colton had promised to let him help on the case, and the boy's cup of happiness was full. The Fee had but two heroes: Thornley Colton in real life; Nick Carter in his favourite fiction.

'We'll go to police headquarters first,' decided Colton. 'The prisoners will be there this morning, and I'd like to question Rogers.' Then he got from Sydney all the details the papers had given of Cartwright's murder.

The Fee found a friendly doorman when they reached

police headquarters and prepared to have the time of his life. Colton's card secured them grudging admittance to the office of the chief of detectives. The chief, like his men, had all the professional's scorn for the amateur, but he knew the blind man, with his wide acquaintance with influential people, was not a person to antagonize. And the police had found Rogers a different proposition from the youth whose infatuation had led him to the dark box and the murder charge. The lawyer was well known, and his story demanded respect despite the utter impossibility of the thing he described. Of course, the barman and the waiter had been arrested as witnesses, but they had not seen the actual shooting. The barman had been dozing, and the waiter had been busy in a front booth. The shot had aroused them.

'Going to give us some more pointers?' asked the chief tolerantly, when he had shaken hands with Colton and nodded curtly to Sydney.

'I'd like to look into that double-murder case a bit,' confessed the problemist, paying no attention to the tone.

'You mean the two murders committed last night,' corrected the chief gruntingly. 'Nothing to 'em. We've got the goods on young Nelson. Twenty people in the three front rows saw him do it. And Rogers's fool story is enough to hang any man.' The real detective's scorn for the criminal whose methods are crude came to his voice. 'He might have got away with a suicide story – Cartwright was all broken up about the girl – but Rogers swears it wasn't suicide, because the manager's hands were not near the pistol when it was fired. He says Cartwright's look was one of horror, as if he'd seen his end coming, and couldn't get away from it.'

'He did see his death coming,' put in Colton quietly; 'and I think that during the last instant he lived he realized at whose hand it came.'

'You think he got wise to Rogers at the end, eh?' guessed the chief.

'No!' The negative was sharp. 'Rogers had no more to do with the murder than you or I. Cartwright was killed by a man who

114

had been planning the murder for years; the death of the girl was a terrible mistake.'

The chief jumped from his chair. 'What do you know?' he demanded.

'Nothing – definitely. With a little help from you I think I can show you the real murderer.'

'You can't show me any murderer but Rogers and Nelson,' snapped the chief, with an air of finality. 'Because you can't convince me or anybody else that a man could see what Rogers says he saw. A pistol with no hand near it. It's impossible! It's dam' foolishness!' He snorted.

Unconsciously Sydney Thames found himself nodding confirmation. That was the whole thing: an impossibility. No one had been near Cartwright but Rogers. The girl had been shot in the back, and no one could have been behind her but Nelson. This last Sydney knew, and had seen.

'Let me see the pistols which killed Cartwright and the girl, and I'll convince you that the same man murdered both,' offered Colton.

'Duplicate guns aren't so rare,' instantly resented the chief. This man was practically telling him that he didn't know his business!

'Those two pistols – and others that may be in the possession of the murderer – are the only ones of their kind in the world!'

'Look at 'em, then.' The chief grabbed them from his desk. 'They're a standard German make, single-shot target pistols, blued steel, with barrels six inches long, numbered and sold all over Europe.'

Colton took the two pistols, and Sydney drew his chair closer to see.

'In the first place,' began the blind man, as his thin, supersensitive fingers examined one gun, while the other lay on his knees, 'murderers don't usually have this kind of pistol. They can't be carried in any ordinary pocket, and' – his forefinger-tip rested over the shallow slot near the muzzle – 'you never before saw target pistols without front sights!'

'Took 'em off so they wouldn't catch in the pocket,' grunted the chief knowingly.

Colton's lips curved in a smile. 'An ingenious theory,' he grunted. 'Have you one to fit the banged-up appearance of these butts?' He held out the pistol and indicated the nicks and scratches.

'Been used to hammer nails,' declared the chief, exaggerated weariness in his voice. 'Gun owners use 'em that way sometimes, like a woman uses a hairbrush. Nothing to that.'

'Yes there is! No gun owner in the world ever drove a nail by holding a gun vertically, hand on the barrel, and pounding it up and down like a pile driver! See, the hard usage doesn't show on the bottom of the butt, as it would have done had the pistol been swung as a hammer. The dents and scratches are all on the outside edge!'

The chief took the extended gun. The sarcastic smile on his lips faded as he tried the two ways of holding it. The blind man was right! No driving of nails could have made nicks and scratches where they were on this pistol! 'What's that got to do with the murder?' he growled.

'Everything,' answered the problemist shortly. He took the other pistol on his palm. 'Didn't it strike you that these were two finely balanced pistols, even for target use?' Before the chief could reply Colton shot another inquiry: 'Didn't you wonder at the fact that both triggers had been filed to a hair so that the slightest jar would cause the hammer to fall? See!' He cocked the pistol and jammed the muzzle against the chief's desk.

The hammer clicked down sharply. He tried it again, this time jamming the butt down on a chair arm. Once more the hammer snapped on the empty chamber.

The chief's jaw dropped. 'That's how those nicks were made!' he ejaculated, shocked from his supercilious attitude. The lightning-like questions, the proving of fact after fact by Colton, had disconcerted him. In ten minutes the man who was sightless had shown him details that neither his keen eyes nor the eyes of his hundred men had seen, and Colton had made of those details startling, vivid possibilities.

'May I speak to Mr Rogers?' Colton asked the question quietly, simply, but under his voice was a subtle note that was dominantly compelling; a note that had made bigger and stronger men than the chief of the New York detective bureau bow to his wishes.

'That's all very interesting stuff,' began the chief pompously, 'but Rogers is the man who shot Cartwright, and we know that Cartwright held a dozen thousand dollars' worth of his paper.'

The door opened to admit an attaché, and Sydney hid a grin with his hand. He had seen the chief press the call button even before he began to speak.

'Bring Rogers here,' grunted the head of the detective bureau.

The lawyer came in a moment later, and the two men who accompanied him were curtly ordered out.

The strong face of the prisoner was marred by lines indicating loss of sleep; his lips were shut grimly, a scowl creased his forehead, his eyes, sharp and piercing, were fixed on the chief.

'This is Mr Colton, Rogers,' introduced the detective shortly. 'He's got a sort of a theory on the Cartwright murder.'

'If it's the right one he'll save you a lot of trouble,' snapped the lawyer ungraciously. He turned to Colton. 'I've heard of your work on the Villers case.' His tone was almost amiable; then into it came dull wonder. 'But that was simplicity itself beside this. I saw that revolver before the shot was fired, unsupported by human hands, against Jim Cartwright's shirt front. It must have flown there on invisible wings!'

The chief grunted sarcastically, as he had grunted at each repetition of that unvarying statement.

Thornley Colton, tapping his foot lightly with his thin stick, looked up. 'That is just what it did do!' he said. The three men stared blankly. The blind man continued: 'According to the newspapers, Mr Rogers, you said that something caused you to jerk up your head in time to see that picture. Do you know what it was?'

'I do not.' Rogers shook his head. 'I can only describe it as some inner impulse.'

'Wasn't it' – Thornley Colton's tone was impressive – 'wasn't it a shadow, a swift-passing shadow, your eyes saw on the floor?'

Rogers leaped to his feet. 'By Heaven, it was!' he shouted. 'I remember now!' His voice trembled with excitement. 'I had lowered my head, and across the streak of light between the seat edge and table flew a shadow – like a bird passing overhead.' He stopped suddenly, the bewildered look on his face telling the sudden realization of his words. 'How could you know that?' he burst out.

'The human brain is a curious thing,' explained the blind man slowly. 'It unconsciously records impressions the eyes give, but they are instantly forgotten – because the giving is so automatic – until something recalls them. Without sight I have been compelled to figure all things in my brain. Even the steps that you take without seeing must be mentally visualized by me. I knew it must have been a shadow that caused you to look up. To you it was merely one of the thousand unconscious-conscious things your eyes see during the day which are locked up in the brain until some outside influence brings them back.'

'You can solve this thing!' Rogers shot out the words as if he had just made a wonderful discovery. The blind man's conscious power in himself had won the confidence of the lawyer; made him realize that there was some logical explanation for the thing which his eyes had seen, and which his reason refused to accept. He forgot that he was a prisoner formally charged with murder, he paced the room nervously. And the chief, scowling down at his desk, was silent. 'If you can find the man who killed Jim Cartwright!' The excitement died from Roger's voice, a new tone came. 'I knew him for thirty years, yet I never knew him until last night!'

'I want to bring to justice the man that could kill a girl whose soul held the music of Miss Reynolds's.' There was unconscious rebuke in the problemist's voice. All his powers he had brought to avenge the innocent girl; but he knew his efforts must be concentrated on the Cartwright murder because that was the key, the only key that would lead to the murderer.

'The love-crazed kid did that! He –' Rogers stopped, his eyes saw the two pistols side by side on the commissioner's desk. Instantly his keen brain recognised the significance. 'They're the same!' he exclaimed.

'What were Cartwright's relations with Miss Reynolds?' It was a command, as Colton put it.

Rogers lifted his eyes from the two pistols.

'You wrong Jim Cartwright,' he said quietly. 'You've accepted the general opinion of him; the opinion he never cared enough about to refute. He wasn't an angel, but he wasn't the devil a thousand jealousies have painted him. I'm going to tell you the story he told me last night.' And he did, with all the deep feeling of his friendship, splendidly, simply.

As the men listened they understood the tragedy of Cartwright's love for the woman who had been killed in the first moments of her new-found happiness – and his; of the little girl he had taken from her dead mother's arms to work for, to protect, to give the happiness the mother had been denied – only to see her foully murdered when her cup of joy had but just been filled. The fiendishness of it held them spell-bound. The two beings that Cartwright had loved had been snatched from him, and he had been killed, knowing in the last instant of his life that the real murderer of the girl was not even suspected, could not be suspected, because of the devilish ingenuity of his crime.

'Kelly, the drunken magician, is the man who killed Cartwright!' ejaculated the chief.

Rogers was startled for a moment, but Colton, with an inscrutable smile on his thin lips, put a question:

'The father of the girl is dead, isn't he?'

Rogers glanced at the blind man in surprise.

'Yes,' he admitted. 'He died in the alcoholic ward of a Chicago hospital three months after his wife was killed. He was buried in the potters' field.'

'Where did you find that out?' scowlingly demanded the chief.

'That I didn't proves the fact,' answered the blind man crisply. 'If Cartwright hadn't known he was dead you'd have heard of him before. Do you want me to go on?' he asked.

'Might as well,' granted the chief. 'Maybe this is your lucky day.'

'Then I'd like to ask a few questions of the boy who was arrested as Miss Reynolds's murderer.'

The chief gave the order, but there was a light of triumphant anticipation in his eyes as he waited. Unlike the murderer of

119

Cartwright, there was nothing mysterious in the killing of the girl, despite the clever efforts of the blind man to prove differently. A score of persons had seen the flash of the pistol from the rear of the box. His men had examined the velvet-hung wall toward which the girl's back had been, and there was not a break in it, not a crack.

When the boy – he was little more – was led in by two detectives there came a look of pity to the faces of Sydney and Rogers. He staggered to a chair when the men released his arms. His lips were purple and torn where Cartwright had beaten him to the floor the night before. A haunting look of terror was in his eyes; his face was pasty white.

'I didn't do it! I didn't! I didn't!' he whispered hoarsely, when he had wet his dry lips to make even the whisper possible.

Colton put his hand on the boy's shoulder. 'I know you didn't,' he said, and there was a world of sympathy in his voice. A new look came to the boy's eyes, a trembling hand sought that of the blind man.

'I loved her and she loved me,' he said chokingly. 'We were going to be married – but that Cartwright –' Shrill vehemence came to the tone, and he stopped.

Colton's hand quieted him. 'Listen closely now, Mr Nelson, and tell me if this is what happened: You groped your way to the box with your right hand on the wall. You felt the black velvet hangings, stopped, and the pistol went off while your right hand was stretched above you, on the hangings, and you were facing the door that led back off the stage.'

'I remember that!' interjected Sydney. 'His left side was towards Cartwright and the girl!'

'Yet you said that the pistol flash crossed his body.'

'It did!' broke in the boy. 'It was not twelve inches ahead of me! My right foot was extended to take another step, and the pistol fell on my toe!'

Colton turned to the three listening men. 'To have fired that shot he would have had to double his left arm behind him and have shot around his body – a physical impossibility, even with a long-barrelled pistol.' He placed his hand gently on the boy's shoulder once more. 'Go outside to the men who brought you in,' he said. 'You will be free in a few hours.'

Silently the boy obeyed. When Colton faced them again there was a curious expression on his face; the expression of a man who has seen a thoughtless boy destroy a priceless work of art by his clumsiness.

'He killed that girl as surely as if he had placed the pistol at her back,' he said sadly. 'Yet he is as innocent of her murder as a child unborn!'

Eager questions, demands for an explanation of that cryptic remark, were fairly hurled at the blind man by the excited Rogers. What did he mean? How could the boy have killed Miss Reynolds and not be guilty of her murder? How had she been killed? By whom? Sydney Thames forbore the questions he knew would not be answered. The chief scowled down at the two pistols, silent, thoughtful. Colton's statement regarding the firing of the pistol across the boy's body had struck him like a dash of cold water. It was true! The boy could not have fired the shot that killed the girl! Once more the blind man's unerring instinct for truth had torn down the case he and his men had been building for hours. In less than five minutes the sightless problemist had proved a fact that twenty pairs of eyes had failed to see.

'Where are the two men who were arrested in the rathskeller?' asked Colton curtly, utterly ignoring the questions.

'Bailed by their boss,' answered the chief. 'They can only establish details anyway.'

'I want to interview at least one of them,' declared Colton. 'I also want to visit the rathskeller. Can Mr Rogers go, in your company, of course? '

'Yes.' The chief took the responsibility unhesitatingly. He realized that he must see the thing through now.

'Is your machine down here? I want to send my boy on an errand with mine.'

'Outside, waiting.' The chief took his hat and coat from the tree. 'I'll go with Rogers while he gets his,' he added, as he opened the door.

The blind man hurried out, feet unerringly retracing the steps his brain had registered when they entered. The red-haired boy ran from the group of detectives he had been entertaining.

'Shrimp!' The blind man used the name he always called the boy, and took him aside. He whispered instructions, thrust two or three bills into the other's hand. The youngster darted for the machine, and jumped up beside the driver as the chief and Rogers came from the front door.

In silence the quartet climbed into the car; in silence they made the journey to the rathskeller, where James Cartwright had been shot a few hours before. The waiter who had been on duty early in the morning was again on hand, heavy-eyed. The barman was at his home.

'Where's the booth you occupied?' asked Colton of Rogers, when the chief had established their identity with the nervous proprietor.

The lawyer went to it, stopped at the table, and stared down at the dark stain that could not be removed.

'This is where we were,' he said huskily.

Colton stepped in between the table and the seat edge, and sat down, facing the rear of the rathskeller. 'Cartwright was seated at the end of the seat, like this?' He illustrated.

Rogers nodded. 'He was on the extreme end, so he could assure himself that no one would hear.'

Colton rose, and with only the slim stick to guide him, made his way to a booth that faced the front of the rathskeller, at right angles to the one where the watching men still stood.

'Who was in this booth when Cartwright was shot?' It was snapped out like the crack of a whip to the waiter.

'Nobody,' faltered the serving man, wincing under the battery of eyes.

'There was!' The voice held accusation. 'A man was in this booth, and he entered a moment or so before Mr Rogers and Mr Cartwright!'

The waiter brushed his dry lips with the back of his hand. 'He couldn't have had nothin' to do with it,' he mumbled, fingers twisting and untwisting the napkin in his hands.

'No one said he did!' said the blind man sharply. 'You've

been a witness in a murder case before, haven't you?'

The watching men saw a look of alarm come to the man's eyes. The chief stepped toward him menacingly. 'Yes, sir,' muttered the waiter, shrinking. 'I saw a man shot while I was at the Royal. The police kept me in the detention for three months, and I lost my job.'

There was a grim smile on Colton's lips as he nodded understandingly. 'You weren't going to take a chance on that again, were you?' His tone was less brusque. 'I'll assure you that you won't be held a minute if you give me a description of the man.'

The chief opened his mouth, then closed it with a snap.

'Then I'll tell you,' consented the waiter eagerly. 'He was a good-sized guy, with a yellow, old-lookin' face, bald-headed, with a scar on the top, and he had eyes that was like slits. He came in that door.' He pointed to one that opened at the rear corner of the rathskeller, apparently on a side street. 'He was so drunk he couldn't hardly walk, and he almost fell into the seat. I was goin' to put him out, we closed in half an hour, an' I didn't want to have to throw no drunks in the street. But he wanted a whisky and –' The waiter flushed and stopped.

'Go on,' prodded Colton.

The waiter looked at the proprietor and gulped nervously. 'He gave me a five-spot, an' told me to keep the change. I was bringin' the drink when the other two came in. I got theirs, and went up front to figger my checks. Then I heard the shot. When I thought of the drunk again he was gone. But he couldn't 'a' done nothin'. He had a horrible bun, an' we seen the gun layin' in front of this guy.' He indicated Rogers. 'Me an' the bartender figgered we wouldn't say nothin' about him. If we did the police'd put us in the detention till they found him. His gettin' out like that would 'a' looked suspicious to them if it didn't to nobody else. He was scared sober an' beat it quick. That's my idear.'

'Probably he'd had an experience in the house of detention, too,' declared the blind man dryly; then: 'You never saw him before?'

'No, sir.'

'That's all. Let's go, chief. There's a detail I want to clear up at the theatre. I've got to prove that girl's murder.' Again there was the ominous ring in the problemist's voice.

The chief glowered at the waiter. 'You stay right here till I want you,' he warned. 'If you try to beat it you go up the river.' He turned to Colton. 'Wait a minute, until I call up headquarters. I'll give 'em the description of that drunk, and have every man in the city on his trail.'

'And spend a week following up clues,' snapped the blind man impatiently. 'I'll show you where he is in less than an hour!'

He paid no further attention to the gaping chief of detectives, but made his way out of the place, the silent Sydney Thames at his elbow, the latter's coat sleeve lightly touching that of Thornley Colton. And the chief followed meekly.

The blind man climbed into the front seat with the driver, and Sydney realized that he wanted to avoid interrogation; to figure out the last steps alone. But in the tonneau the men could not resist voicing the questions that filled their minds. Who had killed Miss Reynolds, and what could have been the object of the murder? What connection could a drunken man have with the murder of Cartwright; with a pistol that had been fired without the aid of human hands?

They were at the theatre. The box-office had just been opened for the day, and the manager took them into the darkened house. The big interior, dim and tomblike, sent a shudder through Sydney Thames. Last night there had been brilliant lights, happy men, laughing women – and the girl of the violin. Today the great stage gaped before them, huge, untenanted; the seats were covered with their white dust cloths; voices sounded eerie in the barnlike emptiness. The velvet hangings at the rear of the box, which had looked so striking with their sleek blackness the night before, now appeared worn and dusty. The overturned chairs had been righted, the blood-stained carpet had been replaced.

Thornley Colton's thin stick located the chairs. His right hand groped along the wall, so that the velvet moved under it. He thrust his slim cane under his arm, and the wonderful fingers went over the velvet inch by inch, sometimes so strongly that the thick stuff moved under them, then the pressure was so light that not a quiver of the loose velvet betrayed their presence. Inch by inch the feeling fingers made their way, as the men watched breathlessly.

Rogers could stand it no longer.

'Was the murderer concealed behind those hangings?' he asked excitedly.

'No,' Colton answered him, without moving. 'The pistol flash came from this side of the velvet.'

Silence came again. The slow-moving fingers stopped. The blind man looked up; then his doubly keen ears caught the sound of hurrying footsteps coming toward them down the aisle.

'A telephone message for me?' he asked, as the attaché stopped.

'Mr Colton?'

'Yes.' He turned to the others. 'Come! I think this is the last detail.'

They were at his heels as he entered the boxlike office. Tense, expectant, though they knew not for what, they listened to the one-sided conversation.

'Yes. Good. Did you see him? No, that's all right. Stay there until we come.' He spoke an aside to the ticket-seller: 'Will you please take this address for me?' The man picked up his pencil and drew a small pad toward him. 'Nine hundred and ninety-seven West Forty-fourth.' The blind man hung up the receiver.

'What is it?' The question was chorused by the excited men.

'The address of the man who murdered Cartwright and Miss Reynolds!'

IV

Before the gasps of amazement, the ejaculations of incredulity could become coherent questions, Thornley Colton had turned and made his way from the office, light stick dangling idly from his fingers. Dazedly they followed him from the theatre and into the waiting automobile. He had located the murderer of Cartwright and the girl! They were dumb with the wonder of it. Swiftly, unerringly, the blind man had found the murderer whose very being they had not suspected a short time before. To the men who had followed every step of the problemist, who had seen things that he could not see, the finding seemed magic comparable only to the magic of the pistol that had apparently flown from the air to deal its death. There was a new expression on the face of the chief of detectives now. The scowl was gone; the sarcastic curve of lips had vanished. In their place had come wonder, tinged with awe toward the man who had builded a wonderful structure of truth from the pieces he and his hundred men had either discarded or had not seen.

The car turned into Forty-fourth, passed the brownstone houses where every door bore its sign: 'Table Board. Furnished Rooms.' A red-headed boy ran out into the street, and the chauffeur slowed up.

'It's t'ree houses down, Mr Colton.' The Fee's voice fairly trembled with excitement. 'He's on the top floor. Kin I go with yuh?'

Colton nodded and stepped down from the machine. 'We'll walk the rest of the way,' he told them. He started, the bright-eyed boy at his elbow.

They mounted the steps of a brownstone house, and Colton rang the bell. A frowsy-haired lady in a grease-spotted kimono opened the door. The smell of cooking onions assailed their nostrils; somewhere within a piano banged out a ragtime tune; a raucous voice screeched: 'I call her Little Hy'cinth, but her name's M'Swigg'; from the depths of the house a squeaky clarinet piped off-key opera.

'Profesh'n?' snapped the lady of the kimono suspiciously before anyone had a chance to speak.

'We want to see Signor Delvetoi,' said the blind man quietly.

Sydney Thames never remembered the short colloquy that followed; never recollected just how they entered the house. Signor Delvetoi! That name drove everything else from his mind. Once more he saw the black-clothed, black-bearded man at the theatre; again he saw the whirling knives flashing from the darkness into the beam of the calcium to bury their points beside the woman of the golden frame; once more came to his mind the wonderful skill that had directed those keen-pointed knives toward their target of living flesh – to brush a cheek and not even scratch it.

Then he found himself following the others up the narrow stairs. In the second floor hallway a fat, greasy-faced woman murmured husky endearments to a monkey in her arms, while a goose waddled at her side. A dozen discordant tunes came from the closed rooms. This was the place they had come to arrest a murderer!

On the third floor Thornley Colton stopped and knocked on a door panel. Thames could feel the tenseness of the men's bodies as they crowded up close to the door as it slowly opened. Standing before them, framed in the light that came into the hallway from the room, stood a big man in a stained red bath-robe that trailed the floor behind the worn carpet-slippers. His head was bald, and across the skull ran a livid scar; his face was a deep-lined, jaundiced yellow.

'We want you for the murder of Cartwright and the girl at the theatre.' That was all Colton said, and his voice was low.

For an instant the face of the man went a fish-belly white; then murderous red rage leaped to the cheeks, and darted from the slit eyes.

'You devils!' he shrieked.

The red robe was flung back; but with a movement as quick as light itself Colton's hand darted out, closed with a grip of steel on a wrist, and the red robe whirled as the man spun to his knees.

'Better handcuff him,' advised the blind man quietly, as he pushed aside the fallen knife with the thin cane that had warned him of the murderous movement. The handcuffs clicked on the knife-thrower's wrists as the chief dragged him to a chair.

'So you're the one, eh?' The detective chief tried to make his tone casual, but he could not keep the wonder from his eyes, or voice.

'Oh, you got me right,' sneered the knife-thrower.

'How did you do it?' put in Rogers dazedly. The picture he had seen the night before was still in his mind.

A cunning light leaped to the half-closed eyes of the red-robed man. 'D'you want to hear the whole thing?' he asked. 'You might as well,' he boasted. 'I'll never swing for it.'

'Go ahead,' growled the chief, drawing his chair up closer and placing his revolver on his knees. The knife-thrower grinned sneeringly.

'Well,' he began, and his evil eyes seemed to gloat at them. 'I'm the only man in the world that could have pulled the trick. It took years of practice to get it down pat, but there's Indian blood in me, mixed with the Irish. They don't know much about me in this country, and I didn't want them to, till I got Jim Cartwright. But in Europe I'm the best in the business, and I'm the only one that could ever plant five knives in a spot the size of a half-dollar at thirty feet, and do it on the level.'

There was boasting in the tone, but to Sydney Thames, who had seen his amazing work of the night before, it was not idle boasting.

'The story of why I killed Cartwright is the same old game: I had a woman and he took her. She wasn't much good, only a doll-faced fool, and there was a squalling kid that got on my nerves; but she was mine, body and soul.' The listening men gritted their teeth at the tone, and he sneered at them for it. 'Cartwright took her, and I went after them both. I had a little money, I was headin' the olio in a burlesque. Before I started I went in a place along the river front in Chicago, where I was. I musta showed my roll, because – now I don't expect you to believe what's comin', and I don't give a damn whether you do or not!' There was sullen defiance in the voice. 'But I woke up in a hospital I never saw before, and the nurse talked German! It was in Berlin, and it was ten years after! Oh, it wasn't anything new, the doctors told me. One of the Windy City thugs had lead-piped me for my roll; you can see the scar I got. Something cracked in my head then, and when I woke I'd just been in a German train smash-up. The doctors said the bump I got there straightened me out.

'I remembered everything after a while. I was doin' a knife-throwin' act. Some wop had picked me up when I didn't know my own name, and brought me to Europe with him. Somehow the kink had kept me off the booze, and I was even better than him, and he was the best in the world, bar none. He died a few months after I got out, and I copped his layout. We'd been rehearsin' a stunt that was going to make 'em all sit up. The Flyin' Death, we called it, and we threw pistols instead of knives. We had a blank board at one end of the stage, and a target at the other. We'd stand in the centre, let it fly at the blank board, duck, and the butt striking would jar down the trigger, and the bullet'd go over our heads and hit the bull's-eye three times out of five. It was big stuff! But I wasn't satisfied, because I wanted to hit the bull's-eye every time. I was goin' to play that act fer one man; the one that stole my wife and ten years out of my life. So I put in two more years on the Continent, still practisin'. If you looked at the nicks in the pistol-butts you can see how many times they'd been used.

'When I got so I couldn't go wrong I came to the States. I learned I was dead – one of the thugs that got my coin and papers, I guess. But that suited me right down to the ground. I found Cartwright was the big cheese in the business, but I couldn't find the wife, or the kid. I wanted to get them, too; ten years don't make no difference to me.' Again came the sneer to the evil, yellow face, as his eyes caught their looks of horror and disgust. 'I spent a year touring here before I could book Cartwright's house. I wanted to get him right before everybody's eyes. That's why I had that dark act. He was up to the rehearsal in the mornin' with a kid that looked something like the woman he stole, but it wasn't my kid, because he made it plain he was only her manager. You can bet he'd a showed it if he had claims. I heard him make a date for the box after her act, and that looked good to me, because I'd get him right beside her.

'Under the knives for the spotlight act was the pistol with a real cartridge, of course. I only used minichure ones with a pinch of powder for the act. The guns was balanced special in Germany, and the front sights was off the barrels so they could slide out of my hand. I could see the white of the girl's waist and his shirt between every knife-throw, because I waited a few seconds each time to get 'em right. Then, when I knew I couldn't make a mistake, I let the gun fly. I was goin' to have the butt hit the wall in back of him, and the bullet catch him between the shoulders. It was easy, because I was above him on the stage, and I thought there couldn't be any suspicion because I was in front of him, and he'd be shot in the back. But that darn' fool kid,' he spat out snarlingly, 'had to have his hands on the hanging just when the gun hit, and throw it off enough to kill the girl.'

Sydney Thames gasped audibly.

'It wasn't my fault she was in the way, but a little thing like that wasn't going to keep me from gettin' the man I wanted. I got another of the guns out of my prop trunk and went after him. I couldn't get him right until I heard the other feller arguin' with him in front of the rathskeller. I ducked around to the side-door. I'd been in there before, but I'd had my black stage-whiskers and wig on, and the waiter didn't know me. I played drunk, and gave the waiter a five-spot for a drink, and told him not to turn on the booth-light.

'Cartwright faced my booth, but I was in the dark. They started to whisper. The waiter was out of sight, and the bartender was sleepin'. I had the gun ready for five minutes. This man bent down – and I let her fly. There wasn't going to be any mistake this time, because I was going to put another half turn on the gun and make it jam its muzzle against his heart. No chance of missin' that way! And he saw the gun comin' when it was too late to dodge! And he knew me then! And the last thing he ever saw was me grinnin' at him! It was a cinch to slope out in the excitement after.'

There was silence in the room when he had finished. From beyond the closed door came the discordant medley of the tinny piano, the screeching clarinet, the hoarse-voiced singers. Before them a manacled man, with sneers in his voice, and boasts, and snarls, had just told them of the man whose death he had accomplished with such fiendish cunning; of the innocent girl whose life he had destroyed.

'Do you mean to say that you could fling those pistols as accurately as all that?' demanded the chief, who was a policeman, first, last, and all the time. The case, to him, had ceased to be one of human emotions, of sorrow and tragedy; it was a matter of proof, of conviction. Such is the policeman's philosophy of life – and death.

'Do you want me to prove it?' taunted the murderer. 'There's the other pistol for the act on the bureau. It ain't loaded. Get it and I'll show you.'

'Better take his word,' suggested Colton warningly.

'I'll see that he plays no tricks,' boasted the chief. It was his case now. He got the pistol from the bureau. 'I'll take one cuff off, and I'll have this gun on you every second!' he snapped.

The knife-thrower leered at him with his bloodless lips, and the slit eyes shone with an exultant gleam. He took a stubby pencil from his bath-robe pocket and drew a small circle on the blank wall. He walked to the other end of the room, the chief watching him like a hawk. The pistol dangled from the man's hand as he turned. A snap of the arm, and it became a flying whirl of blue. The muzzle struck the exact centre of the small circle, the hammer snapped down, and for an instant the gun seemed suspended against the wall before it jangled to the floor.

'God! That's what I saw last night!' choked Rogers.

The knife-thrower picked up the pistol. 'It's just as easy to make the butt strike first, with the muzzle pointed at me, as it should have pointed at Cartwright's back last night.'

The commissioner watched every move as he walked to the end of the room.

Suddenly Colton's voice rang out:

'Don't let him throw that pistol!'

The chief jumped from his chair as the red arm swung.

A line of fire leaped from the blank wall toward the scarlet-robed figure across the room. The explosion echoed and re-echoed in the room. The pistol clattered on the bare boards under the small circle it had struck so unerringly. On the butt were flakes of the white plaster where it had been driven into the wall. The red robe seemed slowly to crumple as the knife-thrower sank to the floor; and as they ran to where he lay, the lips twisted in an evil leer of triumph, the slit eyes gleamed their gloating.

'I told you I'd never swing for it!' he sneered up at them. 'Palming that cartridge was easy. I used to be a magician – when my name was – Kelly!'

V

'Yes, Sydney, he paid the price the State puts on murder, and I guess it is just as well.' A fleeting smile crossed Colton's thin lips for an instant. 'But the chief is naturally angry that such a spectacular murderer should escape his clutches so easily. My keen ears caught the click of the breech as he put in the cartridge. But I was too late; he had waited until the last second.'

The two men were in the library of the old-fashioned house, where the blind man had come to spend his regular afternoon four hours in darkness that meant insurance against the splitting headaches too-long-continued light on his sensitive, sightless eyes always caused. The knife-thrower had lived but a few minutes, for his skill had not failed him, and the bullet had pierced one of his lungs. Rogers had gone to arrange for the funerals of Cartwright and the daughter he had loved. They were to be side by side in death, and the story would go to their graves. On that the men had agreed in the big bare room where the last act of the tragedy had been played.

'How did you ever connect the knife-thrower with the murders?' asked Sydney finally.

'Your story of the shooting in the box, as you told it to me while we were waiting for the panic to cease in the theatre, gave me the first clue,' explained the blind man thoughtfully. 'The fact that you saw the face of Nelson so plainly told me that the flash must have crossed his body, and, in groping his way in the darkness, his right hand must have been on the hangings. Shrimp's enthusiastic description of the knife-thrower's act told me how wonderful it was, and – he was the possibility.

'Then the murder of Cartwright was the proof needed. There could be no explanation but that of a thrown pistol for the thing Rogers saw. And the two pistols being identical was the last link. But no one would believe the theory without irrefutable proof. That I got, first by the nicked-up butts of the guns, showing how long they had been used in practice. Then Rogers's story of Cartwright told me the guilty person. But then came the necessity of explaining where he had been all the years. I sent

Shrimp to the stage entrance to get the knife-thrower's address and locate him. He did, and, being a boy, he aroused not the slightest suspicion when he made an inquiry at the house. I knew also that at least one of the two employees of the rathskeller must have known another man had been on hand when the murder was committed. I had to go there to see why they had withheld the information from the police. The explanation was logical enough, but the police would never have seen it. Then I had to go to the theatre and find the place where the butt of the gun had struck on the wall. The finding was more of a job than I thought. In his excitement the boy must have moved the hangings a foot, for the scar in the velvet was a foot lower than I should have found it. And you must remember that it was a scar that no eye could have seen, one that could only be found with a microscope, or supersensitive fingertips like mine. Then came the message from Shrimp, whom I had told to call me up either at the rathskeller or the theatre.'

Silence came in the darkened room. When Thornley Colton spoke again his voice was low, solemn, its tone one of reverent wonder. 'The death of that girl is one of the higher mysteries, Sydney. Was she murdered because of a terrible mistake, or did a merciful Providence send a thoughtless, foolish boy to grope in the darkness at just the right instant to deflect that pistol, and send the bullet into her back? She died in the happiest moment of her life; joy was in her heart and on her lips. If the pistol had not been turned by the moving velvet, Cartwright would have died. Her whole story would have had to come out then; she would have heard it bandied by unclean lips on the street-corners; to know that her father, the father who did not even recognize her, was a murderer. A merciful Providence? I'll always wonder, Sydney.'

LEDROIT CONNERS

Created by Samuel Gardenhire (1855–1923)

Conners, an upper-crust private investigator working in New York, is, in many ways, a very Holmes-like figure, although Conan Doyle's great detective would be unlikely to approve of this American counterpart's methods. Conners depends on intuition rather than deduction, rapidly forming his conclusions about a case and then working backwards to get the evidence to confirm them. He is a sophisticated, metropolitan man but his background is, to say the least, unusual. He was born in the Canadian wilderness where his Native American mother died, the victim of a wolf attack, and was then brought up by his father. The eight stories featuring LeDroit Conners, told by a Watson-like associate and admirer, were first published in The Saturday Evening Post *in 1905 and then collected in a single volume entitled* The Long Arm *the following year. They were the work of Samuel Gardenhire, a Missouri-born lawyer who had turned to writing fiction in middle age. His first novel,* Lux Crucis, *a historical epic about St Paul, was published in 1904. The tales of LeDroit Conners are untypical of Gardenhire's fiction – he wrote no other crime stories – but they remain very readable.*

THE PARK SLOPE MYSTERY

The proximity of his office to my studio enabled me to see LeDroit Conners almost daily, and I consequently soon came to be on terms of intimacy with this remarkable man. Yet it was a tragedy which touched my own little family that first cemented our association and made me, in the end, his companion in so many curious adventures. Upon the occasion to which I allude I had finished my morning bath and was standing before the mirror, razor in hand, when a cry from the dining room below startled me. It was followed by such confusion, that before I could collect my startled wits I had inflicted a sharp wound upon my cheek, yet, scarcely conscious of any pain, I ran to the head of the stairs to send down an answering call. Then, razor and all, with my features besmeared with blood and lather, I made my appearance in the breakfast room, where my wife, Jennie, stood with the morning paper in her grasp, and her mother, Mrs Barrister, with pallid face and staring eyes, sat rigid upon the sofa.

'What is it?' I asked, excitedly, dashing the razor among the breakfast things and going to Jennie's side.

She thrust the paper into my hand, indicating an article under black headlines, and seated herself beside her mother. Stripped of its sensational introduction, which naturally 'featured' the chief events of the tragedy, the article read as follows:

'One day last week a handsome woman, nearing middle age, appeared at the Park Slope Police Station, evidently for the purpose of making a complaint. Her face showed traces of tears, and her manner was that of one suffering from fright. Before she could make her wishes known to the sergeant in charge, an elderly gentleman came upon the scene. He arrived in a carriage which was driven hastily to the door, and as he entered and saw the woman an exclamation either of anger or apprehension escaped him. He was recognized by the sergeant as a prominent citizen of the vicinity, and was not interrupted when he drew the woman to one side and conversed with her in a low tone.

'Mollified or reassured by what was said to her, she recovered her composure and consented to accompany the gentleman from the station. Her companion remained long enough to explain to the officer that the coming of the woman was a mistake, which she regretted, and that both desired no publicity about the matter. These persons were Dr Charles Haslam, an old and well-known resident of the Park Slope, and Mrs Martha Sands, his housekeeper. The significance of this visit will appear when it is learned that last night, at half-past nine o'clock, Dr Haslam shot the woman to death. The murder took place at the handsome residence of the doctor on Banning Street, a fashionable thoroughfare in Brooklyn's most aristocratic neighbourhood.

'The crime in its details was as gruesome as though committed by some ruffian in the slums, the head of the unfortunate woman being blown to pieces by a charge from a heavily loaded shotgun.

'Immediately prior to the tragedy, officers Flynn and Davis were walking up Banning Street towards the Park, when they were startled by the explosion of a gun, evidently in the second story of the Haslam house. They were at that time directly in front of the entrance. Fearful of either an accident or worse, they ran up the steps to make inquiry. The answer to their ring was delayed, but finally Edward Gray, the butler, opened the door. Pale and frightened, in answer to their questions he informed them that he did not know the meaning of the noise; that Dr Jerome Sadler, an adopted son of Dr Haslam, had gone upstairs to investigate, and that he, Gray, had remained behind only to answer the call at the door. Mystified by the man's demeanour, the officers entered the hall, and immediately encountered Dr Sadler coming down the main stairway, greatly agitated. In a shaking voice he told them that Dr Haslam had killed the housekeeper, the murder having taken place in the study on the second floor.

'Proceeding at once to the room in which the tragedy occurred, the officers found the body of the unfortunate woman lying upon the floor, the head in a pool of blood. The face was shattered almost beyond recognition, and death must have been instantaneous. The weapon with which the crime had been committed was leaning against an angle of the mantel. All possibility of an accident was excluded by the high state of feeling which had for some time existed between Dr Haslam and the woman, and by the fact that Dr Sadler surprised the murderer standing beside the body of his victim, contemplating his work with malevolent satisfaction.

'The stricken son, in the face of the early arrival of the officers, made no attempt to shield his erring parent. At the exclamation of horror which Dr Sadler uttered upon entering the room immediately following the crime, the murderer placed the weapon in the position in which it was found, coolly turned away, and, by descending the back stairway, made his escape from the house at the moment the officers entered from the street. A general alarm has been sent out for his apprehension, and he will doubtless be taken before morning. The police feel confident of this, as he was in his dressing-gown and slippers at the moment of departure, and had little time to effect a change of garments or make provision for flight.

'Dr Haslam is a man of wealth and a physician of large practice. Of late he has been something of a recluse, his failing health having caused a partial abandonment of his professional duties, which were largely assumed by his adopted son. Little is known of the unfortunate woman. She was of unusual personal attraction, English, and, so far as known, had no relatives in this country.'

Here was the story, told with little elaboration, and I stood aghast and, for a moment, speechless. Dr Haslam was the brother of Mrs Barrister and the uncle of my wife.

We were somewhat familiar with his domestic affairs, although there was little cordiality between the fashionable house on Banning Street and my retired residence on Staten Island. The reason lay in Dr Jerome Sadler. A warm affection had existed between Mrs Barrister and her brother, but when Dr Haslam, in his rounds of the hospitals, at which he was a welcome demonstrator, found the young student whom he had taken so closely into his household and subsequently educated, a breach had occurred which had never healed. This, in part, grew out of the fact that the young man became a suitor for Jennie's hand, and her preference for myself greatly disappointed her uncle. But the young man from the first was odious to Mrs Barrister, and Jennie shared the feelings of her mother.

Of Mrs Sands, the murdered woman, we knew little, and yet her presence in the home of Dr Haslam had been a matter of uneasiness. Neither Mrs Barrister nor Jennie had lost interest in their relative, and, with that feminine observance which is quick to note details, they suspected coming trouble – not trouble in the nature of the horrible event of which we had just been apprised, but in the possibility of an ill-advised marriage to be followed by the consequences of an old man's folly. They fancied that Dr Sadler feared this, too, and their hope of seeing it averted lay in the fact of his natural opposition to such a union. They knew him to be selfish, suspected him to be base, and, although both detested him cordially, they held him in nothing like the apprehension with which they regarded the woman, whom Mrs Bàrrister did not hesitate to regard as an adventuress. Deep as was our grief, and firm as had been our confidence in the high character of the man to whom both Jennie and her mother bore the relationship of blood, we had no reason to doubt the facts as told so coolly in the columns of the morning paper.

Gathering my scattered wits together, I sought to calm the weeping women, thinking at the time, with some grimness, of how little there was to say. Mrs Barrister desired to go at once to the scene of the trouble, and Jennie clamoured to accompany her, but to this I would not consent; my wife's presence could do no good.

Yielding, finally, to my wishes, Jennie helped to make her mother ready, and, oppressed by the gloom of our mission, we set out for Banning Street.

Something of the anticipated horror of our visit was kindly spared us. I had looked forward to a fearful inspection, of the body and a pathetic meeting between Mrs Barrister and her brother – doubtless he was now in custody and would be brought to the scene of his crime. I supposed there might be some judicial proceedings in which we would be called upon to participate, and which must be necessarily trying for Jennie's mother.

But upon our arrival we found the house quiet, with only a few curious figures lingering about the corners of the vicinity. Dr Sadler greeted us with a fishy clasp, striving to twist his cold countenance into an expression of sympathy; in the shadow of the tragedy he could afford to be polite. The servants stood about like statues, dazed by the event, and Dr Sadler himself ushered us into the parlour, from which the light was excluded by the closely drawn curtains. But our visit was to be free from any horror; the coroner had held an early inquest, and the body had been taken to the rooms of a neighbouring undertaker. Dr Haslam had not been found.

We met this statement with an exclamation of surprise, and Mrs Barrister sobbed her relief. Dr Sadler had a theory; he stated it in a colourless voice and with a demeanour which I sought to attribute to the influence of the horrible crime. The papers had spoken truly, he observed, when they said that Dr Haslam was unprepared for flight; and he could, of course, find no one to harbour him from the authorities. He had made his way to the river, so he believed, and the police would find him when the waters gave up their dead.

The conclusion was a natural one, although it added to Mrs Barrister's grief. Vainly she sought the cause of such a tragedy in the life of such a man as her brother. What had happened so to change a nature that had been always kind? Was it true that the man had become infatuated with the unfortunate woman whom he had slain?

She plied young Sadler with questions, but he was dumb and stolid. He was as surprised, he said, as she was; he could not understand it; naturally, he shared her grief, and had not yet been able to consider the matter calmly; it was almost useless to find excuses in the light of the horrible facts; he did not know whether his adopted father had left a will, but he did know that there was no insurance; when he could bring himself to think upon the subject he would give these things his attention.

So he answered her, speaking with scarcely a trace of feeling; and, even in my own confusion, I regarded him with increased aversion. He was a hypocrite – but that mattered little.

In response to questions from me, he spoke with more directness. Mrs Sands had been an inmate of the house prior to his coming there; it was only recently that he had suspected an infatuation for her on the part of his adopted father. He had ventured on one occasion to mention the matter to Dr Haslam, but the suggestion had been received with indignation. He dared say no more, but mentioned the matter to the butler – the servants had observed nothing. The tragedy had fallen upon all like a thunderbolt.

Our visit was over. Dr Haslam had probably little need of the sympathy or affection of a sister. We returned to our home, and the two women sank under the sense of disgrace which they fancied the tragedy brought upon them. They held a portion of the stain of blood-guiltiness because of their nearness to the murderer, and although I strove to move them from such a feeling, my efforts were without avail. The gloom of the affair oppressed my own spirits in spite of my struggle to throw it off, and for days I remained closely at home, anxious to be near Jennie, who clung to me like a child frightened at the dark.

The papers dealt further with the Park Slope murder, as it came to be called, because of the prominence of Dr Haslam. Those who had known him best could not reconcile this frantic deed with any propensity of his past life; a man of scrupulous and Christian character, the crime of murder was the last of which they would have suspected him to be guilty. His disappearance also caused wonder, for no trace of him could be found. From the frightful moment when he had slipped into the night from his house, the gloom seemed to have swallowed him. The house and stable on Banning Street had both been searched with a thoroughness which satisfied the police that he had not lingered near his home. The lakes in the Park were dragged until no spot was left unexplored. In all the throngs that intervened between his dwelling and the river, or the sea, no eye could be found that had seen an elderly man, strangely garbed for the street, fleeing in gown and slippers from the scene of his crime.

The search of the police brought to light other facts as revealed by the papers, but scarcely essential in view of the known details of the murder and the motive. Dr Haslam had been ill during the week preceding the crime, and confined closely to his room, this indisposition following his visit to the police station in search of Mrs Sands. There had been high words between himself and his adopted son growing out of this trouble with the housekeeper; the servants had heard the discussion, and the young man admitted it with sorrow. Dr Haslam, under the influence of his passion, had been growing irritable. Certain improvements in the stable had necessitated the laying of a cement floor, and the teamsters, in hauling material into the yard, had broken down one of the concrete stone gate-posts at the side entrance. The doctor was furious, exhibiting unusual rage. He stormed about the premises until the servants were frightened, but under the entreaties of Dr Sadler he finally grew calm. The young man had promised to see personally to the reconstruction of the damaged post, and at once to order the making of a mould in which the great stone should be cast, with which to replace the broken member of the gate.

Strangely subdued, Dr Haslam had retired to his chamber, and there seemingly lost interest in the work which had before engrossed his attention. It progressed to completion, and, though he remained indifferent, he consented to accompany Mrs Sands and Dr Sadler to inspect it. Confined to his room for several days, they had been anxious to persuade him to take the air. The workmen had gone, but the coachman was present when the three entered the stable, and spoke with them. He also heard the old gentleman give directions to Dr Sadler as to the demolished post, the stone for which was ready. It lay upon the floor beside the cement barrels and concrete from which it had been fashioned, and with which the stable paving had been done. It was a circumstance that the coachman had absented himself for two days from that time, and the butler deposed that this was Dr Haslam's last appearance to any member of the household except the murdered woman, until the moment his adopted son had come upon him, standing above the body of his victim.

Meantime, Dr Sadler announced the finding of a will among the papers in the study safe, which he had turned over to the family lawyer. No one doubted that the young man was the heir, but the question of the disposition of the property of the fugitive must wait upon the legal knowledge of his death. While his complete disappearance gave colour to the belief that he had made away with himself, the police were puzzled, and again searched every nook of his dwelling from attic to cellar.

Personally, I was resentful that Dr Sadler, an intruder as it seemed to me in a household where he had no moral right, should sit quietly in possession of property in which my people should have had a share. We had inherited the shame and the disgrace, and it seemed unfair that the law should deprive us of some portion of the worldly goods. Of this, Jennie and Mrs Barrister took no thought, but they continued in a state of such depression that I went with them for a trip South, remaining away for several weeks. The journey brought some of the colour back to Jennie's cheeks, and in a measure benefited Mrs Barrister, so I returned with something of the gloom lifted from my spirits, and finally reappeared at my office.

After greeting Jeffries, and looking at the mail which had accumulated on my desk, I stepped along the hall and opened the door of Conners's studio. An unfinished picture sat as usual on his easel, but he was not before it. The paintings, glowing in all the colours of his fancy, looked at me from the walls, and the raven poised above the bust of Poe seemed to extend to me a grim greeting. Alone, I found myself wondering at his fancy for the apostle of the pessimistic, and studying the countenance that he had given to the three pictures near the statue. They were three conceptions of the Chevalier Dupin, a character he much admired.

As I stood waiting he entered from his bedroom and came forward with a smile. His face expressed his welcome, but I knew from his serious eyes that he understood my absence, and had thought of me with sympathy.

'Back at last, my dear fellow?' he cried, cheerily. 'You have been missed, of course. I know the anxiety you have experienced, and should have sought you if you had been alone. But I could not intrude upon your family circle. As the trouble was mainly theirs, I let you bear it in their company. I endeavour to avoid women.'

I glanced again at his pictures, where sylph and siren, Venus in nature with Venus à la mode, showed every phase of beauty to the eye. He saw my gaze, and understood it.

'These do not count,' he smiled, as he waved his hand about him. 'You recall the temptation of St Anthony? I hold discipline to be good for a man. These I may love – none other.'

I looked at him curiously, struck by the sudden gloom of his manner; but almost immediately his demeanour changed.

'Where have you been?' he inquired.

I told him, and, cheered by the sympathy which looked from his eyes, I spoke of the grief of my wife, and how deeply the matter of our trouble had affected Mrs Barrister. He listened in silence until I had finished.

'I know it all,' he said, finally. 'I have the papers here; every detail has been noted, while the articles are arranged in order. I have studied the matter carefully, wondering how much you knew of it.'

'I believe all is known,' I replied, 'except the fate of my wife's unfortunate uncle.'

'Sit down,' he said, kindly, looking at me with eyes which now displayed another and deeper interest. 'You cannot understand how strongly such matters appeal to me. It is a faculty with me almost to know the solution of a crime when the leading circumstances connected with it are revealed. I form my conclusion first, and, confident of its correctness, hunt for evidence to sustain it. I do this because I am never wrong. It is not magic, telepathy, nor any form of mental science; it is a moral consciousness of the meaning of related facts, impressed upon my mind with unerring certainty.'

'I do not understand you,' I said.

'When I am given certain figures,' he replied, 'the process of addition is instantaneous and sure. So, when I know of established incidents relating to a matter, they group themselves in my mind in such a manner as to reveal to me their meaning. You are grieved that your family must bear the shame of this crime of which Dr Haslam stands charged, that you can discover no trace of him. May I help you?'

'Help me, indeed!' I replied, earnestly. 'From the facts, as you have read them, would you say that he is dead?'

'Not altogether from the facts as I read them,' Conners replied, 'but from the facts not to be denied, he is dead without doubt. He was a man of character, made through a series of years, and intimately known to the best people of his vicinity; guilty or not of this crime, he was never a man to flee. He was a physician, and entirely sane – a man who would eagerly seek, rather than avoid, an explanation of any act he might commit. Whatever his connection with this murder, he would have remained to justify or deny it.'

'That was, in fact, his character,' I replied, eagerly.

'Even though he had fled, his nature suddenly changed, or his mind suffering from a sudden shock,' continued Conners, 'he would have surrendered himself later to the authorities. He is dead, or detained in some spot against his will. Since the latter theory is scarcely tenable, the conviction is certain that he is dead.'

'You believe, then, that he has made away with himself?' I asked.

'It is the first thing that I doubted,' answered Conners, slowly, 'and in your interest I hastened to investigate the matter. I found the task a light one. Why should Dr Haslam flee from his house to make away with himself? He had drugs about him with which he might have made a painless end. The facts as stated were hard to reconcile. Here was a man incapable of murder, who does murder; a man incapable of flight, who flees; a man with every healthy conviction against suicide, drowning himself in the river or ocean – a method of death which required a journey of several miles in night attire through busy thoroughfares or along lighted avenues, against a simpler method of drug or pistol, thus reflecting upon the logic of his whole lifetime. The woman is slain by a gunshot, in the upper story of your kinsman's dwelling; Dr Sadler is below stairs with the butler, and every inmate of the house but the slayer and his victim is positively accounted for as absent from the scene; and Dr Haslam disappears at that instant, as is stated, since which time no trace of him is seen.'

'Yes,' I answered, 'and Dr Sadler saw him at the moment following the commission of his crime.'

'The doctor said so,' returned Conners, significantly. 'It seems to have occurred to no one to doubt his statement. The police are not usually so credulous.'

I made an involuntary movement under the influence of the suggestion, the blood mounting to my cheek; then I experienced as quickly a revulsion of feeling.

'Sadler is treacherous enough and possibly a liar, but that has little bearing here,' I responded, gloomily. 'The woman is dead, Dr Haslam gone – doubtless dead, also, as you have stated. I can conceive of no possible solution of the matter in view of what we know, other than the conclusion of the police. Sane or mad, Dr Haslam can never speak in explanation, and, since every witness who can possibly know of the matter has been fully heard, the case is closed to us.'

'I confess that it is confusing, in the matter of proof,' replied Conners, 'but let us investigate. I already know everything that the reporters can tell us. I should like to know something on my own account.'

'What?' I asked.

'Let us visit Dr Sadler, and, if he will permit, inspect the premises.'

'Surely,' I replied. 'Sadler does not love me, and may resent our coming, but we will go.'

'Let him resent it,' answered Conners, with a peculiar smile. 'I think myself that he will do so.'

'When shall we go?' I asked.

He laughed as he threw aside his studio-jacket.

'Now,' he answered.

I was silent during our ride to Banning Street, but Conners talked cheerfully of many things. He had seemingly studied the matter, and, having arrived at some conclusion, sought to cheer me as best he could until we reached the place. In spite of this, my spirits fell, and I was not reassured as we mounted the steps of the now depressing house with its chill air and its closed shutters. Dr Sadler had done nothing to lighten the gloom which hung over it; the blinds were drawn even at the back windows, and the gate, hung to the new stone of the great post, was shut and bolted.

Our ring was answered by the familiar face of Edward Gray. The new master had evidently retained him. He ushered us into the hall, and then into the parlour. I told him to announce me and a friend.

In a few minutes Sadler entered the room, looking with some surprise at my companion, but greeting me with an attempt at warmth. He made inquiry as to the health of Mrs Barrister and my wife; he had heard of our departure, and expressed his pleasure at our return. Having said so much, he waited to learn my business, eying Conners from under his flabby lids and evidently suspecting an attorney. I could see that he was preparing to meet a declaration of war which might involve some question of property. The subject of the crime with him had become a matter of the past.

He heard my opening statement with evident relief, for his manner assumed an unusual frankness.

'Mr Conners, Doctor, is my friend,' I said. 'I have told him of the depression under which we continue to labour, and how much Mrs Barrister and my wife have suffered. He is good enough to sympathize with me. He suggested that by this time you might have something to offer in the way of news. I have, therefore, ventured to bring him with me to visit you.'

'He is very welcome, as you are,' was the unexpected answer, 'but, alas! I have learned nothing. The police were diligent enough at first, and now know that there is really nothing to discover but the remains of our unfortunate relative. Therefore, they seem to have lost interest in the matter.'

'You were, of course, much distressed by the occurrence, Doctor?' said Conners.

'Naturally, sir,' replied the young man.

'Where were you when the gun was fired?'

'I was in the lower hall, with Edward Gray, the butler. He can testify to that, and has done so.

Mrs Sands entered from the rear of the house and I asked her to go to the study for a book. She met Dr Haslam there as he came from his apartments. He had evidently heard her step in the hall and, prepared for the fateful moment, stood waiting. He killed her ruthlessly. At the noise of the report I ran upstairs to find her dead. The explosion seemed to shake the house, and the butler was too frightened to accompany me. Two officers were outside, and heard it also. Their ring at the door prevented Gray from following me.'

'Did you ask Gray to remain below?'

The young man smiled.

'Why, yes. I saw how he trembled, and my first thought was of burglars. It occurred to me that someone should remain below.'

'There were other servants?'

The doctor looked annoyed. He made no reply.

'The butler was spared the terrifying sight which afflicted you,' continued Conners, dryly. 'May we look over the house, Doctor? The police have done that thoroughly, of course, but I fancy you could tell us graphically of the matter, upon the very scene.'

I saw that Sadler now suspected the detective in my companion, and his eyes glittered balefully. The hatred he had always felt for me showed in every line of his face. But apparently he had nothing to conceal, and, wishing to render every assistance in his power to the authorities, he speedily rose to comply with our request.

'I remember it very graphically, at all events,' he replied. 'Come, gentlemen.'

We followed him up the stairs and into the room where the murder had taken place. It was darkened, but he stepped to the window and pulled up the shade.

'There is a stain beneath that rug near you,' he said. 'We have been unable to remove it, even with acids. I shall have to have a section of the floor taken up. It is not a pleasant thing to see.'

Conners looked about the chamber critically.

'Where was the gun found?'

'Here,' and the doctor indicated the spot at the corner of the mantel.

'How did the piece of brass wire become attached to the stock, which the officers noticed when they first entered the room?'

'Which officer noticed it?' asked Sadler.

'I believe it was Flynn who spoke of it. You were present at the inquest?'

Sadler smiled.

'This is the first I have heard of it,' he said.

'Of the wire?'

'No; of the fact that it was noticed. It was a loop used to hold back a refractory shutter yonder, and it must have fallen from the frame about the gun when Dr Haslam placed it upon the floor. It was not a very gentle deed which he had just perpetrated, and his actions were not studied. The matter has no significance.'

'Do you think that Dr Haslam was concealed – ?'

'Concealed?' The young man answered quickly, with his note of query.

'I mean, do you think he entered from his rooms at the moment of Mrs Sands's coming, or was he waiting for her here in the study?'

Dr Sadler looked at him scornfully.

'It surely matters little, but Dr Haslam could come or go at pleasure in his own house; and he had little difficulty in seeing Mrs Sands at any moment. He would have killed her in the parlour, in the presence of the whole world, having once resolved to do so. He made no attempt at concealment.'

'But he fled.'

The lids of the young man drooped.

'It is the habit of criminals to flee,' he replied.

'Have you learned to think of your benefactor in the light of a criminal?'

The eyes of the young man flashed, but he held his temper in check. I saw, however, that it was by an effort, and that he resented the question.

'I shall always think of him with gratitude,' he answered, 'criminal or not.'

'Did Dr Haslam speak to you?'

'He said nothing, but looked unutterable things.'

'I have thought it strange,' observed Conners, musingly, and I fancied his manner assumed, 'that the doctor should have escaped so readily from the house.'

The young man gave a whiff of disgust.

'Who are here who would have presumed to stop him?' he said. 'No one knew of a crime.'

I thought the observation a trivial one myself, but my companion continued his questions.

'Did the servants speak to Dr Haslam as he passed through the kitchen – did they not inquire of him the meaning of the gunshot they had heard?'

Dr Sadler hesitated. He fumbled with his handkerchief, which he had taken from his pocket, and stared vacantly at the floor.

'It is difficult to recall all these details,' he replied, 'but not the one in question. I have thought it strange that the police did not make that inquiry. The truth is that Dr Haslam left the house unseen. The officers took it for granted that he left the house by the back stairway, because I said so; and I thought so until I found out differently. I did not fail to question the servants as to this.'

'Did not the servants ask this question of their fellow, Gray,

Doctor? What the murderer said, and how he acted, as he passed through the front?'

The eyes of the young man flashed viciously.

'It is quite possible,' he answered. 'As I have said, it is difficult to recall these details.'

'You appear to have attached some importance to this yourself,' persisted Conners.

'Of course,' replied Dr Sadler. 'It was natural that I should, since I found that I was mistaken in the manner in which my benefactor, as you designate him, made his escape.'

'How did he escape?' asked Conners.

The young man did not resent the question, and I listened with intense interest. I could not anticipate what was coming, and I expected little; but the facts were revealing themselves in strangely different form. I knew, of course, that this could matter little, but to me the whole subject was absorbing.

'The police found every window bolted,' said the doctor, speaking slowly, and choosing his words carefully. 'As I stated to them that my father passed down the back stairway, they presumed it to be true, and that ended it. I thought it the truth myself until, as I have said, I learned differently from the servants. There was but one other mode of egress, since the windows were bolted, and that was by means of a trap in the attic roof. It is low to the eaves, and a ladder leads from the main structure to the back building. The descent from here to the yard is without difficulty. There is a trellis near, upon which vines grow. I investigated, and found that Dr Haslam had used this avenue of escape. The vines on the trellis were torn and pulled aside, and I discovered his slipper on the roof of the back building. It is here.'

He stepped to a closet and, taking the slipper from a shelf, exhibited it to us.

'You did not think it necessary to correct the erroneous impression of the police?' observed Conners.

'No,' returned Sadler, coolly. 'It was entirely unimportant, and you must recollect that I was deeply attached to Dr Haslam. I preferred that it be thought that the deed was done in a moment of aberration of mind, as I in truth believe.'

'Very singular,' muttered Conners, 'when, as you say. Dr Haslam was master in his own house and could have left by means of the front door – if he had liked.'

'No,' said Sadler, with a smile; 'not when you have thought about the matter. Dr Haslam may have heard the entry of the officers, and – criminals become frightened.'

'Did Dr Haslam look frightened when you saw him?'

'No,' replied the young man, reflectively. 'But I found the slipper where I stated, and he left by means of the roof. Come, I will show you.'

He led us to the attic, and as he ascended the stairs he furtively touched his eyes with his handkerchief. It was done with an obvious effort at concealment, but I was conscious of the fact that he wished us to believe that he was affected.

'Here is the door through which he passed,' he said, indicating a trap, before which we paused. 'I found it unlatched on the following morning, and took pains to close it.'

Conners turned away almost instantly.

'This is unimportant,' he said. 'Let us go into the yard and inspect the trellis. Dr Sadler can also point out to us the position of the trap-door from the outside.'

The young man led the way downstairs with evident alacrity, and, passing through the rear of the house, we came to the paved space of yard between the back entrance and the stable. Here the doctor eagerly indicated the trellis and pointed to the mark of the opening in the roof.

'An obvious way of escape,' was the comment of Conners. 'I think the papers stated that Dr Haslam had been ailing for a week prior to this matter. Was that correct?'

'Quite correct,' replied Dr Sadler. 'He ventured downstairs, however, two days before the killing, coming with me to inspect some paving which had been completed in the stable.'

'Was Mrs Sands with you?'

'Yes,' replied the young man, a malevolent light in his eyes; 'if the information is of importance to you – Mrs Sands was with us.'

We entered the stable, pausing at the threshold to note a sheet of cemented floor stretching to the farther wall. A great block of white stone lay near the entrance, and about it were some half-filled barrels of lime or composition. A pile of concrete was upon the dirt floor of an adjacent room, and thrown upon it was a huge box. I judged it to be probably ten feet long, with a depth of two or three feet, and perhaps as many wide. All the surroundings appeared to me to be without significance, but Conners tapped the pavement sharply with his heel.

'The police, in their search, would scarcely neglect to remember that a man who has disappeared as completely as has your adopted father might safely lie under so excellent a covering,' he said, blandly.

Dr Sadler smiled.

'They did not forget it,' he replied. 'They sounded every foot of space here, in spite of the fact that he was seen by every person in the house a day after the job was completed and the workmen gone. Dr Haslam's visit to the stable was to inspect the work. Why the police did this was a mystery to me; and it remains so, since they have not explained. Having killed himself, Dr Haslam could hardly bury his own body under a bed of cement that was set and hard while he was yet in the flesh. We should have been glad enough to have found him to bury him in a Christian manner, to say nothing of obtaining peace of mind regarding his fate.'

'Of course,' said Conners. 'What is this stone?'

The doctor coughed slightly as Conners kicked a huge block of granite with his foot, and instantly my friend brought him under his keen eyes; they dwelled for a burning moment upon a face that flushed and then paled, while the green orbs that answered his danced shiftily.

'A stone brought to repair a broken gate-post outside. It was a trifle large and white, by comparison with the fellow it was to serve. Dr Haslam concluded to use it as a carriage-block in front and provide another. There is nothing under it, you may be sure,' and the young man paused to laugh softly. 'As ponderous as it is, the police turned it over, because they gave attention to every incident which last had Dr Haslam's attention. But the gate-post was not repaired until after the killing of Mrs Sands and the disappearance of my adopted father.'

'Yes,' said Conners, quietly. 'I observed the gate-post as we passed it, and I also saw some light pieces of a broken framework amid a tangle of wires thrown in a large box in the inner room of the stable we have just left. What is it, Doctor?'

'I cannot say,' was the reply. 'The servants can perhaps tell you. I observed the fragments myself, and thought they resembled a device upon which to dry clothes.'

'Very likely, Doctor,' responded Conners, cheerfully. 'If you can now tell us what has become of the piecè of wire which was wrapped about the stock of the gun when the police first saw it, and whether or not you have ever travelled in Persia, I think we may call our visit over.'

I started at the change which took place in Sadler's countenance. He swung around as though stung to the quick, facing Conners with an expression of such rage that I thought for a moment he meant to leap at him. But the calm eyes that met his chilled by their depth, and, shaking himself as though to recover his shattered faculties by some physical exertion, he replied in a voice which trembled in spite of his efforts to steady it:

'I have never travelled in Persia, sir,' he said. 'The question is a strange one, and has so little application to any of the matters we have considered that I must regard it as an intent to affront me. If so' – and he grew white again with rage that threatened to break through his control – 'you may, indeed, consider your visit over.'

'This is very strange,' said Conners, still regarding him closely, and nowise abashed. 'I have myself travelled in Persia, and while in the study I saw a book there on Eastern travel, with the contents of which I am familiar. Hence, my inquiry was a natural one.'

The lids above the shifty eyes again fluttered.

'I beg your pardon,' half stammered the young man. 'I did not understand.'

'I am the more surprised,' continued Conners, coolly, 'because of the fact that the book in question was the volume for which you sent Mrs Sands.'

The young man uttered a shriek of dismay. He trembled violently and then lifted a menacing finger.

'All this is idle and foolish!' he cried. 'But now I know that you are here to annoy and insult me. You show little consideration,' he continued, turning on me fiercely, 'in bringing this person here in the time of my affliction to pick at me with insane guesses about an incident which we should both treat with delicacy. You will not be welcomed again!'

'Very singular, truly, this sudden rage against us on the part of Dr Sadler,' said Conners, speaking to me, but evidently seeking to disturb the young man further. 'Let us go.'

'This way,' cried Sadler, violently, as Conners turned towards the exit to the side street. 'I do not accompany my guests through the rear entrance. This way!'

He walked behind us to the front hall, and laid his hand on the door as we passed to the front stoop.

'One moment, Doctor!' cried Conners, lifting his hand as though he had forgotten something, and speaking suddenly. 'You are a married man, are you not?'

The denial came through set teeth and with a muttered oath.

'Alas!' said Conners, pausing upon the top step. 'I have guessed the sad truth: you are a widower.'

The door slammed upon another shriek, to me an expression of uncontrollable rage, and my companion chuckled softly as we descended to the sidewalk.

'Come,' he said, taking me by the arm and turning about the house from Banning Street.

'Let us linger for a moment where you may inspect this gatepost, set reverently up to complete the work which the untimely happenings relating to Dr Haslam unfortunately delayed. You will observe that it is a made stone, of cement, and of a colour not in serious contrast with its older fellow. This is not wholly an excuse to let you understand that I am watching the house, but if you will lift your eyes to the rear upper window you will see that our late host is still interested in our movements.'

I followed his suggestion, and instantly an abrupt movement at the upper window brought the curtain violently down. My companion laughed softly, and, turning away, bent his steps in the direction of the car-line.

'What does this mean?' I asked, as we waited at a street corner. 'I knew already that Sadler was a knave, and I am surprised to find that he was deceitful to the police. Of course he would be insolent to us; we were fortunate to get into the house at all. But what have we discovered?'

Conners's response to my question was entirely irrelevant.

'The Indians have a humane method of disposing of their dead,' he observed – 'humane in that it does not shock the sensibilities of the living. They do not chill them in a tomb, nor hide them in the earth as food for worms. They wrap them in skins and furs and elevate them upon a platform above the grass to wither and dry in the sunshine.'

'What are you talking about?' I asked, in astonishment.

'Nothing of the slightest importance,' he answered with a laugh. 'But I think I am tired, no matter what disposition I may have to be philosophical; and I suspect that you are also. Here comes a car.'

He lapsed into one of his customary fits of silence, and I did not speak to him again until we had reached his quarters. Once more in his studio, his demeanour changed. He threw aside his street coat and, donning the loose and comfortable garment which he always wore in his rooms, he surveyed his pictures with his wonted fondness.

'Some day,' he said, 'I shall read you a homily on feminine beauty, but at present I must ask you to admire the countenance of my brave Dupin. Had he been with us we should scarcely have needed a visit to the house on Banning Street. We have three propositions, however, which are certain:

'1. The murderer of Mrs Sands did not leave the house after the committal of the deed;

'2. Yet the search of the police revealed apparently every person therein;

'3. And Dr Sadler was undoubtedly below-stairs at the time Mrs Sands was killed above.

'A confusing array of absolute circumstances, without others to

154

explain them. You are already in comfortable property, I believe, my friend, but Dr Haslam was reputed rich. Your wife's mother will inherit something.'

I stared at him blankly.

'There is a will,' I replied, finally. 'Of course Sadler is the heir.'

'Never, as a matter of fact; but we must not get into questions of law. Even his relatives would scarcely contest with Mrs Barrister under the circumstances – granting the will to run in his favour.'

'Even his rela – Why, my dear Conners, the man is living, and years younger than Mrs Barrister!'

'Living – perhaps. But let us consider our case. Dr Sadler spoke falsely when he stated that he saw your wife's uncle immediately following the murder. If that were true, the police would have seen him also, for it is clear that they made an immediate and thorough search. He spoke falsely when he stated that Dr Haslam escaped from the house by means of the trap-door in the roof. Our surprise was that he should flee at all. I left the attic quickly when I discovered at a glance that the trap in question was fastened with a rusty padlock, both lock and hasp covered by the cobwebs of months. There was no possible room for error, and I feared that Dr Sadler would note this, too; had he done so, and suspected me, he would have grown cautious in consequence. The police, accepting his story as he told it, did not force him to the alternative of the roof-trap theory.'

'But, my dear friend,' I protested, 'where does this lead us? The conclusions which follow cannot possibly be correct, and why did you suggest to Sadler that he was a widower?'

'Because it was true,' replied Conners. 'I was interested in the case, as I stated to you, and, before your return, I looked it up somewhat. From the facts stated in the newspapers, the significance of which I carefully analysed, my suspicions were aroused. I went far enough to learn that he was married about six months ago. He subsequently lost his wife very suddenly.'

Conners's manner attracted my attention, and he looked at me with an expression almost like humour upon his face. I had scarcely anticipated a jest from him on such a subject, and, as he averted his eyes, I said nothing, waiting for him to continue.

'I think we have accomplished enough for today,' he said; 'I want to assemble the facts as I have gathered them, and perhaps submit them to my friend Inspector Paul. He is a great detective – within limits. You may say to Mrs Barrister and your wife that your family will not rest long under the stigma which they suppose is attached to it.'

'That is cheering,' I replied, doubtfully. 'I know they have a great deal of confidence in you.'

'That is cheering, too,' he laughed.

I left the studio, and as I passed along the hall I heard the bell of his telephone ring sharply. Wondering how much he would have to suggest to the Inspector, I entered my office, and shortly after took my way home.

I did not tell Jennie or anyone else of my visit to Banning Street, nor did I give them the message sent by Conners. What I had heard only tended to confuse me. Nothing had occurred to indicate the whereabouts of Dr Haslam or in any wise mitigate the heinous character of his crime. I could not see that the fact that Sadler was a reprobate had anything whatever to do with it.

The night which passed was a restless one for me. Jennie and Mrs Barrister were both indisposed, and, in consequence, I slept late the following morning, appearing with the others in the breakfast room somewhat ruffled in temper. Our habits seemed to have become demoralised since our return, and I thought, somewhat morosely, of our former state of contentment, and looked regretfully at the sad countenances of the two women at the table.

But the morning paper had another surprise for me in an article which I read aloud, and with an excitement which made my words incoherent, and necessitated many repetitions because of the eager questions and excited exclamations with which my two companions interrupted me. The article in question was under black headlines. It read as follows:

'The mystery of the disappearance of Dr Charles Haslam has been solved at last. Far from being the murderer of his housekeeper, Mrs Martha Sands, as has been generally supposed, Dr Haslam was himself the victim of an assassin. His body was yesterday discovered in a cement gate-post at his late residence, and Dr Jerome Sadler, Dr Haslam's own adopted son, has, by committing suicide, practically confessed himself guilty of the murder of the man who so befriended him, and of a woman whom, only a short time ago, he made his wife.

'As a whole, this tragedy makes one of the most sensational chapters in the criminal history of this city. Seldom has there been chronicled a more horrible and repulsive series of facts than those which relate to the killing of Mrs Martha Sands at the house of Dr Charles Haslam, on Banning Street, in Brooklyn. The terrible crime that sent the unfortunate woman to her grave has now been followed by a ghastly suicide, and three persons are dead as a result of the evil and ingratitude of a wretch whom a generous and confiding old man took into his confidence and affection. Until yesterday it was believed by the public and police that Mrs Sands had died at the hands of Dr Haslam. An obscure page from the records of a Westchester magistrate; a book of Oriental travel pierced by a scarcely perceptible hole through which was drawn a piece of brass wire; an ingenious mechanism constructed to hold a gun at the deadly level of a human head, masked by a green cloth; certain marks where it was attached to the study floor in Dr Haslam's house; the presence of fragments of brass wire about the breech of the fatal gun while it was yet smoking from its discharge; together with other unearthed evidence – which discloses a depth of human depravity – all shrewdly fitted together, have tended to reveal the truth and tell a story which reads like a page from an Italian romance of the Middle Ages.

'Here are the facts: Nearly two years ago Dr Charles Haslam, attracted by the person and talents of a young medical student by the name of Jerome Sadler, took him into his household, and later made him his son by adoption. The inmates of the Banning Street house consisted at that time of Dr Haslam and four servants, including the housekeeper, Mrs Martha Sands, a woman of unusual personal attractions. Although some years older than the young man who was the subject of Dr Haslam's favour, this difference in age did not prevent the development of a singular regard between them, of which fact Dr Haslam became recently advised.

'The young man had firmly entrenched himself in the affections of his lonely patron, and by duplicity and adroitness he was enabled to mislead him. He denied the existence of any intimate relationship between himself and the handsome housekeeper, and insisted that the suspicion was a grave injustice to the woman. The displeasure of his benefactor was thus allayed. Later, however, the woman openly declared that the young man had married her; and that since, under the fear of discovery, which might mean the loss of his position in the house of his adopted father, he had attempted her life by poison. She even sought the police with a view of making her charge public, when Dr Haslam, to save scandal and prevent a rumour of his disturbed domestic relations from becoming known in the neighbourhood, intervened as a peacemaker.

'The strain upon the old man resulted in a fit of illness, during which time a reconciliation was apparently effected between himself and his adopted son. Upon this same afternoon Dr Haslam, feeling better, accompanied Dr Sadler downstairs and went with him to the stable, where some paving had been finished in the carriage room. The coachman, who was present, left at that moment, and the stable-hands were absent. The time was propitious for the crime. A fiendish opportunity for concealing the deed appealed to the young man, and he hastened to take advantage of it. Striking his adopted father down from behind by a blow with a hatchet, he killed him instantly. It is believed, and there is evidence to sustain the theory, that he was assisted in this work by the wretched woman who was to suffer death so shortly herself.

'Secure now in the possession of the premises, and while the servants supposed that Dr Haslam was in the retirement of his chamber, still suffering from the indisposition which had kept him within doors for the previous week, Dr Sadler erected an infernal trap designed to destroy his unhappy accomplice. This consisted of a framework made of lathing, arranged to carry a gun at the proper height and discharge it by means of a wire. The whole was concealed by a green cloth thrown over the structure. The wire, which connected with the set trigger, passed beneath a table before the muzzle of the concealed weapon attached to a book that was placed thereon. The terrible contrivance was erected so as to make failure impossible, and well calculated to deceive and mislead by its results. A chair and a sofa were placed before the table so that the intended victim, to reach the book, must of necessity present herself directly in front of the masked weapon. His trap secure, the murderer set it when alone, and, descending to the lower floor of the house, he remained in the company of the butler while Mrs Sands was carelessly requested to fetch him a book lying on the table in the study above. The woman obeyed and met her instant death.

'Frightened by the explosion, the butler readily obeyed the injunction of his master to wait below while the cause of the disturbance was investigated by himself; and, hurrying to the scene of his work. Dr Sadler removed the deadly mechanism from before the body of his victim, and calmly asserted that the deed was done by his adopted father.

'Here follows a statement which must beggar human belief. When Dr Haslam was murdered in the stable every facility was at hand for a remarkable concealment of the body. It immediately suggested itself to the unnatural murderer, if, indeed, he had not reasoned it out before and beguiled the old man to the spot for the very purpose of perpetrating the crime. A large box-mould, used by the workmen in mixing the cement for a broken gate-post, lay in the stable. Its form was strangely appropriate for the fell purpose for which it was subsequently used, and its bottom was well covered with the liquid mixture. Into this the murderer threw the body, and, covering it carefully with the sand and cement that lay about, smoothed the plastic mass in the mould.

'Here the body lay within the hardening cement until the following day, when the murderer had the now solid block removed from the box. The workmen who had laid the cement floor of the stable were recalled, and the block was erected at the entrance to the yard.

'The unravelling of the mystery attached to the murder of the woman and the discovery of the appalling crime which makes this murder distinctive were due to the marvellous detective skill of

Inspector Paul. This efficient officer, from the first, was dissatisfied with the conclusion that Dr Haslam was guilty of the killing of his housekeeper. The high character of the doctor was at variance with both the crime and the guilty flight.

'The strange hiding-place selected by the murderer for the body of his victim was discovered in a manner to reflect lasting credit upon the deductive mind that reasoned it out, and will rank Inspector Paul among the safest of our secret guardians of the public safety. During a visit to the house in Banning Street he happened carelessly upon a book of Oriental travel pierced by a piece of brass wire. Remembering that this was similar to the wire which enveloped the breech of the fatal shotgun, he was enabled to connect it with the broken fragments of the trap found in the stable, and later to put together the theory which the facts proved to be true. But in the book in question he found a well-thumbed chapter which told a grim story of a method of torture in Persia; it detailed a practice on the part of the cruel authorities of enveloping criminals in a mould of plaster of Paris, or cement, and letting the substance set about their bodies until the unfortunate victims were lost, entombed forever in a solid mass. Inquiry developed that the book was a favourite one of Dr Sadler's.

'Dr Jerome Sadler killed himself by taking prussic acid in the library of the Banning Street residence late yesterday afternoon, immediately following the demolition of the gate-post by the authorities. The coroner will hold an inquest this morning.'

ELINOR FROST

Created by Carolyn Wells (1862–1942)

Born in New Jersey, Carolyn Wells began her writing career as a poet and children's author but turned to crime fiction in her forties. The Clue, the first of her novels featuring the master detective Fleming Stone, was published in 1909 and she went on to write dozens more, the last two appearing in the year of her death. Now mostly forgotten (although one of the Fleming Stone books was recently republished in the Collins Crime Club series), Wells was one of the most popular writers of crime fiction in America during her heyday. In 1913, she produced a guide to the genre entitled The Technique of the Mystery Story *and she also published both a number of novels featuring detectives other than Fleming Stone and a variety of short stories. One of these is 'Christabel's Crystal' which first appeared in 1905. It is essentially a clever parody of the traditional detective story, already well enough established to have recognisable themes and motifs at which Wells can poke gentle fun. Her narrator Elinor Frost herself has the deductive gifts of the great detective, although it's left to the drawling, monocled English aristo Lord Hammerton to explain the elaborate, improbable logic he uses to identify, completely by accident, the criminal.*

CHRISTABEL'S CRYSTAL

Of all the unexpected pleasures that have come into my life, I think perhaps the greatest was when Christabel Farland asked me to be bridesmaid at her wedding.

I always had liked Christabel at college, and though we hadn't seen much of each other since we were graduated, I still had a strong feeling of friendship for her, and besides that I was glad to be one of the merry house party gathered at Farland Hall for the wedding festivities.

I arrived the afternoon before the wedding-day, and found the family and guests drinking tea in the library. Two other bridesmaids were there, Alice Fordham and Janet White, with both of whom I was slightly acquainted. The men, however, except Christabel's brother Fred, were strangers to me, and were introduced as Mr Richmond, who was to be an usher; Herbert Gay, a neighbor, who chanced to be calling; and Mr Wayne, the tutor of Christabel's younger brother Harold. Mrs Farland was there too, and her welcoming words to me were as sweet and cordial as Christabel's.

The party was in frivolous mood, and as the jests and laughter grew more hilarious, Mrs Farland declared that she would take the bride-elect away to her room for a quiet rest, lest she should not appear at her best the next day.

'Come with me, Elinor,' said Christabel to me, 'and I will show you my wedding-gifts.'

Together we went to the room set apart for the purpose, and on many white-draped tables I saw displayed the gorgeous profusion of silver, glass and bric-a-brac that are one of the chief component parts of a wedding of today.

I had gone entirely through my vocabulary of ecstatic adjectives and was beginning over again when we came to a small table which held only one wedding-gift.

'That is the gem of the whole collection,' said Christabel, with a happy smile, 'not only because Laurence gave it to me, but because of its intrinsic perfection and rarity.'

I looked at the bridegroom's gift in some surprise. Instead of the conventional diamond sunburst or heart-shaped brooch, I saw a crystal ball as large as a fair-sized orange.

I knew of Christabel's fondness for Japanese crystals and that she had a number of small ones of varying qualities; but this magnificent specimen fairly took my breath away. It was poised on the top of one of those wavecrests, which the artisans seem to think appropriately interpreted in wrought-iron. Now, I haven't the same subtle sympathy with crystals that Christabel always has had; but still this great, perfect, limpid sphere affected me strangely.

I glanced at it at first with a calm interest; but as I continued to look I became fascinated, and soon found myself obliged (if I may use the expression) to tear my eyes away.

Christabel watched me curiously. 'Do you love it too?' she said, and then she turned her eyes to the crystal with a rapt and rapturous gaze that made her appear lovelier than ever. 'Wasn't it dear of Laurence?' she said. 'He wanted to give me jewels of course; but I told him I would rather have this big crystal than the Koh-i-noor. I have six others, you know; but the largest of them isn't one-third the diameter of this.'

'It is wonderful,' I said, 'and I am glad you have it. I must own it frightens me a little.'

'That is because of its perfection,' said Christabel simply. 'Absolute flawless perfection always is awesome. And when it is combined with perfect, faultless beauty, it is the ultimate perfection of a material thing.'

'But I thought you liked crystals because of their weird supernatural influence over you,' I said.

'That is an effect, not a cause,' Christabel replied. 'Ultimate perfection is so rare in our experiences that its existence perforce produces consequences so rare as to be dubbed weird and supernatural. But I must not gaze at my crystal longer now, or I shall forget that it is my wedding-day. I'm not going to look at it again until after I return from my wedding-trip; and then, as I tell Laurence, he will have to share my affection with his wedding-gift to me.'

Christabel gave the crystal a long parting look, and then ran away to don her wedding-gown. 'Elinor,' she called over her shoulder, as she neared her own door, 'I'll leave my crystal in your special care. See that nothing happens to it while I'm away.'

'Trust me!' I called back gaily, and then went in search of my sister bridesmaids.

The morning after the wedding began rather later than most mornings. But at last we all were seated at the breakfast-table and enthusiastically discussing the events of the night before. It seemed strange to be there without Christabel, and Mrs Farland said that I must stay until the bridal pair returned, for she couldn't get along without a daughter of some sort.

This remark made me look anywhere rather than at Fred Farland, and so I chanced to catch Harold's eye. But the boy gave me such an intelligent, mischievous smile that I actually blushed and was covered with confusion. Just at that moment Katy the parlor-maid came into the dining room, and with an anxious expression on her face said: 'Mrs Farland, do you know anything about Miss Christabel's glass ball? It isn't in the present room.'

'No,' said Mrs Farland; 'but I suppose Mr Haley put it in the safe with the silver and jewelry.'

'I don't think so, ma'am; for he asked me was he to take any of the cut glass, and I told him you had said only the silver and gold, ma'am.'

'But that crystal isn't cut glass, Katy; and it's more valuable than all Miss Christabel's silver gifts put together.'

'Oh, my! Is it, ma'am? Well, then, won't you please see if it's all right, for I'm worried about it.'

I wish I could describe my feelings at this moment. Have you ever been in imminent danger of a fearful catastrophe of any kind, and while with all your heart and soul you hoped it might be averted, yet there was one little, tiny, hidden impulse of your mind that craved the excitement of the disaster? Perhaps it is only an ignoble nature that can have this experience, or there may be a partial excuse for me in the fact that I am afflicted with what sometimes is called the 'detective instinct.' I say afflicted, for I well know that anyone else who has this particular mental bias will agree with me that it causes far more annoyance than satisfaction.

Why, one morning when I met Mrs Van Allen in the market, I said 'It's too bad your waitress had to go out of town to attend the funeral of a near relative, when you were expecting company to luncheon.' And she was as angry as could be, and called me an impertinent busy-body.

But I just had deduced it all from her glove. You see, she had on one brand-new black-kid glove, and the other, though crumpled up in her hand, I could see never had been on at all. So I knew that she wouldn't start to market early in the morning with such gloves if she had any sort of half-worn black ones at all.

And I knew that she had given away her next-best pair recently – it must have been the night before, or she would have tried them on sooner; and as her cook is an enormous woman, I was sure that she had given to her waitress. And why would she, unless the maid was going away in great haste? And what would require such a condition of things except a sudden call to a funeral. And it must have been out of town, or she would have waited until morning, and then she could have bought black gloves for herself. And it must have been a near relative to make the case so urgent. And I knew that Mrs Van Allen expected luncheon guests, because her fingers were stained from paring apples, and why would she pare her own apples so early in the morning except to assist the cook in some hurried preparations? Why, it was all as plain as could be, and every bit true; but Mrs Van Allen wouldn't believe my explanation, and to this day she thinks I made my discoveries by gossiping with her servants.

Perhaps all this will help you to understand why I felt a sort of nervous exhilaration that had in it an element of secret pleasure when we learned that Christabel's crystal really was missing.

Mr Haley, who was a policeman, had remained in the present room during all of the hours devoted to the wedding celebration, and after the guests had gone he had packed up the silver, gold and jewels and put them away in the family safe, which stood in a small dressing room between Mrs Farland's bedroom and Fred's. He had worn civilian's dress during the evening, and few if any of the guests knew that he was guarding the valuable gifts. The mistake had been in not telling him explicitly to care for the crystal as the most valuable gem of all; but this point had been overlooked, and the ignorant officer had assumed that it was merely a piece of cut glass, of no more value than any of the carafes or decanters. When told that the ball's intrinsic value was many thousands of dollars, and that it would be next to impossible to duplicate it at any price, his amazement was unbounded and he appeared extremely grave.

'You ought to have told me,' he said. 'Sure, it's a case for the chief now!' Haley had been hastily telephoned for to come to Farland Hall and tell his story, and now he telephoned for the chief of police and a detective.

I felt a thrill of delight at this, for I always had longed to see a real detective in the act of detecting.

Of course everybody was greatly excited, and I just gave myself up to the enjoyment of the situation, when suddenly I remembered that Christabel had said that she would leave her crystal in my charge, and that in a way I was responsible for its safety. This changed my whole attitude, and I realized that, instead of being an idly curious observer, I must put all my detective instinct to work immediately and use every endeavor to recover the crystal.

First, I flew to my own room and sat down for a few moments to collect my thoughts and lay my plans. Of course, as the windows of the present room were found in the morning fastened as they were left the night before, the theft must have been committed by someone in the house. Naturally it was not one of the family or the guests of the house. As to the servants, they all were honest and trustworthy – I had Mrs Farland's word for that. There was no reason to suspect the policeman, and thus my process of elimination brought me to Mr Wayne, Harold's tutor.

Of course it must have been the tutor. In nine-tenths of all the detective stories I ever have read the criminal proved to be a tutor or secretary or some sort of gentlemanly dependent of the family; and now I had come upon a detective story in real life, and here was the regulation criminal ready to fit right into it. It was the tutor of course; but I should be discreet and not name him until I had collected some undeniable evidence.

Next, I went down to the present room to search for clues. The detective had not arrived yet, and I was glad to be first on the ground, for I remembered how much importance Sherlock Holmes always attached to the search. I didn't really expect that the tutor had left shreds of his clothing clinging to the table-legs, or anything absurd like that; but I fully expected to find a clue of some sort. I hoped that it wouldn't be cigar ashes; for though detectives in fiction always can tell the name and price of cigar from a bit of ash, yet I'm so ignorant about such things that all ashes are alike to me.

I hunted carefully all over the floor, but I couldn't find a thing that seemed the least bit like a clue, except a faded white carnation. Of course that wasn't an unusual thing to find, the day after a wedding; but it was the very flower I had given to Fred Farland the night before, and he had worn it in his buttonhole. I recognized it perfectly, for it was wired and I had twisted it a certain way when I adjusted it for him. This didn't seem like strong evidence against the tutor; but it was convincing to me, for if Mr Wayne was villain enough to steal Christabel's crystal, he was wicked enough to manage to get Fred's boutonniere and leave it in the room, hoping thereby to incriminate Fred. So fearful was I that this trick might make trouble for Fred that I said nothing about the carnation; for I knew that it was in Fred's coat when he said goodnight, and then we all went directly to our rooms. When the detective came he examined the room, and I know that he didn't find anything in the way of evidence; but he tried to appear as if he had, and he frowned and jotted down notes in a book after the most approved fashion.

Then he called in everybody who had been in the house overnight and questioned each one. I could see at once that his questions to the family and guests were purely perfunctory, and that he too had his suspicions of the tutor.

Finally, it was Mr Wayne's turn. He always was a nervous little man, and now he seemed terribly flustered. The detective was gentle with him, and in order to set him more at ease began to converse generally on crystals. He asked Mr Wayne if he had travelled much, if he had ever been to Japan, and if he knew much about the making and polishing of crystal balls.

The tutor fidgeted around a good deal and seemed disinclined to look the detective in the eye; but he replied that he never had been to Japan, and that he never had heard of a Japanese rock crystal until he had seen Miss Farland's wedding-gift, and that even then he had no idea of its great value until since its disappearance he had heard its price named.

This sounded well; but his manner was so embarrassed, and he had such an effect of a guilty man, that I felt sure my intuitions were correct and that he himself was the thief.

The detective seemed to think so too, for he said at last: 'Mr Wayne, your words seem to indicate your innocence; but your attitudes do not. Unless you can explain why you are so agitated and apparently afraid, I shall be forced to the conclusion that you know more about this than you have admitted.'

Then Mr Wayne said: 'Must I tell all I know about it, sir?'

'Certainly,' said the detective.

'Then,' said Mr Wayne, 'I shall have to state that when I left my room late last night to get a glass of water from the ice-pitcher, which always stands on the hall-table, I saw Mr Fred Farland just going into the sitting room, or present room, as it has been called for the last few days.'

There was a dead silence. This, then, was why Mr Wayne had acted so embarrassed; this was the explanation of my finding the white carnation there; and I think the detective thought that the sudden turn affairs had taken incriminated Fred Farland.

I didn't think so at all. The idea of Fred's stealing his own sister's wedding-gift was too preposterous to be considered for a moment.

'Were you in the room late at night, Mr Farland?' asked the detective.

'I was,' said Fred.

'Why didn't you tell me this before?'

'You didn't ask me, and as I didn't take I saw no reason for referring to the fact that I was in the room.'

'Why did you go there?'

'I went,' said Fred coolly, 'with the intention of taking the crystal and hiding it, as a practical joke on Christabel.'

'Why did you not do so?'

'Because the ball wasn't there. I didn't think then that it had been stolen, but that it had been put away safely with the other valuables. Since this is not so, and the crystal is missing, we all must get to work and find it somehow before my sister returns.'

The tutor seemed like a new man after Fred had spoken. His face cleared, and he appeared intelligent, alert and entirely at his ease. 'Let me help,' he said. 'Pray command my services in any way you choose.'

But the detective didn't seem so reassured by Fred's statements. Indeed, I believe he really thought that Christabel's brother was guilty of theft.

But I believed implicitly every word Fred had uttered, and begging him to come with me, I led the way again to the sitting room. Mr Wayne and Janet White came too, and the four of us scrutinized the floor, walls and furniture of the room over and over again. 'There's one thing certain,' I said thoughtfully: 'The crystal was taken either by someone in the house or someone out of it. We've been confining our suspicions to those inside. Why not a real burglar?'

'But the windows are fastened on the inside,' said Janet.

'I know it,' I replied. 'But if a burglar could slip a catch with a thin-bladed knife – and they often do – then he could slip it back again with the same knife and so divert suspicion.'

'Bravo, Miss Frost!' said Mr Wayne, with an admiring glance at me. 'You have the true detective instinct. I'll go outside and see if there are any traces.'

A moment later he was on the veranda and excitedly motioning us to raise the window. Fred pushed back the catch and opened the long French window that opened on the front veranda.

'I believe Miss Frost has discovered the mystery,' said Mr Wayne, and he pointed to numerous scratches on the sash-frame. The house had been painted recently, and it was seen easily that the fresh scratches were made by a thin knife-blade pushed between the sashes.

'By Jove!' cried Fred, 'that's it, Elinor; and the canny fellow had wit enough to push the catch back in place after he was outside again.'

I said nothing, for a moment. My thoughts were adjusting themselves quickly to the new situation from which I must make my deductions. I realized at once that I must give up my theory of the tutor, of course, and anyway I hadn't had a scrap of evidence against him except his fitness for the position. But, given the surety of burglars from outside, I knew just what to do: look for footprints, to be sure.

I glanced around for the light snow that always falls in detective stories just before the crime is committed, and is testified, usually by the village folk, to have stopped just at the crucial moment. But there wasn't a sign of snow or rain or even dew. The veranda showed no footprints, nor could the smooth lawn or flagged walks be expected to. I leaned against the veranda railing in despair, wondering what Sherlock Holmes would do in a provoking absence of footprints, when I saw in the flower-bed beneath several well-defined marks of a man's shoes.

'There you are, Fred!' I cried, and rushed excitedly down the steps.

They all followed, and, sure enough, in the soft earth of the wide flower-bed that surrounded the veranda were strong, clear prints of large masculine footgear.

'That clears us, girls,' cried Janet gleefully, as she measured her daintily shod foot against the depressions.

'Don't touch them!' I cried. 'Call Mr Prout the detective.'

Mr Prout appeared, and politely hiding his chagrin at not having discovered these marks before I did, proceeded to examine them closely.

'You see,' he said in a pompous and dictatorial way, 'there are four prints pointing toward the house, and four pointing toward the street. Those pointing to the street are superimposed upon those leading to the house, hence we deduce that they were made by a burglar who crossed the flower-bed, climbed the veranda, stepped over the rail and entered at the window. He then returned the same way, leaving these last footprints above the others.'

As all this was so palpably evident from the facts of the case, I was not impressed much by the subtlety of his deductions and asked what he gathered from the shape of the prints.

He looked at the well-defined prints intently. 'They are of a medium size,' he announced at last, 'and I should say that they were made by a man of average height and weight, who had a normal-sized foot.'

Well, if that wasn't disappointing! I thought of course that he would tell the man's occupation and social status even if he didn't say that he was left-handed or that he stuttered, which is the kind of thing detectives in fiction always discover.

So I lost all interest in that Prout man, and began to do a little deducing on my own account. Although I felt sure, as we all did, that the thief was a burglar from outside, yet I couldn't measure the shoes of an absent and unidentified burglar, and somehow I felt an uncontrollable impulse to measure shoes.

Without consulting anybody, I found a tape-measure and carefully measured the footprints. Then I went through the house and measured all the men's shoes I could find, from the stable-boy's up to Fred's.

It's an astonishing fact, but nearly all of them fitted the measurements of the prints on the flower-bed. Men's feet are so nearly universal in size, or rather their shoes are, and too, what with extension soles and queer-shaped lasts, you can't tell anything about the size or style of a man from his footprints.

So I gave up deducing and went to talk to Fred Farland.

'Fred,' I said simply, 'did you take Christabel's crystal?'

'No,' he answered with equal simplicity, and he looked me in the eyes so squarely and honestly that I knew he spoke the truth.

'Who did?' I next inquired.

'It was a professional burglar,' said Fred, 'and a mighty cute one; but I'm going to track him and get that crystal before Christabel comes home.'

'Let me help!' I cried eagerly. 'I've got the true detective instinct, and I know I can do something.'

'You?' said Fred incredulously. 'No, you can't help; but I don't mind telling you my plan. You see I expect Lord Hammerton down to make me a visit. He's a jolly young English chap that I chummed with in London. Now, he's a first-rate amateur detective, and though I didn't expect him till next month, he's in New York, and I've no doubt that he'd be willing to come right off. No one will know he's doing any detecting; and I'll wager he'll lay his hands on that ball in less than a week.'

'Lovely!' I exclaimed. 'And I'll be here to see him do it!'

'Yes, the mater says you're to stay a fortnight or more; but mind, this is our secret.'

'Trust me,' I said earnestly; 'but let me help if I can, won't you?'

'You'll help most by not interfering,' declared Fred, and though it didn't altogether suit me, I resolved to help that way rather than not at all.

A few days later Lord Hammerton came. He was not in any way

an imposing-looking man. Indeed, he was a typical Englishman of the Lord Cholmondeley type, and drawled and used a monocle most effectively. The afternoon he came we told him all about the crystal. The talk turned to detective work and detective instinct.

Lord Hammerton opined in his slow languid drawl that the true detective mind was not dependent upon instinct, but was a nicely adjusted mentality that was quick to see the cause back of an effect.

Herbert Gay said that while this doubtless was so, yet it was an even chance whether the cause so skilfully deduced was the true one.

'Quite so,' agreed Lord Hammerton amiably, 'and that is why the detective in real life fails so often. He deduces properly the logical facts from the evidence before him; but real life and real events are so illogical that his deductions, though true theoretically, are false from mere force of circumstances.'

'And that is why,' I said, 'detectives in story-books always deduce rightly, because the obliging author makes the literal facts coincide with the theoretical ones.'

Lord Hammerton put up his monocle and favored me with a truly British stare. 'It is unusual,' he remarked slowly, 'to find such a clear comprehension of this subject in a feminine mind.'

They all laughed at this; but I went on: 'It is easy enough to make the spectacular detective of fiction show marvellous penetration and logical deduction when the antecedent circumstances are arranged carefully to prove it all; but place even Sherlock Holmes face to face with a total stranger, and I, for one, don't believe that he could tell anything definite about him.'

'Oh, come now! I can't agree to that,' said Lord Hammerton, more interestedly than he had spoken before. 'I believe there is much in the detective instinct besides the exotic and the artificial. There is a substantial basis of divination built on minute observation, and which I have picked up in some measure myself.'

'Let us test that statement,' cried Herbert Gay. 'Here comes Mr Wayne, Harold's tutor. Lord Hammerton never has seen him, and before Wayne even speaks let Lord Hammerton tell us some detail, which he divines by observation.'

All agreed to this, and a few minutes later Mr Wayne came up. We laughingly explained the situation to him and asked him to have himself deduced.

Lord Hammerton looked at Arthur Wayne for a few minutes, and then said, still in his deliberate drawl: 'You have lived in Japan for the past seven years, in government service in the interior, and only recently have returned.'

A sudden silence fell upon us all — not so much because Lord Hammerton made deductions from no apparent evidence, but because we all knew Mr Wayne had told Detective Prout that he never had been in Japan.

Fred Farland recovered himself first, and said: 'Now that you've astonished us with your results, tell us how you attained them.'

'It is simple enough,' said Lord Hammerton, looking at young Wayne, who had turned deathly white. 'It is simple enough, sir. The breast-pocket on the outside of your coat is on the right-hand side. Now it never is put there. Your coat is a good one — Poole, or some London tailor of that class. He never made a coat with an outer breast-pocket on the right side. You have had the coat turned — thus the original left-hand pocket appears now on the right side.

'Looking at you, I see that you have not the constitution which could recover from an acute attack of poverty. If you had it turned from want, you would not have your present effect of comfortable circumstances. Now, you must have had it turned because you were in a country where tailoring is not frequent, but sewing and delicate manipulation easy to find. India? You are not bronzed. China? The same. Japan? Probable; but not treaty ports — there are plenty of tailors there. Hence, the interior of Japan.

'Long residence, to make it incumbent on you to get the coat turned, means government service, because unattached foreigners are allowed only as tourists. Then the cut of the coat is not so very old, and as contracts run seven or fourteen years with the Japanese, I repeat that you probably resided seven years in the interior of Japan, possibly as an irrigation engineer.'

I felt sorry then for poor Mr Wayne. Lord Hammerton's deductions were absolutely true, and coming upon the young man so suddenly he made no attempt to refute them.

And so as he had been so long in Japan, and must have been familiar with rock crystals for years, Fred questioned him sternly in reference to his false statements.

Then he broke down completely and confessed that he had taken Christabel's crystal because it had fascinated him.

He declared that he had a morbid craving for crystals; that he had crept down to the present room late that night, merely to look at the wonderful, beautiful ball; that it had so possessed him that he carried it to his room to gaze at for a while, intending to return with it after an hour or so. When he returned he saw Fred Farland, and dared not carry out his plan.

'And the footprints?' I asked eagerly.

'I made them myself,' he explained with a dogged shamefacedness. 'I did have a moment of temptation to keep the crystal, and so tried to make you think that a burglar had taken it; but the purity and beauty of the ball itself so reproached me that I tried to return it. I didn't do so then, and since –'

'Since?' urged Fred, not unkindly.

'Well, I've been torn between fear and the desire to keep the ball. You will find it in my trunk. Here is the key.'

There was a certain dignity about the young man that made him seem unlike a criminal, or even a wrong-doer.

As for me, I entirely appreciated the fact that he was hypnotized by the crystal and in a way was not responsible. I don't believe that man would steal anything else in the world.

Somehow the others agreed with me, and as they had recovered the ball, they took no steps to prosecute Mr Wayne.

He went away at once, still in that dazed, uncertain condition. We never saw him again; but I hope for his own sake that he never was subjected to such a temptation.

Just before he left, I said to him out of sheer curiosity: 'Please explain one point, Mr Wayne. Since you opened and closed that window purposely to mislead us, since you made those footprints in the flower-bed for the same reason, and since to do it you must have gone out and then come back, why were the outgoing footprints made over the incoming ones?'

'I walked backward on purpose,' said Mr Wayne simply.

PHILO GUBB

Created by Ellis Parker Butler (1869-1937)

Philo Gubb works as a paper-hanger in a small town in Iowa. He is also an enthusiast for the Sherlock Holmes stories who is taking a correspondence course in how to be a 'deteckative'. Whenever the opportunity arises, he tries to put into practice what he is learning, adopting a series of disguises which fool nobody and solving crimes more through amiable persistence and good luck than any deductive skills. Gubb himself is said to commit 'a major crime during every case on which he works: the murder of the English language'. Comic crime stories rarely work very well. Comic crime stories that are more than a century old should be very nearly unreadable but the tales featuring Philo Gubb retain their charm. They were the work of Ellis Parker Butler, Iowa-born but long resident in New York, who, in addition to a successful career in banking, was also a prolific writer of novels and short stories. The first Philo Gubb story appeared in The Red Book *magazine in 1913. Several dozen others followed, mostly in the next four years, although Butler returned to the character on a handful of occasions in the 1920s and 1930s. Gubb was popular enough to appear in several short films in the silent era and for the stories to be regularly reprinted.*

PHILO GUBB'S GREATEST CASE

Philo Gubb, wrapped in his bathrobe, went to the door of the room that was the headquarters of his business of paper-hanging and decorating as well as the office of his detective business, and opened the door a crack. It was still early in the morning, but Mr Gubb was a modest man, and, lest anyone should see him in his scanty attire, he peered through the crack of the door before he stepped hastily into the hall and captured his copy of the *Riverbank Daily Eagle*. When he had secured the still damp newspaper, he returned to his cot bed and spread himself out to read comfortably.

It was a hot Iowa morning. Business was so slack that if Mr Gubb had not taken out his set of eight varieties of false whiskers daily and brushed them carefully, the moths would have been able to devour them at leisure.

P Gubb opened the *Eagle*. The first words that met his eye caused him to sit upright on his cot. At the top of the first column of the first page were the headlines.

MYSTERIOUS DEATH OF HENRY SMITZ

Body Found In Mississippi River By Boatman Early This AM.

Foul Play Suspected

Mr Gubb unfolded the paper and read the item under the headlines with the most intense interest. Foul play meant the possibility of an opportunity to put to use once more the precepts of the Course of Twelve Lessons, and with them fresh in his mind Detective Gubb was eager to undertake the solution of any mystery that Riverbank could furnish. This was the article:

> Just as we go to press we receive word through Policeman Michael O'Toole that the well-known mussel-dredger and boatman, Samuel Fliggis (Long Sam), while dredging for mussels last night just below the bridge, recovered the body of Henry Smitz, late of this place.

Mr Smitz had been missing for three days and his wife had been greatly worried. Mr Brownson, of the Brownson Packing Company, by whom he was employed, admitted that Mr Smitz had been missing for several days.

The body was found sewed in a sack. Foul play is suspected.

'I should think foul play would be suspected,' exclaimed Philo Gubb, 'if a man was sewed into a bag and deposited into the Mississippi River until dead.'

He propped the paper against the foot of the cot bed and was still reading when someone knocked on his door. He wrapped his bathrobe carefully about him and opened the door. A young woman with tear-dimmed eyes stood in the doorway.

'Mr P Gubb?' she asked. 'I'm sorry to disturb you so early in the morning, Mr Gubb, but I couldn't sleep all night. I came on a matter of business, as you might say. There's a couple of things I want you to do.'

'Paper-hanging or deteckating?' asked P Gubb.

'Both,' said the young woman. 'My name is Smitz – Emily Smitz. My husband –'

'I'm aware of the knowledge of your loss, ma'am,' said the paper-hanger detective gently.

'Lots of people know of it,' said Mrs Smitz. 'I guess everybody knows of it – I told the police to try to find Henry, so it is no secret. And I want you to come up as soon as you get dressed, and paper my bedroom.'

Mr Gubb looked at the young woman as if he thought she had gone insane under the burden of her woe.

'And then I want you to find Henry,' she said, 'because I've heard you can do so well in the detecting line.'

Mr Gubb suddenly realized that the poor creature did not yet know the full extent of her loss. He gazed down upon her with pity in his bird-like eyes.

'I know you'll think it strange,' the young woman went on, 'that I should ask you to paper a bedroom first, when my husband is lost; but if he is gone it is because I was a mean, stubborn thing. We never quarrelled in our lives, Mr Gubb, until I picked out the wall-paper for our bedroom, and Henry said parrots and birds-of-paradise and tropical flowers that were as big as umbrellas would look awful on our bedroom wall. So I said he hadn't anything but Low Dutch taste, and he got mad. "All right, have it your own way," he said, and I went and had Mr Skaggs put the paper on the wall, and the next day Henry didn't come home at all.

'If I'd thought Henry would take it that way, I'd rather had the wall bare, Mr Gubb. I've cried and cried, and last night I made up my mind it was all my fault and that when Henry came home he'd find a decent paper on the wall. I don't mind telling you, Mr Gubb, that when the paper was on the wall it looked worse than it looked in the roll. It looked crazy.'

'Yes'm,' said Mr Gubb, 'it often does. But, however, there's something you'd ought to know right away about Henry.'

The young woman stared wide-eyed at Mr Gubb for a moment; she turned as white as her shirtwaist.

'Henry is dead!' she cried, and collapsed into Mr Gubb's long, thin arms.

Mr Gubb, the inert form of the young woman in his arms, glanced around with a startled gaze. He stood miserably, not knowing what to do, when suddenly he saw Policeman O'Toole coming toward him down the hall. Policeman O'Toole was leading by the arm a man whose wrists bore clanking handcuffs.

'What's this now?' asked the policeman none too gently, as he saw the bathrobed Mr Gubb holding the fainting woman in his arms.

'I am exceedingly glad you have come,' said Mr Gubb. 'The only meaning into it, is that this is Mrs H Smitz, widow-lady, fainted onto me against my will and wishes.'

'I was only askin',' said Policeman O'Toole politely enough.

'You shouldn't ask such things until you're asked to ask,' said Mr Gubb.

After looking into Mr Gubb's room to see that there was no easy means of escape, O'Toole pushed his prisoner into the room and took the limp form of Mrs Smitz from Mr Gubb, who entered the room and closed the door.

'I may as well say what I want to say right now,' said the handcuffed man as soon as he was alone with Mr Gubb. 'I've heard of Detective Gubb, off and on, many a time, and as soon as I got into this trouble I said, "Gubb's the man that can get me out if any one can." My name is Herman Wiggins.'

'Glad to meet you,' said Mr Gubb, slipping his long legs into his trousers.

'And I give you my word for what it is worth,' continued Mr Wiggins, 'that I'm as innocent of this crime as the babe unborn.'

'What crime?' asked Mr Gubb.

'Why, killing Hen Smitz – what crime did you think?' said Mr Wiggins. 'Do I look like a man that would go and murder a man just because –'

He hesitated and Mr Gubb, who was slipping his suspenders over his bony shoulders, looked at Mr Wiggins with keen eyes.

'Well, just because him and me had words in fun,' said Mr Wiggins, 'I leave it to you, can't a man say words in fun once in a while?'

'Certainly sure,' said Mr Gubb.

'I guess so,' said Mr Wiggins. 'Anybody'd know a man don't mean all he says. When I went and told Hen Smitz I'd murder him as sure as green apples grow on a tree, I was just fooling. But this fool policeman –'

'Mr O'Toole?'

'Yes. They gave him this Hen Smitz case to look into, and the first thing he did was to arrest me for murder. Nervy, I call it.'

Policeman O'Toole opened the door a crack and peeked in. Seeing Mr Gubb well along in his dressing operations, he opened the door wider and assisted Mrs Smitz to a chair. She was still limp, but she was a brave little woman and was trying to control her sobs.

'Through?' O'Toole asked Wiggins. 'If you are, come along back to jail.'

'Now, don't talk to me in that tone of voice,' said Mr Wiggins angrily. 'No, I'm not through. You don't know how to treat a gentleman like a gentleman, and never did.'

He turned to Mr Gubb.

'The long and short of it is this: I'm arrested for the murder of Hen Smitz, and I didn't murder him and I want you to take my case and get me out of jail.'

'Ah, stuff!' exclaimed O'Toole. 'You murdered him and you know you did. What's the use talkin'?'

Mrs Smitz leaned forward in her chair.

'Murdered Henry?' she cried. 'He never murdered Henry. I murdered him.'

'Now, ma'am,' said O'Toole politely, 'I hate to contradict a lady, but you never murdered him at all. This man here murdered him, and I've got the proof on him.'

'I murdered him!' cried Mrs Smitz again. 'I drove him out of his right mind and made him kill himself.'

'Nothing of the sort,' declared O'Toole. 'This man Wiggins murdered him.'

'I did not!' exclaimed Mr Wiggins indignantly. 'Some other man did it.'

It seemed a deadlock, for each was quite positive. Mr Gubb looked from one to the other doubtfully.

'All right, take me back to jail,' said Mr Wiggins. 'You look up the case, Mr Gubb; that's all I came here for. Will you do it? Dig into it, hey?'

'I most certainly shall be glad to so do,' said Mr Gubb, 'at the regular terms.'

O'Toole led his prisoner away.

For a few minutes Mrs Smitz sat silent, her hands clasped, staring at the floor. Then she looked up into Mr Gubb's eyes.

'You will work on this case, Mr Gubb, won't you?' she begged. 'I have a little money – I'll give it all to have you do your best. It is cruel – cruel to have that poor man suffer under the charge of murder when I know so well Henry killed himself because I was cross with him. You can prove he killed himself – that it was my fault. You will?'

'The way the deteckative profession operates onto a case,' said Mr Gubb, 'isn't to go to work to prove anything particularly especial. It finds a clue or clues and follows them to where they lead to. That I shall be willing to do.'

'That is all I could ask,' said Mrs Smitz gratefully.

Arising from her seat with difficulty, she walked tremblingly to the door. Mr Gubb assisted her down the stairs, and it was not until she was gone that he remembered that she did not know the body of her husband had been found – sewed in a sack and at the bottom of the river. Young husbands have been known to quarrel with their wives over matters as trivial as bedroom wall-paper; they have even been known to leave home for several days at a time when angry; in extreme cases they have even been known to seek death at their own hands; but it is not at all usual for a young husband to leave home for several days and then in cold blood sew himself in a sack and jump into the river. In the first place there are easier ways of terminating one's life; in the second place a man can jump into the river with perfect ease without going to the trouble of sewing himself in a sack; and in the third place it is exceedingly difficult for a man to sew himself into a sack. It is almost impossible.

To sew himself into a sack a man must have no little skill, and he must have a large, roomy sack. He takes, let us say, a sack-needle, threaded with a good length of twine; he steps into the sack and pulls it up over his head; he then reaches above his head, holding the mouth of the sack together with one hand while he sews with the other hand. In hot anger this would be quite impossible.

Philo Gubb thought of all this as he looked through his disguises, selecting one suitable for the work he had in hand. He had just decided that the most appropriate disguise would be 'Number 13, Undertaker,' and had picked up the close black wig, and long, drooping mustache, when he had another thought. Given a bag sufficiently loose to permit free motion of the hands and arms, and a man, even in hot anger, might sew himself in. A man, intent on suicidally bagging himself, would sew the mouth of the bag shut and would then cut a slit in the front of the bag large enough to crawl into. He would then crawl into the bag and sew up the slit, which would be immediately in front of his hands. It could be done! Philo Gubb chose from his wardrobe a black frock coat and a silk hat with a wide band of crape. He carefully locked his door and went down to the street.

On a day as hot as this day promised to be, a frock coat and a silk hat could be nothing but distressingly uncomfortable. Between his door and the corner, eight various citizens spoke to Philo Gubb, calling him by name. In fact, Riverbank was as accustomed to seeing P Gubb in disguise as out of disguise, and while a few children might be interested by the sight of Detective Gubb in disguise, the older citizens thought no more of it, as a rule, than of seeing Banker Jennings appear in a pink shirt one day and a blue striped one the next. No one ever accused Banker Jennings of trying to hide his identity by a change of shirts, and no one imagined that P Gubb was trying to disguise himself when he put on a disguise. They considered it a mere business custom, just as a butcher tied on a white apron before he went behind his counter.

This was why, instead of wondering who the tall, dark-garbed stranger might be, Banker Jennings greeted Philo Gubb cheerfully.

'Ah, Gubb!' he said. 'So you are going to work on this Smitz case, are you? Glad of it, and wish you luck. Hope you place the crime on the right man and get him the full penalty. Let me tell you there's nothing in this rumor of Smitz being short of money. We did lend him money, but we never pressed him for it. We never even asked him for interest. I told him a dozen times he could have as much more from us as he wanted, within reason, whenever he wanted it, and that he could pay me when his invention was on the market.'

'No report of news of any such rumor has as yet come to my hearing,' said P Gubb, 'but since you mention it, I'll take it for less than it is worth.'

'And that's less than nothing,' said the banker. 'Have you any clue?'

'I'm on my way to find one at the present moment of time,' said Mr Gubb.

'Well, let me give you a pointer,' said the banker. 'Get a line on Herman Wiggins or some of his crew, understand? Don't say I said a word – I don't want to be brought into this – but Smitz was afraid of Wiggins and his crew. He told me so. He said Wiggins had threatened to murder him.'

'Mr Wiggins is at present in the custody of the county jail for killing H Smitz with intent to murder him,' said Mr Gubb.

'Oh, then – then it's all settled,' said the banker. 'They've proved it on him. I thought they would. Well, I suppose you've got to do your little bit of detecting just the same. Got to air the camphor out of the false hair, eh?'

The banker waved a cheerful hand at P Gubb and passed into his banking institution.

Detective Gubb, cordially greeted by his many friends and admirers, passed on down the main street, and by the time he reached the street that led to the river he was followed by a large and growing group intent on the pleasant occupation of watching a detective detect.

As Mr Gubb walked toward the river, other citizens joined the group, but all kept a respectful distance behind him. When Mr Gubb reached River Street and his false moustache fell off, the interest of the audience stopped short three paces behind him and stood until he had rescued the moustache and once more placed its wires in his nostrils. Then, when he moved forward again, they too moved forward. Never, perhaps, in the history of crime was a detective favored with a more respectful gallery.

On the edge of the river, Mr Gubb found Long Sam Fliggis, the mussel-dredger, seated on an empty tar-barrel with his own audience ranged before him listening while he told, for the fortieth time, the story of his finding of the body of H Smitz. As Philo Gubb approached, Long Sam ceased speaking, and his audience and Mr Gubb's gallery merged into one great circle which respectfully looked and listened while Mr Gubb questioned the mussel-dredger.

'Suicide?' said Long Sam scoffingly. 'Why, he wan't no more a suicide than I am right now. He was murdered or wan't nothin'! I've dredged up some suicides in my day, and some of 'em had stones tied to 'em, to make sure they'd sink, and some thought they'd sink without no ballast, but nary one of 'em ever sewed himself into a bag, and I give my word,' he said positively, 'that Hen Smitz couldn't have sewed himself into that burlap bag unless someone done the sewing. Then the feller that did it was an assistant-suicide, and the way I look at it is that an assistant-suicide is jest the same as a murderer.'

The crowd murmured approval, but Mr Gubb held up his hand for silence.

'In certain kinds of burlap bags it is possibly probable a man could sew himself into it,' said Mr Gubb, and the crowd, seeing the logic of the remark applauded gently but feelingly.

'You ain't seen the way he was sewed up,' said Long Sam, 'or you wouldn't talk like that.'

'I haven't yet took a look,' admitted Mr Gubb, 'but I aim so to do immediately after I find a clue onto which to work up my case. An A-1 deteckative can't set forth to work until he has a clue, that being a rule of the game.'

'What kind of a clue was you lookin' for?' asked Long Sam. 'What's a clue, anyway?'

'A clue,' said P Gubb, 'is almost anything connected with the late lamented, but generally something that nobody but a deteckative would think had anything to do with anything whatsoever. Not infrequently often it is a button.'

'Well, I've got no button except them that is sewed onto me,' said Long Sam, 'but if this here sack-needle will do any good –'

He brought from his pocket the point of a heavy sack-needle and laid it in Philo Gubb's palm. Mr Gubb looked at it carefully. In the eye of the needle still remained a few inches of twine.

'I cut that off'n the burlap he was sewed up in,' volunteered Long Sam, 'I thought I'd keep it as a sort of nice little souvenir. I'd like it back again when you don't need it for a clue no more.'

'Certainly sure,' agreed Mr Gubb, and he examined the needle carefully.

There are two kinds of sack-needles in general use. In both, the point of the needle is curved to facilitate pushing it into and out of a closely filled sack; in both, the curved portion is somewhat flattened so that the thumb and finger may secure a firm grasp to pull the needle through; but in one style the eye is at the end of the shaft while in the other it is near the point. This needle was like neither; the eye was midway of the shaft; the needle was pointed at each end and the curved portions were not flattened. Mr Gubb noticed another thing – the twine was not the ordinary loosely twisted hemp twine, but a hard, smooth cotton cord, like carpet warp.

'Thank you,' said Mr Gubb, 'and now I will go elsewhere to investigate to a further extent, and it is not necessarily imperative that everybody should accompany along with me if they don't want to.'

But everybody did want to, it seemed. Long Sam and his audience joined Mr Gubb's gallery and, with a dozen or so newcomers, they followed Mr Gubb at a decent distance as he walked toward the plant of the Brownson Packing Company, which stood on the riverbank some two blocks away.

It was here Henry Smitz had worked. Six or eight buildings of various sizes, the largest of which stood immediately on the river's edge, together with the 'yards' or pens, all enclosed by a high board fence, constituted the plant of the packing company, and as Mr Gubb appeared at the gate the watchman there stood aside to let him enter.

'Good morning, Mr Gubb,' he said pleasantly. 'I been sort of expecting you. Always right on the job when there's crime being done, ain't you? You'll find Merkel and Brill and Jokosky and the rest of Wiggins's crew in the main building, and I guess they'll tell you just what they told the police. They hate it, but what else can they say? It's the truth.'

'What is the truth?' asked Mr Gubb.

'That Wiggins was dead sore at Hen Smitz,' said the watchman. 'That Wiggins told Hen he'd do for him if he lost them their jobs like he said he would. That's the truth.'

Mr Gubb – his admiring followers were halted at the gate by the watchman – entered the large building and inquired his way to Mr Wiggins's department. He found it on the side of the building toward the river and on the ground floor. On one side the vast room led into the refrigerating room of the company; on the other it opened upon a long but narrow dock that ran the width of the building.

Along the outer edge of the dock were tied two barges, and into these barges some of Wiggins's crew were dumping mutton – not legs of mutton but entire sheep, neatly sewed in burlap. The large room was the packing and shipping room, and the work of Wiggins's crew was that of sewing the slaughtered and refrigerated sheep carcasses in burlap for shipment. Bales of burlap stood against one wall; strands of hemp twine ready for the needle hung from pegs in the wall and the posts that supported the floor above. The contiguity of the refrigerating room gave the room a pleasantly cool atmosphere.

Mr Gubb glanced sharply around. Here was the burlap, here were needles, here was twine. Yonder was the river into which Hen Smitz had been thrown. He glanced across the narrow dock at the blue river. As his eye returned he noticed one of the men carefully sweeping the dock with a broom – sweeping fragments of glass into the river. As the men in the room watched him curiously, Mr Gubb picked up a piece of burlap and put it in his pocket, wrapped a strand of twine around his finger and pocketed the twine, examined the needles stuck in improvised needle-holders made by boring gimlet holes in the wall, and then walked to the dock and picked up one of the pieces of glass.

'Clues,' he remarked, and gave his attention to the work of questioning the men.

Although manifestly reluctant, they honestly admitted that Wiggins had more than once threatened Hen Smitz – that he hated Hen Smitz with the hatred of a man who has been threatened with the loss of his job. Mr Gubb learned that Hen Smitz had been the foreman for the entire building – a sort of autocrat with, as Wiggins's crew informed him, an easy job. He had only to see that the crews in the building turned out more work this year than they did last year. ''Ficiency' had been his motto, they said, and they hated ''Ficiency'.

Mr Gubb's gallery was awaiting him at the gate, and its members were in a heated discussion as to what Mr Gubb had been doing. They ceased at once when he appeared and fell in behind him as he walked away from the packing house and toward the undertaking establishment of Mr Holworthy Bartman, on the main street. Here, joining the curious group already assembled, the gallery was forced to wait while Mr Gubb entered. His task was an unpleasant but necessary one. He must visit the little 'morgue' at the back of Mr Bartman's establishment.

The body of poor Hen Smitz had not yet been removed from the bag in which it had been found, and it was to the bag Mr Gubb gave his closest attention. The bag – in order that the body might be identified – had not been ripped, but had been cut, and not a stitch had been severed. It did not take Mr Gubb a moment to see that Hen Smitz had not been sewed in a bag at all. He had been sewed in burlap – burlap 'yard goods,' to use a shopkeeper's term – and it was burlap identical with that used by Mr Wiggins and his crew. It was no loose bag of burlap – but a close-fitting wrapping of burlap; a cocoon of burlap that had been drawn tight around the body, as burlap is drawn tight around the carcass of sheep for shipment, like a mummy's wrappings.

It would have been utterly impossible for Hen Smitz to have sewed himself into the casing, not only because it bound his arms tight to his sides, but because the burlap was lapped over and sewed from the outside. This, once and for all, ended the suicide theory. The question was: Who was the murderer?

As Philo Gubb turned away from the bier, Undertaker Bartman entered the morgue.

'The crowd outside is getting impatient, Mr Gubb,' he said in his soft, undertakery voice. 'It is getting on toward their lunch hour, and they want to crowd into my front office to find out what you've learned. I'm afraid they'll break my plate glass windows, they're pushing so hard against them. I don't want to hurry you, but if you would go out and tell them Wiggins is the murderer they'll go away. Of course there's no doubt about Wiggins being the murderer, since he has admitted he asked the stock-keeper for the electric-light bulb.'

'What bulb?' asked Philo Gubb.

'The electric-light bulb we found sewed inside this burlap when we sliced it open,' said Bartman. 'Matter of fact, we found it in Hen's hand. O'Toole took it for a clue and I guess it fixes the murder on Wiggins beyond all doubt. The stock-keeper says Wiggins got it from him.'

'And what does Wiggins remark on that subject?' asked Mr Gubb.

'Not a word,' said Bartman. 'His lawyer told him not to open his mouth, and he won't. Listen to that crowd out there!'

'I will attend to that crowd right presently,' said P Gubb, sternly. 'What I should wish to know now is why Mister Wiggins went and sewed an electric-light bulb in with the corpse for.'

'In the first place,' said Mr Bartman, 'he didn't sew it in with any corpse, because Hen Smitz wasn't a corpse when he was sewed in that burlap, unless Wiggins drowned him first, for Dr Mortimer says Hen Smitz died of drowning; and in the second place, if you had a live man to sew in burlap, and had to hold him while you sewed him, you'd be liable to sew anything in with him.

'My idea is that Wiggins and some of his crew jumped on Hen Smitz and threw him down, and some of them held him while the others sewed him in. My idea is that Wiggins got that electric-light bulb to replace one that had burned out, and that he met Hen Smitz and had words with him, and they clinched, and Hen Smitz grabbed the bulb, and then the others came, and they sewed him into the burlap and dumped him into the river.

'So all you've got to do is to go out and tell that crowd that Wiggins did it and that you'll let them know who helped him as soon as you find out. And you better do it before they break my windows.'

Detective Gubb turned and went out of the morgue. As he left the undertaker's establishment the crowd gave a slight cheer, but Mr Gubb walked hurriedly toward the jail. He found Policeman O'Toole there and questioned him about the bulb; and O'Toole, proud to be the center of so large and interested a gathering of his fellow citizens, pulled the bulb from his pocket and handed it to Mr Gubb, while he repeated in more detail the facts given by Mr Bartman. Mr Gubb looked at the bulb.

'I presume to suppose,' he said, 'that Mr Wiggins asked the stock-keeper for a new bulb to replace one that was burned out?'

'You're right,' said O'Toole. 'Why?'

'For the reason that this bulb is a burned-out bulb,' said Mr Gubb.

And so it was. The inner surface of the bulb was darkened slightly, and the filament of carbon was severed. O'Toole took the bulb and examined it curiously.

'That's odd, ain't it?' he said.

'It might so seem to the non-deteckative mind,' said Mr Gubb, 'but to the deteckative mind, nothing is odd.'

'No, no, this ain't so odd, either,' said O'Toole, 'for whether Hen Smitz grabbed the bulb before Wiggins changed the new one for the old one, or after he changed it, don't make so much difference, when you come to think of it.'

'To the deteckative mind,' said Mr Gubb, 'it makes the difference that this ain't the bulb you thought it was, and hence consequently it ain't the bulb Mister Wiggins got from the stock-keeper.'

★★★★

Mr Gubb started away. The crowd followed him. He did not go in search of the original bulb at once. He returned first to his room, where he changed his undertaker disguise for Number Six, that of a blue woolen-shirted laboring-man with a long brown beard. Then he led the way back to the packing house.

Again the crowd was halted at the gate, but again P Gubb passed inside, and he found the stock-keeper eating his luncheon out of a tin pail. The stock-keeper was perfectly willing to talk.

'It was like this,' said the stock-keeper. 'We've been working overtime in some departments down here, and Wiggins and his crew had to work overtime the night Hen Smitz was murdered. Hen and Wiggins was at outs, or anyway I heard Hen tell Wiggins he'd better be hunting another job because he wouldn't have this one long, and Wiggins told Hen that if he lost his job he'd murder him – Wiggins would murder Hen, that is. I didn't think it was much of anything but loose talk at the time. But Hen was working overtime too. He'd been working nights up in that little room of his on the second floor for quite some time, and this night Wiggins come to me and he says Hen had asked him for a fresh thirty-two-candle-power bulb. So I give it to Wiggins, and then I went home. And, come to find out, Wiggins sewed that bulb up with Hen.'

'Perhaps maybe you have sack-needles like this into your stockroom,' said P Gubb, producing the needle Long Sam had given him. The stock-keeper took the needle and examined it carefully.

'Never had any like that,' he said.

'Now, if,' said Philo Gubb – 'if the bulb that was sewed up into the burlap with Henry Smitz wasn't a new bulb, and if Mr Wiggins had given the new bulb to Henry, and if Henry had changed the new bulb for an old one, where would he have changed it at?'

'Up in his room, where he was always tinkering at that machine of his,' said the stock-keeper.

'Could I have the pleasure of taking a look into that there room for a moment of time?' asked Mr Gubb.

The stock-keeper arose, returned the remnants of his luncheon to his dinner-pail and led the way up the stairs. He opened the door of the room Henry Smitz had used as a workroom, and P Gubb walked in. The room was in some confusion, but, except in one or two particulars, no more than a workroom is apt to be. A rather cumbrous machine – the invention on which Henry Smitz had been working – stood as the murdered man had left it, all its levers, wheels, arms, and cogs intact. A chair, tipped over, lay on the floor. A roll of burlap stood on a roller by the machine. Looking up, Mr Gubb saw, on the ceiling, the lighting fixture of the room, and in it was a clean, shining thirty-two-candle-power bulb. Where another similar bulb might have been in the other socket was a plug from which an insulated wire, evidently to furnish power, ran to the small motor connected with the machine on which Henry Smitz had been working.

The stock-keeper was the first to speak.

'Hello!' he said. 'Somebody broke that window!' And it was true. Somebody had not only broken the window, but had broken every pane and the sash itself. But Mr Gubb was not interested in this. He was gazing at the electric bulb and thinking of Part Two, Lesson Six of the Course of Twelve Lessons – 'How to Identify by Finger-Prints, with General Remarks on the Bertillon System.' He looked about for some means of reaching the bulb above his head. His eye lit on the fallen chair. By placing the chair upright and placing one foot on the frame of Henry Smitz's machine and the other on the chair-back, he could reach the bulb. He righted the chair and stepped onto its seat. He put one foot on the frame of Henry Smitz's machine; very carefully he put the other foot on the top of the chair-back. He reached upward and unscrewed the bulb.

The stock-keeper saw the chair totter. He sprang forward to steady it, but he was too late. Philo Gubb, grasping the air, fell on the broad, level board that formed the middle part of Henry Smitz's machine.

The effect was instantaneous. The cogs and wheels of the machine began to revolve rapidly. Two strong, steel arms flopped down and held Detective Gubb to the table, clamping his arms to his side. The roll of burlap unrolled, and as it unrolled, the loose end was seized and slipped under Mr Gubb and wrapped around him and drawn taut, bundling him as a sheep's carcass is bundled. An arm reached down and back and forth, with a sewing motion, and passed from Mr Gubb's head to his feet. As it reached his feet a knife sliced the burlap in which he was wrapped from the burlap on the roll.

And then a most surprising thing happened. As if the board on which he lay had been a catapult, it suddenly and unexpectedly raised Philo Gubb and tossed him through the open window. The stock-keeper heard a muffled scream and then a great splash, but when he ran to the window, the great paper-hanger detective had disappeared in the bosom of the Mississippi.

Like Henry Smitz he had tried to reach the ceiling by standing on the chair-back; like Henry Smitz he had fallen upon the newly invented burlaping and loading machine; like Henry Smitz he had been wrapped and thrown through the window into the river; but, unlike Henry Smitz, he had not been sewn into the burlap, because Philo Gubb had the double-pointed shuttle-action needle in his pocket.

Page Seventeen of Lesson Eleven of the Rising Sun Detective Agency's Correspondence School of Detecting's Course of Twelve Lessons, says: –

In cases of extreme difficulty of solution it is well for the detective to re-enact as nearly as possible the probable action of the crime.

Mr Philo Gubb had done so. He had also proved that a man may be sewn in a sack and drowned in a river without committing wilful suicide or being the victim of foul play.

CLARE KENDALL

Created by Arthur B Reeve (1880-1936)

Arthur B Reeve was one of the most popular and widely read writers of crime fiction in early twentieth-century America. His most famous character was Craig Kennedy, 'The Scientific Detective', one of whose adventures is recorded in the next story in this anthology. Reeve was a prolific author and also created a number of other detectives, including two female sleuths. The better known of these is Constance Dunlap who appeared in a 1913 collection of interlinked short stories. In that same year, Reeve also published a series of magazine stories about Clare Kendall, who works as a private investigator. He returned to the character occasionally in later work and she even plays a role in a Craig Kennedy tale, 'The Woman Detective', where she is described as 'a tall, striking, self-reliant young woman with an engaging smile'. 'The Mystery of the Stolen Da Vinci' is an intriguing and entertaining period piece. Describing the theft of a Da Vinci portrait, it was written at a time when the artist's most famous work had indeed been stolen. The Mona Lisa *went missing from the Louvre in 1911 and was only recovered in November 1913. The story also shows that Clare Kendall had the same interest in cutting-edge technology as Reeve's more famous detective, Craig Kennedy. She solves the mystery using a telegraphone, a device for recording sound which had, as she remarks in the narrative, been recently patented by Valdemar Poulsen, 'The Danish Edison'.*

THE MYSTERY OF THE STOLEN DA VINCI

'Cut from the frame, the most precious treasure of my whole collection – da Vinci's lost *Ginevra Benci*.'

Lawrence Osgood, the American Medici, as the press called him, was standing with Clare Kendall in his private gallery, ruefully regarding a heavy gilt frame which now enclosed nothing but jagged ends of canvas fringing the careful backing on which had hung the famous portrait.

'And today I received this letter,' he added, spreading out on a sixteenth-century table a note in a cramped foreign script. 'What do you make of it?'

It bore neither date nor heading, but as Clare read the signature, she exclaimed, 'La Mano Nera – the Black Hand!' Hastily she ran through it:

'We have heard,' it read, 'that you have lost a famous painting. It can be restored to you if you will see Pierre Jacot of Jacot & Cie, the Fifth Avenue dealers. Jacot knows nothing of it yet but this afternoon a woman will let him know how the picture can be secured. It will be returned on payment of $50,000 as we direct. It is useless to try to trace this letter, the messengers we employ or any other means we take to communicate. Such an effort or any dealings with the police will provoke a tragedy and the picture will be lost to you forever. – La Mano Nera.'

'A woman will let him know,' repeated Clare, turning the letter over and looking at it carefully. 'Apparently there is nothing about this note that gives a clue, not even the postmark.'

'Do you think Jacot himself could have anything to do with it?' asked Osgood slowly. 'I have known Jacot a long time, but I didn't think he knew I owned *La Ginevra*.'

'What do you mean?' asked Clare in surprise.

'It was the companion picture to *Mona Lisa*, painted about the same time,' explained Osgood thoughtfully. 'It disappeared a few years after da Vinci died and was only recently discovered, after centuries, in an old chapel in Italy. *Mona Lisa* was stolen; now *Mona Ginevra* is gone also.'

'Was anything else taken?' asked Clare, surveying the rich store of loot collected from all ages.

'I don't know yet. Until my curator, Dr Grimm, and his assistant, Miss Latham, have gone over the catalogue and checked things up. It looks now as if the thief, whoever he was, had confined his attention to this fifteenth- and sixteenth-century Italian corner. The modern crook, you know, has an eye for pictures. Anyhow, this one went straight for the da Vinci which cost me a quarter of a million at a secret sale in London.'

'Secret?'

'Yes, that is why I didn't say anything to the police or the newspapers. The crook must have known the facts. It was smuggled out of Italy by a London dealer after its discovery; they have very strict laws there about taking such things out of the country. You see, I hoped in some way to have it fixed up so that I would get a clear title in the end, for I can't afford to have people make me out a pirate. I could have fixed that, all right. Here's a photograph of the canvas.'

Clare swiftly studied the face which the master had painted as a companion to the famous portrait which had hung so long and attracted so many worshipers at the Louvre. There was a hard, cruel sensuousness about the beautiful mouth which the painter seemed to have captured beneath the very oils. Masked cleverly in the penetrating hazel eyes was a sort of Medusa-like cunning, a cunning which combined with the ravishing curves of the neck and chin transfixed the observer even of a photograph.

Osgood saw that Clare, with her woman instinct, had caught the spirit of the portrait, as that subtle fascination over the human mind which is exercised by the art relics of the past.

'What crimes a man might commit under the spell of a woman like that!' he mused, then added, half smiling, 'Even for her portrait I was ready to risk a certain degree of reputation. Now someone risks his own liberty to kidnap her.'

'The infatuation in this case,' commented Clare quietly, scanning the letter again, 'is of the kind that holds for ransom, not for love. I should like very much to look over your museum. Have you any idea how the thief gained entrance?'

'No, that is another inexplicable feature. Apparently everything was safely locked, and as for Dr Grimm, I would trust him with the whole collection. Shall I ask him to accompany us about?'

'By all means.'

Narrowly she watched the curator as they proceeded, chatting, from room to room of wonders. Dr Grimm was a middle-aged man, rather good-looking in spite of his huge tortoise-shell spectacles and the slight stoop to his shoulders. He had an air that suggested the savant and epicurean combined.

Carefully Clare went over every lock and bolt of the big private gallery. At last in the basement, after what had seemed a fruitless search, they came to a strong door by which rubbish was removed to the street. A low exclamation from Clare called attention to some steel filings which had collected in a corner and had evidently been overlooked by someone in cleaning.

She began tapping the door. Suddenly with her nail she dug directly into what looked on the surface like painted steel. There, over the lock, was a little hole in the heavy door, puttied up and carefully painted over.

'How could that have been done?' exclaimed Osgood.

'By an electric drill,' she answered, glancing about. 'It must have been attached to that light socket up there outside the door. Very clever, too.'

Dr Grimm said nothing, but it was evident from his face that he felt relieved that the robbery had no longer the appearance of being an inside job.

'What would you advise me to do!' inquired Osgood, as they retraced their steps.

'Negotiate,' decided Clare tersely. 'Offer half the demand at first. Only, don't pay – yet.'

'I wonder if Jacot did have anything to do with it?' reiterated Osgood.

'I should like to see him before you begin negotiations,' answered Clare noncommitally. 'By the way, from your end I would suggest that it is safer to put the matter in the hands of Dr Grimm and let him manage it with Jacot.'

That afternoon Clare and Billy Lawson, with a small grip, sat in the lobby of the Prince Henry, just around the corner from Jacot's. She had telephoned hastily to Lawson and had briefly stated the facts in the case.

'You will stay here, Billy,' she planned in conclusion. 'Keep this grip of mine. I will call up from Jacot's, if I need you; and will have you paged as Mr Winterhouse. Then bring the grip over.'

Jacot's, enjoying an excellent patronage, opened on Fifth Avenue just a few feet below the street level. Jacot himself was a slim Frenchman, well preserved, faultlessly dressed.

'I am the agent of Mr Winterhouse, a western mine owner and connoisseur,' volunteered Clare on entering the shop. 'May I look around?'

'*Avec plaisir, m'amselle,*' returned the suave Frenchman with both hands interlocking. 'In what is Mr Winterhouse most interested? In furniture? In pictures? In –'

'Nearly everything,' she confided, looking the dealer frankly in the eye. 'And he is not particular about the price, if he wants a thing. As for me I am particular about one thing. A rebate on the bill, a commission, you understand? The price is immaterial, but not my – er – commission. *Comprenez-vous?*'

'*Parfaitement,*' smiled the little Frenchman. 'I can arrange all that. Trust me.'

An hour perhaps Clare spent wandering up and down the long aisles of the store, admiring, pricing, absorbing facts that might serve to captivate the fictitious Mr Winterhouse.

Suddenly she glanced at her little wrist watch, giving a suppressed exclamation. 'Oh – is it after four? At four I was to meet Mr Winterhouse up town. He is waiting now. What shall I do?'

'Can mademoiselle not telephone?' suggested Jacot, in genuine solicitude to please a prospective customer.

'Oh – may I?'

'Assuredly, *voilà* – the booth in the office.'

'Billy,' she almost whispered in the transmitter, 'you'd better call a taxi. Have a messenger carry that grip. I've told some whoppers here. You're at least a billionaire. Only you must say "No" to every suggestion I make. Then agree to reconsider tomorrow when you have time. Get me?'

'I'm on.'

A few minutes later Lawson arrived and with marked respect was greeted by Jacot and conducted to the office where Clare waited.

'I was so fascinated in looking over this wonderful collection,' she apologized, 'that I forgot the time, and then I thought perhaps you might be interested in some exquisite seventeenth-century silverware. You may leave the grip here, boy,' she concluded to the messenger.

Lawson dropped into a chair with feigned exhaustion. 'Tired to death,' he sighed. 'Still, I'll look at it.'

With a hasty glance about, Clare noted that the office was in a corner and that no one could see it except Jacot.

'Could you not bring the silver service in here for inspection?' she asked.

'Delighted,' bowed Jacot. 'If mademoiselle and monsieur will make themselves at home here I am sure it will not take long.'

Jacot retired backward. Instantly Clare was on her knees opening the grip.

'Move that cabinet beside the telephone booth out just a bit, Billy,' she whispered, quickly removing the covering from a mahogany box and placing it on a table. It was a peculiar box with a sort of dial in the front face, and as Clare opened and shut it for an instant she closed what looked like two discs or spools of wire.

Quietly Lawson edged the cabinet out. Clare closed the box and a moment later she placed it carefully on the floor, leaving two wires exposed. Footsteps down the aisle warned them that Jacot and an assistant were returning with the silver service.

'Push the cabinet back, Billy,' whispered Clare, shoving the wires out of sight. 'I'll finish when you have turned down the silver service.'

Lawson had moved the cabinet and restored the status quo by lounging into the easy chair with a half yawn. Clare consumed several minutes urging the merits of the silver service as compared with one they had seen in London. Lawson parried.

'Perhaps you would be interested in the new importation of Chinese cloisonné which Mr Jacot showed me?'

'Bring it out, so long as we are here.'

Again Jacot disappeared. Clare found the loose wires and deftly cut in and attached them to the wires of the telephone in the shadow of the cabinet where they would not be observed.

The cloisonné satisfied Lawson even less than the silver service. Still, taking the cue from Clare that her plan, whatever it was, had worked well so far, he assumed an air of cordiality toward Jacot and asked to call the next day.

As they arose to go, Lawson observed that Clare had left her parasol in a corner. Before he could hand it to her he caught a fleeting frown and a shake of her head. She evidently intended to forget it.

'What do you make of the little Frenchman?' he asked when they had reached the waiting taxicab. 'Is he playing a "fence" or is he on the square with Osgood?'

'I'm not guessing,' she answered, 'at least not until I have had a chance to return for my parasol before he closes. I think I'll go alone. Meanwhile, I'll let you know if anything develops.'

That night Clare and Lawson sat comfortably chatting in an obscure corner of the parlor at the Ritz.

'How did you get the clue?' asked Lawson with surprise and admiration.

'Never mind, Billy, there's Jacot, now. See, he is evidently looking for someone.'

Just then Jacot caught sight of a tastefully gowned woman, obviously a foreigner, who had been seated alone in an alcove at the other end of the room. As he advanced toward her, she hesitantly recognized him, arose, and then received him with cordiality, extending a jewelled hand.

As Clare studied the face of the woman, it flashed on her that something beneath the olive beauty of her complexion resembled that enigmatical look in the photograph of *La Ginevra*. Jacot himself was evidently much taken with her. They chatted with animation, and when he made his adieux, he bent so low over her hand that his lips almost touched the rings on her fingers.

'Follow Jacot, Billy,' whispered Clare. 'I don't think it will lead to much, but there's no use taking chances.'

A moment later she wished she had not sent him away. A stranger, in evening clothes of pronounced continental tone, sauntered through the lobby as if seeking someone, caught sight of the woman, alone, turned to the desk to recall a card he had just given the clerk, and made his way quickly to her side.

The greeting between the two left no doubt but that the man was infatuated; and she, as they talked, seemed utterly oblivious of the gay throng of diners passing through the lobby.

Clare sauntered to the desk.

'What, please, is that lady's name?' she asked casually.

'Signora Giulia Ascoli,' replied the clerk.

'And by the way, do you know who is with her?'

'Dr Vaccaro was on the card – Giorgio Vaccaro, I think.'

The woman had turned. Her wonderful eyes had divined that the clerk was talking about her. Yet without showing the least perturbation the Signora and Dr Vaccaro quietly moved toward the carriage entrance. It was useless to try to follow them. In fact it would have been fatal. Instead Clare decided to see her millionaire principal and discover what had happened during the afternoon.

'Has Dr Grimm called up Jacot?' she asked, as Osgood conducted her into his spacious library.

'Yes, several times, I believe. First he told Jacot that I was willing to pay for the return of *La Ginevra*, but not fifty thousand, as you advised. Jacot agreed, I understand, to carry to them my offer of twenty-five thousand and Grimm is to hear from them tonight.'

'I have just seen Jacot at the Ritz,' remarked Clare casually, 'talking with a woman whose name I believe is Giulia Ascoli. Later a Dr Vaccaro –'

'Vaccaro?' cried Osgood wheeling in his chair. 'Why, he is an acquaintance of Dr Grimm. That complicates things exceedingly. Vaccaro – yes, he might have heard of *La Ginevra*. Where in heaven will this thing end? Vaccaro is a dreamer, a critic, one of the foremost art connoisseurs of Italy. I should never have thought he could be mixed up in such a thing.'

The door opened and the butler announced Dr Grimm. The curator appeared to be very much excited.

'They have agreed at last to compromise on twenty-five thousand,' he announced, coming directly to the point. 'I have just had a message from Jacot.'

'How and where is it to be paid?'

'I am sworn not to tell, except that I am to be on a certain corner with the money at a certain time tonight and I am to hand it over to a person in a motor car who drives up and – no, no, I cannot tell more. I dare not. Miss Kendall might follow.' He was trembling apprehensively. 'They would take my life if you followed – no – no!'

'What shall I do?' asked Osgood in genuine solicitude.

'I should advise paying,' counselled Clare.

Osgood looked at her quickly. It was not for the purpose of surrender that he had retained her, and this was surrender. Clare said nothing. With a man Osgood would probably have disputed the policy. But even he, accustomed to dealing directly with affairs, saw that this was a case which called for finesse. Without further ado he opened a little spherical safe in the corner, took out and counted twenty-five crisp one thousand dollar bills and handed them to the curator.

'You may depend on me, Mr Osgood,' remarked Grimm, 'to execute this as carefully as if it were my own mission.'

'I do, doctor, and good luck to you,' rejoined Osgood heartily, as if no suspicion had entered his mind.

'I wonder,' mused the millionaire, when the door closed, 'whether Grimm and these people can be in league with each other? To tell you the truth, I think there is no Black Hand about this thing at all. I think it is blackmail. Or perhaps it is just a scheme to return the picture to Italy and double-cross me at the same time?'

Absorbed in studying an antique paper-weight which had once been an Indian crystal ball, Clare absently remarked, 'I wish you would let me know at once the outcome of Dr Grimm's expedition,' rising to go. 'I shall give them until tomorrow before we act in the open. If the picture is returned, then we shall get them without jeopardizing it. If not, we shall get them anyhow.'

'Where did Jacot go?' she telephoned Lawson from the nearest pay station.

'To his office. I waited outside. Then he went home.'

'I thought so. We may expect something soon, but had better not act until morning. Then I'll call you. And thank you ever so much, Billy, for your trouble. Goodbye.'

Her telephone was tinkling insistently the next morning.

'Hello – is this Miss Kendall?' called Osgood in great agitation. 'What do you think has happened? Dr Grimm has just been discovered dead in a doorway on the lower West Side and the money is gone.'

Clare nearly dropped the receiver at this tragic turn of events. 'I hardly thought they would dare go as far as murder,' she managed to reply. Her mind was working in flashes.

To her hasty inquiry Osgood answered that the body had been removed by the coroner to a nearby undertaking establishment. There was no word of reproach in his tone; but it was evident he felt bitterly that he himself had misjudged Grimm. Clare said nothing.

'Within an hour, Mr Osgood,' she concluded, 'please be in your library.'

Hurriedly telephoning Dr Lawson, she asked him to meet her as soon as possible at the West Side undertaker's. Then followed a short parley with the detective bureau at Headquarters, and she was speeding to investigate the tragic death of the unfortunate Dr Grimm.

Lawson was waiting when she arrived. Already he had seen the body. Long and intently he looked on the strangely contorted face of the curator. It had an indescribable look – half of passion, half of horror.

'Not a mark,' he commented, 'except on the back of the neck, just a little scratch.'

'What did it? Poison?'

'Ricinus, I think, one of the most recent of poisons and one of the most powerful,' was the reply. 'A gram of it would kill a million guinea pigs, and it surpasses prussic acid and other commonly known drugs of the sort. They probably thought in this way to get away with the picture, the money and the witness.'

'Then we must act quickly before another blow falls,' decided Clare, leading the way to the cab in which she had come. 'Jacot's on Fifth Avenue.'

It was still early and Jacot was not there, but the clerks had just opened the place, and remembered them.

Without waiting Clare led the way to the office and before Lawson could help her had moved out the heavy cabinet and lifted up the curious mahogany box. It took scarcely a moment to detach the wires, slip the box in the grip which she had brought and direct the chauffeur to the Osgood house.

Jacot arrived a few minutes afterward, protesting, in the custody of a Central Office man who had forced an entrance into his apartment.

'Says he doesn't know a thing about it,' whispered the detective to Clare, 'and acts as though he didn't either. I went to the Ritz and the clerk tells me that the Ascoli woman left suddenly late last night. I can't make this one out, though – he's too smooth for me.'

Jacot was standing with open-eyed surprise at seeing his prospective customers under such circumstances.

'Mr Osgood, we are ready now,' began Clare after she had introduced Lawson and his discovery of the ricinus had been told.

She had opened the grip and taken out the mahogany box. There now rested on the table a machine of wheels and spools of steel wire like piano wire, batteries and clockwork, and a sort of horn. She took out the spool of wire already in it, laid it carefully aside and dropped in another which she had brought packed in a case.

She turned a switch. From the horn came a distinct voice.

'Hello. This is Mrs Burridge. Yesterday I ordered a vase –'

'We'll skip that,' interrupted Clare, moving the wire forward on the spool.

'What is it?' asked Osgood, mystified.

'A telegraphone,' explained Clare. 'An instrument invented by Poulsen, the Danish Edison, by which the human voice can be recorded on a wire or a steel disc by means of a new principle involving the use of minute localized electric charges. I can't stop to tell you the principle of the thing, but I can get a local or long distance conversation, thirty minutes of it in all, on one of these spools.'

Several times she interrupted the routine conversations recorded. Then came a soft musical voice.

'Italian,' commented Clare, as all listened intently, 'and a woman's voice, too.'

'Hello,' *purred the voice in the machine. 'Is this Mr Pierre Jacot, the art dealer?'*

'Yes, this is Mr Jacot. What can I do for you?'

A pause.

'Have you had any offer from Mr Osgood for La Ginevra?'

'Ah!' *prolonged Jacot, in either well-simulated or genuine surprise. 'So this is what his curator, Dr Grimm, meant.'*

'How is that?' *asked the voice.*

'He is willing to pay twenty-five thousand for the return of the painting and no questions asked or —'*

'Diavolo! It cannot be. Fifty thousand — it is the lowest price. It is worth it. It —'*

'I should like to see you, madame. Where can I? I will see what I can do and report to you then. It is so much more satisfactory than over the telephone. You can trust me. I will betray nothing.'*

'Absolutely? ...'*

'Absolutely! On my honor.'*

'Then call at the Ritz tonight, about eight. I have not the picture, but I can tell all about how to secure it. I shall be in the alcove of the parlor, alone. You can recognize me by my cream-colored evening gown, and one large American Beauty rose. Wear a rose yourself. Now, remember, no word to the polizia or, by the saints. it will go hard with you, with all, monsieur.'*

'Bien. Never fear.'*

The telegraphone trailed off into other conversations of no significance.

'That is where I got my first clue which took me up to the Ritz, Billy,' remarked Clare, removing the spool which she had been using and substituting the one she had just laid aside which contained the records of what was said afterward.

The second spool bore several hasty business calls, then one from Jacot to Dr Grimm:

'Dr Grimm? This is Jacot.'*

'Yes?'*

'They agree.'*

'For twenty-five? Good?'*

'*You are to have the cash at midnight. Stand at the corner below Luigi's restaurant — you know where it is? — just off Washington Square? A car will drive up. If a lady leans out and asks, "Are you waiting for Ginevra?" you are to answer, "Si, Signora." Then she will embrace you. The money is to be in a flat package which you are to slip into her hand. La Ginevra will be given to you rolled up in a long brass tube. You understand?*'

'*Perfectly. I shall be there, to the dot.*'

'*Alone — and no police.*'

'*Exactly.*'

'Evidently, late as it was,' commented Clare, 'Jacot returned to his office, shadowed by Dr Lawson otherwise Mr Winterhouse. I suppose he did not trust to the public telephones. His own was the worst he could have trusted, however.'

She had set the machine in motion again. There was only a slight pause this time:

'*Is this 2330? The apartment of Signor Vaccaro, please. Hello — who is this — Oh, Signora — how do you do? I did not expect to find you here. Is Signor Vaccaro out?*'

'*Yes, I will take the message.*'

'*I wish I might deliver it in person.*'

'*It is impossible — tonight. Tell me — quickly.*'

'*I have told Dr Grimm that your friends will take twenty-five thousand and he says he will have the money tonight.*'

'*Good! You told him what to do?*'

'*Yes. He will be there at midnight. For one part of the transaction, Signora, I would willingly change places with him.*'

A silvery laugh was recorded.

'*Ah, monsieur, for what you have done I could wish to have you change places. Over the telephone I kiss you.*'

'*Without the telephone — ma chérie — tomorrow?*' hinted Jacot in his most gallantly insinuating tone.

'*Perhaps. We shall see. Ah — quick — monsieur. Goodbye. I hear Georgio coming to my room.*'

The receiver at the other end had evidently been hung up at the most interesting point of the little flirtation.

Jacot was now trembling like a leaf.

'Before God, Mr Osgood,' he cried, 'it's all true enough. But

I know no more about it now than you know. I did nothing – nothing. I was only the agent of Dr Grimm who met this woman, the agent of the others. She led me on – like a fool – women, women –'

'Let me see,' interrupted Clare. 'The number 2330 is not the Ritz, of course. Hello. Information. What is the street address of 2330? The York Arms – Fifty-eighth. Thank you. Mr Osgood – your car, please.'

They pulled up with a jolt before the York Arms and the hall boy was subsidized to show them to the Vaccaro apartments.

As Lawson and Osgood half tumbled into a sitting room, they stopped short before Signora Ascoli, tall, imperious, in a diaphanous morning gown.

It needed no word from any of them to tell her that she was cornered. There was Jacot himself cringing in the rear. Facing her was the woman she had seen at the Ritz who had caused her hasty departure and had aroused suspicion that after all Dr Grimm might have spoken with the hated *polizia*.

Quickly she glided, almost like a serpent, to a stand and seized a bottle of acid. Before she could pour it into a long brass tube, Lawson with his heavy cane had dashed the bottle to the floor where the acid ate into and blackened the wood.

Another moment and Clare had seized the tube itself. From it she drew a long strip of canvas. As it unwound Osgood cried in delight, 'At last! My lost *Ginevra Benci* safe!'

'*Subito… Giorgio… Urgenzia…*' cried the woman, dashing into a bedroom, through another door.

They followed. There stood Vaccaro – his escape cut off. With a hasty sentence or two in low Italian, she flung her arms about his neck. For one long moment they held each other in a passionate embrace.

'He is the thief,' cried Jacot who had heard and translated the words. 'He planned it from his knowledge of art: he did it under the spell of those eyes – eyes like those in the painting itself – for which a man would risk all – honor, life. I see it. This meant money for both – love.'

Jacot paused, horrified. The faces of the lovers had changed even as he was speaking. Together, locked in an unrelaxing grasp they sank back on the divan.

Staring at the intruders lay Vaccaro unable to move a muscle, hearing but powerless to speak, as if ebbing away. Lawson looked quickly from one to the other of the pair. The already hardening features of Giulia Ascoli told the story.

'Ricinus again,' he muttered. 'The poison by which they killed others.'

Clare had reached down and withdrawn carefully from the jewelled hand of the Ascoli woman a little ring which she held out to Osgood.

'The poison ring of the Borgias,' he cried in amazement, 'taken from my own collection. See, it has a hollow in the part that encircles the stone, with a point and a little concealed spring. It is a formidable and easy weapon – see – the fatal scratch could be given while shaking hands while blinded by the passion of the embrace.'

'It was that poisoned fang that sent your faithful curator to his death,' remarked Clare, quietly regarding the awesome ring. 'It would have sent others, too, who knew too much about the stolen picture, the money, the murder.'

Jacot was in a palsy.

'Another day and I should have followed Grimm,' he shivered, turning to Clare with a new respect that even the susceptible little art dealer had never felt for the sex. 'Mademoiselle, I owe you my life.'

CRAIG KENNEDY

Created by Arthur B Reeve (1880–1936)

Known as 'The Scientific Detective', Craig Kennedy is barely remembered today but he was once enormously popular, particularly in the USA. He appeared not only in short stories and novels but silent film serials and comic strips. As late as 1952, there was a 26-episode TV series entitled Craig Kennedy, Criminologist. *A professor of chemistry who applied his knowledge of science and an array of technological inventions to the solution of baffling crimes, Kennedy was the brainchild of Arthur B Reeve. Born in New York State and educated at Princeton, Reeve originally intended to be a lawyer but turned instead to journalism. After writing a series of articles about the use of cutting-edge science in detective work, he was inspired to create Kennedy who made his debut in a short story published in the magazine* Cosmopolitan *in December 1910. More than eighty further stories and over a dozen novels followed. The Kennedy stories, narrated by the scientific detective's admiring sidekick, the journalist Walter Jameson, can often seem dated today. The technology that Reeve proclaims as close to miraculous is often very old hat (X-rays, lie detectors, Dictaphones) but the tales themselves remain entertaining and lively.*

THE AZURE RING

Files of newspapers and innumerable clippings from the press bureaus littered Kennedy's desk in rank profusion. Kennedy himself was so deeply absorbed that I had merely said good evening as I came in and had started to open my mail. With an impatient sweep of his hand, however, he brushed the whole mass of newspapers into the waste-basket.

'It seems to me, Walter,' he exclaimed in disgust, 'that this mystery is considered insoluble for the very reason which should make it easy to solve – the extraordinary character of its features.'

Inasmuch as he had opened the subject, I laid down the letter I was reading. 'I'll wager I can tell you just why you made that remark, Craig,' I ventured. 'You're reading up on that Wainwright-Templeton affair.'

'You are on the road to becoming a detective yourself, Walter,' he answered with a touch of sarcasm. 'Your ability to add two units to two other units and obtain four units is almost worthy of Inspector O'Connor. You are right and within a quarter of an hour the district attorney of Westchester County will be here. He telephoned me this afternoon and sent an assistant with this mass of dope. I suppose he'll want it back,' he added, fishing the newspapers out of the basket again. 'But, with all due respect to your profession, I'll say that no one would ever get on speaking terms with the solution of this case if he had to depend solely on the newspaper writers.'

'No?' I queried, rather nettled at his tone.

'No,' he repeated emphatically. 'Here one of the most popular girls in the fashionable suburb of Williston, and one of the leading younger members of the bar in New York, engaged to be married, are found dead in the library of the girl's home the day before the ceremony. And now, a week later, no one knows whether it was an accident due to the fumes from the antique charcoal-brazier, or whether it was a double suicide, or suicide and murder, or a double murder, or – or – why, the experts haven't even been able to agree on whether they have discovered poison or not,' he continued, growing as excited as the city editor did over my first attempt as a cub reporter.

'They haven't agreed on anything except that on the eve of what was, presumably, to have been the happiest day of their lives two of the best known members of the younger set are found dead, while absolutely no one, as far as is known, can be proved to have been near them within the time necessary to murder them. No wonder the coroner says it is simply a case of asphyxiation. No wonder the district attorney is at his wits' end. You fellows have hounded them with your hypotheses until they can't see the facts straight. You suggest one solution and before –'

The door-bell sounded insistently, and without waiting for an answer a tall, spare, loose-jointed individual stalked in and laid a green bag on the table.

'Good evening, Professor Kennedy,' he began brusquely. 'I am District Attorney Whitney, of Westchester. I see you have been reading up on the case. Quite right.'

'Quite wrong,' answered Craig. 'Let me introduce my friend, Mr Jameson, of the *Star*. Sit down. Jameson knows what I think of the way the newspapers have handled this case. I was about to tell him as you came in that I intended to disregard everything that had been printed, to start out with you as if it were a fresh subject and get the facts at first-hand. Let's get right down to business. First tell us just how it was that Miss Wainwright and Mr Templeton were discovered and by whom.'

The district attorney loosened the cords of the green bag and drew out a bundle of documents. 'I'll read you the affidavit of the maid who found them,' he said, fingering the documents nervously. 'You see, John Templeton had left his office in New York early that afternoon, telling his father that he was going to visit Miss Wainwright. He caught the three-twenty train, reached Williston all right, walked to the Wainwright house, and, in spite of the bustle of preparation for the wedding, the next day, he spent the rest of the afternoon with Miss Wainwright. That's where the mystery begins. They had no visitors. At least, the maid who answers the bell says they had none. She was busy with the rest of the family, and I believe the front door was not locked – we don't lock our doors in Williston, except at night.'

He had found the paper and paused to impress these facts on our minds.

'Mrs Wainwright and Miss Marian Wainwright, the sister, were busy about the house. Mrs Wainwright wished to consult Laura about something. She summoned the maid and asked if Mr Templeton and Miss Wainwright were in the house. The maid replied that she would see, and this is her affidavit. Ahem! I'll skip the legal part: "I knocked at the library door twice, but obtaining no answer, I supposed they had gone out for a walk or perhaps a ride across country as they often did. I opened the door partly and looked in. There was a silence in the room, a strange, queer silence. I opened the door further and, looking toward the davenport in the corner, I saw Miss Laura and Mr Templeton in such an awkward position. They looked as if they had fallen asleep. His head was thrown back against the cushions of the davenport, and on his face was a most awful look. It was discoloured. Her head had fallen forward on his shoulder, sideways, and on her face, too, was the same terrible stare and the same discolouration. Their right hands were tightly clasped.

'"I called to them. They did not answer. Then the horrible truth flashed on me. They were dead. I felt giddy for a minute, but quickly recovered myself, and with a cry for help I rushed to Mrs Wainwright's room, shrieking that they were dead. Mrs Wainwright fainted. Miss Marian called the doctor on the telephone and helped us restore her mother. She seemed perfectly cool in the tragedy, and I do not know what we servants should have done if she had not been there to direct us. The house was frantic, and Mr Wainwright was not at home.

'"I did not detect any odour when I opened the library door. No glasses or bottles or vials or other receptacles which could have held poison were discovered or removed by me, or to the best of my knowledge and belief by anyone else."'

'What happened next?' asked Craig eagerly.

'The family physician arrived and sent for the coroner immediately, and later for myself. You see, he thought at once of murder.'

'But the coroner, I understand, thinks differently,' prompted Kennedy.

'Yes, the coroner has declared the case to be accidental. He says that the weight of evidence points positively to asphyxiation. Still, how can it be asphyxiation? They could have escaped from the room at any time; the door was not locked. I tell you, in spite of the fact that the tests for poison in their mouths, stomachs, and blood have so far revealed nothing, I still believe that John Templeton and Laura Wainwright were murdered.'

Kennedy looked at his watch thoughtfully. 'You have told me just enough to make me want to see the coroner himself,' he mused. 'If we take the next train out to Williston with you, will you engage to get us a half-hour talk with him on the case, Mr Whitney?'

'Surely. But we'll have to start right away. I've finished my other business in New York. Inspector O'Connor – ah, I see you know him – has promised to secure the attendance of anyone whom I can show to be a material witness in the case. Come on, gentlemen: I'll answer your other questions on the train.'

As we settled ourselves in the smoker, Whitney remarked in a low voice, 'You know, someone has said that there is only one thing more difficult to investigate and solve than a crime whose commission is surrounded by complicated circumstances and that is a crime whose perpetration is wholly devoid of circumstances.'

'Are you so sure that this crime is wholly devoid of circumstances?' asked Craig.

'Professor,' he replied, 'I'm not sure of anything in this case. If I were I should not require your assistance. I would like the credit of solving it myself, but it is beyond me. Just think of it: so far we haven't a clue, at least none that shows the slightest promise, although we have worked night and day for a week. It's all darkness. The facts are so simple that they give us nothing to work on. It is like a blank sheet of paper.'

Kennedy said nothing, and the district attorney proceeded: 'I don't blame Mr Nott, the coroner, for thinking it an accident. But to my mind, some master criminal must have arranged this very baffling simplicity of circumstances. You recall that the front door was unlocked. This person must have entered the house unobserved, not a difficult thing to do, for the Wainwright house is somewhat isolated. Perhaps this person brought along some poison in the form of a beverage, and induced the two victims to drink. And then, this person must have removed the evidences as swiftly as they were brought in and by the same door. That, I think, is the only solution.'

'That is not the only solution. It is one solution,' interrupted Kennedy quietly.

'Do you think someone in the house did it?' I asked quickly.

'I think,' replied Craig, carefully measuring his words, 'that if poison was given them it must have been by someone they both knew pretty well.'

No one said a word, until at last I broke the silence. 'I know from the gossip of the *Star* office that many Williston people say that Marian was very jealous of her sister Laura for capturing the catch of the season. Williston people don't hesitate to hint at it.'

Whitney produced another document from that fertile green bag. It was another affidavit. He handed it to us. It was a statement signed by Mrs Wainwright, and read:

'Before God, my daughter Marian is innocent. If you wish to find out all, find out more about the past history of Mr Templeton before he became engaged to Laura. She would never in the world have committed suicide. She was too bright and cheerful for that, even if Mr Templeton had been about to break off the engagement. My daughters Laura and Marian were always treated by Mr Wainwright and myself exactly alike. Of course they had their quarrels, just as all sisters do, but there was never, to my certain knowledge, a serious disagreement, and I was always close enough to my girls to know. No, Laura was murdered by someone outside.'

Kennedy did not seem to attach much importance to this statement. 'Let us see,' he began reflectively. 'First, we have a young woman especially attractive and charming in both person and temperament. She is just about to be married and, if the reports are to be believed, there was no cloud on her happiness. Secondly, we have a young man whom everyone agrees to have been of an ardent, energetic, optimistic temperament. He had everything to live for, presumably. So far, so good. Everyone who has investigated this case, I understand, has tried to eliminate the double-suicide and the suicide-and-murder theories. That is all right, providing the facts are as stated. We shall see, later, when we interview the coroner. Now, Mr Whitney, suppose you tell us briefly what you have learned about the past history of the two unfortunate lovers.'

'Well, the Wainwrights are an old Westchester family, not very wealthy, but of the real aristocracy of the county. There were only two children, Laura and Marian. The Templetons were much the same sort of family. The children all attended a private school at White Plains, and there also they met Schuyler Vanderdyke. These four constituted a sort of little aristocracy in the school. I mention this because Vanderdyke later became Laura's first husband. This marriage with Templeton was a second venture.'

'How long ago was she divorced?' asked Craig attentively.

'About three years ago. I'm coming to that in a moment. The sisters went to college together, Templeton to law school, and Vanderdyke studied civil engineering. Their intimacy was pretty well broken up, all except Laura's and Vanderdyke's. Soon after he graduated he was taken into the construction department of the Central Railroad by his uncle, who was a vice-president, and Laura and he were married. As far as I can learn he had been a fellow of convivial habits at college, and about two years after their marriage his wife suddenly became aware of what had long been well known in Williston, that Vanderdyke was paying marked attention to a woman named Miss Laporte in New York.

'No sooner had Laura Vanderdyke learned of this intimacy of her husband,' continued Whitney, 'than she quietly hired private detectives to shadow him, and on their evidence she obtained a divorce. The papers were sealed, and she resumed her maiden name.

'As far as I can find out, Vanderdyke then disappeared from her life. He resigned his position with the railroad and joined a party of engineers exploring the upper Amazon. Later he went to Venezuela. Miss Laporte also went to South America about the same time, and was for a time in Venezuela, and later in Peru.

'Vanderdyke seems to have dropped all his early associations completely, though at present I find he is back in New York raising capital for a company to exploit a new asphalt concession in the interior of Venezuela. Miss Laporte has also reappeared in New York as Mrs Ralston, with a mining claim in the mountains of Peru.'

'And Templeton?' asked Craig. 'Had he had any previous matrimonial ventures?'

'No, none. Of course he had had love affairs, mostly with the country-club set. He had known Miss Laporte pretty well, too, while he was in law school in New York. But when he settled down to work he seems to have forgotten all about the girls for a couple of years or so. He was very anxious to get ahead, and let nothing stand in his way. He was admitted to the bar and taken in by his father as junior member of the firm of Templeton, Mills & Templeton. Not long ago he was appointed a special master to take testimony in the get-rich-quick-company prosecutions, and I happen to know that he was making good in the investigation.'

Kennedy nodded. 'What sort of fellow personally was Templeton?' he asked.

'Very popular,' replied the district attorney, 'both at the country club and in his profession in New York. He was a fellow of naturally commanding temperament – the Templetons were always that way. I doubt if many young men even with his chances could have gained such a reputation at thirty-five as his. Socially he was very popular, too, a great catch for all the sly mamas of the country club who had marriageable daughters. He liked automobiles and outdoor sports, and he was strong in politics, too. That was how he got ahead so fast.

'Well, to cut the story short, Templeton met the Wainwright girls again last summer at a resort on Long Island. They had just returned from a long trip abroad, spending most of the time in the Far East with their father, whose firm has business interests in China. The girls were very attractive. They rode and played tennis and golf better than most of the men, and this fall Templeton became a frequent visitor at the Wainwright home in Williston.

'People who know them best tell me that his first attentions were paid to Marian, a very dashing and ambitious young woman. Nearly every day Templeton's car stopped at the house and the girls and some friend of Templeton's in the country club went for a ride. They tell me that at this time Marian always sat with Templeton on the front seat. But after a few weeks the gossips – nothing of that sort ever escapes Williston – said that the occupant of the front seat was Laura. She often drove the car herself and was very clever at it. At any rate, not long after that the engagement was announced.'

As he walked up from the pretty little Williston station Kennedy asked: 'One more question, Mr Whitney. How did Marian take the engagement?'

The district attorney hesitated. 'I will be perfectly frank, Mr Kennedy,' he answered. 'The country-club people tell me that the girls were very cool toward each other. That was why I got that statement from Mrs Wainwright. I wish to be perfectly fair to everyone concerned in this case.'

We found the coroner quite willing to talk, in spite of the fact that the hour was late. 'My friend, Mr Whitney, here, still holds the poison theory,' began the coroner, 'in spite of the fact that everything points absolutely toward asphyxiation. If I had been able to discover the slightest trace of illuminating-gas in the room I should have pronounced it asphyxia at once. All the symptoms accorded with it. But the asphyxia was not caused by escaping illuminating-gas.

'There was an antique charcoal-brazier in the room, and I have ascertained that it was lighted. Now, anything like a brazier will, unless there is proper ventilation, give rise to carbonic oxide or carbon monoxide gas, which is always present in the products of combustion, often to the extent of from five to ten per cent. A very slight quantity of this gas, insufficient even to cause an odour in a room, will give a severe headache, and a case is recorded where a whole family in Glasgow was poisoned without knowing it by the escape of this gas. A little over one per cent of it in the atmosphere is fatal, if breathed for any length of time. You know, it is a product of combustion, and is very deadly – it is the much-dreaded white damp or afterdamp of a mine explosion.

'I'm going to tell you a secret which I have not given out to the press yet. I tried an experiment in a closed room today, lighting the brazier. Some distance from it I placed a cat confined in a cage so it could not escape. In an hour and a half the cat was asphyxiated.'

The coroner concluded with an air of triumph that quite squelched the district attorney.

Kennedy was all attention. 'Have you preserved samples of the blood of Mr Templeton and Miss Wainwright?' he asked.

'Certainly. I have them in my office.'

The coroner, who was also a local physician, led us back into his private office.

'And the cat?' added Craig.

Doctor Nott produced it in a covered basket.

Quickly Kennedy drew off a little of the blood of the cat and held it up to the light along with the human samples. The difference was apparent.

'You see,' he explained, 'carbon monoxide combines firmly with the blood, destroying the red colouring matter of the red corpuscles. No, Doctor, I'm afraid it wasn't carbonic oxide that killed the lovers, although it certainly killed the cat.'

Doctor Nott was crestfallen, but still unconvinced. 'If my whole medical reputation were at stake,' he repeated, 'I should still be compelled to swear to asphyxia. I've seen it too often, to make a mistake. Carbonic oxide or not, Templeton and Miss Wainwright were asphyxiated.'

It was now Whitney's chance to air his theory.

'I have always inclined toward the cyanide-of-potassium theory, either that it was administered in a drink or perhaps injected by a needle,' he said. 'One of the chemists has reported that there was a possibility of slight traces of cyanide in the mouths.'

'If it had been cyanide,' replied Craig, looking reflectively at the two jars before him on the table, 'these blood specimens would be blue in colour and clotted. But they are not. Then, too, there is a substance in the saliva which is used in the process of digestion. It gives a reaction which might very easily be mistaken for a slight trace of cyanide. I think that explains what the chemist discovered; no more, no less. The cyanide theory does not fit.'

'One chemist hinted at nux vomica,' volunteered the coroner. 'He said it wasn't nux vomica, but that the blood test showed something very much like it. Oh, we've looked for morphine chloroform, ether, all the ordinary poisons, besides some of the little known alkaloids. Believe me, Professor Kennedy, it was asphyxia.'

I could tell by the look that crossed Kennedy's face that at last a ray of light had pierced the darkness. 'Have you any spirits of turpentine in the office?' he asked.

The coroner shook his head and took a step toward the telephone as if to call the drug-store in town.

'Or ether?' interrupted Craig. 'Ether will do.'

'Oh, yes, plenty of ether.'

Craig poured a little of one of the blood samples from the jar into a tube and added a few drops of ether. A cloudy dark precipitate formed. He smiled quietly and said, half to himself, 'I thought so.'

'What is it?' asked the coroner eagerly. 'Nux vomica?'

Craig shook his head as he stared at the black precipitate. 'You were perfectly right about the asphyxiation, Doctor,' he remarked slowly, 'but wrong as to the cause. It wasn't carbon monoxide or illuminating-gas. And you, Mr Whitney, were right about the poison, too. Only it is a poison neither of you ever heard of.'

'What is it?' we asked simultaneously.

'Let me take these samples and make some further tests. I am sure of it, but it is new to me. Wait till tomorrow night, when my chain of evidence is completed. Then you are all cordially invited to attend at my laboratory at the university. I'll ask you, Mr Whitney, to come armed with a warrant for John or Jane Doe. Please see that the Wainwrights, particularly Marian, are present. You can tell Inspector O'Connor that Mr Vanderdyke and Mrs Ralston are required as material witnesses – anything so long as you are sure that these five persons are present. Goodnight, gentlemen.'

We rode back to the city in silence, but as we neared the station, Kennedy remarked: 'You see, Walter, these people are like the newspapers. They are floundering around in a sea of unrelated facts. There is more than they think back of this crime. I've been revolving in my mind how it will be possible to get some inkling about this concession of Vanderdyke's, the mining claim of Mrs Ralston, and the exact itinerary of the Wainwright trip in the Far East. Do you think you can get that information for me? I think it will take me all day tomorrow to isolate this poison and get things in convincing shape on that score. Meanwhile if you can see Vanderdyke and Mrs Ralston you can help me a great deal. I am sure you will find them very interesting people.'

'I have been told that she is quite a female high financier,' I replied, tacitly accepting Craig's commission. 'Her story is that her claim is situated near the mine of a group of powerful American capitalists, who are opposed to having any competition, and on the strength of that story she has been raking in the money right and left. I don't know Vanderdyke, never heard of him before, but no doubt he has some equally interesting game.'

'Don't let them think you connect them with the case, however,' cautioned Craig.

Early the next morning I started out on my quest for facts, though not so early but that Kennedy had preceded me to his work in his laboratory. It was not very difficult to get Mrs Ralston to talk about her troubles with the government. In fact, I did not even have to broach the subject of the death of Templeton. She volunteered the information that in his handling of her case he had been very unjust to her, in spite of the fact that she had known him well a long time ago. She even hinted that she believed he represented the combination of capitalists who were using the government to aid their own monopoly and prevent the development of her mine. Whether it was an obsession of her mind, or merely part of her clever scheme, I could not make out. I noted, however, that when she spoke of Templeton it was in a studied, impersonal way, and that she was at pains to lay the blame for the governmental interference rather on the rival mine owners.

It quite surprised me when I found from the directory that Vanderdyke's office was on the floor below in the same building. Like Mrs Ralston's, it was open, but not doing business, pending the investigation by the Post-Office Department.

Vanderdyke was a type of which I had seen many before. Well dressed to the extreme, he displayed all those evidences of prosperity which are the stock in trade of the man with securities to sell. He grasped my hand when I told him I was going to present the other side of the Post-Office cases and held it between both of his as if he had known me all his life. Only the fact that he had never seen me before prevented his calling me by my first name. I took mental note of his stock of jewellery, the pin in his tie that might almost have been the Hope diamond, the heavy watch chain across his chest, and a very brilliant seal ring of lapis lazuli on the hand that grasped mine. He saw me looking at it and smiled.

'My dear fellow, we have deposits of that stuff that would make a fortune if we could get the machinery to get at it. Why, sir, there is lapis lazuli enough on our claim to make enough ultramarine paint to supply all the artists to the end of the world. Actually we could afford to crush it up and sell it as paint. And that is merely incidental to the other things on the concession. The asphalt's the thing. That's where the big money is. When we get started, sir, the old asphalt trust will simply melt away, melt away.'

He blew a cloud of tobacco smoke and let it dissolve significantly in the air.

When it came to talking about the suits, however, Vanderdyke was not so communicative as Mrs Ralston, but he was also not so bitter against either the Post-Office or Templeton.

'Poor Templeton,' he said. 'I used to know him years ago when we were boys. Went to school with him and all that sort of thing, you know, but until I ran across him, or rather he ran across me, in this investigation I hadn't heard much about him. Pretty clever fellow he was, too. The state will miss him, but my lawyer tells me that we should have won the suit anyhow, even if that unfortunate tragedy hadn't occurred. Most unaccountable, wasn't it? I've read about it in the papers for old time's sake, and can make nothing out of it.'

I said nothing, but wondered how he could pass so lightheartedly over the death of the woman who had once been his wife. However, I said nothing. The result was he launched forth again on the riches of his Venezuelan concession and loaded me down with 'literature,' which I crammed into my pocket for future reference.

My next step was to drop into the office of a Spanish-American paper whose editor was especially well informed on South American affairs.

'Do I know Mrs Ralston?' he repeated, thoughtfully lighting one of those black cigarettes that look so vicious and are so mild. 'I should say so. I'll tell you a little story about her. Three or four years ago she turned up in Caracas. I don't know who Mr Ralston was – perhaps there never was any Mr Ralston. Anyhow, she got in with the official circle of the Castro government and was very successful as an adventuress. She has considerable business ability and represented a certain group of Americans. But, if you recall, when Castro was eliminated pretty nearly everyone who had stood high with him went, too. It seems that a number of the old concessionaires played the game on both sides. This particular group had a man named Vanderdyke on the anti-Castro side. So, when Mrs Ralston went, she just quietly sailed by way of Panama to the other side of the continent, to Peru – they paid her well – and Vanderdyke took the title role.

'Oh, yes, she and Vanderdyke were very good friends, very, indeed. I think they must have known each other here in the States. Still they played their parts well at the time. Since things have settled down in Venezuela, the concessionaires have found no further use for Vanderdyke either, and here they are, Vanderdyke and Mrs Ralston, both in New York now, with two of the most outrageous schemes of financing ever seen on Broad Street. They have offices in the same building, they are together a great deal, and now I hear that the state attorney-general is after both of them.'

With this information and a very meagre report of the Wainwright trip to the Far East, which had taken in some out-of-the-way places apparently, I hastened back to Kennedy. He was surrounded by bottles, tubes, jars, retorts, Bunsen burners, everything in the science and art of chemistry, I thought.

I didn't like the way he looked. His hand was unsteady, and his eyes looked badly, but he seemed quite put out when I suggested that he was working too hard over the case. I was worried about him, but rather than say anything to offend him I left him for the rest of the afternoon, only dropping in before dinner to make sure that he would not forget to eat something. He was then completing his preparations for the evening. They were of the simplest kind, apparently. In fact, all I could see was an apparatus which consisted of a rubber funnel, inverted and attached to a rubber tube which led in turn into a jar about a quarter full of water. Through the stopper of the jar another tube led to a tank of oxygen.

There were several jars of various liquids on the table and a number of chemicals. Among other things was a sort of gourd, encrusted with a black substance, and in a corner was a box from which sounds issued as if it contained something alive.

I did not trouble Kennedy with questions, for I was only too glad when he consented to take a brisk walk and join me in a thick porterhouse.

It was a large party that gathered in Kennedy's laboratory that night, one of the largest he had ever had. Mr and Mrs Wainwright and Miss Marian came, the ladies heavily veiled. Doctor Nott and Mr Whitney were among the first to arrive. Later came Mr Vanderdyke and last of all Mrs Ralston with Inspector O'Connor. Altogether it was an unwilling party.

'I shall begin,' said Kennedy, 'by going over, briefly, the facts in this case.'

Tersely he summarised it, to my surprise laying great stress on the proof that the couple had been asphyxiated.

'But it was no ordinary asphyxiation,' he continued. 'We have to deal in this case with a poison which is apparently among the most subtle known. A particle of matter so minute as to be hardly distinguishable by the naked eye, on the point of a needle or a lancet, a prick of the skin scarcely felt under any circumstances and which would pass quite unheeded if the attention were otherwise engaged, and not all the power in the world – unless one was fully prepared – could save the life of the person in whose skin the puncture had been made.'

Craig paused a moment, but no one showed any evidence of being more than ordinarily impressed.

'This poison, I find, acts on the so-called endplates of the muscles and nerves. It produces complete paralysis, but not loss of consciousness, sensation, circulation, or respiration until the end approaches. It seems to be one of the most powerful sedatives I have ever heard of. When introduced in even a minute quantity it produces death finally by asphyxiation – by paralysing the muscles of respiration. This asphyxia is what so puzzled the coroner.

'I will now inject a little of the blood serum of the victims into a white mouse.'

He took a mouse from the box I had seen, and with a needle injected the serum. The mouse did not even wince, so lightly did he touch it, but as we watched, its life seemed gently to ebb away, without pain and without struggle. Its breath simply seemed to stop.

Next he took the gourd I had seen on the table and with a knife scraped off just the minutest particle of the black licorice-like stuff that encrusted it. He dissolved the particle in some alcohol and with a sterilised needle repeated his experiment on a second mouse. The effect was precisely similar to that produced by the blood on the first.

It did not seem to me that anyone showed any emotion except possibly the slight exclamation that escaped Miss Marian Wainwright. I fell to wondering whether it was prompted by a soft heart or a guilty conscience.

We were all intent on what Craig was doing, especially Doctor Nott, who now broke in with a question.

'Professor Kennedy, may I ask a question? Admitting that the first mouse died in an apparently similar manner to the second, what proof have you that the poison is the same in both cases? And if it is the same can you show that it affects human beings in the same way, and that enough of it has been discovered in the blood of the victims to have caused their death? In other words, I want the last doubt set aside. How do you know absolutely that this poison which you discovered in my office last night in that black precipitate when you added the ether – how do you know that it asphyxiated the victims?'

If ever Craig startled me it was by his quiet reply. 'I've isolated it in their blood, extracted it, sterilised it, and I've tried it on myself.'

In breathless amazement, with eyes riveted on Craig, we listened.

'Altogether I was able to recover from the blood samples of

both of the victims of this crime six centigrams of the poison,' he pursued. 'Starting with two centigrams of it as a moderate dose, I injected it into my right arm subcutaneously. Then I slowly worked my way up to three and then four centigrams. They did not produce any very appreciable results other than to cause some dizziness, slight vertigo, a considerable degree of lassitude, and an extremely painful headache of rather unusual duration. But five centigrams considerably improved on this. It caused a degree of vertigo and lassitude that was most distressing, and six centigrams, the whole amount which I had recovered from the samples of blood, gave me the fright of my life right here in this laboratory this afternoon.

'Perhaps I was not wise in giving myself so large an injection on a day when I was overheated and below par otherwise because of the strain I have been under in handling this case. However that may be, the added centigram produced so much more on top of the five centigrams previously taken that for a time I had reason to fear that that additional centigram was just the amount needed to bring my experiments to a permanent close.

'Within three minutes of the time of injection the dizziness and vertigo had become so great as to make walking seem impossible. In another minute the lassitude rapidly crept over me, and the serious disturbance of my breathing made it apparent to me that walking, waving my arms, anything, was imperative. My lungs felt glued up, and the muscles of my chest refused to work. Everything swam before my eyes, and I was soon reduced to walking up and down the laboratory with halting steps, only preventing falling on the floor by holding fast to the edge of this table. It seemed to me that I spent hours gasping for breath. It reminded me of what I once experienced in the Cave of the Winds of Niagara, where water is more abundant in the atmosphere than air. My watch afterward indicated only about twenty minutes of extreme distress, but that twenty minutes is one never to be forgotten, and I advise you all, if you ever are so foolish as to try the experiment, to remain below the five-centigram limit.

'How much was administered to the victims, Doctor Nott, I cannot say, but it must have been a good deal more than I took.

Six centigrams, which I recovered from these small samples, are only nine-tenths of a grain. Yet you see what effect it had. I trust that answers your question.'

Doctor Nott was too overwhelmed to reply.

'And what is this deadly poison?' continued Craig, anticipating our thoughts. 'I have been fortunate enough to obtain a sample of it from the Museum of Natural History. It comes in a little gourd, or often a calabash. This is in a gourd. It is blackish brittle stuff encrusting the sides of the gourd just as if it was poured in in the liquid state and left to dry. Indeed, that is just what has been done by those who manufacture this stuff after a lengthy and somewhat secret process.'

He placed the gourd on the edge of the table where we could all see it. I was almost afraid even to look at it.

'The famous traveller, Sir Robert Schomburgh, first brought it into Europe, and Darwin has described it. It is now an article of commerce and is to be found in the United States Pharmacopoeia as a medicine, though of course it is used in only very minute quantities, as a heart stimulant.'

Craig opened a book to a place he had marked:

'At least one person in this room will appreciate the local colour of a little incident I am going to read – to illustrate what death from this poison is like. Two natives of the part of the world whence it comes were one day hunting. They were armed with blowpipes and quivers full of poisoned darts made of thin charred pieces of bamboo tipped with this stuff. One of them aimed a dart. It missed the object overhead, glanced off the tree, and fell down on the hunter himself. This is how the other native reported the result:

'"Quacca takes the dart out of his shoulder. Never a word. Puts it in his quiver and throws it in the stream. Gives me his blowpipe for his little son. Says to me goodbye for his wife and the village. Then he lies down. His tongue talks no longer. No sight in his eyes. He folds his arms. He rolls over slowly. His mouth moves without sound. I feel his heart. It goes fast and then slow. It stops. Quacca has shot his last woorali dart."'

We looked at each other, and the horror of the thing sank deep into our minds. Woorali. What was it? There were many travellers in the room who had been in the Orient, home of poisons, and in South America. Which one had run across the poison?

'Woorali, or curare,' said Craig slowly, 'is the well-known poison with which the South American Indians of the upper Orinoco tip their arrows. Its principal ingredient is derived from the Strychnos toxifera tree, which yields also the drug nux vomica.'

A great light dawned on me. I turned quickly to where Vanderdyke was sitting next to Mrs Ralston, and a little behind her. His stony stare and laboured breathing told me that he had read the purport of Kennedy's actions.

'For God's sake, Craig,' I gasped. 'An emetic, quick – Vanderdyke.'

A trace of a smile flitted over Vanderdyke's features, as much as to say that he was beyond our interference.

'Vanderdyke,' said Craig, with what seemed to me a brutal calmness, 'then it was you who were the visitor who last saw Laura Wainwright and John Templeton alive. Whether you shot a dart at them I do not know. But you are the murderer.'

Vanderdyke raised his hand as if to assent. It fell back limp, and I noted the ring of the bluest lapis lazuli.

Mrs Ralston threw herself toward him. 'Will you not do something? Is there no antidote? Don't let him die!' she cried.

'You are the murderer,' repeated Kennedy, as if demanding a final answer.

Again the hand moved in confession, and he feebly moved the finger on which shone the ring.

Our attention was centred on Vanderdyke. Mrs Ralston, unobserved, went to the table and picked up the gourd. Before O'Connor could stop her she had rubbed her tongue on the black substance inside. It was only a little bit, for O'Connor quickly dashed it from her lips and threw the gourd through the window, smashing the glass.

'Kennedy,' he shouted frantically, 'Mrs Ralston has swallowed some of it.'

Kennedy seemed so intent on Vanderdyke that I had to repeat the remark.

Without looking up, he said: 'Oh, one can swallow it – it's strange, but it is comparatively inert if swallowed even in a pretty good-sized quantity. I doubt if Mrs Ralston ever heard of it before except by hearsay. If she had, she'd have scratched herself with it instead of swallowing it.'

If Craig had been indifferent to the emergency of Vanderdyke before, he was all action now that the confession had been made. In an instant Vanderdyke was stretched on the floor and Craig had taken out the apparatus I had seen during the afternoon.

'I am prepared for this,' he exclaimed quickly. 'Here is the apparatus for artificial respiration. Nott, hold that rubber funnel over his nose, and start the oxygen from the tank. Pull his tongue forward so it won't fall down his throat and choke him. I'll work his arms. Walter, make a tourniquet of your handkerchief and put it tightly on the muscles of his left arm. That may keep some of the poison in his arm from spreading into the rest of his body. This is the only antidote known – artificial respiration.'

Kennedy was working feverishly, going through the motions of first aid to a drowned man. Mrs Ralston was on her knees beside Vanderdyke, kissing his hands and forehead whenever Kennedy stopped for a minute, and crying softly.

'Schuyler, poor boy, I wonder how you could have done it. I was with him that day. We rode up in his car, and as we passed through Williston he said he would stop a minute and wish Templeton luck. I didn't think it strange, for he said he had nothing any longer against Laura Wainwright, and Templeton only did his duty as a lawyer against us. I forgave John for prosecuting us, but Schuyler didn't, after all. Oh, my poor boy, why did you do it? We could have gone somewhere else and started all over again – it wouldn't have been the first time.'

At last came the flutter of an eyelid and a voluntary breath or two. Vanderdyke seemed to realise where he was. With a last supreme effort he raised his hand and drew it slowly across his face. Then he fell back, exhausted by the effort.

But he had at last put himself beyond the reach of the law. There was no tourniquet that would confine the poison now in the scratch across his face. Back of those lack-lustre eyes he heard and knew, but could not move or speak. His voice was gone, his limbs, his face, his chest, and, last, his eyes. I wondered if it were possible to conceive a more dreadful torture than that endured by a mind which so witnessed the dying of one organ after another of its own body, shut up, as it were, in the fullness of life, within a corpse.

I looked in bewilderment at the scratch on his face. 'How did he do it?' I asked.

Carefully Craig drew off the azure ring and examined it. In that part which surrounded the blue lapis lazuli, he indicated a hollow point, concealed. It worked with a spring and communicated with a little receptacle behind, in such a way that the murderer could give the fatal scratch while shaking hands with his victim.

I shuddered, for my hand had once been clasped by the one wearing that poison ring, which had sent Templeton, and his fiancée and now Vanderdyke himself, to their deaths.

MADELYN MACK

Created by Hugh Cosgro Weir (1884–1934)

A fascinating female Sherlock, Madelyn Mack is a young and glamorous American woman with a genius for criminology who works as a private detective in New York. (Although the story below is set in Boston.) Like Conan Doyle's character, she is possessed of startling deductive abilities. She has her own Watson in the journalist Nora Noraker, who narrates her adventures, and, also like Holmes, she has her eccentricities and foibles. She collects gramophone records, commissioning exclusive performances from famous musicians. During particularly difficult cases, she stores cola berries in a locket around her neck, using them to keep herself awake for days on end. Her creator was Hugh Cosgro Weir, born in Illinois, who had a varied career as a writer, advertising guru, Hollywood screenwriter and magazine publisher. His stories about her first appeared in magazines and then were collected in the volume Miss Madelyn Mack, Detective *in 1914. Weir may have based his character on a real-life woman detective named Mary E Holland who was a well-known figure in Chicago in the first two decades of the twentieth century. Madelyn Mack, now nearly forgotten, was popular enough in her day to be the heroine of several films starring Alice Joyce, an actress who appeared in more than 200 movies during the silent era.*

CINDERELLA'S SLIPPER

I

Raymond Rennick might have been going to his wedding instead of to his – death. Spick and span in a new spring suit, he paused just outside the broad arched gates of the Duffield estate and drew his silver cigarette case from his pocket. A self-satisfied smile flashed across his face as he struck a match and inhaled the fragrant odour of the tobacco. It was good tobacco, very good tobacco – and Senator Duffield's private secretary was something of a judge!

For a moment Rennick lingered. It was a day to banish uncomfortable thoughts, to smooth the rough edges of a man's problems – and burdens. As the secretary glanced up at the soft blue sky, the reflection swept his mind that his own future was as free from clouds. It was a pleasing reflection. Perhaps the cigarette, perhaps the day helped to deepen it as he swung almost jauntily up the winding driveway toward the square white house commanding the terraced lawn beyond.

Just ahead of him a maple tree, standing alone, rustled gaily in its spring foliage like a woman calling attention to her new finery. It was all so fresh and beautiful and innocent! Rennick felt a tingling thrill in his blood. Unconsciously he tossed away his cigarette. He reached the rustling maple and passed it...

From behind the gnarled trunk, a shadow darted. A figure sprang at his shoulders, with the long blade of a dagger awkwardly poised. There was a flash of steel in the sunlight...

It was perhaps ten minutes later that they found him. He had fallen face downward at the edge of the driveway, with his body half across the velvet green of the grass. A thin thread of red, creeping from the wound in his breast, was losing itself in the sod.

One hand was doubled, as in a desperate effort at defence. His glasses were twisted under his shoulders. Death must have been nearly instantaneous. The dagger had reached his heart at the first thrust. One might have fancied an expression of overpowering amazement in the staring eyes. That was all. The weapon had caught him squarely on the left side. He had evidently whirled toward the assassin almost at the instant of the blow.

Whether in the second left him of life he had recognized his assailant, and the recognition had made the death-blow the quicker and the surer, were questions that only deepened the horror of the noon-day.

As though to emphasize the hour, the mahogany clock in Senator Duffield's library rang out its twelve monotonous chimes as John Dorrence, his valet, beat sharply on the door. The echo of the nervous tattoo was lost in an unanswering silence. Dorrence repeated his knock before he brought an impatient response from beyond the panels.

'Can you come, sir?' the valet burst out. 'Something awful has happened, sir. It's, it's —'

The door was flung open. A ruddy-faced man with thick white hair and grizzled moustache, and the hints of a nervous temperament showing in his eyes and voice, sprang into the hall. Somebody once remarked that Senator Duffield was Mark Twain's double. The Senator took the comparison as a compliment, perhaps because it was a woman who made it.

Dorrence seized his master by the sleeve, which loss of dignity did more to impress the Senator with the gravity of the situation than all of the servant's excitable words.

'Mr Rennick, sir, has been stabbed, sir, on the lawn, and Miss Beth, sir —'

Senator Duffield staggered against the wall. The valet's alarm swerved to another channel.

'Shall I get the brandy, sir?'

'Brandy?' the Senator repeated vaguely. The next instant, as though grasping the situation anew, he sprang down the hall with the skirts of his frock coat flapping against his knees. At the door of the veranda, he whirled.

'Get the doctor on the 'phone, Dorrence — Redfield, if Scott is out. Let him know it's a matter of minutes! And, Dorrence —'

'Yes, sir!'

'Tell the telephone girl that, if this leaks to the newspapers, I will have the whole office discharged!'

A shifting group on the edge of the lawn, with that strange sense of awkwardness which sudden death brings, showed the scene of the tragedy.

The circle fell back as the Senator's figure appeared. On the grass, Rennick's body still lay where it had fallen — suggesting a skater who has ignominiously collapsed on the ice rather than a man stabbed to the heart. The group had been wondering at the fact in whispered monosyllables.

A kneeling girl was bending over the secretary's body. It was not until Senator Duffield had spoken her name twice that she glanced up. In her eyes was a grief so wild that for a moment he was held dumb.

'Come, Beth,' he said, gently, 'this is no place for you.'

At once the white-faced girl became the central figure of the situation. If she heard him, she gave no sign. The Senator caught her shoulder and pushed her slowly away. One of the women-servants took her arm. Curiously enough, the two were the only members of the family that had been called to the scene.

The Senator swung on the group with a return of his aggressiveness.

'Someone, who can talk fast and to the point, tell me the story. Burke, you have a ready tongue. How did it happen?'

The groom – a much-tanned young fellow in his early twenties – touched his cap.

'I don't know, sir. No one knows. Mr Rennick was lying here, stabbed, when we found him. He was already dead.'

'But surely there was some cry, some sound of a scuffle?'

The groom shook his head. 'If there was, sir, none of us heard it. We all liked Mr Rennick, sir. I would have gone through fire and water if he needed my help. If there had been an outcry loud enough to reach the stable, I would have been there on the jump!'

'Do you mean to tell me that Rennick could have been struck down in the midst of fifteen or twenty people with no one the wiser? It's ridiculous, impossible!'

Burke squared his shoulders, with an almost unconscious suggestion of dignity. 'I am telling you the truth, sir!'

The Senator's glance dropped to his secretary's body and he looked up with a shudder. Then, as though with an effort, his eyes returned to the huddled form, and he stood staring down at the dead man, with a frown knitting his brow. Once he jerked his head toward the gardener with the curt question, 'Who found him?' Jenkins shambled forward uneasily. 'I did, sir. I hope you don't think I disturbed the body?'

The Senator shrugged his shoulders impatiently. He did not raise his head again until the sound of a motor in the driveway broke the tension. The surgeon had arrived. Almost at the same moment there was a cry from Jenkins.

The gardener stood perhaps a half a dozen yards from the body, staring at an object hidden in the grass at his feet. He stooped and raised it. It was a woman's slipper!

As a turn of his head showed him the eyes of the group turned in his direction, he walked across to Senator Duffield, holding his find at arm's length, as though its dainty outlines might conceal an adder's nest.

The slipper was of black suede, high-heeled and slender, tied with a broad, black ribbon. One end of the ribbon was broken and stained as though it had tripped its owner. On the thin sole were cakes of the peculiar red clay of the driveway.

It might have been unconscious magnetism that caused the Senator suddenly to turn his eyes in the direction of his daughter. She was swaying on the arm of the servant.

Throwing off the support of the woman, she took two quick steps forward, with her hand flung out as though to tear the slipper from him. And then, without a word, she fell prone on the grass.

II

The telephone in my room must have been jangling a full moment before I struggled out of my sleep and raised myself to my elbow. It was with a feeling of distinct rebellion that I slipped into my kimono and slippers and shuffled across to the sputtering instrument in the corner. From eight in the morning until eight in the evening, I had been on racking duty in the Farragut poison trial, and the belated report of the wrangling jury, at an hour which made any sort of a meal impossible until after ten, had left me worn out physically and mentally. I glanced at my watch as I snapped the receiver to my ear. It lacked barely fifteen minutes of midnight. An unearthly hour to call a woman out of bed, even if she is past the age of sentimental dreams! 'Well?' I growled.

A laugh answered me at the other end of the wire. I would have flung the receiver back to the hook and myself back to bed had I not recognized the tones. There is only one person in the world, except the tyrant at our city editor's desk, who would arouse me at midnight. But I had thought this person separated from me by twelve hundred miles of ocean.

'Madelyn Mack!' I gasped.

The laughter ceased. 'Madelyn Mack it is!' came back the answer, now reduced to a tone of decorous gravity. 'Pardon my merriment, Nora. The mental picture of your huddled form —'

'But I thought you in Jamaica!' I broke in, now thoroughly awake.

'I was — until Saturday. Our steamer came out of quarantine at four o'clock this afternoon. As it develops, I reached here at the psychological moment.'

I kicked a rocker to my side and dropped into it with a rueful glance at the rumpled sheets of the bed. With Madelyn Mack at the telephone at midnight, only one conclusion was possible; and such a conclusion shattered all thought of sleep.

'Have you read the evening dispatches from Boston, Nora?'

'I have read nothing — except the report of the Farragut jury!' I returned crisply. 'Why?'

'If you had, you would perhaps divine the reason of my call. I have been retained in the Rennick murder case. I'm taking the one-thirty sleeper for Boston. I secured our berths just before I telephoned.'

'Our berths!'

'I am taking you with me. Now that you are up, you may as well dress and ring for a taxicab. I will meet you at the Roanoke hotel.'

'But,' I protested, 'don't you think —'

'Very well, if you don't care to go! That settles it!'

'Oh, I will be there!' I said with an air of resignation. 'Ten minutes to dress, and fifteen minutes for the taxi!'

'I will add five minutes for incidentals,' Madelyn replied and hung up the receiver.

The elevator boy at 'The Occident,' where I had my modest apartment, had become accustomed to the strange hours and strange visitors of a newspaper woman during my three years' residence. He opened the door with a grin of sympathy as the car reached my floor. As though to give more active expression to his feelings he caught up my bag and gave it a place of honour on his own stool.

'Going far?' he queried as I alighted at the main corridor.

'I may be back in twenty-four hours and I may not be back for twenty-four days,' I answered cautiously – I knew Madelyn Mack! As I waited for the whir of the taxicab, I appropriated the evening paper on the night clerk's desk. The Rennick murder case had been given a three-column head on the front page. If I had not been so absorbed in the Farragut trial, it could not have escaped me. I had not finished the headlines, however, when the taxi, with a promptness almost uncanny, rumbled up to the curb.

I threw myself back against the cushions, switched on the electric light, and spread my paper over my knee, as the chauffeur turned off toward Fifth Avenue. The story was well written and had made much of a few facts. Trust my newspaper instinct to know that! I had expected a fantastic puzzle – when it could spur Madelyn into action within six hours after her landing – but I was hardly anticipating a problem such as I could read between rather than in the lines of type before me. Long before the 'Roanoke' loomed into view, I had forgotten my lost sleep.

The identity of Raymond Rennick's assassin was as baffling as in the first moments of the discovery of the tragedy. There had been no arrests – nor hint of any. From the moment when the secretary had turned into the gate of the Duffield yard until the finding of his body, all trace of his movements had been lost as effectually as though the darkness of midnight had enveloped him, instead of the sunlight of noon. More than ten minutes could not have elapsed between his entrance into the grounds and the discovery of his murder – perhaps not more than five – but they had been sufficient for the assassin to effect a complete escape.

There was not even the shadow of a motive. Raymond Rennick was one of those few men who seemed to be without an enemy. In an official capacity, his conduct was without a blemish. In a social capacity, he was admittedly one of the most popular men in Brookline – among both sexes. Rumour had it, apparently on unquestioned authority, that the announcement of his engagement to Beth Duffield was to have been an event of the early summer. This fact was in my mind as I stared out into the darkness.

On a sudden impulse, I opened the paper again. From an inside page the latest photograph of the Senator's daughter, taken at a fashionable Boston studio, smiled up at me. It was an excellent likeness as I remembered her at the inaugural ball the year before – a wisp of a girl, with a mass of black hair, which served to emphasize her frailness. I studied the picture with a frown. There was a sense of familiarity in its outlines, which certainly our casual meeting could not explain. Then, abruptly, my thoughts flashed back to the crowded court room of the afternoon – and I remembered.

In the prisoner's dock I saw again the figure of Beatrice Farragut, slender, fragile, her white face, her sombre gown, her eyes fixed like those of a frightened lamb on the jury which was to give her life – or death.

'She poison her husband?' had buzzed the whispered comments at my shoulders during the weary weeks of the trial. 'She couldn't harm a butterfly!' Like a mocking echo, the tones of the foreman had sounded the answering verdict of murder – in the first degree. And in New York this meant –

Why had Beatrice Farragut suggested Beth Duffield? Or was it Beth Duffield who had suggested – I crumpled the paper into a heap and tossed it from the window in disgust at my morbid imagination. B-u-r-r-h! And yet they say that a New York newspaper woman has no nerves!

A voice hailed us from the darkness and a white-gowned figure sprang out on to the walk. As the chauffeur brought the machine to a halt, Madelyn Mack caught my hands.

Her next two actions were thoroughly characteristic.

Whirling to the driver, she demanded shortly, 'How soon can you make the Grand Central Station?'

The man hesitated. 'Can you give me twenty minutes?'

'Just! We will leave here at one sharp. You will wait, please!'

Having thus disposed of the chauffeur – Madelyn never gave a thought to the matter of expense! – she seized my arm and pushed me through the entrance of the 'Roanoke' as nonchalantly as though we had parted six hours before instead of six weeks.

'I hope you enjoyed Jamaica?' I ventured.

'Did you read the evening papers on the way over?' she returned as easily as though I had not spoken.

'One,' I answered shortly. Madelyn's habit of ignoring my queries grated most uncomfortably at times.

'Then you know what has been published concerning the case?'

I nodded. 'I imagine that you can add considerable.'

'As a matter of fact, I know less than the reporters!' Madelyn threw open the door of her room. 'You have interviewed Senator Duffield on several occasions, have you not, Nora?'

'You might say on several delicate occasions if you cared to!'

'You can tell me then whether the Senator is in the habit of polishing his glasses when he is in a nervous mood?'

A rather superior smile flashed over my face. 'I assure you that Senator Duffield never wears glasses on any occasion!'

Something like a chuckle came from Madelyn.

'Perhaps you can do as well on another question. You will observe in these newspapers four different photographs of the murdered secretary. Naturally, they bear many points of similarity – they were all taken in the last three years – but they contain one feature in common which puzzles me. Does it impress you in the same way?'

I glanced at the group of photographs doubtfully. Three of them were obviously newspaper 'snap-shots,' taken of the secretary while in the company of Senator Duffield. The fourth was a reproduction showing a conventional cabinet photograph. They showed a clean-shaven, well-built young man of thirty or thereabouts; tall, and I should say inclined to athletics. I turned from the newspapers to Madelyn with a shrug.

'I am afraid I don't quite follow you,' I admitted ruefully. 'There is nothing at all out of the ordinary in any of them that I can catch.'

Madelyn carefully clipped the pictures and placed them under the front cover of her black morocco note-book. As she did so, a clock chimed the hour of one. We both pushed back our chairs.

As we stepped into the taxicab, Madelyn tapped my arm. 'I

wonder if Raymond Rennick polished his glasses when he was nervous?' she asked musingly.

III

Boston, from the viewpoint of the South Station at half past seven in the morning, suggests to me a rheumatic individual climbing stiffly out of bed. Boston distinctly resents anything happening before noon. I'll wager that nearly every important event that she has contributed to history occurred after lunch-time!

If Madelyn Mack had expected to have to find her way to the Duffield home without a guide, she was pleasantly disappointed. No less a person than the Senator himself was waiting for us at the train-gate – a somewhat dishevelled Senator, it must be confessed, with the stubble of a day-old beard showing eloquently how his peace of mind and the routine of his habits had been shattered. As he shook hands with us he made an obvious attempt to recover something of his ease of manner.

'I trust that you had a pleasant night's rest,' he ventured, as he led the way across the station to his automobile.

'Much pleasanter than you had, I fear,' replied Madelyn.

The Senator sighed. 'As a matter of fact, I found sleep hopeless; I spent most of the night with my cigar. The suggestion of meeting your train came as a really welcome relief.'

As we stepped into the waiting motor, a leather-lunged newsboy thrust a bundle of heavy-typed papers into our faces. The Senator whirled with a curt dismissal on his tongue when Madelyn thrust a coin toward the lad and swept a handful of flapping papers into her lap.

'There is absolutely nothing new in the case, Miss Mack, I assure you,' the Senator said impatiently. 'The reporters have pestered me like so many leeches. The sight of a headline makes me shiver.'

Madelyn bent over her papers without comment. As I settled into the seat by her side, however, and the machine whirled around the corner, I saw that she was not even making a pretence of reading. I watched her with a frown as she turned the pages. There was no question of her interest, but it was not the type that held her attention. I doubted if she was perusing a line of the closely-set columns. It was not until she reached the last paper that I solved the mystery. It was the illustrations that she was studying!

When she finished the heap of papers, she began slowly and even more thoughtfully to go through them again. Now I saw that she was pondering the various photographs of Senator Duffield's family that the newspapers had published. I turned away from her bent form and tapping finger, but there was a magnetism in her abstraction that forced my eyes back to her in spite of myself. As my gaze returned to her, she thrust her gloved hand into the recesses of her bag and drew out her black morocco notebook. From its pages she selected the four newspaper pictures of the murdered secretary that she had offered me the night before. With a twinkle of satisfaction she grouped them about a large, black-bordered picture which stared up at her from the printed page in her lap.

Our ride to the Duffield gate was not a long one. In fact I was so absorbed by my furtive study of Madelyn Mack that I was startled when the chauffeur slackened his speed, and I realized from a straightening of the Senator's bent shoulders that we were nearing our destination.

At the edge of the driveway, a quietly dressed man in a grey suit, who was strolling carelessly back and forth from the gate to the house, eyed us curiously as we passed, and touched his hat to the Senator. I knew at once he was a detective. (Trust a newspaper woman to 'spot' a plain-clothes man, even if he has left his police uniform at home!) Madelyn did not look up and the Senator made no comment.

As we stepped from the machine, a tall girl with severe, almost classical features and a profusion of nut-brown hair which fell away from her forehead without even the suggestion of a ripple, was awaiting us. 'My daughter, Maria,' Senator Duffield announced formally.

Madelyn stepped forward with extended hand. It was evident that Miss Duffield had intended only a brief nod. For an instant she hesitated, with a barely perceptible flush. Then her fingers dropped limply into Madelyn Mack's palm. (I chuckled inwardly at the ill grace with which she did it!)

'This must be a most trying occasion for you,' Madelyn said with a note of sympathy in her voice, which made me stare. Effusiveness of any kind was so foreign to her nature that I frowned as we followed our host into the wide front drawing room. As we entered by one door, a black-gowned, white-haired woman, evidently Mrs Duffield, entered by the opposite door.

In spite of the reserve of the society leader, whose sway might be said to extend to three cities, she darted an appealing glance at Madelyn Mack that melted much of the newspaper cynicism with which I was prepared to greet her. Madelyn crossed the room to her side and spoke a low sentence, that I did not catch, as she took her hand. I found myself again wondering at her unwonted friendliness. She was obviously exerting herself to gain the good will of the Duffield household. Why?

A trim maid, who stared at us as though we were museum freaks, conducted us to our rooms – adjoining apartments at the front of the third floor. The identity of Madelyn Mack had already been noised through the house, and I caught a saucer-eyed glance from a second servant as we passed down the corridor. If the atmosphere of suppressed curiosity was embarrassing my companion, however, she gave no sign of the fact. Indeed, we had hardly time to remove our hats when the breakfast gong rang.

The family was assembling in the old-fashioned dining room when we entered. In addition to the members of the domestic circle whom I have already indicated, my attention was at once caught by two figures who entered just before us. One was a young woman whom it did not need a second glance to tell me was Beth Duffield. Her white face and swollen eyes were evidence enough of her overwrought condition, and I caught myself speculating why she had left her room.

Her companion was a tall, slender young fellow with just the faintest trace of a stoop in his shoulders. As he turned toward us, I saw a handsome though self-indulgent face, to a close observer suggesting evidence of more dissipation than was good for its owner. And, if the newspaper stories of the doings of Fletcher Duffield were true, the facial index was a true one – if I remember rightly, Senator Duffield's son more than once had made prim old Boston town rub her spectacled eyes at the tales of his escapades!

Fletcher Duffield bowed rather abstractedly as he was presented to us, but during the eggs and chops he brightened visibly, and put several curious questions to Madelyn as to her methods of work, which enlivened what otherwise would have been a rather dull half-hour.

As the strokes of nine rang through the room, my companion pushed her chair back.

'What time is the coroner's inquest, Senator?'

Mr Duffield raised his eyebrows at the change in her attitude. 'It is scheduled for eleven o'clock.'

'And when do you expect Inspector Taylor of headquarters?'

'In the course of an hour, I should say, perhaps less. His man, Martin, has been here since yesterday afternoon – you probably saw him as we drove into the yard. I can telephone Mr Taylor, if you wish to see him sooner.'

'That will hardly be necessary, thank you.'

Madelyn walked across to the window. For a moment she stood peering out on to the lawn. Then she stooped, and her hand fumbled with the catch. The window swung open with the noiselessness of well-oiled hinges, and she stepped out on to the verandah, without so much as a glance at the group about the table.

I think the Senator and I rose from our chairs at the same instant. When we reached the window, Madelyn was half across the lawn. Perhaps twenty yards ahead of her towered a huge maple, rustling in the early morning breeze.

I realized that this was the spot where Raymond Rennick had met his death.

In spite of his nervousness, Senator Duffield did not forget his old-fashioned courtliness, which I believe had become second nature to him. Stepping aside with a slight bow, he held the window open for me, following at my shoulder. As we reached the lawn, I saw that the scene of the murder was in plain view from at least one of the principal rooms of the Duffield home.

Madelyn was leaning against the maple when we reached her.

Senator Duffield said gravely, as he pointed to the gnarled trunk, 'You are standing just at the point where the woman waited, Miss Mack.'

'Woman?'

'I refer to the assassin,' the Senator rejoined a trifle impatiently. 'Judging by our fragmentary clues, she must have been hidden behind the trunk when poor Rennick appeared on the driveway. We found her slipper somewhat to the left of the tree – a matter of eight or ten feet, I should say.'

'Oh!' said Madelyn listlessly. I fancied that she was somewhat annoyed that we had followed her.

'An odd clue, that slipper,' the Senator continued with an obvious attempt to maintain the conversation. 'If we were disposed to be fanciful, it might suggest the childhood legend of Cinderella.' Madelyn did not answer. She stood leaning back against the tree with her eyes wandering about the yard. Once I saw her gaze flash down the driveway to the open gate, where the detective, Martin, stood watching us furtively.

'Nora,' she said, without turning, 'will you kindly walk six steps to your right?'

I knew better than to ask the reason for the request. With a shrug, I faced toward the house and came to a pause at the end of the stipulated distance.

'Is Miss Noraker standing where Mr Rennick's body was found, Senator?'

'She will strike the exact spot, I think, if she takes two steps more.'

I had hardly obeyed the suggestion when I caught the swift rustle of skirts behind me. I whirled to see Madelyn's lithe form darting toward me with her right hand raised as though it held a weapon.

'Good!' she cried. 'I call you to witness, Senator, that I was fully six feet away when she turned! Now I want you to take Miss Noraker's place. The instant you hear me behind you – the instant, mind you – I want you to let me know.' She walked back to the tree as the Senator reluctantly changed places with me. I could almost picture the murderess dashing upon her victim as

Madelyn bent forward. The Senator turned his back to us with a rather ludicrous air of bewilderment.

My erratic friend had covered perhaps half of the distance between her and our host when he spun about with a cry of discovery. She paused with a long breath.

'Thank you, Senator. What first attracted your attention to me?'

'The rustle of your dress, of course!' Madelyn turned to me with the first smile of satisfaction I had seen since we entered the Duffield gate.

'Was the same true in your case, Nora?'

I nodded. 'The fact that you are a woman hopelessly betrayed you. If you had not been hampered by petticoats –' Madelyn broke in upon my sentence with that peculiar freedom which she always reserves to herself. 'There are two things I would like to ask of you, Senator, if I may.'

'I am at your disposal, I assure you.'

'I would like to borrow a Boston directory, and the services of a messenger.'

We walked slowly up the driveway, Madelyn again relapsing into her preoccupied silence and Senator Duffield making no effort to induce her to speak.

IV

We had nearly reached the verandah when there was the sound of a motor at the gate, and a red touring car swept into the yard. An elderly, clean-shaven man, in a long frock coat and a broad-brimmed felt hat, was sharing the front seat with the chauffeur. He sprang to the ground with extended hand as our host stepped forward to greet him. The two exchanged half a dozen low sentences at the side of the machine, and then Senator Duffield raised his voice as they approached us.

'Miss Mack, allow me to introduce my colleague, Senator Burroughs.'

'I have heard of you, of course, Miss Mack,' the Senator said genially, raising his broad-brimmed hat with a flourish. 'I am very glad, indeed, that you are able to give us the benefit of your experience in this, er – unfortunate affair. I presume that it is too early to ask if you have developed a theory?'

'I wonder if you would allow me to reverse the question?' Madelyn responded as she took his hand.

'I fear that my detective ability would hardly be of much service to you, eh, Duffield?'

Our host smiled faintly as he turned to repeat to a servant Madelyn's request for a directory and a messenger. Senator Burroughs folded his arms as his chauffeur circled on toward the garage. There was an odd suggestion of nervousness in the whole group. Or was it fancy?

'Have you ever given particular study to the legal angle in your cases, Miss Mack?' The question came from Senator Burroughs as we ascended the steps.

'The legal angle? I am afraid I don't grasp your meaning.'

The Senator's hand moved mechanically toward his cigar case. 'I am a lawyer, and perhaps I argue unduly from a lawyer's viewpoint. We always work from the question of motive, Miss Mack. A professional detective, I believe – or, at least, the average professional detective – tries to find the criminal first and establish his motive afterward.'

'Now, in a case such as this, Senator –'

'In a case such as this, Miss Mack, the trained legal mind would delve first for the motive in Mr Rennick's assassination.'

'And your legal mind, Senator, I presume, has delved for the motive. Has it found it?'

The Senator turned his unlighted cigar reflectively between his lips. 'I have not found it! Eliminating the field of sordid passion and insanity, I divide the motives of the murderer under three heads – robbery, jealousy and revenge. In the present case, I eliminate the first possibility at the outset. There remain then only the two latter.'

'You are interesting. You forget, however, a fourth motive – the strongest spur to crime in the human mind!'

Senator Burroughs took his cigar from his mouth.

'I mean the motive of – fear!' Madelyn said abruptly, as she

243

swept into the house. When I followed her, Senator Burroughs had walked over to the railing and stood staring down at the ground below. He had tossed his cigar away.

In the room where we had breakfasted, one of the stable boys stood awkwardly awaiting Madelyn Mack's orders, while John Dorrence, the valet, was just laying a city directory on the table.

'Nora,' she said, as she turned to the boy, 'will you kindly look up the list of packing houses?'

'Pick out the largest and give me the address,' she continued, as I ran my finger through the closely typed pages. With a growing curiosity, I selected a firm whose prestige was advertised in heavy letters. Madelyn's fountain pen scratched a dozen lines across a sheet of her note-book, and she thrust it into an envelope and extended it to the stable lad.

As the youth backed from the room, Senator Duffield appeared at the window.

'I presume it will be possible for me to see Mr Rennick's body, Senator?' Madelyn Mack asked.

Our host bowed.

'Also, I would like to look at his clothes – the suit he was wearing at the time of his death, I mean – and, when I am through, I want twenty or thirty minutes alone in his room. If Mr Taylor should arrive before I am through, will you kindly let me know?'

'I can assure you, Miss Mack, that the police have been through Mr Rennick's apartment with a microscope.'

'Then there can be no objection to my going through it with mine! By the way, Mr Rennick's glasses – the pair that was found under his body – were packed with his clothes, were they not?'

'Certainly,' the Senator responded.

I did not accompany Madelyn into the darkened room where the corpse of the murdered man was reposing. To my surprise, she rejoined me in less than five minutes.

'What did you find?' I queried as we ascended the stairs.

'A five-inch cut just above the sixth rib.'

'That is what the newspapers said.'

'You are mistaken. They said a three-inch cut. Have you ever tried to plunge a dagger through five inches of human flesh?'

'Certainly not.'

Accustomed as I was to Madelyn Mack's eccentricities, I stood stock still and stared into her face.

'Oh, I'm not a murderess! I refer to my dissecting room experiences.'

We had reached the upper hall when there was a quick movement at my shoulder, and I saw my companion's hand dart behind my waist. Before I could quite grasp the situation, she had caught my right arm in a grip of steel. For an instant I thought she was trying to force me back down the stairs. Then the force of her hold wrung a low cry of pain from my lips. She released me with a rueful apology.

'Forgive me, Nora! For a woman, I pride myself that I have a strong wrist!'

'Yes, I think you have!'

'Perhaps now you can appreciate what I mean when I say that even I haven't strength enough to inflict the wound that killed Raymond Rennick!'

'Then we must be dealing with an Amazon.'

'Would Cinderella's missing slipper fit an Amazon?' she answered drily.

As she finished her sentence, we paused before a closed door which I rightly surmised led into the room of the murdered secretary. Madelyn's hand was on the knob when there was a step behind us, and Senator Duffield joined us with a rough bundle in his hands.

'Mr Rennick's clothes,' he explained. Madelyn nodded.

'Inspector Taylor left them in my care to hold until the inquest.'

Madelyn flung the door open without any comment and led the way inside. Slipping the string from the bundle, she emptied the contents out on to the counterpane of the bed. They comprised the usual warm weather outfit of a well-dressed man, who evidently avoided the extremes of fashion, and she deftly sorted the articles into small neat piles. She glanced up with an expression of impatience.

'I thought you said they were here, Mr Duffield!'

'What?'

'Mr Rennick's glasses! Where are they?'

Senator Duffield fumbled in his pocket. 'I beg your pardon, Miss Mack. I had overlooked them,' he apologized, as he produced a thin paper parcel.

Madelyn carried it to the window and carefully unwrapped it.

'You will find the spectacles rather badly damaged, I fear. One lens is completely ruined.'

Madelyn placed the broken glasses on the sill, and raised the blind to its full height. Then she dropped to her knees and whipped out her microscope. When she arose, her small, black-clad figure was tense with suppressed excitement.

A fat oak chiffonier stood in the corner nearest her. Crossing to its side, she rummaged among the articles that littered its surface, opened and closed the top drawer, and stepped back with an expression of annoyance. A writing table was the next point of her search, with results which I judged to be equally fruitless. She glanced uncertainly from the bed to the three chairs, the only other articles of furniture that the room contained. Then her eyes lighted again as they rested on the broad, carved mantel that spanned the empty fire-place.

It held the usual collection of bric-a-brac of a bachelor's room. At the end farthest from us, however, there was a narrow red case, of which I caught only an indistinct view, when Madelyn's hand closed over it.

She whirled toward us. 'I must ask you to leave me alone now, please!'

The Senator flushed at the peremptory command. I stepped into the hall and he followed me, with a shrug. He was closing the door when Madelyn raised her voice. 'If Inspector Taylor is below, kindly send him up at once!'

'And what about the inquest, Miss Mack?'

'There will be no inquest – today!'

Senator Duffield led the way downstairs without a word. In the hall below, a ruddy-faced man, with grey hair, a thin grey beard and moustache, and a grey suit – suggesting an army officer in civilian clothes – was awaiting us. I could readily imagine that Inspector Taylor was something of a disciplinarian in the Boston police department. Also, relying on Madelyn Mack's estimate, he was one of the three shrewdest detectives on the American continent.

Senator Duffield hurried toward him with a suggestion of relief. 'Miss Mack is upstairs, Inspector, and requested me to send you to her the moment you arrived.'

'Is she in Mr Rennick's room?'

The Senator nodded. The Inspector hesitated as though about to ask another question and then, as though thinking better of it, bowed and turned to the stairs.

Inspector Taylor was one of those few policemen who had the honour of being numbered among Madelyn Mack's personal friends, and I fancied that he welcomed the news of her arrival.

Fletcher Duffield was chatting somewhat aimlessly with Senator Burroughs as we sauntered out into the yard again. None of the ladies of the family was visible. The plain-clothes man was still lounging disconsolately in the vicinity of the gate. There was a sense of unrest in the scene, a vague expectancy. Although no one voiced the suggestion, we might all have been waiting to catch the first clap of distant thunder.

As Senator Duffield joined the men, I wandered across to the dining room window. I fancied the room was deserted, but I was mistaken. As I faced about toward the driveway, a low voice caught my ear from behind the curtains.

'You are Miss Mack's friend, are you not? No, don't turn around, please!'

But I had already faced toward the open door. At my elbow was a white-capped maid – with her face almost as white as her cap – whom I remembered to have seen at breakfast.

'Yes, I am Miss Mack's friend. What can I do for you?'

'I have a message for her. Will you see that she gets it?'

'Certainly.'

'Tell her that I was at the door of Senator Duffield's library the night before the murder.'

My face must have expressed my bewilderment. For an instant

I fancied the girl was about to run from the room. I stepped through the window and put my arm about her shoulders. She smiled faintly.

'I don't know much about the law, and evidence, and that sort of thing – and I'm afraid! You will take care of me, won't you?'

'Of course, I will, Anna. Your name is Anna, isn't it?'

The girl was rapidly recovering her self-possession. 'I thought you ought to know what happened Tuesday night. I was passing the door of the library – it was fairly late, about ten o'clock, I think – when I heard a man's voice inside the room. It was a loud angry voice like that of a person in a quarrel. Then I heard a second voice, lower and much calmer.'

'Did you recognize the speakers?'

'They were Mr Rennick and Senator Duffield!'

I caught my breath. 'You said one of them was angry. Which was it?'

'Oh, it was the Senator! He was very much excited and worked up. Mr Rennick seemed to be speaking very low.'

'What were they saying, Anna?' I tried to make my tones careless and indifferent, but they trembled in spite of myself.

'I couldn't catch what Mr Rennick said. The Senator was saying some dreadful things. I remember he cried, "You swindlers!" And then a bit later, "I have evidence that should put you and your thieving crew behind the bars!" I think that is all. I was too bewildered to –'

A stir on the lawn interrupted the sentence. Madelyn Mack and Inspector Taylor had appeared. At the sound of their voices, the girl broke from my arm and darted toward the door.

Through the window, I heard the Inspector's heavy tones, as he announced curtly, 'I am telephoning the coroner, Senator, that we are not ready for the inquest today. We must postpone it until tomorrow.'

V

The balance of the day passed without incident. In fact, I found the subdued quiet of the Duffield home becoming irksome as evening fell. I saw little of Madelyn Mack. She disappeared shortly after luncheon behind the door of her room, and I did not see her again until the dressing bell rang for dinner. Senator Duffield left for the city with Mr Burroughs at noon, and his car did not bring him back until dark. The women of the family remained in their apartments during the entire day, nor could I wonder at the fact. A morbid crowd of curious sight-seers was massed about the gates almost constantly, and it was necessary to send a call for two additional policemen to keep them back. In spite of the vigilance, frequent groups of newspaper men managed to slip into the grounds, and, after half a dozen experiences in frantically dodging a battery of cameras, I decided to stick to the shelter of the house.

It was with a feeling of distinct relief that I heard the door of Madelyn's room open and her voice called to me to enter. I found her stretched on a lounge before the window, with a mass of pillows under her head.

'Been asleep?' I asked.

'No – to tell the truth, I've been too busy.'

'What? In this room!'

'This is the first time I've been here since noon!'

'Then where –'

'Nora, don't ask questions!'

I turned away with a shrug that brought a laugh from the lounge. Madelyn rose and shook out her skirts. I sat watching her as she walked across to the mirror and stood patting the great golden masses of her hair.

A low tap on the door interrupted her. Dorrence, the valet, stood outside as she opened it, extending an envelope. Madelyn fumbled it as she walked back. She let the envelope flutter to the floor and I saw that it contained only a blank sheet of paper. She thrust it into her pocket without explanation.

'How would you like a long motor ride, Nora?'

'For business or pleasure?'

'Pleasure! The day's work is finished. I don't know whether you agree with me or not, but I am strongly of the opinion that a whirl out under the elms of Cambridge, and then on to Concord and Lexington, would be delightful in the moonlight. What do you say?'

The clock was hovering on the verge of midnight and the household had retired when we returned. Madelyn was in singularly cheery spirits. The low refrain which she was humming as the car swung into the grounds – Schubert's *Serenade*, I think it was – ceased only when we stepped on to the verandah, and realized that we were entering the house of the dead.

I turned off my lights in silence, and glanced undecidedly from the bed to the rocker by the window. The cool night breeze beckoned me to the latter, and I drew the chair back a pace and cuddled down among the cushions. The lawn was almost silver under the flood of the moonlight, recalling vaguely the sweep of the ocean on a midsummer night. Back and forth along the edge of the gate the figure of a man was pacing like a tired sentinel. It was the plain-clothes officer from headquarters. His figure suggested a state of siege. We might have been surrounded by a skulking enemy. Or was the enemy within, and the sentinel stationed to prevent his escape? I stumbled across to the bed and to sleep, with the question echoing oddly through my brain.

When I opened my eyes, the sun was throwing a yellow shaft of light across my bed, but it wasn't the sun that had wakened me. Madelyn was standing in the doorway, dressed, with an expression on her face which brought me to my elbow.

'What has happened now?'

'Burglars!'

'Burglars?' I repeated dully.

'I am going down to the library. Someone is making news for us fast, Nora. When will it be our turn?'

I dressed in record-breaking time, with my curiosity whetted by sounds of supressed excitement which forced their way into the upper hall. The Duffield home not only was early astir, but was rudely jarred out of its customary routine.

When I descended, I found a nervous group of servants clustered about the door of the library. They stood aside to let me pass, with attitudes of uneasiness which I surmised would mean a wholesale series of 'notices' if the strange events in the usually well-regulated household continued.

Behind the closed door of the library were Senator Duffield, his son Fletcher, and Madelyn Mack. It was easy to appreciate at a glance the unusual condition of the room. At the right, one of the long windows, partly raised, showed the small round hole of a diamond cutter just over the latch. It was obvious where the clandestine entrance and exit had been obtained. The most noticeable feature of the apartment, however, was a small square safe in the corner, with its heavy lid swinging awkwardly ajar, and the rug below littered with a heap of papers, that had evidently been torn from its neatly tabulated series of drawers. The burglarious hands either had been very angry or very much in a hurry. Even a number of unsealed envelopes had been ripped across, as though the pillager had been too impatient to extract their contents in the ordinary manner. To a man of Senator Duffield's methodical habits, it was easy to imagine that the scene had been a severe wrench.

Madelyn was speaking in her quick, incisive tones as I entered.

'Are you quite sure of that fact, Senator?' she asked sharply, as I closed the door and joined the trio.

'Quite sure, Miss Mack!'

'Then nothing is missing, absolutely nothing?'

'Not a single article, valuable or otherwise.'

'I presume then there were articles of more or less value in the safe?'

'There was perhaps four hundred dollars in loose bills in my private cash drawer, and, so far as I know, there is not a dollar gone.'

'How about your papers and memoranda?'

The Senator shook his head 'There was nothing of the slightest use to a stranger. As a matter of fact, just two days ago, I took pains to destroy the only portfolio of valuable documents in the safe.'

Madelyn stooped thoughtfully over the litter of papers on the rug. 'You mean three evenings ago, don't you?'

'How on earth, Miss Mack —'

'You refer to the memoranda that you and Mr Rennick were working on the night before his death, do you not?'

'Of course!' And then I saw Senator Duffield was staring at his curt questioner as though he had said something he hadn't meant to.

'I think you told me once before that the combination of your safe was known only to yourself and Mr Rennick?'

'You are correct.'

'Then, to your knowledge, you are the only living person, who possesses this information at the present time?'

'That is the case. It was a rather intricate combination, and we changed hardly a month ago.'

Madelyn rose from the safe, glancing reflectively at a huge leather chair, and sank into its depths with a sigh.

'You say nothing has been stolen, Senator, that the burglar's visit yielded him nothing. For your peace of mind I would like to agree with you, but I am sorry to inform you that you are mistaken.'

'Surely, Miss Mack, you are hasty! I am confident that I have searched my possessions with the utmost care.'

'Nevertheless, you have been robbed!'

Senator Duffield glanced down at the small lithe figure impatiently. 'Then, perhaps, you will be good enough to tell me of what my loss consists?'

'I refer to the article for which your secretary was murdered! It was stolen from this room last night.'

Had the point of a dagger pressed against Senator Duffield's shoulders, he could not have bounded forward in greater consternation. His composure was shattered like a pane of glass crumbling.

He sprang toward the safe with a cry like a man in sudden fear or agony. Jerking back its door, he plunged his hand into its lower left compartment. When he straightened, he held a long, wax phonograph record.

His dismay had vanished in a quick blending of relief and anger, as his eyes swept from the cylinder to the grave figure of Madelyn Mack.

'I fail to appreciate your joke, Miss Mack – if you call it a joke to frighten a man without cause as you have me!'

'Have you examined the record in your hand, Senator?'

Fletcher Duffield and I stared at the two. There was a suggestion of tragedy in the scene as the impatience and irritation gradually faded from the Senator's

'It is a substitute!' he groaned. 'A substitute! I have been tricked, victimized, robbed!'

He stood staring at the wax record as though it were a heated iron burning into his flesh. Suddenly it slipped from his fingers and was shattered on the floor.

But he did not appear to notice the fact as he burst out, 'Do you realize that you are standing here inactive while the thief is escaping? I don't know how your wit surprised my secret, and don't care now, but you are throwing away your chances of stopping the burglar while he may be putting miles between himself and us! Are you made of ice, woman? Can't you appreciate what this means? In the name of heaven, Miss Mack –'

'The thief will not escape, Mr Duffield!'

'It seems to me that he has already escaped.'

'Let me assure you, Senator, that your missing property is as secure as though it were locked in your safe at this moment!'

'But do you realize that, once a hint of its nature is known, it will be almost worthless to me?'

'Better perhaps than you do – so well that I pledge myself to return it to your hands within the next half hour!'

Senator Duffield took three steps forward until he stood so close to Madelyn that he could have reached over and touched her on the shoulder.

'I am an old man, Miss Mack, and the last two days have brought me almost to a collapse. If I have appeared unduly sharp, I tender you my apologies – but do not give me false hopes! Tell me frankly that you cannot encourage me. It will be a kindness. You will realize that I cannot blame you.'

Senator Duffield's imperious attitude was so broken that I could hardly believe it possible that the same man who ruled a great political party, almost by the sway of his finger, was speaking. Madelyn caught his hand with a grasp of assurance.

'I will promise even more.' She snapped open her watch. 'If you will return to this room at nine o'clock, not only will I restore your stolen property – but I will deliver the murderer of Raymond Rennick!'

'Rennick's murderer?' the Senator gasped.

Madelyn bowed. 'In this room at nine o'clock.'

I think I was the first to move toward the door. Fletcher Duffield hesitated a moment, staring at Madelyn, then he turned and hurried past me down the hall.

His father followed more slowly. As he closed the door, I saw Madelyn standing where we had left her, leaning back against her chair, and staring at a woman's black slipper. It was the one which had been found by Raymond Rennick's dead body.

I made my way mechanically toward the dining room, and was surprised to find that the members of the Duffield family were already at the table. With the exception of Madelyn, it was the same breakfast group as the morning before. In another house, this attempt to maintain the conventions in the face of tragedy might have seemed incongruous; but it was so thoroughly in keeping with the self-contained Duffield character that, after the first shock, I realized it was not at all surprising. I fancy that we all breathed a sigh of relief, however, when the meal was over.

We were rising from the table, when a folded note addressed to the Senator, was handed to the butler from the hall. He glanced through it hurriedly, and held up his hand for us to wait.

'This is from Miss Mack. She requests me to have all of the members of the family, and those servants who have furnished any evidence in connection with the, er – murder' – the Senator winced as he spoke the word – 'to assemble in the library at nine o'clock. I think that we owe it both to ourselves and to her to obey her instructions to the letter. Perkins, will you kindly notify the servants?'

As it happened, Madelyn's audience in the library was increased by two spectators she had not named. The tooting of a motor sounded without, and the tall figure of Senator Burroughs met us as we were leaving the dining room. Senator Duffield took his arm with a glance of relief, and explained the situation as he forced him to accompany us.

VI

In the library, we found for the first time that Madelyn was not alone. Engaged in a low conversation with her, which ceased as we entered, was Inspector Taylor. He had evidently been designated as the spokesman of the occasion. 'Is everybody here?' he asked.

'I think so,' Senator Duffield replied. 'There are really only five of the servants who count in the case.'

Madelyn's eyes flashed over the circle.

'Close the door, please, Mr Taylor. I think you had better lock it also.'

'There are fourteen persons in this room,' she continued, 'counting, of course, Inspector Taylor, Miss Noraker and myself. We may safely be said to be outside the case. There are then eleven persons here connected in some degree with the tragedy. It is in this list of eleven that I have searched for the murderer. I am happy to tell you that my search has been successful!'

Senator Duffield was the first to speak. 'You mean to say, Miss Mack, that the murderer is in this room at the present time?'

'Correct.'

'Then you accuse one of this group –'

'Of dealing the blow which killed your secretary, and, later, of plundering your safe.'

Inspector Taylor moved quietly to a post between the two windows. Escape from the room was barred. I darted a stealthy glance around the circle in an effort to surprise a trace of guilt in the faces before me, and was startled to find my neighbours engaged in the same furtive occupation. Of the women of the family, the Senator's wife had compressed her lips as though, as mistress of the house, she felt the need of maintaining her composure in any situation. Maria was toying with her bracelet, while Beth made no effort to conceal her agitation.

Senator Burroughs was studying the pattern of the carpet with a face as inscrutable as a mask. Fletcher Duffield was sitting back in his chair, his hands in his pockets. His father was leaning against the locked door, his eyes flashing from face to face. With the exception of Dorrence, the valet, and Perkins, the butler, who I do not think would have stirred out of their stolidness had the ceiling fallen, the servants were in an utter panic. Two of the maids were plainly bordering on hysterics.

Such was the group that faced Madelyn in the Duffield library. One of the number was a murderer, whom the next ten minutes were to brand as such. Which was it? Instinctively my eyes turned again toward the three women of the Duffield family, as Madelyn walked across to a portiere which screened a corner of the apartment.

Jerking it aside, she showed, suspended from a hook in the ceiling, a quarter of fresh veal.

On an adjoining stand was a long, thin-bladed knife, which might have been a dagger, ground to a razor-edge. Madelyn held it before her as she turned to us.

'This is the weapon which killed Mr Rennick.' I fancied I heard a gasp as she spoke. Although I whirled almost on the instant, however, I could detect no signs of it in the faces behind me.

'I propose to conduct a short experiment, which I assure you is absolutely necessary to my chain of reasoning,' Madelyn continued. 'You may or may not know that the body of a calf practically offers the same degree of resistance to a knife as the body of a man. Dead flesh, of course, is harder and firmer than living flesh, but I think that, adding the thickness of clothes, we may take it for granted that in the quarter of veal before us, we have a fair substitute for the body of Raymond Rennick. Now watch me closely, please!'

Drawing back her arm, she plunged her knife into the meat with a force which sent it spinning on its hook. She drew the knife out, and examined it reflectively.

'I have made a cut of only a little more than three and a half inches. The blow which killed Mr Rennick penetrated at least five inches.

'Here we encounter a singularly striking feature of our case, involving a stratagem which I think I can safely say is the most unique in my experience. To all intents, it was a woman who killed Mr Rennick. In fact, it has been taken for granted that he met his death at the hand of a female assassin. We must dispose of this conclusion at the outset, for the simple reason that it was physically impossible for a woman to have dealt the death blow!'

I chanced to be gazing directly at Fletcher Duffield as Madelyn made the statement. An expression of such relief flashed into his face that instinctively I turned about and followed the direction of his glance. His eyes were fixed on his sister, Beth.

Madelyn deposited the knife on the stand.

'Indeed, I may say there are few men – perhaps not one in ten – with a wrist strong enough to have dealt Mr Rennick's death blow,' she went on. 'There is only one such person among the fourteen in this room at the present time.

'Again you will recall that the wound was delivered from the rear just as Mr Rennick faced about in his own defence. Had he been attacked by a woman, he would have heard the rustle of her dress several feet before she possibly could have reached him. I think you will recall my demonstration of that fact yesterday morning, Mr Duffield.

'Obviously then, it is a man whom we must seek if we would find the murderer of your secretary, and a man of certain peculiar characteristics. Two of these I can name now. He possessed a wrist developed to an extraordinary degree, and he owned feet as small and shapely as a woman's. Otherwise, the stratagem of wearing a woman's slippers and leaving one of them near the scene of the crime to divert suspicion from himself, would never have occurred to him!'

Again I thought I heard a gasp behind me, but its owner escaped me a second time.

'There was a third marked feature among the physical characteristics of the murderer. He was near-sighted – so much so that it was necessary for him to wear glasses of the kind known technically as a "double lens". Unfortunately for the assassin, when his victim fell, the latter caught the glasses in his hand, and they were broken under his body. The murderer may have been thrown into a panic, and feared to take the time to recover his spectacles; but it was a fatal blunder. Fortune, however, might have helped him even then in spite of this fact, for those who found the body fell into the natural error of considering the glasses to be the property of the murdered man. Had it not been for two minor details, this impression might never have been contradicted.'

Madelyn held up a packet of newspaper illustrations. Several of them I recognized as the pictures of the murdered secretary that she had shown me at the 'Roanoke'. The others were also photographs of the same man.

'If Mr Rennick hadn't been fond of having his picture taken, the fact that he never wore glasses on the street might not have been noticed. None of his pictures, not even the snap-shots, showed a man in spectacles. It is true that he did possess a pair, and it is here where those who discovered the crime went astray. But they were for reading purposes only, the kind termed a .125 lens, while those of his assailant were a .210 lens. To clinch the matter, I later found Mr Rennick's own spectacles in his room where he had left them the evening before.'

Madelyn held up the red leather case she had found on the mantelpiece, and tapped it musingly as she gave a slight nod to Inspector Taylor.

'We have now the following description of the murderer – a slenderly built man, with an unusual wrist, possibly an athlete at one time, who possesses a foot capable of squeezing into a woman's shoe, and who is handicapped by near-sightedness. Is there an individual in this room to whom this description applies?'

There was a new glitter in Madelyn's eyes as she continued.

'Through the co-operation of Inspector Taylor, I am enabled to answer this question. Mr Taylor has traced the glasses of the assassin to the optician who gave the prescription for them. I am not surprised to find that the owner of the spectacles tallies with the owner of these other interesting articles.'

With the words, she whisked from the stand at her elbow, the long, narrow-bladed dagger, and a pair of soiled, black suede slippers.

There was a suggestion of grotesque unreality about it all. It was much as though I had been viewing the denouement of a play from the snug vantage point of an orchestra seat, waiting for the lights to flare up and the curtain to ring down. A shriek ran through my ears, jarring me back to the realization that I was not a spectator, but a part, of the play.

A figure darted toward the window. It was John Dorrence, the valet.

The next instant Inspector Taylor threw himself on the fleeing man's shoulders, and the two went to the floor.

'Can you manage him?' Madelyn called.

'Unless he prefers cold steel through his body to cold steel about his wrists,' was the rejoinder.

'I think you may dismiss the other servants, Senator,' Madelyn said. 'I wish, however, that the family would remain a few moments.'

As the door closed again, she continued, 'I promised you also, Senator, the return of your stolen property. I have the honour to make that promise good.'

From her stand, which was rapidly assuming the proportions of a conjurer's table, she produced a round, brown paper parcel.

'Before I unwrap this, have I your permission to explain its contents?'

'As you will, Miss Mack.'

'Perhaps the most puzzling feature of the tragedy is the motive. It is this parcel which supplies us with the answer.

'Your secretary, Mr Duffield, was an exceptional young man. Not only did he repeatedly resist bribery such as comes to few men, but he gave his life for his trust.

'At any time since this parcel came into his possession, he could have sold it for a fortune. Because he refused to sell it he was murdered for it. Perhaps every reader of the newspapers is more or less familiar with Senator Duffield's investigations of the ravages of a certain great Trust. A few days ago, the Senator came into possession of evidence against the combine of such a drastic nature that he realized it would mean nothing less than the annihilation of the monopoly, imprisonment for the chief officers, and a business sensation such as this country has seldom known.

'Once the officers of the Trust knew of his evidence, however, they would be forearmed in such a manner that its value would be largely destroyed. The evidence was a remarkable piece of detective work. It consisted of a phonographic record of a secret directors' meeting, laying bare the inmost depredations of the corporation.'

Madelyn paused as the handcuffed valet showed signs of a renewed struggle. Inspector Taylor without comment calmly snapped a second pair of bracelets about his feet.

'The Trust was shrewd enough to appreciate the value of a spy in the Duffield home. Dorrence was engaged for the post, and from what I have learned of his character, he filled it admirably. How he stumbled on Senator Duffield's latest coup is immaterial. The main point is that he tried to bribe Mr Rennick so persistently to betray his post that the latter threatened to expose him. Partly in the fear that he would carry out his threat, and partly in the hope that he carried memoranda which might lead to the discovery of the evidence that he sought, Dorrence planned and carried out the murder.

'In the secretary's pocket he discovered the combination of the safe, and made use of it last night. I found the stolen phonograph record this morning behind the register of the furnace pipe in Dorrence's room. I had already found that this was his cache, containing the dagger which killed Rennick, and the second of Cinderella's slippers. The pair was stolen some days ago from the room of Miss Beth Duffield.'

★★★★

The swirl of the day was finally over. Dorrence had been led to his cell; the coroner's jury had returned its verdict; and all that was mortal of Raymond Rennick had been laid in its last resting place. Madelyn and I had settled ourselves in the homeward bound Pullman as it rumbled out of the Boston station in the early dusk.

'There are two questions I want to ask,' I said reflectively.

Madelyn looked up from her newspaper with a yawn.

'Why did John Dorrence bring you back a blank sheet of paper when you despatched him on your errand?'

'As a matter of fact, there was nothing else for him to bring back. Mr Taylor kept him at police headquarters long enough to give me time to carry my search through his room. The message was a blind.'

'And what was the quarrel that the servant girl, Anna, heard in the Duffield library?'

'It wasn't a quarrel, my dear girl. It was the Senator preparing the speech with which he intended to launch his evidence against the Trust. The Senator is in the habit of dictating his speeches to a phonograph. Some of them I am afraid, are rather fiery.'

JIGGER MASTERS

Created by Anthony M Rud (1893–1942)

Born in Chicago, the son of two doctors, Anthony M Rud studied at medical college himself as a young man but soon turned to writing. He became one of the many prolific, versatile authors who wrote chiefly for the pulp magazines. He produced dozens and dozens of stories in a variety of genres. He also worked as editor of Detective Story Magazine *and* Adventure. *Probably his best remembered tales fall into the broad categories of horror or science fiction ('Ooze', reprinted many times, appeared in the first issue of the legendary* Weird Tales*) but he wrote plenty of detective fiction. The adventures of his crime fighter Jigger Masters were published in 1918 in* The Green Book Magazine *with enticing titles such as 'The Vengeance of the Wah Fu Tong' and 'The Giant Footprints'. According to* The Green Book, *'Not since Sherlock Holmes has any fiction detective done such interesting things as our friend Masters'. This is exaggeration and hype, of course, but perhaps forgivable. In truth, the Jigger Masters stories, narrated by his Watson, the artist Bert Hoffman, are fairly standard issue crime fiction of the time but they remain good fun to read and their red-blooded, patriotic hero is a likeable character.*

THE AFFAIR AT STEFFEN SHOALS

The bell rang insistently. Knowing that Central would have me fully awake in five minutes anyway, I rose and yanked down the receiver, prepared to bite the head off the individual who had nerve enough to rout me out at three in the morning.

'Bert?' The quick question forestalled the savage growl I was summoning as I leaned over the transmitter. I straightened instantly from my belligerent slouch, for it was the one voice in the world I most wanted to hear.

'Jigger!' I exclaimed, as wide awake suddenly as if it had been noon. 'Where are you? Where have you been? I'd given you up for dead two months ago!' This was literally the truth, for Masters had been out of town nearly four months, and because I knew his sledge-hammer methods in dealing with his quarries and the risks he delighted in taking, I had pictured him lying somewhere in the mud of the East River, or hacked to pieces by some of the alien criminals he sought.

'Not yet, Hoffman!' he chuckled. 'Can't answer your questions over the wire, though. Are you very busy?'

'Lord no!' If I had been painting the Queen of England at the moment, I would have answered in the same way. As it was, I had two portrait appointments for the following week, but I knew these could be postponed.

'Same old Bert!' he laughed. 'Well, meet me at the 5:32 Grand Central.'

'This morning?'

'Yes. Oh, and bring your golf sticks, if you can find them. We may be able to get in eighteen holes. I'm anxious for a game.'

'All right.' I knew that Masters was chaffing, for he scarcely knew a driver from a sammy iron, but behind the lightest of his jests there lay always a serious side. 'Any – other weapons?' I asked, thinking of the two automatics that had lain unused in my bureau drawer for so long.

'Of course,' he replied. 'That's always understood.' As he dropped the receiver. I sprang to my feet, thrilling with delight at the prospect of action. I needed it badly, for my work had fallen off in quality of late. The impetus and inspiration of an adventure with Masters was just what I wanted.

★★★★

I gathered a few pieces of clean linen, in case I should be away longer than the day, and crammed them into my leather bag. I started to put the automatics on top, but changed my mind.

Masters's affairs often developed with such startling suddenness that it was unwise not to be fully prepared. I placed one in the pocket of my jacket and the other on my right hip. My breakfast was a hurried affair, not because there was any particular reason for rush but because I was burning with impatience. As a result I got to Grand Central nearly a half-hour early.

I was lighting my second panatella when I spied Masters. He was approaching briskly from the subway stairs, dressed as I had never seen him before. His angular frame was revealed more than usual by a back-fitted tweed coat, and the material advertised by garish checks the fact that the new American dyes were not yet complete successes. The soft collar of his shirt, though pinned together carefully over the tie, left his bony neck unprotected. Always previously he had worn the highest linen procurable. Completely engulfing his mat of black hair was a checked cap, pulled down too far toward his ears. I thought he seemed a little paler and thinner than on the last occasion I had accompanied him – the time we chased the family ghost for Lew Macey.

'Jigger!' I cried, seizing his hand warmly. He did not speak for a second, but I saw the curious expression creep into his blue eyes that was his nearest approach to sentiment.

'I'm glad to see you, old man!' he answered, a moment later, crushing my fingers. 'Thought I never was going to get back to New York.'

'So did I! Well, what's the assignment that gets us up before the roosters this morning?'

And this was all the spoken greeting between us. I think that it would have been the same had Masters been away for ten years instead of a few months; each of us knew exactly what the other thought and felt, yet both were unable to phrase our genuine gladness.

Masters purchased our tickets, signifying by a gesture that he would tell me the story as soon as possible. When he came back, we made for the smoker, and took the seat farthest forward. The train had just been made up, so we were the first in the car.

'It has been a tangled skein, Bert,' began Masters, when we had arranged our baggage, 'the hardest case to get at I've ever tackled.

I have one end of the thread in hand now, and because I know how you delight in being on hand at the finish, I've asked you out with me.

'Over fourteen weeks ago I was called to Washington. I couldn't tell you, for I was asked to keep my own counsel strictly. It seems that for some months they have been cognizant of certain information leaks. News reached the Germans before our own troops in France knew it.'

'You mean that there were spies in our own departments?'

'Yes, were and are!' he nodded emphatically. 'That's nothing unusual, of course. Every nation has to contend with that problem. The feature about it that caused me to be called in was that such a quick and comprehensive chain for the revealing of ordnance and construction secrets had been established that the Germans actually were using our newest war weapons against us about as quickly as we could bring them into play ourselves.

'One of the most striking examples of this was the chloropicrin-phosgene gas mine. This was an American invention, but the Germans knew all about it and brought it up on the Toul front only ten days after we used it first. Since it takes at least a month to make one of these terrible agents of destruction, you can see readily how soon the Germans must have heard of it.'

'I should think we would begin to investigate!' I replied. 'What was this gas-mine apparatus?'

'A huge tank-bomb arrangement for use underground,' replied Masters. 'I won't trouble you with a description of it except to say that it was placed in territory about to be evacuated. When the enemy occupied the position it was exploded. First it gave off terrific clouds of chloropicrin gas: this is an agent that makes every soldier sicker than he was his first trip on the ocean. Naturally every man takes off his gas mask when he gets sick – chloropicrin gets through the mask – and that leaves him an easy mark for the phosgene. The latter gas comes from the mine five minutes after the chloropicrin. Since the inhalation of a microscopic quantity of phosgene is immediately fatal, taking off the masks at this time allows the phosgene to get in its deadly work. Most of the victims of chloropicrin are too sick to care, anyway.'

I shuddered. 'Ghastly thing, isn't it?' I said.

'Yes.' Masters shrugged his shoulders. 'They have found, though, that the only way to fight the Huns successfully is to beat them to it. Because the Germans are learning our secrets as fast as we can invent new machines and methods, though, is exactly the reason you and I are here.'

'Where are we bound for this morning?'

'Jaques Corners, Rhode Island,' answered Masters promptly.

'Sounds rural,' I commented. 'What are we going to find there?' I noticed that our train had started.

'Well, I am told that the Weekapang Country Club near there has an excellent golf course.'

'Oh, don't be tight!' I exclaimed. 'What are we after? Where are these outlandish places?'

Masters smiled. 'You can find Weekapang on the map, down in the southernmost corner of Rhode Island. The golf course –'

'Oh, hang that! What about Jakeville, or whatever you called it? Jaques Corners, wasn't it?'

Masters's expression became serious. 'That is a war town, put up entirely by the government for the construction of war machines and munitions. I have traced my skein that far, and I have a hint of the next coil of the strand. I think they call the town by that hick name just to avoid suspicion. I have three men in high positions in our war organization who are going to face a firing squad before another month has passed. It is only because I do not care to let the method go undiscovered that I have not had them court-martialled already. They have confederates and some method of conveying news to Germany that is novel, to say the least. In all the time I have watched them not one of the crowd has sent a wireless message, mailed a letter or engaged in intimate conversation with any people outside their own homes. And I have made certain that members of the family have not carried the messages on.'

'Then why do you suspect them? They sound blameless.'

'Yes, entirely too much so!' Masters's tone was savage. 'An innocent man posts a letter now and then. He also gets chummy with other men. These men don't. Besides – and I'll admit that this feature occurred to me after I had them nailed down — I have evidence to prove that the specifications of the chloropicrin-phosgene mine passed through these particular hands, not to mention other documents that Hindenburg would pay millions to possess. The last snarl in the thread I am following is a Mr Mesnil Phillips, a government inspector of ordnance. I am convinced that through him the news reaches the Germans, though how he does it I cannot pretend to say just yet.

'The manner in which I have pinned down these men has not been spectacular in the least. Only five persons saw the specifications of the gas mine before it was taken to the ordnance factory at Jaques Corners. One of these was the President. Another was the Secretary of War.'

'That leaves three possible suspects.' I commented.

'Yes,' answered Masters in a solemn voice, 'and it is a dreadful thing to know that individuals even in these lesser positions of trust can prove traitors.'

I moved uneasily. 'But are you certain?' I asked. 'It seems to me that there ought to be plenty of chance for some mechanic or foreman or someone like that out at the manufacturing plant to send on the news.'

Masters shook his head. 'No, it's not possible. On the twelfth of November, 1917, the plans of this mine were submitted by one of our greatest military inventors.

'He had worked alone on the project, and is a man who appreciates thoroughly the fact that secrecy is a prime factor in the success of any new machine. On the twenty-seventh of November the approved plans were placed in a time-lock safe at the factory. On the fourth of January of this year the first of the mines arrived at our front in France. On the evening of the thirteenth of January the Germans exploded an identical mine near St Mihiel. Making every allowance for the transmission of the plans, the lesser time required for transporting from Essen or Brandenburg, the finger points unerringly at the fifteen-day period elapsing before the plans reached the factory.'

'Sounds a little shaky!' I remarked dubiously.

'In one case, yes,' returned Masters. 'I have followed through the gas mine with you because I mentioned it first. The infrangible part of the reasoning rests in the law of averages, however. I have established the same chain in no less than four other important instances. Even at that I never would dare to prefer charges of this sort without having every loophole covered. In the past three months I have directed a body of sixty picked secret-service agents. These have made it their business to know every movement during every second of waking time of all of the individuals who even might have obtained access to the plans at any time, but with negative results. I have data in hand to show what all of these have done every day – with one exception. That exception is Mr Mesnil Phillips, one of the original three, and concerns his recreation periods.'

'Golf, you mean?'

'Yes.' Masters's face was drawn and serious. 'I know that it is possible for me to make mistakes, Bert, but I have given this case the very best I have, and without hurry. I have eliminated all the factors but one. That one must materialize!' The long fingers of his right hand clenched with unconscious emphasis.

'Have you baited any trap?' I asked.

He nodded slowly. 'Yes. That is what makes success just at this time absolutely necessary. A certain construction secret is going through now that a thousand men in Washington would give their lives to prevent the Germans from receiving. Because I have given my solemn promise of its protection, I have prevailed on the Secretary of War to send it by the usual channels!' He regarded me quietly. 'It's up to us, Bert,' he said in a strained tone.

Our conversation turned to my personal affairs. Rather I should say that Masters directed it thus. Perceiving that he did not care to discuss the case further at the time, I related the work I had accomplished in his absence. After a time I saw an impersonal stare creeping into his eyes, the old symptom of concentration. Since I knew that he was not listening, I picked up a newspaper.

We did not stop in the town of Weekapang, but took the station bus directly to the country club. 'I thought you said Jaques Corners,' I mentioned, as we were jogging along over the macadam road.

'Yes. There's no station there for passengers, though. See!' And

Masters pointed to the north, where I discerned a cloud of smoke over the tree-tops. 'That's Jaques Corners,' he said.

★★★★

The Weekapang Country Club proved to be a frame building set in a small grove of oaks. Toward the ocean the land rolled away as clipped fair green, artistically bunkered and pitted.

While Masters introduced himself to the secretary, I captured a pair of caddies and practiced with my driver. The moment Masters appeared, however, he dismissed the boys, flipping them a quarter each. 'We may play this course too irregularly to suit caddies,' he said when we were well toward the first hole. 'The secretary tells me that our friend, Mr Mesnil Phillips, is out alone. He is wearing a white felt hat and white flannel trousers, and has no caddie.'

'Because this is Thursday we probably won't have any difficulty locating him.' I said. 'Not many matches play during the week.'

Masters scanned the broad expanse of grass. 'No one in sight just now,' he commented. Removing a small field-glass from the pocket of his coat he swept the circle. At a point southwest from where we stood the binoculars rested.

'Think I see him,' he remarked. 'He's up beyond, probably playing the second nine.'

'What will we do, cut in behind him?' I asked.

'No, not yet. We'll play the second. That doubles parallel to the way he's shooting. All I want to do is to keep him in sight all of the time. When I am playing, you keep your eyes on him.' At the moment all I could distinguish was a white speck, far off in the direction Masters indicated, but as we went on, the two courses converged, nearing the ocean. Fifteen minutes later we could follow the man's actions without glasses.

★★★★

As he played along, I saw him stop two or three times and study the landscape before him, as if in doubt as to which club to play. Always he dubbed his shots, however, for as he approached the fifteenth green, I saw him use his mashie three times, yet the man did not look like a beginner. He was lean and bronzed from the sun, and he possessed an easy, certain swing that spoke of long practice.

He acted sincerely disgusted after his last mashie shot. Throwing down his club he unbuckled the strap of the pocket on his bag and drew out another ball. Dropping this in the approximate position of his last shot he again faced the green.

He was still angry, apparently, for when he addressed the ball he swung on it with entirely unnecessary strength. The gutta-percha sphere mounted in a perfect arch, soaring high above the flag. It floated far over the rough beyond toward a little clump of oaks, beside which an employee was raking up leaves.

'Fore!' I heard Phillips call sharply. The man in overalls started as the ball narrowly missed his head, impinging among the tree-trunks beyond. Masters got so excited at this that he holed out a putt he never could have made in a conscious moment. As the two of us picked up our balls and scored, we saw the employee gaze about him, and then recover the ball that had so nearly hit him. He did not throw it back as we expected, but dropped it into his pocket. Phillips paid no attention to this, but calmly sought his first ball, and played up to the green.

Though we watched him feverishly as we teed off on the third hole, he never made any sign that he had seen the theft. He holed out and then teed off on the sixteenth, playing directly away from us.

'Didn't care much about eighty-five cents!' I commented, knowing that the incident had some bearing on the case, but willing to let Masters give me the correct version, when it pleased him.

'That ball was worth quite a bit more than that,' said my friend, hurrying on. 'Yes, I imagine Phillips would have spent a long time looking if he had really lost it.' His tone was excitedly triumphant, and I eyed him inquiringly.

★★★★

He wasted no time in explanations, however. As soon as we had a bunker between us and the man in overalls, Masters stopped. 'You stay right here!' he commanded. 'Take a good rest and watch that employee. If he does anything with that ball, you follow the ball. Don't let them know you're watching, either, or it will all be spoiled!'

'What are you going to do?' I asked.

'Going in to interrogate the secretary again,' he answered shortly, and swung away into his long, graceless stride.

I watched him depart with mixed feelings. I was going to miss luncheon and anticipated a dull, hot time out in the sand-pit, watching our quarry; still, if Masters really was only going to see the club secretary, I was nearer to the action than he would be. I poked my head out beside the bunker, and looked for the man in overalls.

I was just in time. He was making his way down toward the beach, having deserted his rake. In a moment the bank would have shut him off from my view. I seized the ball I had been playing with and hurled it with all my strength toward the clump of trees. It bounced into the rough, and I hurried after it, seizing the first club that came to hand.

Using this as an excuse, I approached the edge of the bank. The man in overalls was looking straight out over the bay, seemingly interested in the white stone lighthouse two miles out to sea. As bad luck would have it I tiptoed that instant upon a dry stick. At the snap which resulted the man in overalls whirled about. I did my best to register absorption in the business of finding my ball, but out of the tail of my eye I saw him glowering at me. A second later he strode up the hill.

'Are you a member of this club?' he demanded, approaching me.

'No, a guest,' I replied, assuming as innocent an expression as I could summon.

'Who introduced you?' His tone was curt and aggressive, and his words left me at a total loss. Jigger had not mentioned the member through whom we had obtained the right to play.

'Mr – er – Smith,' I rejoined hesitatingly. 'Did you see a ball come over here?' I stamped about in the long grass, hoping to divert his attention.

His expression grew blacker, and I saw him glance hastily over his shoulder. 'Mr Smith died last month!' he growled, and a shiver danced down my spine. Could there be only one Smith in the club?

'Harry Smith is the one I mean,' I explained.

'There ain't any Harry Smith!' he retorted. 'Now you get out, and get out quick!' He extended a muscled arm in the direction of the gateway, and came toward me.

'Now see here, my man,' I began in an attempt to be dictatorial. It did not work, however. He dived for a hold on my collar and made me duck to avoid him. Seeing there was to be no other way out of it I brought my mashie niblick down upon the crown of his head. It was not a hard blow, as I had no intention whatever of killing him, but he sank to the ground without a word. I examined him hastily, but could not tell for certain whether or not I had fractured his skull.

★★★★

The far-away throbbing of a marine engine caused me to look up. Midway between the distant lighthouse and the shore a white chip of a motorboat was dancing on the rollers. It was headed in my direction, and as I gazed, the idea flashed through my mind that a connection might exist between my victim and the little craft. I thought immediately of the golf ball, and feverishly explored the pockets of his overalls for this.

The moment I had it in hand, however, I knew that there was something peculiar about it. The sphere was less than one third the normal weight of a ball! I turned it over, examining the surface. Sure enough, a curved line was distinguishable where a flap had been fastened down with rubber adhesive. My penknife soon sliced through this, exposing the hollow core. The interior of the ball was literally stuffed with paper!

I pulled this out and put it in my pocket, and then glanced again at the motorboat. It was approaching steadily, and I knew that in a very few minutes the occupants would be looking for the man in overalls. On impulse I turned again to him. Stripping him of the blue suit I pulled it over my golfing attire, and pulled his battered felt hat over my eyes. Then I went down to the protection of the last clump of bushes near the water's edge, and waited. I had some hope of being shielded sufficiently from the observation of those who would land to allow me to get the drop on them with my revolvers.

As they drew near, however, it became apparent that they did not intend to land at all. Keeping just outside the line of breakers they hummed along parallel to the shore. I got the idea. The golf ball would float! The next second the sphere was flying outward in a long parabola, to fall a few yards in front of the bow of the motorboat. The lone occupant dipped it out of the water deftly, waved his hand and passed on.

****

Just as the ball left my hand, I heard a gasp behind me. 'My heavens, Bert!' protested the voice of Masters. 'You didn't give them that ball after all, did you?' He was looking up at me in genuine consternation, and I noticed that the course employee lay beside him in a crumpled position different from that in which I had left him.

Masters said nothing more for an instant; I saw that he was truly disgusted. 'Here,' I answered at last, unable to keep the secret longer, 'are the papers that were inside the ball!' I held out the crumpled roll.

Masters pounced upon this and examined it hastily. 'Bravo, Bert!' he exclaimed. 'I had thought you stupid for the moment.' A peculiar expression crept into his blue eyes. 'Guess I won't have to explain much of this case to you,' he commented. 'You must have got to the bottom of it pretty well in the ten minutes I was away.'

'Well,' I said, 'you can explain to me what you did when you got back here.' And I pointed to the prostrate figure beside us.

'Killed him,' rejoined Masters. 'I came up just in time to see him creeping up on you with a golf club. I reached him first; that's all.

'You have the chain pretty well in hand now,' he went on, changing his tone. 'That golf ball goes out to Steffen Shoals lighthouse. What becomes of the message then?'

'I – I suppose they send it to Germany by wireless,' I returned doubtfully.

'No. That wouldn't work long. How would you like to see the dénouement and the answer to it all at the same time?'

'Lead on!'

'Well, no hurry,' he answered, smiling. 'There's nothing doing till evening. I thought, as soon as I saw the way the golf ball was being passed around, that I had come to the last snarl of the chain. We'll go down now and get a boat for Block Island.'

'Won't he – the chap in the boat, I mean – find out that the message has been extracted from the ball and come back for it?' I asked as we gained the clubhouse.

Masters nodded sharply. 'Correct, Bert!' he said. 'I'll get a posse to wait down there for him.'

****

At seven that evening we boarded a United States torpedo-boat destroyer at Block Island. The speedy vessel moved quietly out into the ocean and was joined by two more of the rakish gray craft. Though dusk was settling on the water, the destroyers showed no lights. At a speed which could not have been more than seven or eight knots an hour the three silent defenders crept toward Steffen Shoals. As they approached, their speed slackened still more, until it seemed that they were scarcely moving. As the tower of the lighthouse became dimly perceptible in the distance. Masters clutched my arm. 'We may have to wait awhile,' he said in a low tone, 'but the show is due to start at any minute!'

Fifteen minutes later it did start. On the side of the lighthouse tower a steady light flashed out. This burned for perhaps ten minutes. Then it began certain gyrations that were both unaccountable and unintelligible to me, whirling about in a semicircle to the right, going back to the horizontal, going to the left twice and then continuing the dizzy whirl until I lost count entirely.

'Semaphore signals!' whispered Masters. The second he spoke three immense searchlights flared from the decks of the destroyers, throwing the ocean at the foot of the lighthouse into a light far brighter than day. Motionless, perhaps six hundred yards in front of us, I saw a grayish shape lying on the water, like an immense elongated whale come to the surface.

'A U-boat!' I cried, as Masters pushed his hand over my mouth. As it proved, there was no necessity for silence. Fifteen three-inch semi-automatic cannon, trained on the marauder, spoke almost in unison. Every second thereafter one or more of the pieces sent a shell into the splendid target.

It lasted only a minute or so, but during that time the gray back of the U-boat was kept well illuminated by the fires of bursting shells as well as by the searchlights. Huge fragments were knocked off before the commander could even think of submerging, and as I watched, deafened but thrilled to the depth of my soul, the sea monster turned on one side and sank.

Masters left me at that moment, and while the vessels were patrolling the circle he was in conference with the captain. The two joined me a half-hour later, and Masters's face was glowing. 'It's really a big success, Bert!' he exclaimed. 'We got one U-boat, and the captain thinks that more will call around here each day or so. They will trap every one of them!'

'But how about Mr Mesnil Phillips and the rest of his chain of spies?' I asked.

Masters frowned. 'Nobody will ever hear of them again!' he answered shortly.

QUINCY ADAMS SAWYER

Created by Charles Felton Pidgin (1844-1923)

In the course of a varied career, Charles Felton Pidgin worked as a statistician for the state of Massachusetts, wrote musical comedies for the stage and patented a number of inventions. (His most successful was a machine for tabulating statistics; his silliest, a never-used method of displaying dialogue in silent films which involved inflated text balloons emerging from the actors' mouths.) In his fifties, he turned to fiction and wrote more than a dozen novels, including an interesting work of 'alternate history' in which the politician Aaron Burr, disgraced and exiled after a fatal duel in reality, becomes President of the USA and abolishes slavery half-a-century before Lincoln. Pidgin's most famous creation was Quincy Adams Sawyer, a young attorney and the title character in his first and bestselling novel, published in 1900. The tale was twice adapted by Hollywood in the silent era and Pidgin returned several times to Sawyer in later books. By the time of the short stories collected in The Chronicles of Quincy Adams Sawyer, Detective, *the character had become a professional private investigator, clearly influenced by Sherlock Holmes. The stories, as the example below shows, are all engaging and well written.*

THE AFFAIR OF LAMSON'S COOK

Quincy sauntered slowly along the street, enjoying the sunny warmth of an early June morning. Few cases had been presented to him of late, and the resulting inactivity had served to stock him, both mentally and physically, with unusual energy. His keen eyes, restless with inaction, flashed hither and thither over the small throng of hurrying pedestrians, as though in search of something on which to exercise his peculiar talents. But the people surrounding him seemed productive of anything other than mysteries. They comprised mainly the usual throng of hurrying clerks, stenographers and other employees, all rushing toward their individual desks or stations, and whatever secrets might be buried in their minds were for the present, at least, successfully forgotten or covered. With a deep sigh at the possibility of another day of quiet and solitude, Quincy turned slowly in the direction of his own office, but paused sharply as the sound of a call reached his ears.

'Sawyer! Oh, I say, Sawyer!' came the half-suppressed shout, and Quincy's eyes, flashing sharply over the street, instantly picked out the source of the call.

Slowly bearing down on him, through the press of market wagons, trucks and other early morning vehicles, came a handsome touring car. At the wheel sat an impassive French chauffeur and in the tonneau a fat, puffy little man danced frantically about for all the world like a huge bullfrog in a net. Quincy recognized the man as Herbert Lamson, prominent clubman, first-nighter, and society leader in general, and wondered vaguely what unseemly occurrence could have brought Lamson out at that early hour of the morning. He halted and stood smiling interrogatively as the machine drew up at the curb.

'Oh, I say, Sawyer!' Lamson puffed, as soon as the car had been brought to a halt. 'It's lucky I found you, you know. I want you to come right out to my house without a moment's delay. We've had a frightful occurrence there. Frightful!'

'Which house?' Quincy inquired, ignoring the door which Lamson held invitingly open.

'My country house, Sawyer. The one at Beverly. Come right away, won't you? It's an awful thing and I simply must have help!'

'But, what is it? What has happened?' Quincy questioned, not relishing the idea of being dragged down to Beverly to discover who had thrown a pebble through one of Lamson's plate glass windows, which possibility, knowing Lamson as well as he did, Quincy deemed not improbable.

'It's murder, Sawyer, murder!' Lamson spluttered, spitting out the word as though it choked him and gazing helplessly at Quincy through his round, sheep-like eyes. 'Somebody brutally murdered my cook last night and she could cook the best fish dinners I ever tasted.'

Quincy barely suppressed a desire to laugh at the incongruity of the two statements, knowing well that the only method of endearing oneself to Lamson was through the medium of the latter's digestive system. For a moment only he hesitated, then, swinging into the car beside Lamson, he settled back for the ride to Beverly.

'Now, Lamson,' he said, when the car had drawn away from the mid-city tumult, 'give me some of the details of this case so that I may be prepared to act when we arrive. Just when, so far as you can tell, did the murder take place?'

'I can't say just when,' Lamson informed him. 'I was away from the house from five o'clock in the afternoon until late last night. It might have been done while I was away, or after I returned, because she was not discovered until early this morning. One of the maids, according to custom, went to call her in time to prepare breakfast, and found her dead. I was immediately notified and, not knowing what else to do, I hurried up after you. I'll catch that murderer, Sawyer, if it costs me my entire fortune,' he broke off savagely. 'That woman was a downright shrew, but she could cook. Lord bless you! she could cook! And now I must spend a year or two hunting another cook, and I shall probably be obliged to live on all manner of horrible dishes during my search. I know I can never find another who will be able to cook fish the way she could!' He seemed saddened, almost to the point of breaking down, at the last thought.

'I understand, Lamson,' said Quincy, after a protracted coughing fit behind his hand. 'But I want to get the facts of the case itself, the murder. How was she murdered, and do you suspect anybody? Now, give me something of that sort to work on. First, what was her name, where did she come from, and how long had she been with you?'

'Her name,' said Lamson in a saddened voice, apparently engendered by the thought of the fish dinners which were to be his no more, 'was Mrs Elizabeth Buck. She had been with me as cook for about twelve years, but I have no idea where she came from originally. You see, I was obliged to hire her rather hastily at a time when I was giving a dinner and my other cook –'

'Yes, yes,' Quincy hurriedly interrupted, 'but had she any relatives or friends who wrote to her, or with whom she visited?'

'Nobody of whom I ever heard. In fact, from the time when I first engaged her, I do not believe she has been away from my house a single day. Her sharp temper would rather preclude the possibility of her having any friends, and I doubt if there was a person in the world, outside myself, in whom she felt the slightest interest.'

'Now,' said Quincy approvingly, 'you are started right. Give me all the details you can up to the time when the body was discovered.'

'Well, she was a woman who, as I said, apparently had neither friends nor acquaintances. Therefore, I do not think that the affair occurred because of some old grudge a previous associate may have owed her. Since I have been talking with you a possibility, which hitherto had not occurred to me, has come into my mind. I paid her well, very well, and, as I never knew of her spending much money at a time, she must have been able to lay by quite a bit in the last twelve years. Of course she may have kept her money in a savings bank, but it is equally possible that her distrustful nature led her to hide it somewhere about her house. She did not room in my house, but in a little cottage which stood on the grounds, living by herself. Now the possibility I mentioned, and which, at the time when I left, had not been investigated, is that somebody may have murdered her for her money. Damn 'em! I'd have given them an equal amount gladly, if they'd only have let her live to cook for me.

'In person she was a small woman of perhaps fifty, although she was so wizened and dried-up by nature that she might have been either more or less. In fact, her appearance has never changed since I have known her. She was very small in stature, and, although I think she would have been capable of putting up a stiff fight, she would have been no match, of course, for an ordinarily strong man. Last night, the servants say, she retired to her cottage at her usual time, and nothing was heard of her during the evening. Very early this morning one of the maids went to call her and, receiving no response to her knock, pushed open the door and found the body.

'The woman had been stabbed, and the place was in a terrible state of disorder; but that part of it you can see for yourself when we get there. I left orders that nobody should enter the building, and that nothing was to be disturbed until I returned. On making the discovery, the maid rushed from the house screaming, and fell on the lawn in a dead faint. I was at once called, and, by the time the maid had regained her senses, I was on the spot. As soon as she had told her story I looked hastily into the woman's house to verify the facts, and hurried to Boston to secure your services. You are, of course, to do whatever you think best in the matter, and I give you full authority to act in any way you may deem necessary on my premises.'

For a few moments, following the recital, Quincy was silent, knowing well that little further information was to be gained until he should arrive at the grounds and be able to examine the premises in person.

'How did you come to employ the woman when you had absolutely no knowledge of her, or of her previous state of life?' he asked, after a time.

'Why, I told you that I was obliged to have a cook in great haste at that time,' Lamson protested. 'She was well recommended as a cook by the employment agency, and consequently I hired her with very little question. I have never had any trouble whatever with her and, in the twelve years, I had come to look on her as being scrupulously honest and trustworthy in every way. But wait, we are nearly there now, and you will soon have an opportunity to judge this matter at first hand.'

Quincy stared unseeingly at the low and dirty wooden buildings which lined the street along which the machine was speeding. The case appealed strongly to him as it had been rehearsed, and he could not suppress a certain intangible feeling that it would grow yet more interesting as it progressed. Of course, he considered, in the case of a murder for the purpose of robbery, at the possibility of which Lamson hinted, the case would undoubtedly degenerate into a mere police routine affair in which he could take no part. But, on the other hand, the very air of mystery which appeared to surround the woman, herself, gave a vague promise of possibilities into which he would be able to dig and search to his heart's content. He glanced once more at his surroundings, and discovered that they were now in more open country and that the dirty little buildings had given place to the more imposing residences of Beverly's summer colony. The machine turned abruptly, and he discovered that they were rolling up a curved driveway to what was undoubtedly Lamson's house.

A much agitated servant hurried up to the machine as they alighted and, after a somewhat doubtful glance at Quincy, reported in a rapid undertone:

'The police are here, sir, and the medical examiner. I told them of my orders against allowing anybody to enter the cook's house until you had returned with a detective, and they consented to wait. They are down under the tree by the house now.'

'All right, Higgins,' Lamson replied, turning once more toward Quincy. 'Now, Mr Sawyer, if you will come right down we can all examine the rooms together. I am somewhat surprised that the police consented to await my return. They are usually little inclined to await the convenience of a private detective, are they not?'

'Unfortunately, they are,' Quincy replied with a dry smile. 'The police in a large city would not have done so, under any circumstances; but it is probable that in these smaller towns the police and all other municipal officials are more ready to pay heed to the wishes of their wealthy residents. It is out of respect to you, and through no regard for me, that they are waiting.'

Quincy carefully examined the exterior of the cook's former place of residence as they approached. It was a pretty little cottage, painted a conservative white and standing in a location considerably removed from the residence of Lamson himself. The cottage was of fair dimensions, containing, he judged, about six rooms; but it appeared dwarfed because of the giant horse-chestnut trees which towered above it on every side. From beneath one of these trees three men arose, and came forward to meet them, Quincy having an excellent opportunity to examine the officials as they advanced.

The foremost of the trio he judged, by reason of the bountiful supply of gold braid sprinkled over his uniform, to be the chief of the local department. The second, who followed at a respectful distance, was evidently a member of the force, while the last, a rather small, dark-faced man in plain clothes, was undoubtedly the medical examiner. As Quincy and Lamson halted before the house, the chief bustled up to them, a smile, which was evidently intended to be courteous, playing across his ordinarily pompous features.

'We have been waiting some time for you, Mr Lamson,' he remarked; 'but under the circumstances we were willing to delay our work until your return. The affair undoubtedly will prove a simple one, and it is too bad you have gone to the expense of importing a private detective.' With the concluding words he shot a brief, but unfriendly, glance in Quincy's direction.

Lamson made no reply to the speech, other than by a brief nod of recognition, and, stepping quickly to the door, he unlocked it and threw it open, standing aside to allow the entrance of the officials. Like a pack of hounds unleashed the local men dived through the door, and into what was apparently a living room, Quincy and Lamson following in their rear. On entering the room all paused abruptly and stared about them, the scene well warranting the sudden halt.

The room was, indeed, in a terrible state of disorder. Furniture had been overturned, some had been broken, all had been misplaced, and on every hand were to be seen signs of violence and confusion. The main feature, however, was to be found in the figure of a little woman who lay almost in the very middle of the room. The body lay face down, the hair dishevelled and the clothing somewhat disarranged from the struggle, while from its side and several inches below the left armpit protruded the hilt of a heavy and strong-bladed knife. There were very few signs of blood, as the wound had evidently bled inwardly; but the scene was ghastly enough without that.

Exercising the prerogative of his office, the medical examiner strode forward and knelt at the side of the body, gently turning it over. As he did so the watchers instinctively started, for on the woman's face was revealed such an expression of fierce and malignant hatred as it is seldom the misfortune of any person to gaze on. The lips were drawn back in a snarl of rage which left exposed the worn and ragged teeth, and the eyes, fixed and staring, seemed to hold in their depths a fury scarcely human.

'Lord!' muttered Lamson, repressing a shudder. 'She surely didn't die with any love of man in her heart.'

The medical examiner grimly held up the knife. 'From here on it's your work, gentlemen,' he observed. 'Make what you can of this.'

The chief took the knife, and all stared curiously at it. It was an ordinary wooden-hilted knife of the kind to be found in any market and, from the thinness of the blade, it had evidently known long service and many grindings. After nodding his head over it several times, the chief passed the knife on to Quincy with the air of a man wishing to be courteous, although hardly recognizing the possibility of any value in the act. To Quincy, judging from his expression, the knife meant much or nothing. He glanced at it keenly, turned it over several times and then, without comment, returned it to the chief.

The search for clues then started in earnest, the two members of the regular force burrowing amidst the debris in the room like terriers after a rat. They pulled open every drawer, peered under or through every article of furniture, and minutely examined every square inch of space in the room. Now and then the chief would pause to glance speculatively at Quincy, as though in fear that the private detective might stumble on a clue that the regulars had overlooked. After each scrutiny, however, he invariably returned to his search, appearing satisfied that Quincy's aimless wanderings would net him nothing of value in the way of clues.

'By the way, Chief,' Quincy interrupted at length, 'may I inquire as to what it is that you expect to find in this room?'

The chief eyed him suspiciously before replying. 'Well, it's not customary to hand our suspicions to outsiders, but, as you are, in a way, one of us, I don't mind telling you. Of course we are looking for possible clues which the murderer may have left behind, but primarily I want to discover whether or not the old woman's hoard of money is missing.'

'I see, Chief; but, unless we know, which we do not, where the money was hidden, how are we to be able to tell whether or not it is gone? We suspect, of course, but we do not know, that there was money hidden in the house. It is hardly likely that the woman would have kept any quantity of it hidden away in a bureau drawer. It strikes me that if she had money to hide she would have placed it in a more secret hiding-place under the floor boards, behind a stone in the cellar wall, or in some similar crevice. We might search a week and still not find the place. And, even if we should chance to find the money, all we should have gained would be a knowledge that the murderer did not take it. Look over the room. There was no search for money previous to our coming. That furniture was all disarranged during the struggle. Either the murderer knew exactly where the money was hidden, and took it from its hiding-place, or else he was actuated by some other motive, entirely, and had neither thought nor regard for the money that might be here.'

The chief listened stolidly to Quincy's summing up of the matter; but he seemed unimpressed.

'You are at liberty to follow any method you please in the conduct of your search,' he said coldly; 'but the regular police must act under my orders, and I see no necessity for changing the orders because of your ingenious theory. I am experienced in these matters, Mr Sawyer, and I judge that you are not; so please don't confuse my men by advancing any other theories. This murder was for the purpose of robbery, and for no other purpose under the sun.'

Quincy meekly accepted the rebuff without reply, but there was a peculiar smile playing about his lips as he turned away. Apparently undisturbed, he wandered nonchalantly out of the room, with Lamson, angered at the treatment his special representative had received, trailing behind. To the remaining rooms on the first floor Quincy paid only the most casual notice, doing little more than to glance into each before ascending the stairs. On the second floor, however, his interest appeared to awaken, especially when the woman's chamber had been reached.

Once within the chamber his aimless wandering ceased, and his every movement appeared to take on a definite purpose. He glanced sharply over the walls, carefully scrutinizing the few pictures with which they were adorned, after which he stepped briskly to the bureau, where he conducted a most minute examination of the contents of every drawer. Once he paused and held up a small packet before the gaze of Lamson, grinning as he did so.

'I imagine our friends downstairs would be interested in this,' he remarked.

'What are they?' Lamson questioned eagerly.

'Bank books. Your late cook evidently patronized several savings banks, instead of hoarding her money as has been suspected. I'll place them back where they were, and let the police discover them when they reach this point in their search. At their present rate of speed they should reach this room in a day or two.'

For some little time, after the discovery of the books, he remained before the bureau, searching every nook and cranny of it. At last, appearing vastly dissatisfied with the result, he arose and stood meditatively in the middle of the room, allowing his eyes to run rapidly over first one article of furniture and then another.

'Did your cook have a trunk when she came here?' he questioned abruptly.

'I don't think so,' said Lamson slowly, as he strived to remember the event of twelve years previous. 'No, I am sure she brought with her one of those old-fashioned canvas extension bags. It must be around here somewhere.'

Quincy's interest appeared to renew itself at the information, and he was immediately deep in his search again. At last, with much shuffling and scuffling of his feet, he emerged backward from a dark nook in the closet, dragging after him the described bag. Placing it on the floor, he arose and stared at Lamson through eyes shining with eagerness.

'Lamson,' he said, 'I expect to find the clue I want in that bag.

There is one thing that no woman, and few men for that matter, regardless of station in life, is without in these days. It may be only the most tantalizing of clues which I shall be able to make nothing of, but I'll stake my reputation that it's there.'

With no further explanation he threw back the cover of the bag, dropped on his knees before it, and dug into its contents. For several moments there was no sound save his eager breathing, echoed by the puffing breaths of Lamson, and the swishing of articles being hastily overturned in the bag. Then, with an almost explosive exhalation, he started back and sprang to his feet, three small articles in his hand.

'I have it, Lamson,' he exclaimed. 'I have it. Now, what can we make of it?'

He strode to the nearest window, with Lamson scuttling at his heels, and held up to the light three small, unmounted photographs. 'You see, Lamson,' he said, 'every woman has a certain degree of sentiment in her makeup. Consequently, in these days of plentiful photographs, there is scarcely a woman anywhere who does not possess photographs of her early home, or associations surrounding it. Here we have the photographs, but, as they are not mounted, and bear no photographer's seal, their value to us will depend on our ability to recognize the places represented.'

Lamson stared incredulously. 'But my dear Sawyer,' he protested, 'those photographs may represent scenes hundreds or thousands of miles from here. How are we to recognize them? '

Quincy lowered the photographs and turned impressively. 'Lamson,' he said, 'I have not yet looked at those photographs closely, but mark my words when I tell you that they will represent scenes within a radius of fifty miles. That woman was not a traveller.'

Without further comment he raised the photographs once more and studied them carefully.

The first depicted a woman, beyond doubt Mrs Buck at a period much earlier in her life, standing before a small cottage of the style of architecture most frequently seen among the houses of the ocean fishermen. The second showed a large open boat, a trawler, fully manned, and lying just below a wharf with the wharf's buildings visible in the background. The last showed two fishermen standing on the steps of a hotel, and holding between them a strange monster of the deep, while, from above, curious guests peered down from over the balcony rail.

'There, Lamson, I think we have our clue.'

'But how? What in the deuce is there to all that stuff that shows you anything?' Lamson was fairly staggered with bewilderment.

'Look here!' Quincy flipped the second photograph into view. 'That trawler indicates, as do all three photographs, a fishing community. Now look at the buildings in the background. On the central building you can dimly distinguish the sign of the fishing company: The Bay State Codfish Company. Now look at this third photograph. Above the fishermen's heads is the sign of the Puritan Hotel. By coupling those two names we have our clue. Both the Bay State Codfish Company and the Puritan Hotel are located in Gloucester. In the photograph of Mrs Buck herself we find her standing before a typical fisherman's cottage. Therefore, does our clue not point toward Gloucester as a starting-point in our search for the woman's identity and that of her murderer? I also have another clue, but I shall leave that out of the matter for the present.'

'Then you will go to Gloucester?' Lamson questioned.

'At once, although I would suggest that you do not mention the fact to the police. It might only serve to further muddle their brains, and they are sufficiently at sea in regard to this case already.'

'You may use my car for the trip if you want to,' Lamson volunteered immediately.

'No, I thank you. I prefer to go in the train. I shall be pleased to have your car take me to the station, though, if that will not inconvenience you.'

As the pair descended the stairs they paused a moment to gaze at the activities of the police. The room remained in much the same condition as when they had originally viewed it, except for the fact that the body had been removed, thus doing away with the most gruesome feature of the case. Seeing them, the chief paused for a moment.

'Giving up so early in the game, Mr Sawyer?' he inquired, a slightly sneering accent in his voice.

'Not exactly giving up, Chief,' Quincy replied, ignoring the tone. 'But my business temporarily calls me elsewhere, and, for the present, I shall be obliged to absent myself. I expect to return here later on, though, unless in the meantime you have been able to solve the mystery. You have found no trace of hidden wealth as yet, I suppose?'

'No, we have found nothing, but there must be some clue to it somewhere. I am about to act on your suggestion and search the cellar.'

'Before you do that, Chief,' said Quincy, smiling frankly, 'I would suggest that you search the woman's chamber. There are some bank books there which will be of interest to you.'

'You mean that her money was deposited in a bank?' the chief demanded sharply.

'It was, and still is, in a bank, or in banks, to be more exact. I fear you will be wasting your time if you search farther for it here.'

For a moment the chief stared silently, but at last a slow grin began to relieve the hard lines of his face. 'Mr Sawyer,' he said, 'you have put one across on us. I held you lightly in the beginning because, several times of late, my department has been considerably hindered by the actions of amateur detectives, and I took you to belong to the same class. I see you know your business, and I apologize for my former abruptness of speech.'

The speech came as a complete surprise to Quincy, but he was not to be outdone in courtesy. 'Chief,' he said, 'I accept your remarks in the spirit in which they were intended. Frankly, I am now starting out on a clue which I think will prove valuable. If I am successful I shall notify you of the fact on my return, and it is highly probable that we may be able to act together in the final scenes.'

The chief regarded him with increased respect. 'I shall be pleased to act with you if you are successful,' he said simply.

In ten minutes' time Quincy was seated in Lamson's car and hurrying toward the railroad station. Shortly afterward he was aboard a train for Gloucester and, bending over the three photographs, was carefully arranging his plans for the campaign he intended to wage in that peculiar city.

All that day, and throughout the night, Lamson and the chief anxiously awaited the return of Quincy or the coming of some word which would indicate his progress. The affair by that time had been spread broadcast through the medium of the press, and the grounds swarmed with reporters, to the disgust of Lamson, who cordially hated the notoriety which was thus being brought to his door. The second forenoon following the murder passed away without result in the desired direction, and Lamson, unused to the necessary tedium of a police investigation, and suffering from the strain involved, was at his wits' end when Quincy suddenly reappeared as unostentatiously as he had departed. Lamson rushed eagerly from the house to greet him, the chief, no less eager, hurrying after, while the handful of reporters clustered around, listening intently for the first hint which might be incorporated in their several stories. Quincy waved them laughingly aside.

'Not yet, boys,' he adjured them. 'I have a good story for you, and you shall have it very shortly, but I must first make my report to Mr Lamson.'

Obediently the reporters fell back, accepting his assurance without question. Lamson and the chief reached him simultaneously and, above the hurried hum of the reporters' voices, rose Lamson's appeal:

'What luck, Sawyer? For heaven's sake tell me the result quickly.'

Quincy took him soothingly by the arm. 'It's settled, Lamson,' he said quietly; 'but my investigation has had a most remarkable result. A most surprising result! Come into the house, and I'll tell you all about it.'

When they were seated in the library, or at least when the chief and Quincy were seated, Lamson being too nervous to do anything other than to fidget about the room, Quincy digressed slightly from the point of the matter in hand.

'I notice that you have gained considerable notoriety, Lamson,' he said.

'Notoriety!' Lamson snorted the word furiously. 'Notoriety! Yes, I certainly have, thanks to the press and its representatives outside! Look at the headlines which have been running. "Wealthy Epicurean's Cook Murdered", "Lamson's Elysium Wrecked by

Murderer" and so on without end! Why in the world must I be dragged into the case in that manner?'

Quincy allowed himself a smile at Lamson's expense before proceeding. 'You are merely the victim of circumstances, Lamson; but that was not what I intended to tell you. I wish to warn you that you are to receive still more notoriety because this case is about to produce one of the greatest sensations the press has had for years.'

Lamson paled at the words, and his agitation increased perceptibly. 'You don't mean,' he stammered, 'that you suspect me of the murder?'

'Oh, no, Lamson, great Scott, no!' Quincy hastened to assure him. 'I have the murderer, and he has confessed. I merely wished to warn you that Mrs Buck, regardless of her own identity, will still continue in the eyes of the public to be Lamson's cook, and as such she will be handled by the press. But sit down, man, nobody suspects you. I'll tell you my story at once, so that your mind may be placed at rest in that direction at least. You know of the photographs which I discovered before going to Gloucester?' he inquired, turning toward the chief.

'Yes, Mr Lamson told me of them,' the chief informed him.

'Very well, then, I wished you to know of them before telling my story, because I desire you to be in possession of the several clues which led me to Gloucester. As you are aware, one of those pictures showed the wharf of the Bay State Codfish Company. Now, Chief, remember. Do you not recall that the knife with which the murder was committed was stamped on the hilt with the letters "B. S. C. Co.?" From that fact I argued that the person connected with the Bay State Codfish Company in whom Mrs Buck was interested years ago must still be there, and that Gloucester was the spot which I must search for the murderer. As I said before, I found him; but in order to place you thoroughly in possession of the facts I am going to retrogress twelve years and begin my story at that point. The discovery of the man after I reached Gloucester was a very simple act, so simple as to hardly be worthy of recognition in the story, while his confession followed almost as a matter of course. He is at present being held by the Gloucester police. I recognized him, Lamson, from his photograph. He is the man on the right of that sea monster in the third picture; he also appears in the second photograph and, as the other does not, I naturally settled on him at once as the man whom I desired to find.

'But now for the story. Twelve years ago Amos Buck and his shrewish wife, Elizabeth, your cook, Lamson, lived in a small cottage at the far end of the Gloucester water-front. Amos was a trawler in the employ of the Bay State Codfish Company and, being a steady, temperate man, was regarded by the heads of his department as being one of their most reliable employees. But in his case, as in that of every other man, his home environment played a great part in the matter of his value to his employers. His wife's shrewish nature developed, and her constant nagging eventually began to play its part in his ultimate downfall, the result being that he finally became a steady patron of the nearest groggery, and it appeared that his complete degeneration would be merely a matter of time. Daily indulgence soon became protracted into sprees of a week's duration, and Mrs Buck became more vituperative than ever.

'Then another link in the peculiar chain of circumstances was forged. Amos brought to his home a widowed cousin, Emma Bray by name, and insisted upon her taking up her permanent residence with himself and his wife. Mrs Bray greatly resembled Mrs Buck in figure, although their features were vastly dissimilar, and their dispositions were as far separated as the poles. The cousin proved to be a pleasant, even-tempered woman, and she showed every desire to alleviate the constant friction between Buck and his wife.

'Her attempts at intervention only added to Mrs Buck's fury, and within a few weeks Mrs Buck had developed a hatred for both her husband and his cousin that was almost inhuman in its intensity. The demeanour of his wife at last had its effect on Buck himself, and, instead of meekly submitting to her verbal assaults, as he had done in the past, he soon commenced to reply in kind, with the result that the house became a veritable inferno. This continued until one day Buck's temper, grown ragged from the constant warfare, gave way entirely and he struck his wife, knocking her down. Then, overcome by the deed, and by the scenes which had led up to it, he rushed from the house to his favourite haunt in a cheap saloon.

'Although naturally a reticent man, his tongue soon became loosened by liquor and, when one of his associates pointed to a fresh cut on the side of Buck's head, inquiring as to its origin, he replied that his wife had made it, but that he had fixed her so she wouldn't do it again. The savage look with which he accompanied the words, and the dark hint which seemed to be contained in them, caused the speech to be remembered. Shortly afterward Buck purchased a quart of raw rum and disappeared, going nobody knew where.

'The next morning he was aroused by the chief of police from the drunken slumber into which he had sunk behind the sheltering piles of a lumber wharf. The rough handling by the chief, together with the black looks and muttered threats of the small body of men who accompanied him, completely sobered Buck, and he demanded the reason of his arrest. The reply was unsatisfactory, being merely a gruff "Guess you know" from the chief, and a volley of threats from the crowd, which was constantly growing larger.

'To Buck's surprise he was taken directly to his own house and, when led indoors, the last trace of liquor was driven out of him, and his surprise was turned to horror. The main room of the cottage was indeed in a terrible state, its floor and walls being covered with blood, its meagre furnishings broken and scattered, and its every appearance being as if a terrific battle had been waged within it. To make the nature of the crime which had been committed doubly sure, a blood-stained axe lay at one side of the room, where it had evidently been thrown by the fleeing murderer. But, whatever hopes the chief may have had of securing a confession from Buck by taking him to the place were speedily dashed, for Buck, instead of breaking down, appeared too utterly stupefied by the scene for speech of any kind.

'No trace of either woman had been found, and there was consequently nothing to do save to hold Buck on suspicion while the search for the bodies was being conducted. The search speedily bore fruit, for, within an hour of Buck's arrest, the body of a woman was found floating in the harbour. The features had been obliterated, being so badly hacked and battered as to make recognition impossible, but the clothing on the body was speedily identified as being that of Mrs Buck. As no trace of the cousin was found it was decided that her body must have floated out to sea on the tide, and Buck was held, charged with the murder of both women.

'At the trial circumstantial evidence figured strongly in securing Buck's conviction, but there was also a beautiful train of circumstantial evidence in his favour. He pointed out that no blood-stains had been found on his clothing, and defied the prosecution to demonstrate a way in which he could have hacked a body as his wife's had been mangled and then have conveyed it to the water without having become stained with blood. He also showed a streak of genius by defying the police to show conclusively that his cousin, Emma Bray, was really dead, as no trace of her body had been found. This part of the indictment was shortly dropped, and he stood accused of only the one murder, that of his wife.

'Of course his rash words in the saloon played an important part against him, but in his favour was the absence of blood-stains upon him and that fact, together with his drunkenness and the well-known frequency with which his wife had assaulted him, both orally and physically, saved him from execution. He was, however, convicted of murder in the second degree, and sentenced to imprisonment for life; but, even after Buck had been imprisoned, there remained many people who did not believe him guilty of the crime. Consequently, after he had served a term of years, a movement was set on foot to have him pardoned, the movement being eventually successful.

'After his release Buck returned to Gloucester and quietly resumed his old life, taking up his residence in his former home and again entering the employ of the Bay State Codfish Company. For two years he lived quietly and then, like a sudden thunderclap, came a piece of news which entirely upset his every thought. An associate came to him, giving him positive assurance that he had seen Mrs Buck in Beverly, and had been told that she was employed by a rich man as a cook. For days Buck brooded over that information, striving to make himself realize that he had not only been sent to prison for a crime which he had never committed, but also for one which, possibly, had never been committed at all.

'At last he could stand the strain no longer, and so set out one night for Beverly, to prove for himself the truth or falsity of the weird rumour. Before starting, moved by some instinct which even he himself cannot define, he secreted one of the company's knives in his coat, giving it no more thought after his departure from Gloucester.

'On his arrival in Beverly he had no difficulty in locating Lamson's estate and, proceeding here at once, he slipped about in the darkness, searching for the woman who might or might not prove to be his wife. He soon stumbled on the cook's cottage, and, peering through one of the lighted windows, he was able to clearly view the woman within and his feelings cannot be described when he realized that she was indeed his wife. Overcome by a blind, insensate fury, he made his way quickly to the front of the house, burst open the door, and confronted her.

'According to his story the woman showed no surprise at seeing him, but merely sat staring into his face with a smile of contempt on her lips. She made no reply when he accused her of allowing him to be falsely imprisoned, but continued to gloat over him with an air that aroused his already nearly uncontrollable fury to a pitch which it had never hitherto reached. He broke into savage denunciation of her, and, at last, stung her into replying to his charges. To his intense surprise she admitted them to be true. Not only that, but she boastfully asserted that she had killed his cousin out of revenge, and had then dressed the body in her own clothes to throw suspicion on him, had dragged it into the water and had then fled from the place in disguise. As she warmed up to the recital she added almost fiendish details, and through it all she continued to glory in her own success and Buck's resulting conviction.

'Naturally such a scene could have but one ending. Buck's temper became more and more savage and at the conclusion of her story he had reached a point but little, if anything, short of insanity. He told her he was going to kill her and that he would be justified in the act. The announcement sobered her and silenced her tongue; but, instead of screaming for help as he had expected her to do, she launched herself fiercely at his throat. You know the result. The struggle was short-lived, and at its conclusion Buck hurried from the place, making his way immediately back to Gloucester, where I found him.

'Now, gentlemen,' and with the words Quincy straightened impressively, 'now we come to the sensational part of the whole affair. The question to be decided, and it is an important one, is: Can Buck be punished for the murder?

'At first glance the natural reply would be that he can; but, can he? Can the courts touch him in any way? When a man is tried and acquitted he cannot again be brought to trial for the same offence, even though it may afterward be shown conclusively that he is guilty. Therefore, can Buck be twice punished for the same offence? He has already paid the penalty, has paid in advance, so to speak, for the privilege of killing his wife. He was convicted when innocent, and, now that he is guilty, can he be again convicted of the same crime for which he has already paid the penalty which was legally demanded of him?

'I freely admit, gentlemen, that it is a question which I cannot answer, and you may rest assured that the press will eagerly await the decision of the Supreme Court if it is considered necessary to carry the matter that far.'

VIOLET STRANGE

Created by Anna Katharine Green (1846-1935)

In 1878, the poet Anna Katharine Green, disappointed that her verse had not received the recognition she had hoped for it, decided to try her hand at fiction. The result was The Leavenworth Case, *often cited (not entirely accurately since there are other claimants) as the first mystery written by an American woman. The book, with its story of a rich man's murder, investigated by a detective from the New York Metropolitan Police Force named Ebenezer Gryce, was a great success and launched Anna Katharine Green on a career as a crime writer that lasted more than forty years. Gryce returned in a dozen further novels, in some of which he was paired with a proto-Miss Marple figure, a nosey spinster with an eye for crime named Amelia Butterworth. Green also wrote other crime novels and published several volumes of short stories.* The Golden Slipper and Other Stories *appeared in 1915 and introduced another character to her readers. Violet Strange is an attractive young woman, a debutante who is at home amongst the upper echelons of New York society. She also leads a secret life as a professional sleuth, investigating crimes of all kinds to provide herself with an income of which her father knows nothing. The Violet Strange stories are not as pioneering as the longer fiction Green wrote decades earlier but they are skilfully crafted and entertaining, and their lively heroine is one of the most engaging of the era's female detectives.*

THE SECOND BULLET

'No. No.'

'She's a most unhappy woman. Husband and child both taken from her in a moment; and now, all means of living as well, unless some happy thought of yours – some inspiration of your genius –

shows us a way of re-establishing her claims to the policy voided by this cry of suicide.'

But the small wise head of Violet Strange continued its slow shake of decided refusal.

'I'm sorry,' she protested, 'but it's quite out of my province. I'm too young to meddle with so serious a matter.'

'Not when you can save a bereaved woman the only possible compensation left her by untoward fate?'

'Let the police try their hand at that.'

'They have had no success with the case.'

'Or you?'

'Nor I either.'

'And you expect –'

'Yes, Miss Strange. I expect you to find the missing bullet which will settle the fact that murder and not suicide ended George Hammond's life. If you cannot, then a long litigation awaits this poor widow, ending, as such litigation usually does, in favour of the stronger party. There's the alternative. If you once saw her –'

'But that's what I'm not willing to do. If I once saw her I should yield to her importunities and attempt the seemingly impossible. My instincts bid me say no. Give me something easier.'

'Easier things are not so remunerative. There's money in this affair, if the insurance company is forced to pay up. I can offer you –'

'What?'

There was eagerness in the tone despite her effort at nonchalance. The other smiled imperceptibly, and briefly named the sum.

It was larger than she had expected. This her visitor saw by the way her eyelids fell and the peculiar stillness which, for an instant, held her vivacity in check.

'And you think I can earn that?'

Her eyes were fixed on his in an eagerness as honest as it was unrestrained.

He could hardly conceal his amazement, her desire was so evident and the cause of it so difficult to understand. He knew she wanted money – that was her avowed reason for entering into this uncongenial work. But to want it so much! He glanced at her person; it was simply clad but very expensively – how expensively it was his business to know. Then he took in the room in which they sat. Simplicity again, but the simplicity of high art – the drawing room of one rich enough to indulge in the final luxury of a highly cultivated taste, viz.: unostentatious elegance and the subjection of each carefully chosen ornament to the general effect.

What did this favoured child of fortune lack that she could be reached by such a plea, when her whole being revolted from the nature of the task he offered her? It was a question not new to him; but one he had never heard answered and was not likely to hear answered now. But the fact remained that the consent he had thought dependent upon sympathetic interest could be reached much more readily by the promise of large emolument – and he owned to a feeling of secret disappointment even while he recognized the value of the discovery.

But his satisfaction in the latter, if satisfaction it were, was of very short duration. Almost immediately he observed a change in her. The sparkle which had shone in the eye whose depths he had never been able to penetrate, had dissipated itself in something like a tear and she spoke up in that vigorous tone no one but himself had ever heard, as she said:

'No. The sum is a good one and I could use it; but I will not waste my energy on a case I do not believe in. The man shot himself. He was a speculator, and probably had good reason for his act. Even his wife acknowledges that he has lately had more losses than gains.'

'See her. She has something to tell you which never got into the papers.'

'You say that? You know that?'

'On my honour, Miss Strange.'

Violet pondered; then suddenly succumbed.

'Let her come, then. Prompt to the hour. I will receive her at three. Later I have a tea and two party calls to make.'

Her visitor rose to leave. He had been able to subdue all evidence of his extreme gratification, and now took on a formal air. In dismissing a guest, Miss Strange was invariably the society belle and that only. This he had come to recognize.

The case (well known at the time) was, in the fewest possible words, as follows:

On a sultry night in September, a young couple living in one of the large apartment houses in the extreme upper portion of Manhattan were so annoyed by the incessant crying of a child in the adjoining suite that they got up, he to smoke, and she to sit in the window for a possible breath of cool air. They were congratulating themselves upon the wisdom they had shown in thus giving up all thought of sleep – for the child's crying had not ceased – when (it may have been two o'clock and it may have been a little later) there came from somewhere near the sharp and somewhat peculiar detonation of a pistol-shot.

He thought it came from above; she, from the rear, and they were staring at each other in the helpless wonder of the moment, when they were struck by the silence. The baby had ceased to cry. All was as still in the adjoining apartment as in their own – too still – much too still. Their mutual stare turned to one of horror. 'It came from there!' whispered the wife. 'Some accident has occurred to Mr or Mrs Hammond – we ought to go –'

Her words – very tremulous ones – were broken by a shout from below. They were standing in their window and had evidently been seen by a passing policeman. 'Anything wrong up there?' they heard him cry. Mr Saunders immediately looked out. 'Nothing wrong here,' he called down. (They were but two stories from the pavement.) 'But I'm not so sure about the rear apartment. We thought we heard a shot. Hadn't you better come up, officer? My wife is nervous about it. I'll meet you at the stair-head and show you the way.'

The officer nodded and stepped in. The young couple hastily donned some wraps, and, by the time he appeared on their floor, they were ready to accompany him.

Meanwhile, no disturbance was apparent anywhere else in the house, until the policeman rang the bell of the Hammond apartment. Then, voices began to be heard, and doors to open above and below, but not the one before which the policeman stood.

Another ring, and this time an insistent one – and still no

response. The officer's hand was rising for the third time when there came a sound of fluttering from behind the panels against which he had laid his ear, and finally a choked voice uttering unintelligible words. Then a hand began to struggle with the lock, and the door, slowly opening, disclosed a woman clad in a hastily donned wrapper and giving every evidence of extreme fright.

'Oh!' she exclaimed, seeing only the compassionate faces of her neighbours. 'You heard it, too! A pistol-shot from there – there – my husband's room. I have not dared to go – I – I – O, have mercy and see if anything is wrong! It is so still – so still, and only a moment ago the baby was crying. Mrs Saunders, Mrs Saunders, why is it so still?'

She had fallen into her neighbour's arms. The hand with which she had pointed out a certain door had sunk to her side and she appeared to be on the verge of collapse.

The officer eyed her sternly, while noting her appearance, which was that of a woman hastily risen from bed.

'Where were you?' he asked. 'Not with your husband and child, or you would know what had happened there.'

'I was sleeping down the hall,' she managed to gasp out. 'I'm not well – I – oh, why do you all stand still and do nothing? My baby's in there. Go! go!' and, with sudden energy, she sprang upright, her eyes wide open and burning, her small well-featured face white as the linen she sought to hide.

The officer demurred no longer. In another instant he was trying the door at which she was again pointing.

It was locked.

Glancing back at the woman, now cowering almost to the floor, he pounded at the door and asked the man inside to open.

No answer came back.

With a sharp turn he glanced again at the wife.

'You say that your husband is in this room?'

She nodded, gasping faintly, 'And the child!'

He turned back, listened, then beckoned to Mr Saunders. 'We shall have to break our way in,' said he. 'Put your shoulder well to the door. Now!'

The hinges of the door creaked; the lock gave way (this special officer weighed two hundred and seventy-five, as he found out, next day), and a prolonged and sweeping crash told the rest.

Mrs Hammond gave a low cry; and, straining forward from where she crouched in terror on the floor, searched the faces of the two men for some hint of what they saw in the dimly-lighted space beyond. Something dreadful, something which made Mr Saunders come rushing back with a shout:

'Take her away! Take her to our apartment, Jennie. She must not see —'

Not see! He realized the futility of his words as his gaze fell on the young woman who had risen up at his approach and now stood gazing at him without speech, without movement, but with a glare of terror in her eyes, which gave him his first realization of human misery.

His own glance fell before it. If he had followed his instinct he would have fled the house rather than answer the question of her look and the attitude of her whole frozen body.

Perhaps in mercy to his speechless terror, perhaps in mercy to herself, she was the one who at last found the word which voiced their mutual anguish.

'Dead?'

No answer. None was needed.

'And my baby?'

O, that cry! It curdled the hearts of all who heard it. It shook the souls of men and women both inside and outside the apartment; then all was forgotten in the wild rush she made. The wife and mother had flung herself upon the scene, and, side by side with the not unmoved policeman, stood looking down upon the desolation made in one fatal instant in her home and heart.

They lay there together, both past help, both quite dead. The child had simply been strangled by the weight of his father's arm which lay directly across the upturned little throat. But the father was a victim of the shot they had heard. There was blood on his breast, and a pistol in his hand.

Suicide! The horrible truth was patent. No wonder they wanted to hold the young widow back. Her neighbour, Mrs Saunders, crept in on tiptoe and put her arms about the swaying, fainting woman; but there was nothing to say – absolutely nothing.

At least, they thought not. But when they saw her throw herself down, not by her husband, but by the child, and drag it out from under that strangling arm and hug and kiss it and call out wildly for a doctor, the officer endeavoured to interfere and yet could not find the heart to do so, though he knew the child was dead and should not, according to all the rules of the coroner's office, be moved before that official arrived. Yet because no mother could be convinced of a fact like this, he let her sit with it on the floor and try all her little arts to revive it, while he gave orders to the janitor and waited himself for the arrival of doctor and coroner.

She was still sitting there in wide-eyed misery, alternately fondling the little body and drawing back to consult its small set features for some sign of life, when the doctor came, and, after one look at the child, drew it softly from her arms and laid it quietly in the crib from which its father had evidently lifted it but a short time before. Then he turned back to her, and found her on her feet, upheld by her two friends. She had understood his action, and without a groan had accepted her fate. Indeed, she seemed incapable of any further speech or action. She was staring down at her husband's body, which she, for the first time, seemed fully to see. Was her look one of grief or of resentment for the part he had played so unintentionally in her child's death? It was hard to tell; and when, with slowly rising finger, she pointed to the pistol so tightly clutched in the other outstretched hand, no one there – and by this time the room was full – could foretell what her words would be when her tongue regained its usage and she could speak.

What she did say was this:

'Is there a bullet gone? Did he fire off that pistol?' A question so manifestly one of delirium that no one answered it, which seemed to surprise her, though she said nothing till her glance had passed all around the walls of the room to where a window stood open to the night – its lower sash being entirely raised. 'There! Look there!' she cried, with a commanding accent, and, throwing up her hands, sank a dead weight into the arms of those supporting her.

No one understood; but naturally more than one rushed to

the window. An open space was before them. Here lay the fields not yet parcelled out into lots and built upon; but it was not upon these they looked, but upon the strong trellis which they found there, which, if it supported no vine, formed a veritable ladder between this window and the ground.

Could she have meant to call attention to this fact; and were her words expressive of another idea than the obvious one of suicide?

If so, to what lengths a woman's imagination can go! Or so their combined looks seemed to proclaim, when to their utter astonishment they saw the officer, who had presented a calm appearance up till now, shift his position and with a surprised grunt direct their eyes to a portion of the wall just visible beyond the half-drawn curtains of the bed. The mirror hanging there showed a star-shaped breakage, such as follows the sharp impact of a bullet or a fiercely projected stone.

'He fired two shots. One went wild; the other straight home.'

It was the officer delivering his opinion.

Mr Saunders, returning from the distant room where he had assisted in carrying Mrs Hammond, cast a look at the shattered glass, and remarked forcibly:

'I heard but one; and I was sitting up, disturbed by that poor infant. Jennie, did you hear more than one shot?' he asked, turning toward his wife.

'No,' she answered, but not with the readiness he had evidently expected. 'I heard only one, but that was not quite usual in its tone. I'm used to guns,' she explained, turning to the officer. 'My father was an army man, and he taught me very early to load and fire a pistol. There was a prolonged sound to this shot; something like an echo of itself, following close upon the first ping. Didn't you notice that, Warren?'

'I remember something of the kind,' her husband allowed.

'He shot twice and quickly,' interposed the policeman, sententiously. 'We shall find a spent bullet back of that mirror.'

But when, upon the arrival of the coroner, an investigation was made of the mirror and the wall behind, no bullet was found either there or anywhere else in the room, save in the dead man's breast. Nor had more than one been shot from his pistol, as five full chambers testified. The case which seemed so simple had its mysteries, but the assertion made by Mrs Saunders no longer carried weight, nor was the evidence offered by the broken mirror considered as indubitably establishing the fact that a second shot had been fired in the room.

Yet it was equally evident that the charge which had entered the dead speculator's breast had not been delivered at the close range of the pistol found clutched in his hand. There were no powder-marks to be discerned on his pyjama-jacket, or on the flesh beneath. Thus anomaly confronted anomaly, leaving open but one other theory: that the bullet found in Mr Hammond's breast came from the window and the one he shot went out of it. But this would necessitate his having shot his pistol from a point far removed from where he was found; and his wound was such as made it difficult to believe that he would stagger far, if at all, after its infliction.

Yet, because the coroner was both conscientious and alert, he caused a most rigorous search to be made of the ground overlooked by the above mentioned window; a search in which the police joined, but which was without any result save that of rousing the attention of people in the neighbourhood and leading to a story being circulated of a man seen some time the night before crossing the fields in a great hurry. But as no further particulars were forthcoming, and not even a description of the man to be had, no emphasis would have been laid upon this story had it not transpired that the moment a report of it had come to Mrs Hammond's ears (why is there always someone to carry these reports?) she roused from the torpor into which she had fallen, and in wild fashion exclaimed:

'I knew it! I expected it! He was shot through the window and by that wretch. He never shot himself.' Violent declarations which trailed off into the one continuous wail, 'O, my baby! my poor baby!'

Such words, even though the fruit of delirium, merited some sort of attention, or so this good coroner thought, and as soon as opportunity offered and she was sufficiently sane and quiet to respond to his questions, he asked her whom she had meant by that wretch, and what reason she had, or thought she had, of attributing her husband's death to any other agency than his own disgust with life.

And then it was that his sympathies, although greatly roused in her favour began to wane. She met the question with a cold stare followed by a few ambiguous words out of which he could make nothing. Had she said wretch? She did not remember. They must not be influenced by anything she might have uttered in her first grief. She was well-nigh insane at the time. But of one thing they might be sure: her husband had not shot himself; he was too much afraid of death for such an act. Besides, he was too happy. Whatever folks might say he was too fond of his family to wish to leave it.

Nor did the coroner or any other official succeed in eliciting anything further from her. Even when she was asked, with cruel insistence, how she explained the fact that the baby was found lying on the floor instead of in its crib, her only answer was: 'His father was trying to soothe it. The child was crying dreadfully, as you have heard from those who were kept awake by him that night, and my husband was carrying him about when the shot came which caused George to fall and overlay the baby in his struggles.'

'Carrying a baby about with a loaded pistol in his hand?' came back in stern retort.

She had no answer for this. She admitted when informed that the bullet extracted from her husband's body had been found to correspond exactly with those remaining in the five chambers of the pistol taken from his hand, that he was not only the owner of this pistol but was in the habit of sleeping with it under his pillow; but, beyond that, nothing; and this reticence, as well as her manner which was cold and repellent, told against her.

A verdict of suicide was rendered by the coroner's jury, and the life-insurance company, in which Mr Hammond had but lately insured himself for a large sum, taking advantage of the suicide clause embodied in the policy, announced its determination of not paying the same.

Such was the situation, as known to Violet Strange and the

general public, on the day she was asked to see Mrs Hammond and learn what might alter her opinion as to the justice of this verdict and the stand taken by the Shuler Life Insurance Company.

The clock on the mantel in Miss Strange's rose-coloured boudoir had struck three, and Violet was gazing in some impatience at the door, when there came a gentle knock upon it, and the maid (one of the elderly, not youthful, kind) ushered in her expected visitor.

'You are Mrs Hammond?' she asked, in natural awe of the too black figure outlined so sharply against the deep pink of the sea-shell room.

The answer was a slow lifting of the veil which shadowed the features she knew only from the cuts she had seen in newspapers.

'You are – Miss Strange?' stammered her visitor; 'the young lady who –'

'I am,' chimed in a voice as ringing as it was sweet. 'I am the person you have come here to see. And this is my home. But that does not make me less interested in the unhappy, or less desirous of serving them. Certainly you have met with the two greatest losses which can come to a woman – I know your story well enough to say that – but what have you to tell me in proof that you should not lose your anticipated income as well? Something vital, I hope, else I cannot help you; something which you should have told the coroner's jury – and did not.'

The flush which was the sole answer these words called forth did not take from the refinement of the young widow's expression, but rather added to it; Violet watched it in its ebb and flow and, seriously affected by it (why, she did not know, for Mrs Hammond had made no other appeal either by look or gesture), pushed forward a chair and begged her visitor to be seated.

'We can converse in perfect safety here,' she said. 'When you feel quite equal to it, let me hear what you have to communicate. It will never go any further. I could not do the work I do if I felt it necessary to have a confidant.'

'But you are so young and so – so –'

'So inexperienced you would say and so evidently a member of what New Yorkers call "society". Do not let that trouble you. My inexperience is not likely to last long and my social pleasures are more apt to add to my efficiency than to detract from it.'

With this Violet's face broke into a smile. It was not the brilliant one so often seen upon her lips, but there was something in its quality which carried encouragement to the widow and led her to say with obvious eagerness:

'You know the facts?'

'I have read all the papers.'

'I was not believed on the stand.'

'It was your manner —'

'I could not help my manner. I was keeping something back, and, being unused to deceit, I could not act quite naturally.'

'Why did you keep something back? When you saw the unfavourable impression made by your reticence, why did you not speak up and frankly tell your story?'

'Because I was ashamed. Because I thought it would hurt me more to speak than to keep silent. I do not think so now; but I did then — and so made my great mistake. You must remember not only the awful shock of my double loss, but the sense of guilt accompanying it; for my husband and I had quarrelled that night, quarrelled bitterly — that was why I had run away into another room and not because I was feeling ill and impatient of the baby's fretful cries.'

'So people have thought.' In saying this, Miss Strange was perhaps cruelly emphatic. 'You wish to explain that quarrel? You think it will be doing any good to your cause to go into that matter with me now?'

'I cannot say; but I must first clear my conscience and then try to convince you that quarrel or no quarrel, he never took his own life. He was not that kind. He had an abnormal fear of death. I do not like to say it but he was a physical coward. I have seen him turn pale at the least hint of danger. He could no more have turned that muzzle upon his own breast than he could have turned it upon his baby. Some other hand shot him, Miss Strange. Remember the open window, the shattered mirror; and I think I know that hand.'

Her head had fallen forward on her breast. The emotion she showed was not so eloquent of grief as of deep personal shame.

'You think you know the man?' In saying this, Violet's voice sunk to a whisper. It was an accusation of murder she had just heard.

'To my great distress, yes. When Mr Hammond and I were married,' the widow now proceeded in a more determined tone, 'there was another man – a very violent one – who vowed even at the church door that George and I should never live out two full years together. We have not. Our second anniversary would have been in November.'

'But –'

'Let me say this: the quarrel of which I speak was not serious enough to occasion any such act of despair on his part. A man would be mad to end his life on account of so slight a disagreement. It was not even on account of the person of whom I've just spoken, though that person had been mentioned between us earlier in the evening, Mr Hammond having come across him face to face that very afternoon in the subway. Up to this time neither of us had seen or heard of him since our wedding-day.'

'And you think this person whom you barely mentioned, so mindful of his old grudge that he sought out your domicile, and, with the intention of murder, climbed the trellis leading to your room and turned his pistol upon the shadowy figure which was all he could see in the semi-obscurity of a much lowered gas-jet?'

'A man in the dark does not need a bright light to see his enemy when he is intent upon revenge.'

Miss Strange altered her tone.

'And your husband? You must acknowledge that he shot off his pistol whether the other did or not.'

'It was in self-defence. He would shoot to save his own life – or the baby's.'

'Then he must have heard or seen –'

'A man at the window.'

'And would have shot there?'

'Or tried to.'

'Tried to?'

'Yes; the other shot first – oh, I've thought it all out – causing my husband's bullet to go wild. It was his which broke the mirror.'

Violet's eyes, bright as stars, suddenly narrowed.

'And what happened then?' she asked. 'Why cannot they find the bullet?'

'Because it went out of the window – glanced off and went out of the window.'

Mrs Hammond's tone was triumphant; her look spirited and intense.

Violet eyed her compassionately.

'Would a bullet glancing off from a mirror, however hung, be apt to reach a window so far on the opposite side?'

'I don't know; I only know that it did,' was the contradictory, almost absurd, reply.

'What was the cause of the quarrel you speak of between your husband and yourself? You see, I must know the exact truth and all the truth to be of any assistance to you.'

'It was – it was about the care I gave, or didn't give, the baby. I feel awfully to have to say it, but George did not think I did my full duty by the child. He said there was no need of its crying so; that if I gave it the proper attention it would not keep the neighbours and himself awake half the night. And I – I got angry and insisted that I did the best I could; that the child was naturally fretful and that if he wasn't satisfied with my way of looking after it, he might try his. All of which was very wrong and unreasonable on my part, as witness the awful punishment which followed.'

'And what made you get up and leave him?'

'The growl he gave me in reply. When I heard that, I bounded out of bed and said I was going to the spare room to sleep; and if the baby cried he might just try what he could do himself to stop it.'

'And he answered?'

'This, just this – I shall never forget his words as long as I live – "If you go, you need not expect me to let you in again no matter what happens."'

'He said that?'

'And locked the door after me. You see I could not tell all that.'

'It might have been better if you had. It was such a natural quarrel and so unprovocative of actual tragedy.'

Mrs Hammond was silent. It was not difficult to see that she had no very keen regrets for her husband personally. But then he was not a very estimable man nor in any respect her equal.

'You were not happy with him,' Violet ventured to remark.

'I was not a fully contented woman. But for all that he had no cause to complain of me except for the reason I have mentioned. I was not a very intelligent mother. But if the baby were living now – O, if he were living now – with what devotion I should care for him.'

She was on her feet, her arms were raised, her face impassioned with feeling. Violet, gazing at her, heaved a little sigh. It was perhaps in keeping with the situation, perhaps extraneous to it, but whatever its source, it marked a change in her manner. With no further check upon her sympathy, she said very softly:

'It is well with the child.'

The mother stiffened, swayed, and then burst into wild weeping.

'But not with me,' she cried, 'not with me. I am desolate and bereft. I have not even a home in which to hide my grief and no prospect of one.'

'But,' interposed Violet, 'surely your husband left you something? You cannot be quite penniless?'

'My husband left nothing,' was the answer, uttered without bitterness, but with all the hardness of fact. 'He had debts. I shall pay those debts. When these and other necessary expenses are liquidated, there will be but little left. He made no secret of the fact that he lived close up to his means. That is why he was induced to take on a life insurance. Not a friend of his but knows his improvidence. I – I have not even jewels. I have only my determination and an absolute conviction as to the real nature of my husband's death.'

'What is the name of the man you secretly believe to have shot your husband from the trellis?'

Mrs Hammond told her.

It was a new one to Violet. She said so and then asked:

'What else can you tell me about him?'

'Nothing, but that he is a very dark man and has a club-foot.'

'Oh, what a mistake you've made.'

'Mistake? Yes, I acknowledge that.'

'I mean in not giving this last bit of information at once to the police. A man can be identified by such a defect. Even his footsteps can be traced. He might have been found that very day. Now, what have we to go upon?'

'You are right, but not expecting to have any difficulty about the insurance money I thought it would be generous in me to keep still. Besides, this is only surmise on my part. I feel certain that my husband was shot by another hand than his own, but I know of no way of proving it. Do you?'

Then Violet talked seriously with her, explaining how their only hope lay in the discovery of a second bullet in the room which had already been ransacked for this very purpose and without the shadow of a result.

A tea, a musicale, and an evening dance kept Violet Strange in a whirl for the remainder of the day. No brighter eye nor more contagious wit lent brilliance to these occasions, but with the passing of the midnight hour no one who had seen her in the blaze of electric lights would have recognized this favoured child of fortune in the earnest figure sitting in the obscurity of an up-town apartment, studying the walls, the ceilings, and the floors by the dim light of a lowered gas-jet. Violet Strange in society was a very different person from Violet Strange under the tension of her secret and peculiar work.

She had told them at home that she was going to spend the night with a friend; but only her old coachman knew who that friend was. Therefore a very natural sense of guilt mingled with her emotions at finding herself alone on a scene whose gruesome mystery she could solve only by identifying herself with the place and the man who had perished there.

Dismissing from her mind all thought of self, she strove to think as he thought, and act as he acted on the night when he found himself (a man of but little courage) left in this room with an ailing child.

At odds with himself, his wife, and possibly with the child

screaming away in its crib, what would he be apt to do in his present emergency? Nothing at first, but as the screaming continued he would remember the old tales of fathers walking the floor at night with crying babies, and hasten to follow suit. Violet, in her anxiety to reach his inmost thought, crossed to where the crib had stood, and, taking that as a start, began pacing the room in search of the spot from which a bullet, if shot, would glance aside from the mirror in the direction of the window. (Not that she was ready to accept this theory of Mrs Hammond, but that she did not wish to entirely dismiss it without putting it to the test.)

She found it in an unexpected quarter of the room and much nearer the bed-head than where his body was found. This, which might seem to confuse matters, served, on the contrary to remove from the case one of its most serious difficulties. Standing here, he was within reach of the pillow under which his pistol lay hidden, and if startled, as his wife believed him to have been by a noise at the other end of the room, had but to crouch and reach behind him in order to find himself armed and ready for a possible intruder.

Imitating his action in this as in other things, she had herself crouched low at the bedside and was on the point of withdrawing her hand from under the pillow, when a new surprise checked her movement and held her fixed in her position, with eyes staring straight at the adjoining wall. She had seen there what he must have seen in making this same turn – the dark bars of the opposite window-frame outlined in the mirror – and understood at once what had happened. In the nervousness and terror of the moment, George Hammond had mistaken this reflection of the window for the window itself, and shot impulsively at the man he undoubtedly saw covering him from the trellis without. But while this explained the shattering of the mirror, how about the other and still more vital question, of where the bullet went afterward? Was the angle at which it had been fired acute enough to send it out of a window diagonally opposed? No; even if the pistol had been held closer to the man firing it than she had reason to believe, the angle still would be oblique enough to carry it on to the further wall.

But no sign of any such impact had been discovered on this

wall. Consequently, the force of the bullet had been expended before reaching it, and when it fell –

Here, her glance, slowly traveling along the floor, impetuously paused. It had reached the spot where the two bodies had been found, and unconsciously her eyes rested there, conjuring up the picture of the bleeding father and the strangled child. How piteous and how dreadful it all was. If she could only understand – suddenly she rose straight up, staring and immovable in the dim light. Had the idea – the explanation – the only possible explanation covering the whole phenomena come to her at last?

It would seem so, for as she so stood, a look of conviction settled over her features, and with this look, evidences of a horror which for all her fast accumulating knowledge of life and its possibilities made her appear very small and very helpless.

A half-hour later, when Mrs Hammond, in her anxiety at hearing nothing more from Miss Strange, opened the door of her room, it was to find, lying on the edge of the sill, the little detective's card with these words hastily written across it:

I do not feel as well as I could wish, and so have telephoned to my own coachman to come and take me home. I will either see or write you within a few days. But do not allow yourself to hope. I pray you do not allow yourself the least hope; the outcome is still very problematical.

When Violet's employer entered his office the next morning it was to find a veiled figure awaiting him which he at once recognized as that of his little deputy. She was slow in lifting her veil and when it finally came free he felt a momentary doubt as to his wisdom in giving her just such a matter as this to investigate. He was quite sure of his mistake when he saw her face, it was so drawn and pitiful.

'You have failed,' said he.

'Of that you must judge,' she answered; and drawing near she whispered in his ear.

'No!' he cried in his amazement.

'Think,' she murmured, 'think. Only so can all the facts be accounted for.'

'I will look into it; I will certainly look into it,' was his earnest reply. 'If you are right – but never mind that. Go home and take a horseback ride in the Park. When I have news in regard to this I will let you know. Till then forget it all. Hear me, I charge you to forget everything but your balls and your parties.'

And Violet obeyed him.

Some few days after this, the following statement appeared in all the papers:

'Owing to some remarkable work done by the firm of –– & ––, the well-known private detective agency, the claim made by Mrs George Hammond against the Shuler Life Insurance Company is likely to be allowed without further litigation. As our readers will remember, the contestant has insisted from the first that the bullet causing her husband's death came from another pistol than the one found clutched in his own hand. But while reasons were not lacking to substantiate this assertion, the failure to discover more than the disputed track of a second bullet led to a verdict of suicide, and a refusal of the company to pay.

'But now that bullet has been found. And where? In the most startling place in the world, viz.: in the larynx of the child found lying dead upon the floor beside his father, strangled as was supposed by the weight of that father's arm. The theory is, and there seems to be none other, that the father, hearing a suspicious noise at the window, set down the child he was endeavouring to soothe and made for the bed and his own pistol, and, mistaking a reflection of the assassin for the assassin himself, sent his shot sidewise at a mirror just as the other let go the trigger which drove a similar bullet into his breast. The course of the one was straight and fatal and that of the other deflected. Striking the mirror at an oblique angle, the bullet fell to the floor where it was picked up by the crawling child, and, as was most natural, thrust at once into his mouth. Perhaps it felt hot to the little tongue; perhaps the child was simply frightened by some convulsive movement of the father who evidently spent his last moment in an endeavour to reach the child, but, whatever the cause, in the quick gasp it gave, the bullet was drawn into the larynx, strangling him.

'That the father's arm, in his last struggle, should have fallen directly across the little throat is one of those anomalies which confounds reason and misleads justice by stopping investigation at the very point where truth lies and mystery disappears.

'Mrs Hammond is to be congratulated that there are detectives who do not give too much credence to outward appearances.'

We expect soon to hear of the capture of the man who sped home the death-dealing bullet.

PROFESSOR AUGUSTUS SFX VAN DUSEN ('THE THINKING MACHINE')

Created by Jacques Futrelle (1875–1912)

Is there a fictional detective even more cerebral than Sherlock Holmes? One more committed to the power of cold, unemotional reasoning? Step forward the extravagantly named Professor Augustus SFX Van Dusen, otherwise known as 'The Thinking Machine'. Van Dusen was the creation of Jacques Futrelle. His most famous appearance is in a much-anthologised story entitled 'The Problem of Cell 13' in which the Professor applies his gigantic brain to the challenge of exiting an apparently escape-proof prison cell. (The story is included in my own anthology, The Rivals of Sherlock Holmes.*) However, Futrelle wrote dozens of other tales about The Thinking Machine between 1905 and 1912, all of which are worth reading. Futrelle himself was born in Georgia and worked as a journalist in Atlanta before moving to New England to write for newspapers in New York and Boston. He began publishing fiction and both his novels and his short stories proved popular. One of the novels,* The Diamond Master, *was adapted for Hollywood three times in the silent era. In 1912, Futrelle visited England and booked passage back to New York on an ocean liner. Unfortunately, the liner was the* Titanic. *When ship met iceberg and sank, he was amongst nearly 1500 who drowned. His detective – brilliant, cantankerous and eccentric – lives on.*

THE PROBLEM OF THE OPERA BOX

Gradually the lights dimmed and the great audience became an impalpable, shadowy mass broken here and there by the vagrant glint of a jewel or the gleam of white shoulders. There was a preliminary blare of horns, then the crashing anvil chorus of *Il*

Trovatore began. Sparks spattered and flashed as the sledges rose and fell in exquisite rhythm while the clangorous music roared through the big theatre.

Eleanor Oliver arose, and moving from the front of the box into the gloom at the rear, leaned her head wearily against the latticed partition. Her mother, beside whom she had been sitting, glanced up inquiringly as did her father and their guest Sylvester Knight.

'What's the matter, my dear?' asked Mrs Oliver.

'Those sparks and that noise give me a headache,' she explained. 'Father, sit in front there if you wish. I'll stay here in the dark until I feel better.'

Mr Oliver took the seat near his wife and Knight immediately lost interest in the stage, turning his chair to face Eleanor. She seemed a little pale and mingled eagerness and anxiety in his face showed his concern. They chatted together for a minute or so and under cover of darkness his hand caught hers and held it a fluttering prisoner.

As they talked the drone of their voices interfered with Mrs Oliver's enjoyment of the music and she glanced back warningly. Neither noticed it for Knight was gazing deeply into the girl's eyes with adoration in his own. She made some remark to him and he protested quickly.

'Please don't,' Mrs Oliver heard him say pleadingly as his voice was raised. 'It won't be long.'

'I'm afraid I'll have to,' the girl replied.

'You mustn't,' Knight commanded earnestly. 'If you insist on it I shall have to do something desperate.'

Mrs Oliver turned and looked back at them reprovingly.

'You children chatter too much,' she said good-naturedly. 'You make more noise than the anvils.'

She turned again to the stage and Knight was silent for a moment. Finally the girl said something else that the mother didn't catch.

'Certainly,' he replied.

He arose quietly and left the box. The swish and fall of the curtain behind him were smothered in the heavy volume of music. The girl sat white and inert. Knight found her in just that position when he returned with a glass of water. He had been out only a minute or so, and the encore to the chorus was just ending.

He offered the glass to Eleanor but she made no move to take it and he touched her lightly on the arm. Still she did not move and he leaned over and looked at her closely. Then he turned quickly to Mrs Oliver.

'Eleanor has fainted, I think,' he whispered uneasily.

'Fainted?' exclaimed Mrs Oliver as she arose. 'Fainted?'

She pushed her chair back and in a moment was beside her daughter chafing her hands. Mr Oliver turned and glanced at them with languid interest.

'What's the matter now?' he inquired.

'We'll have to go,' replied Mrs Oliver. 'Eleanor has fainted.'

'Again?' he asked impatiently.

Knight hovered about anxiously, helplessly as the father and mother worked with the girl. Finally in some way he never understood Eleanor was lifted out, still unconscious and white as death, and removed in a waiting carriage to her home. Two physicians were summoned and disappeared into her boudoir while Knight paced back and forth restlessly between the smoking room and the hall. Mrs Oliver was with her daughter; Mr Oliver sat quietly smoking.

'I wouldn't worry,' he advised the young man after a few minutes. 'She has a trick of fainting like that. You will know more about her after a while – when she is Mrs Knight.'

★★★★

From somewhere upstairs came a scream and Knight started nervously. It was a shrill, penetrating cry that tore straight through him. Mr Oliver took it phlegmatically, even smiled at his nervousness.

'That's my wife fainting,' he explained. 'She always does it that way. You know,' he added confidentially, 'my wife and two daughters are so exhausted with this everlasting social game that they go off like that at any minute. I've talked to them about it but they won't listen.'

Heedless of the idle, even heartless, comments of the father Knight stopped in the hall and stood at the foot of the stairs looking up. After a minute a man came down; it was Dr Brander, one of the two physicians who had been called. On his face was an expression of troubled perplexity.

'How is she?' demanded Knight abruptly.

'Where is Mr Oliver?' asked Dr Brander.

'In the smoking room,' replied the young man. 'What's the matter?'

Without answering the physician went on to the father. Mr Oliver looked up.

'Bring her around all right?' he asked.

'She's dead,' replied the physician.

'Dead?' gasped Knight.

Mr Oliver rose suddenly and gripped the physician fiercely by a shoulder. For an instant he gazed and then his face grew deathly pale. With a distinct effort he recovered himself.

'Her heart?' he asked at last.

'No. She was stabbed.'

Dr Brander looked from one to the other of the two white faces with troubled lines about his eyes.

'Why it can't be,' burst out Knight suddenly. 'Where is she? I'll go to her.'

Dr Brander laid a detaining hand on his shoulder.

'You can do no good,' he said quietly.

For a time Mr Oliver was dumb and the physician curiously watched the struggle in his face. The hand that clung to his shoulder was trembling horribly. At last the father found voice.

'What happened?' he asked.

'She was stabbed,' said Dr Brander again. 'When we examined her we found the knife – a long, keen, short-handled stiletto. It was driven in with great force directly under her left arm and penetrated the heart. She must have been dead when she was lifted from the box at the opera. The stiletto remained in the wound and prevented any flow of blood while its position and the short handle caused it to be overlooked when she was lifted into the carriage. We did not find the knife for several minutes after we arrived. It was covered by her arm.'

'Did you tell my wife?' asked Mr Oliver quickly.

'She was present,' the physician went on. 'She screamed and fainted. Dr Seaver is attending her. Her condition is – is not very good. Where is your 'phone? I must notify the police.'

Mr Oliver started to ask something else, paused and dropped back in his chair only to rise instantly and rush up the stairs. Knight into whose face there had come a deadly calm stood stone-like while Dr Brander used the telephone. At last the physician finished.

'The calling of the police means that Eleanor did not kill herself?' asked the young man.

'It was murder,' was the positive reply. 'She could not have stabbed herself. The knife went straight in, entering here,' and he indicated a spot about four inches below his left arm. 'You see,' he explained, 'it took a very long blade to penetrate the heart.'

There was dull despair in Knight's eyes. He dropped down at a table with his head on his arms and sat motionless for a long time. He looked up once and asked a question.

'Where is the knife?'

'I have it,' replied Dr Brander. 'I shall turn it over to the authorities.'

****

'Now,' began The Thinking Machine in his small, irritated voice as Hutchinson Hatch, reporter, stopped talking and leaned back to listen, 'all problems are merely sums in addition, when reduced to their primary parts. Therefore this one is simply a matter of putting facts together in order to prove that two and two do not sometimes but always make four.'

Professor Augustus SFX Van Dusen, scientist and logician, paused to adjust his head comfortably on the cushion in the big chair, then resumed:

'Your statement of the case, Mr Hatch, gives me these absolute facts: Eleanor Oliver is dead; she died of a stab wound; a stiletto made this wound; it was in such a position that she could hardly have inflicted it herself; and Sylvester Knight, her fiancé, is under arrest. That's all we know isn't it?'

'You forget that she was stabbed while in a box at the opera,' the reporter put in, 'in the hearing of three or four thousand persons.'

'I forget nothing,' snapped the scientist. 'It does not appear at all that she was stabbed while in that box. It appears merely that she was ill and might have fainted. She might have been stabbed while in the carriage, or even after she was in her room.'

Hatch's eyes opened wide at the bare mention of these possibilities.

'The presumption is of course,' The Thinking Machine went on a little less aggressively, 'that she was stabbed while in the box, but we can't put that down as an absolute fact to work on until we know it. Remember, the stiletto was not found until she was in her room.'

This gave the reporter something new to think about and he was silent as he considered it. He saw that either of the possibilities suggested by the scientist was tenable, but on the other hand – on the other hand, and there his mind refused to work.

'You have told me that Knight was arrested at the suggestion of Mr Oliver last night shortly after the police learned of the affair,' The Thinking Machine went on, musingly. 'Now just what have you or the police learned as to him? How do they connect him with the affair?'

'First the police acted on the general ground of exclusive opportunity,' the reporter explained. 'Then Knight was arrested. The stiletto used was not an ordinary one. It had a blade of about seven inches and was very slender, but instead of a guard on it there was only a gold band. The handle is a straight, highly polished piece of wood. Around it, below the gold band where the guard should have been, there were threads as if it had been screwed into something.'

'Yes, yes, I see,' the other interrupted impatiently. 'It was intended to be carried hidden in a walking cane, perhaps, and was screwed down with the blade in the stick. Go on.'

'Detective Mallory surmised that when he saw the stiletto,' the reporter continued, 'so after Knight was locked up he searched his rooms for the other part – the lower end – of the cane.'

'And he found it, without the stiletto?'

'Yes, that's the chain against Knight. First, exclusive opportunity, then the stiletto and the finding of the lower end of the cane in his possession.'

'Exclusive fiddlesticks!' exclaimed the scientist irritably. 'I presume Knight denies that he killed Miss Oliver?'

'Naturally.'

'And where is the stiletto that belongs to his cane? Does he attempt to account for it?'

'He doesn't seem to know where it is – in fact he doesn't deny that the stiletto might be his. He merely says he doesn't know.'

The Thinking Machine was silent for several minutes.

'Looks bad for him,' he remarked at last.

'Thank you,' remarked Hatch dryly. It was one of those rare occasions when the scientist saw a problem exactly as he saw it.

'Miss Oliver and Mr Knight were to be married – when?'

'Three weeks from next Wednesday.'

'I suppose Detective Mallory has the stiletto and cane?'

'Yes.'

The Thinking Machine arose and found his hat.

'Let's run over to police headquarters,' he suggested.

★★★★

They found Detective Mallory snugly ensconced behind a fat cigar with beatific satisfaction on his face.

'Ah, gentlemen,' he remarked graciously – the graciousness of conscious superiority. 'We've nailed it to our friend Knight all right.'

'How?' inquired The Thinking Machine.

The detective gloated a little – twisted his tongue around the dainty morsel – before he answered.

'I suppose Hatch has told you the grounds of the arrest?' he asked. 'Exclusive opportunity and all that? Then you know, too, how I searched Knight's rooms and found the other part of the stiletto cane. Of course that was enough to convict, but early this evening the last link in the chain against him was supplied when Mrs Oliver made a statement to me.'

The detective paused in enjoyment of the curiosity he had aroused.

'Well?' asked The Thinking Machine, at last.

'Mrs Oliver heard – understand me – heard Knight threaten her daughter only a few minutes before she was found dead.'

'Threaten her?' exclaimed Hatch, as he glanced at The Thinking Machine. 'By George!'

Detective Mallory tugged at his moustache complacently.

'Mrs Oliver heard Knight first say something like, "Please don't. It won't be very long." Her daughter answered something she couldn't catch after which she heard Knight say positively, "You mustn't. If you do I shall do something desperate," or something like that. Now as she remembers it the tone was threatening – it must have been raised in anger to be heard above the anvils. Thus the case is complete.'

The Thinking Machine and Hatch silently considered this new point.

'Remember this was only three or four minutes before she was found stabbed,' the detective went on with conviction. 'It all connects up straight from exclusive opportunity to the ownership of the stiletto; from that to the threat and there you are.'

'No motive of course?' asked The Thinking Machine.

'Well, the question of motive isn't exactly clear but our further investigations will bring it out all right,' the detective admitted. 'I should imagine the motive to be jealousy. Of course the story of Knight not knowing where his stiletto is has no weight.'

Detective Mallory was so charmed with himself that he offered cigars to his visitors – an unusual burst of generosity – and Hatch was so deeply thoughtful that he accepted. The Thinking Machine never smoked.

'May I see the stiletto and cane?' he asked instead.

The detective was delighted to oblige. He watched the scientist with keen satisfaction as that astute gentleman squinted at the slender blade, still stained with blood, and then as he examined the lower part of the cane. Finally the scientist thrust the long blade into the hollow stick and screwed the handle in. It fitted perfectly. Detective Mallory smiled.

'I don't suppose you'll try to put a crimp in me this time?' he asked jovially.

'Very clever, Mr Mallory, very clever,' replied The Thinking Machine, and with Hatch trailing he left headquarters.

'Mallory will swell like a balloon after that,' Hatch commented grimly.

'Well, he might save himself that trouble,' replied the scientist crustily. 'He has the wrong man.'

The reporter glanced quickly into the inscrutable face of his companion.

'Didn't Knight do it?' he asked.

'Certainly not,' was the impatient answer.

'Who did?'

'I don't know.'

★★★★

Together they went on to the theatre from which Miss Oliver had been removed the night before. There a few words with the manager gained permission to look at the Oliver box – a box which the Olivers held only on alternate nights during the opera season. It was on the first balcony level, to the left as they entered the house.

The first three rows of seats in the balcony ran around to and stopped at the box, one of four on that level and the furthest from the stage. The Thinking Machine pottered around aimlessly for ten minutes while Hatch looked on. He entered the box two or three times, examined the curtains, the partitions, the floor and the chairs after which he led the way into the lobby.

There he excused himself to Hatch and stopped in the manager's office. He remained only a few minutes, afterwards climbing into a cab in which he and Hatch were driven back to police headquarters.

After some wire pulling and a good deal of red tape The

Thinking Machine and his companion were permitted to see Knight. They found him standing at the barred cell door, staring out with weary eyes and pallid face.

The Thinking Machine was introduced to the prisoner by Hatch who had previously tried vainly to induce the young man to talk.

'I have nothing to say,' Knight declared belligerently. 'See my attorney.'

'I would like to ask three or four questions to which you can have no possible objection,' said The Thinking Machine. 'If you do object of course don't answer.'

'Well?' demanded the prisoner.

'Have you ever travelled in Europe?'

'I was there for nearly a year. I only returned to this country three months ago.'

'Have you ever been interested in any other woman? Or has any other woman ever been interested in you?'

The prisoner stared at his questioner coldly.

'No,' he responded, emphatically.

'Your answer to that question may mean your freedom within a few hours,' said The Thinking Machine quite calmly. 'Tell me the truth.'

'That is the truth – on my honour.'

The answer came frankly, and there came a quick gleam of hope in the prisoner's face.

'Just where in Italy did you buy that stiletto cane?' was the next question.

'In Rome.'

'Rather expensive?'

'Five hundred lira – that is about one hundred dollars.'

'I suppose they are very common in Italy?'

'Yes, rather.'

Knight pressed eagerly against the bars of his cell and gazed deeply but uncomprehendingly into the quiet squinting blue eyes.

'There has never been any sort of a quarrel – serious or otherwise – between you and Miss Oliver?'

'Never,' was the quick response.

'Now, only one more question,' said The Thinking Machine. 'I shall not ask it to hurt you.'

There was a little pause and Hatch waited expectantly. 'Does it happen that you know whether or not Miss Oliver ever had any other love affair?'

'Certainly not,' exclaimed the young man, hotly. 'She was just a girl – only twenty, out of Vassar just a few months ago and – and –'

'You needn't say any more,' interrupted The Thinking Machine. 'It isn't necessary. Make your plans to leave here tonight, not later than midnight. It is now four o'clock. Tomorrow the newspapers will exonerate you.'

The prisoner seemed almost overcome by his emotions. He started to speak, but only extended an open hand through the bars. The Thinking Machine laid his slender fingers in it with a slight look of annoyance, said 'Good day' mechanically and he and Hatch went out.

The reporter was in a sort of a trance, not an unusual condition in him when in the company of his scientific friend. They climbed into the cab again and were driven away. Hatch was thinking too deeply to note the destination when the scientist gave it to the cabby.

'Do you actually anticipate that you will be able to get Knight out of this thing so easily?' he asked incredulously.

'Certainly,' was the response. 'The problem is solved except for one or two minor points. Now I am proving it.'

'But – but –'

'I will make it all clear to you in due time,' interrupted the other.

★★★★

They were both silent until the cab stopped. Hatch glanced out and recognized the Oliver home. He followed The Thinking Machine up the steps and into the reception hall. There the scientist handed a card to the servant.

'Tell Mr Oliver, please, that I will only take a moment,' he explained.

The servant bowed and left them. A short wait and Mr Oliver entered.

'I am sorry to disturb you at such a time, Mr Oliver,' said the scientist, 'but if you can give me just a little information I think perhaps we may get a full light on this unfortunate affair.'

Mr Oliver bowed.

'First, let me ask you to confirm what I may say is my knowledge that your daughter, Eleanor, knew this man. I will ask, too, that you do not mention his name now.'

He scribbled hastily on a piece of paper and handed it to Mr Oliver. An expression of deep surprise came into the latter's face and he shook his head.

'I can answer that question positively,' he said. 'She does not know him. She had never been abroad and he has never been in this country until now.'

The Thinking Machine arose with something nearly akin to agitation in his face, and his slender fingers worked nervously.

'What?' he demanded abruptly. 'What?' Then, after a pause: 'I beg your pardon, sir. It startled me a little. But are you sure?'

'Perfectly sure,' replied Mr Oliver firmly. 'They could not have met in any way.'

For a long time The Thinking Machine stood squinting aggressively at his host with bewilderment plainly apparent in his manner. Hatch looked on with absorbed interest. Something had gone wrong; a cog had slipped; the wheels of logic had been thrown out of gear.

'I have made a mistake, Mr Oliver,' said The Thinking Machine at last. 'I am sorry to have disturbed you.'

Mr Oliver bowed courteously and they were ushered out.

'What is it?' asked Hatch anxiously as they once more took their seats in the cab.

The Thinking Machine shook his head in frank annoyance.

'What happened?' Hatch insisted.

'I've made a mistake,' was the petulant response. 'I'm going home and start all over again. It may be that I shall send for you later.'

Hatch accepted that as a dismissal and went his way wonderingly.

That evening The Thinking Machine called him to the 'phone.

'Mr Hatch?'

'Yes.'

'Did Miss Oliver have any sisters?'

'Yes, one. Her name is Florence. There's something about her in the afternoon papers in connection with the murder story.'

'How old is she?'

'I don't know – twenty-two or -three.'

'Ah!' came a long, aspirated sigh of relief over the wire. 'Run by and bring Detective Mallory up to my place.'

'All right. But what was the matter?'

'I was a fool, that's all. Goodbye.'

Detective Mallory was still delighted with himself when Hatch entered his office.

'What particular line is your friend Van Dusen working?' he asked a little curiously.

The reporter shrugged his shoulders.

'He asked me to come by and bring you up,' he replied. 'He has evidently reached some conclusion.'

'If it's anything that doesn't count Knight in it's all wind,' he said loftily. For once in his life he was confident that he could deliver a blow which would obliterate any theory but his own. In this mood, therefore, he went with Hatch. They found The Thinking Machine pacing back and forth across his small laboratory with his slender hands clasped behind his back. Hatch noted that the perplexed wrinkles had gone.

'In adding up a column of figures,' began the scientist abruptly as he sat down, 'the oversight of even so trivial a unit as one will make a glaring error in the result. You, Mr Mallory, have overlooked a figure one, therefore your conclusion is wrong. In my first consideration of this affair I also overlooked a figure one and my conclusion toppled over just at the moment when it seemed to be corroborated. So I had to start over; I found the one.'

'But this thing against Knight is conclusive,' said the detective explosively.

'Except for the figure one,' added the scientist.

Detective Mallory snorted politely.

'Now here is the logic of the thing,' resumed The Thinking Machine. 'It will show how I overlooked the figure one – that is a vital fact – and how I found it.'

He dropped back into the reflective attitude which was so familiar to his hearers, squint eyes turned upward and with his fingers pressed tip to tip. For several minutes he was silent while Detective Mallory vented his impatience by chewing his moustache.

'In the beginning,' began The Thinking Machine at last, 'we have a girl, pretty, young and wealthy in a box at the opera with her parents and her fiancé. It would seem, at first glance, to be as safe a place as her home would be, yet she is murdered mysteriously. A stiletto is thrust into her heart. We will assume that her death occurred in the box; that the knife thrust came while she was in a dead faint. This temporary unconsciousness would account for the fact that she did not scream, as the heart would have been pierced by a sudden thrust before consciousness of pain was awakened.

'Now the three persons who were with her. There seemed no reason to suspect either the father or mother, so we come to Sylvester Knight, her intended husband. There is always to be found a motive, either real or imaginary, for a man to kill his sweetheart. In this case Knight had the opportunity, but not the exclusive opportunity. Therefore, an unlimited field of speculation was opened up.'

Detective Mallory raised his hand impressively and started to say something, then thought better of it.

'After Mr Knight's arrest,' The Thinking Machine continued, 'your investigation, Mr Mallory, drew a net about him. That's what you wanted to say, I believe. There was the stiletto, the other end of the cane and the alleged threats. I admit all these things. On this statement of the case it looked black for Mr Knight.'

'That's what,' remarked the detective.

'Now a stiletto naturally suggests Italy. The blade with which Miss Oliver was killed bore an Italian manufacturer's mark. I presume you noticed it?'

'Oh, that!' exclaimed the detective.

'Means nothing conclusively,' added The Thinking Machine.

'I agree with you. Still it was a suggestion. Then I saw the thing that did mean something. This was the fact that the handle of the stiletto was not of the same wood as the part of the cane you found in Mr Knight's room. This difference is so slight that you would hardly notice it even now, but it was there and showed a possible clue leading away from Mr Knight.'

Detective Mallory could not readily place his tongue on words to fittingly express his disgust, so he remained silent.

'When I considered what manner of man Mr Knight is and the singular nature of the crime,' resumed the scientist, 'I had no hesitancy in assuring Mr Hatch that you had the wrong man.

'After we first saw you we examined the opera box. It was on the left of the theatre and separated from the next box by a latticed partition. It was against this partition that Miss Oliver was leaning.

'Remember, I saw the box after I examined the stiletto and while I was seeking a method by which another person might have stabbed her without entering the box. I found it. By using a stiletto without a guard it would have been perfectly possible for a person in the next box to have killed her by thrusting the blade through the lattice partition. That is exactly what happened.'

Detective Mallory arose with a mouth full of words. They tumbled out in incoherent surprise and protest, then he sat down again. The Thinking Machine was still staring upward.

'I then took steps to learn who was in the adjoining box at the time of her death,' he continued quietly. 'The manager of the theatre told me it was occupied by Mr and Mrs Franklin Dupree, and their guest an Italian nobleman. Italian nobleman! Italian stiletto! You see the connection?

'Then we saw Mr Knight. He assured me, and I believed him, that he had never had any other love affair, therefore no woman would have had a motive in killing Miss Oliver because of him. He was positive, too, that Miss Oliver had never had any other love affair, yet I saw the possibility of some connecting link between her and the nobleman. It was perfectly possible, indeed probable, that he would not know of it. At the moment I was convinced that there had been such an affair.

'Mr Knight also told me that he bought his stiletto cane in

Rome; and he paid a price that would seem to guarantee that it would be a perfect one, with the same wood in the handle and lower part, and that he and Miss Oliver had never had any sort of a quarrel.'

There was a little pause and The Thinking Machine shifted his position slightly.

'Here I had a motive – jealousy of one man who was thrown over for another; the method of death, through the lattice; a clue to the murderer in the stiletto, and the name of the man. It seemed conclusive but I had overlooked a figure one. I saw that when Mr Oliver assured me that Miss Eleanor Oliver did not know the nobleman whose name I wrote for him; that she could not have known him. The entire structure tumbled. I was nonplussed and a little rude, I fear, in my surprise. Then I had to reconsider the matter from the beginning. The most important of all the connecting links was missing, yet the logic was right. It is always right.

'There are times when imagination has to bridge gaps caused by the absence of demonstrable facts. I considered the matter carefully, then saw where I had dropped the figure one. I 'phoned to Mr Hatch to know if Miss Oliver had a sister. She had. The newspapers to which Mr Hatch referred me told me the rest of it. It was Eleanor Oliver's sister who had the affair with the nobleman. That cleared it. There is the name of the murderer.'

He laid down a card on which was scribbled this name and address: 'Count Leo Tortino, Hotel Teutonic.' Hatch and the detective read it simultaneously, then looked at The Thinking Machine inquiringly.

'But I don't see it yet,' expostulated the detective. 'This man Knight –'

'Briefly it is this,' declared the other impatiently. 'The newspapers carried a story of Florence Oliver's love affair with Count Tortino at the time she was travelling in Europe with her mother. According to what I read she jilted him and returned to this country where her engagement to another man was rumoured. That was several months ago. Now it doesn't follow that because the Count knew Florence Oliver that he knew or even knew of Eleanor Oliver.

'Suppose he came here maddened by disappointment and seeking revenge, suppose further he reached the theatre, as he did, while the anvil chorus was on, the party started into the wrong box and the usher mentioned casually that the Olivers were in there. We presume he knew Mrs Oliver by sight, and saw her. He might reasonably have surmised, perhaps he was told, that the other woman was Miss Oliver – and Miss Oliver meant to him the woman who had jilted him. The lattice work offered a way, the din of the music covered the act – and that's all. It doesn't really appear – it isn't necessary to know – how he carried the stiletto about him, or why.'

The detective was gnawing his moustache. He was silent for several minutes trying to see the tragedy in this new light.

'But the threats Knight made?' he inquired finally.

'Has he explained them?'

'Oh, he said something about the girl being ill and wanting to go home, and he urged her not to. He told her, he says, that she mustn't go, because he would have to do something desperate. Silly explanation I call it.'

'But I dare say it's perfectly correct,' commented The Thinking Machine. 'Men of your profession, Mr Mallory, never believe the simple things. If you would take the word of an accused man at face value occasionally you would have less trouble.' There was a pause, then: 'I promised Mr Knight that he would be free by midnight. It is now ten. Suppose you run down to the Teutonic and see Count Tortino. He will hardly deny anything.'

★★★★

Detective Mallory and Hatch found the Count in his room. He was lying face down across a bed with a bullet hole in his temple. A note of explanation confessed the singular error which had led to the murder of Eleanor Oliver.

It was three minutes of midnight when Sylvester Knight walked out of his cell a heartbroken man, but free.

ACKNOWLEDGEMENTS

Firstly, I would like to thank Ion Mills, Claire Watts, Clare Quinlivan, Lisa Gooding, Hollie McDevitt, and Ellie Lavender at Oldcastle Books for their help while I was compiling this book, and for their hard work in bringing it into print and putting it into the hands of readers. Thanks also to Elsa Mathern who has created just as eyecatching a cover design for the book as she has done for my earlier anthologies. Jayne Lewis has once again demonstrated her brilliant copy-editing skills in making my original manuscript much more readable and error-free and Steven Mair proved, as always, an exceptionally sharp-eyed proof-reader. As always, I am grateful to family and friends for their encouragement while I have been engaged in reading hundred-year-old crime stories. Particular mentions must go to my sister, Lucinda Rennison, my brother-in-law, Wolfgang Lüers, my nieces, Lorna and Milena Lüers, my mother, Eileen Rennison, and to David Jones, a close friend for more than forty years. Finally, I would not have finished this anthology without the love and support I receive each day from my wife, Eve.

ACKNOWLEDGEMENTS